The Secrets of Miryam

Michael Maloney

The Secrets of Miryam is a work of fiction. Characters and events are either biblical, historical, or are products of the author's imagination. Any resemblance to other persons, living or dead, is entirely coincidental.

E2

Cover design: Susan Maloney

ISBN: 0-9906833-1-1
ISBN-13: 978-0-9906833-1-5

To Susan, Maura, Terry, Lisa, Stuart, and Barry, who suffered through early versions of this work, and provided invaluable feedback and encouragement

CONTENTS

Genesis

Yom Shlishi, the third week in the month of Sivan
Late spring in the 3758th year of creation

D avid's sandal slipped at a bend in the path on grass still slick with morning dew. He fell to the side, dropping both of his pails and spilling manure over his feet. "Idiot! Pay attention," he scolded himself aloud. At least he managed to avoid falling into the brambles.

Something sharp jabbed at his left heel.

He picked himself up and scooped the spilled dung back into the buckets, exposing a jagged root from the previous year's crop. With difficulty, he pulled it up and tossed it aside.

When he reached the crest of the ridge, he sat on a rock and wiped the mud from his feet on the moist grass. The wound was neither deep nor serious. He continued his labor.

Now that the late season lentils were planted, the task was to spread compost, rich with sheep dung, among the seedlings. Despite the early hour, the air was already humid and warm. It was going to be another hot day.

When he finished, he hoisted the empty buckets and returned down the winding path to where he had secured his cart. There he rested for a moment, taking a long drink from his water skin. He mentally listed the tasks that lay ahead: Lead the sheep to the fallow grass fields by the stream. In the afternoon while they grazed, he would tend the flax, which was already overgrown with mustard weed.

This field where he now toiled was less familiar to him. It had been part of his wife's dowry, acquired through marriage a little more than five months ago. A good crop would be needed this winter, especially since Mariamne was already with child. She had missed her blood three times now. Soon, the midwife had advised them, it would be time to announce the news to the village.

David reflected on the many changes occurring in his life. It seemed like only yesterday that his cares were those of a child. Now at seventeen, he was married and soon to be a father. He was the eldest son, meaning that he was to inherit his father's farm. Despite these burdens on his young shoulders, David felt lucky. Lucky that, as a landowner, his future would be somewhat secure, or as secure as it *could* be as a peasant farmer under Roman rule. But mostly he felt lucky because he was married to a woman he adored. Nothing that the world threw at him could change that.

David grinned as he recalled an afternoon when he was ten years old. While playing a game with other children, Mariamne chased David into old Sabah's olive orchard. It was late spring, so the trees were thick with fragrant white flowers. David hid behind a wide trunk and sprang out to surprise Mariamne as she ran past. They collided and rolled together down a small bank. She held David captive in her arms, because after all, that was the object of the game. But she continued to hold him longer than necessary. He remembered the look in her dark eyes. Finally, the spell broken, she kissed him quickly on the lips and scampered off. He lay there, surprised and intrigued.

In the subsequent years, Mariamne grew into a beautiful woman. He closed his eyes and pictured her face – her olive complexion, the mole above her lip accentuating her wide smile, the half-moon eyes, half hidden by her dark hair.

David wiped his brow and returned his attention to the present. He passed the rest of the morning in hard work and pleasant memories. As he pushed the heavy cart toward his home his youngest sister, Chunya, ran out to greet him.

"David, David!" Chunya was five, and in many ways she treated David and Mariamne as parents. "Did you pick me any dates?"

"No lamb, you know it's not date season. Are you being silly?"

"No dates. Then did you pick me an apple?"

"No apples. Apples only grow at night," he said with a smile.

Chunya considered this. "Where do the stars go in the day?"

David recognized that Chunya was playing her 'question game'. Whatever answer David gave, Chunya would reply with a new question, growing increasingly nonsensical. "Everyone knows that the stars hide behind rocks in the day," he countered.

"You mean the rocks on top of Mount Morah?" came the new query without hesitation. She was good.

The game continued as David left his cart outside the barn and walked up the steps into the courtyard. Mariamne was there, hanging linens to dry on an olive wood trellis. She came to embrace him, but he held up his hands to fend her off. "I need to clean. I've been working with sheep droppings all morning."

Chunya chanted, "Droppings, drippings, droopings. Why don't you just say turds!"

"Chunya!" scolded Mariamne, "we don't use those words. I don't care if you heard Te'oma bar Sabah say them. Go and help David wash while I prepare his meal."

David and Chunya walked to the far corner of the courtyard where a deep cistern had been dug into the limestone bedrock. It was situated next to the house to capture rainwater that ran off the roof. They used this water mainly for washing, preferring to drink the fresh cool water from the village well.

Chunya waited for David to take her hand before lowering the jug into the water with the rope. Stories of a toddler drowning in such cisterns were circulated among the villages from time to time. Chunya had been given strict orders to never go near it without an adult.

David sat on the low stone wall to undo his sandals. Chunya dribbled cool water over his feet and began to wipe them with a linen rag. "What's that?" She pointed to a cut on the inside of his left heel.

"Oh that," he said. "Just a scrape I got in the fields." Now that David looked at his newly cleansed foot he could see that the cut was deeper than he had thought. "Wash it *extra*, yes?"

"Yes. Yes. Washing, washing, waaaaaashing." The last word was a high, sustained warble with exaggerated vibrato. She continued scrubbing his foot as she hummed a made-up tune. Finally, she remarked: "Te'oma bar Sabah says that his father saw a Roman on a horse going up to the city yesterday, and that he had a sword that was THIS big." She demonstrated by spreading both hands as wide as she could.

"Really! And did this Roman have a helmet with a big brush on the top?"

"Yes. Big big! How did you know?"

"The brush is so that in case he falls from his horse and lands on his head, it will sweep the ground clean so his clothes won't get dirty."

"Really?" asked Chunya, intrigued. "I'll bet Te'oma bar Sabah doesn't know that!"

"Well you can tell him this afternoon. Mariamne tells me that you're going to visit him. Now let's go in and see how our father is getting on today." David and Chunya's father, Adlay, was the official patriarch of the family, although David made most of the decisions (with abundant input from Mariamne, who was never shy about sharing her opinions).

"Abbe is not here," replied Chunya. "He went to visit Sabah."

"Oh? I guess he's feeling better. He was complaining about his stiff old bones when I got up this morning. In that case, let's go eat. I smell bread!"

Chunya made up a song about stiff old bones as they walked hand in hand down the steps and around to the door of the house. David was not tall, but he still had to duck under the stone lintel of the front door. The house was a work in progress, with each generation adding a room or two. The original structure had been built by Adlay's grandfather. Then it was nothing but a crude stone rectangle built in front of the mouth of a cave that descended into the hillside. Now they had several connecting rooms. They still used the cool cave in the hot summer months to store food and wine.

David and Chunya entered in to the front room as Mariamne was tending the brazier in the corner. A stew of fava beans, garlic, onions, vinegar and herbs was boiling in a clay pot. The aroma made his empty stomach grumble in anticipation.

Mariamne stood and faced him. "Have a seat at the table. The bread is already set out."

David sat at the table with Chunya. "When are my brothers due back?"

Mariamne set out three bowls and ladled stew into them. "Not until tomorrow. They plan to stay with my sister in the city tonight."

David had two brothers. Yoceph would reach his sixteenth year next month, and thus would move to the city. The new laws were strictly enforced. A peasant-owned farm could not be divided. It must go to the eldest male. Other siblings must move out when they reach sixteen years. The Romans apparently wanted to limit the number of people that a farm must support so as to be able to take more in taxes.

Although David felt responsible, there was nothing he could do. Yoceph bore his burden in his normal stoic manner, but those who knew him well could tell that he was consumed with worry. And with good reason: prospects were not good for unskilled laborers, even in a bustling city like Sepphoris.

His other brother, Mattanyah, was only twelve, and so had a few years before this fate would befall him. David sat in silence and reached for a hunk of bread. Chunya slapped his hand and scolded officiously: "David, you have to wait. We have to pray first."

They bowed their heads and prayed. Mariamne distributed bowls of stew while David chewed his bread. As usual, she could guess his thoughts. "I wouldn't worry too much. Yoceph is strong and very handy. There are many trades he can learn. And my sister's husband has become quite influential. Natan will help him find something to do and a place to live. He says the tetrarch has big plans for Sepphoris. There will be work in the coming years." Turning to Chunya she asked, "Sweetness, can you carefully pour some wine for David? Half wine, half water."

Chunya skipped to the shelves.

David changed the subject: "I wonder how your sister is getting along with the new baby. It has been what, three months now since Channah was born?"

"Almost five. David, we should visit them soon. We'll hear more tomorrow when your brothers return. I hear that Natan has already promised her in marriage."

Chunya was inching her way back to the table, carrying a goblet with both hands and staring at it intently. She had over-filled it, and was spilling a few drops with each step. David said, "Come here with that, you little Monkey!"

Chunya giggled. By the time she handed him the cup, more than half had spilled onto the earthen floor. "David, when can we go see the monkeys again?"

They had walked into Sepphoris two weeks ago. In the marketplace they had seen a troupe of entertainers from Africa. They had many strange animals including two small monkeys that begged from the crowds while the entertainers played drums and chanted. Chunya had been spellbound and had given the monkeys all of the bread she had brought for herself.

"Maybe on Yom Sheni if the grape harvest is going well. And if Mariamne agrees." David replied.

After lunch and a short period of relaxation, they once again set about their tasks. David took Chunya by the hand and walked the short distance down the lane to where the village elder, Sabah, lived with his two sons, Tahmid and Te'oma. They entered the courtyard at the side of the house. Chunya called excitedly and ran to where Te'oma was examining his latest find. Yesterday it had been a discarded snakeskin. Today, who knew?

"David, come. Join us in the shade for a drink," called Sabah. He and David's father, Adlay, were sitting at a table under an overhanging roof at the side of the courtyard.

"Hello Sabah, I wish I could, but I have sowing to finish and the sheep need tending." He turned to Adlay. "How are you feeling today Abbe?"

"Hah! Better than yesterday but not as good as the day before." He and Sabah clinked their goblets together and took another gulp of wine.

"Uh ... will you two be able to manage here with the children?"

Sabah replied, "David, David, your father is twice your age and I'm almost three times. To us, *you* are still a child." He winked at Adlay, who encouraged him with a toothless grin. "Go and mind your farm. If you see my Tahmid out there, remind him to get the ox cart ready for the grape harvest down the valley tomorrow. That boy would forget his feet if he could walk without them."

David shook his head and returned to his labors. That afternoon his thoughts turned to his father. It was difficult to reconcile his childhood memories of a strong and vibrant Adlay with what he saw now. At thirty-four, the man had the haggard look of an old goat. His face was like burnt leather. He had lost most of his teeth. In the past year, his joints had become swollen and painful, making it difficult for him to get around.

Life had been hard to Adlay. His beloved wife had given him five sons and four daughters in their twelve years of marriage. Five of the children had died, leaving David, Yoceph, Mattanyah and Chunya. Finally, David's mother had succumbed to a fever four years ago. Adlay never quite recovered from this grief. These days he spent most of his time drinking wine with Sabah and talking about old times.

David arrived home just before sundown. He entered the house to find Mariamne once again cooking. Chunya sat at the table stacking wooden blocks. "Why is it so dark in here?" His eyes had not yet adjusted to the meager light provided by the oil lamps set in cavities in the stone walls.

"You always ask that!" taunted Chunya. "Guess what me and Te'oma bar Sabah did today."

"Hmmm, did you climb Mount Tabor?"

"No! We made bread and then we helped clean out the wine press for tomorrow, and then we played with Te'oma's cat. But then I got scratched, see?" She held out her hand to show David the injury.

"That's too bad. It sounds like you had a more exciting day than me."

After a while, Adlay emerged from the back room where he had been napping. They sat around the table, closed their eyes, and bowed their heads. Adlay prayed: "Alilah, now at the start of the new day of Yom R'vi'i make our deepest desires your desires. We thank you for filling us with your breath another day, and for providing this food for us to eat. Watch over my sons and see that they return to us tomorrow."

Then they all intoned, "Alilah Shemaya."

They ate their meal of leftover stew and bread. Mariamne had also picked fresh strawberries. They drank wine, talked, laughed and enjoyed each other's company into the evening, their faces illuminated by the dancing orange light of the lamps.

~

Late that evening, after putting Chunya to bed and making sure that Adlay was comfortable, Mariamne found David standing at the door, thoughtfully gazing into the star-lit fields. She hugged him from behind, resting her cheek against his strong back. "Thank you," she said.

"For what?"

"For all of this. I feel wealthy. What more could I want?"

David turned around to see a tear descending her cheek. He embraced her tenderly. "My dove, you are upset. Have I done something to ..."

He was silenced mid-sentence. She pulled his head down and hungrily kissed his mouth. After a brief moment of surprise, he returned the ardor. He cradled her head in his hand as he kissed her, running his hands through her thick hair, overcome by her intoxicating scent.

She stopped suddenly and pushed him an arm's length away, a mischievous smile spreading across her face. Crossing her arms, she reached down to the hem of her robe and pulled it over her head. She tossed it on the table and stood before him. "How do you like my womanly figure, husband?"

Her body was radiant in the starlight streaming in from the doorway. She had indeed grown more curvaceous in the past month. Her breasts were larger and her belly noticeably swollen. He knelt in front of her and kissed her hard belly, his hands running the length of her muscular legs from her feet to her buttocks. She lifted him up and once again kissed him on the mouth. She took his hand and led him back into the side room where they kept their bed. They made love and lay in each other's arms.

After a while, Mariamne's breathing relaxed into the slow rhythm of sleep. David gently extricated himself from her embrace. He was restless. He donned his tunic and went outside. The air was crisp and clear. He went through the courtyard and climbed the ladder to the flat roof. The red clay was still warm from being baked in the day's sun.

He enjoyed these moments of solitude. He lay on his back and gazed up at the bright stars in the moonless sky. The Romans said that groups of stars formed the shapes of animals and people. He had heard some of the names, like Aries, Cassiopeia, and Orion. He focused on a particularly bright star to the south that he knew was called Sirius. Unlike the lives of men and women, the stars were always the same. He recalled the words of the preacher he had heard as a youth in synagogue meetings, about there being a season for everything, and that all is vanity, and that the best thing a man can do is to take joy in his daily labor. He once again recalled the memory of the first kiss given to him as a boy by Mariamne. It occurred to him that it was this kiss that had set the direction for his life. This kiss had changed everything. He was now married and soon would have a child. Would he have a son or a beautiful daughter? He wondered what the child would be like. He wondered about the strange road that the kiss had set him on, and where it would take him and Mariamne in the years to come.

~

David was awoken by Chunya. She was chattering excitedly because Te'oma bar Sabah was coming to spend the day with her. Mariamne was already up and about. He rubbed the sleep from his eyes, donned his sandals, and arose. He noticed a mild pain in his left foot as he walked out to the courtyard.

He habitually thought of the tasks that awaited him this day. Two days ago, a farmer who lived an hour's walk to the southwest had sent word that he had a huge spring crop of grapes. The fruit had ripened early, due to the unseasonably warm winter. It would need to be harvested right away or would be spoiled. Although there was plenty of work to do here, David, Adlay, Sabah, and his son Tahmid planned to spend the day helping their neighbor.

These kinds of arrangements were common. Farmers assisted each other when they could. In exchange for their help, the southern farmer would give them a portion of the early grapes. Not that they needed it right now – their own harvest had been good. But they could make extra wine and hopefully sell it at a good price in the market in Sepphoris.

After making his toilet, he returned to the courtyard and sat by the cistern to examine his foot in the sunlight. It was pink and a little swollen, but still, just a scratch. He washed it thoroughly and wrapped it in clean linen. He put his sandals back on and reentered the house.

Adlay was up, sitting at the table with Chunya. They were eating yesterday's bread along with nuts, raisins and honeycomb. Chunya was arranging the raisins and nuts into various shapes on her plate.

He sat down and poured himself a goblet of unfermented new wine. "Sabah and Tahmid should be here soon. Are you ready Abbe?"

"Hah? I've been up for hours. Don't sleep much these days." He gummed a crust of bread.

"Abbe, you don't have to go. I'm sure the three of us can manage."

"Want me to lie around wasting away? Don't worry, you'll own this farm soon enough. I'm up to a day of hard work."

David was about to reply when Chunya poked him in the side. "Look! I made a picture of Mariamne!" She tilted her plate so David could see the arrangement of raisins.

"Very pretty, but you know the rabbi says we must not make images. Where is my wife, by the way?"

Adlay answered while Chunya continued her artwork. "Tending the herb garden. You slept quite late. Said she'd be back before we left."

"I guess I was tired. Hard day yesterday." David yawned. "When are my brothers returning?"

"Could be late. Wouldn't count on them for any help."

Another poke from Chunya, "David look: now she has brown hair!"

"I see," he said. "Now you better stop playing and eat. Te'oma bar Sabah will be here soon. What are you two going to do all day?"

"Mariamne said that me and Te'oma bar Sabah can feed the sheep. And then when you get back we can stomp the grapes."

"That sounds fun, but don't go near the ram. He can be mean sometimes, and he's twice as big as you."

They heard the cart rolling up the path and came outside to see Sabah and Tahmid walking astride the ox. In the back of the cart rode Sabah's son, Te'oma. The little boy waved excitedly when he saw Chunya dance out of the house.

Sabah was five years older than Adlay and was in remarkably good shape for a man of forty years. He even still had most of his teeth. What a contrast, David observed. Sabah seemed to have avoided the problem of swollen, painful joints that usually began to afflict farmers in their twenties.

"Good morning David, and a very good morning to you, young Chunya," Sabah called out as they walked up.

Sabah lifted Te'oma down from the ox cart. He was already

telling Chunya about his latest discoveries: three worms in the mud
outside his house, his favorite cat had caught a mouse last night, and
something about the number of seeds in a pomegranate. Te'oma was
seven. He was intelligent and curious. His looks were a bit unusual
because of his light-colored hair, gray eyes, and a large red birthmark
on his forehead. Chunya, who was two years younger, adored him
and already talked about marrying him when she grew up.

Mariamne strolled down the lane with a basket of herbs and
lettuce. She greeted her husband with a warm embrace. "Did you get
the satchel I packed with your lunch? There should be enough for
the four of you. I baked some figs into flatbreads, and I found some
pears that ripened early."

"What about wine?" asked Adlay.

"You and Sabah don't worry," she said with a knowing look. "I
packed three skins. Try not to drink it all before midday."

David and Tahmid remained outside while the others went into
the house. Tahmid was unnecessarily adjusting the straps on the ox.
David walked over. "Are you ready for work, Tahmid? Your father is
a hard master."

Tahmid assumed that this was some kind of challenge. "I can
pick more grapes than you, *little* David." He playfully gave David a
shove. "Why is your foot wrapped up? You an old man already?" He
paused and gave out a loud belch and then laughed loudly.

Tahmid was prone to crudeness. Though the same age as David,
mentally he was a child and probably always would be. He was tall
like his father. His pimply face had odd patches of whiskers growing
here and there. He had long greasy black hair, and if one stood too
close to him it was obvious that he was badly in need of bathing.
When he was idle, which was most of the time, his mouth would
hang open on one side, causing him to drool. In spite of these social
handicaps, it was likely that Tahmid would indeed marry in the next
year or two. He was the eldest boy, and so would inherit Sabah's
land.

David ignored the taunt. "I'll go fetch the water jugs and our
lunch."

A short time later, the four men started on their way. Since they were traveling with an oxcart, the going was slow. After an hour, they entered the broad shallow ravine of a stream known as the Nahal Mizra.

The farmer who owned the land was already hard at work with three others. Sabah greeted him, and after some negotiation they agreed that the four newcomers would harvest the section nearest the stream. In exchange for their labor, they could keep half of what they picked. Looking at the abundance of the vines, David thought this would be substantial.

They set the ox to graze and unloaded the picking baskets. David carefully unwrapped his sharp pruning hook from the oiled cloth where he kept it. He measured the iron blade against his hand as he had done since he was a small boy. His hand was now almost as wide as the hook. He remembered carving the now-worn olive wood handle when he was twelve.

Sabah and Adlay did a little tidying of the cart and the land under the grapevines. They gathered grapes that had already fallen on the ground to use as compost. Then they settled themselves in a shady spot under a tree by the stream to supervise while passing a wineskin back and forth.

It was hard work for Tahmid and David. Each proceeded down a row of vines dragging a waist-high basket. They got into the rhythm of repeated motion: grasp a bunch of grapes, slice the stem, toss it in the basket. When the baskets were full, they would empty one in their own cart and the next in the landowner's.

At midday, their cart was half full. They sat on the ground and unwrapped the food Mariamne had prepared. They feasted on the flatbread, pears and of course, freshly picked grapes.

David poured out a small amount of wine into wooden goblets for himself and Tahmid, which they then filled to the brim with water from a jug. The stream here, being shallow and muddy, was not fit for drinking.

After the meal, they lay in the grass in the shade of a large olive tree. After the hard morning's work and the wine, David felt sleepy and soon dozed off.

He awoke with a start. Cold water splashed on his face. Tahmid stood over him with his now-empty cup, laughing loudly.

David sprang up and chased after Tahmid, who quickly darted off. It was at this point that David realized his left foot had become quite painful. At first, he thought it was just asleep from the way he had been lying in the grass. Then he realized that it was the bandaged foot. It felt swollen and hot. He limped back and leaned against the cart for support.

Sabah shook his head and scolded, "Tahmid! Don't waste water." And then to David: "What's the matter, son? I noticed that your foot was bandaged. It didn't seem to bother you until just now."

"I tripped on a root yesterday. It's nothing."

"Hm... It might be nothing, or it might be something. Let's finish with the harvest here and head home. Maybe you can ride on the cart where it's level, but on the uphill parts, with a cart full of grapes, I don't think this old ox can handle the extra weight."

"I said it's nothing. I can walk fine."

"Fair enough. Just trying to help." Then he called out to Tahmid, "Go and awaken Adlay, but gently! Then come back here. These grapes won't pick themselves."

They worked through the afternoon. Even Adlay and Sabah pitched in and did some actual picking, but it took longer than expected. They would be lucky to arrive home before sundown. There would be no time for winemaking tonight. The children would be disappointed.

As they neared the village, they were greeted on the path by David's brother, Yoceph. "David, why are you limping?"

"He says it's nothing." Adlay answered. "I wanted him to ride on the cart but he insisted on walking. My son is more stubborn than this ox."

David sighed. "I just need to rest for a bit."

Yoceph offered David his shoulder to lean on, and together they walked back to the house. "Mattanyah and I got back from

Sepphoris an hour ago. There's no work to be had now, but the word is that Antipas is going to make the city his capital. There will be lots of building soon. I should do all right."

David gave him a sideward glance as he limped along. "Why don't you stay another year? It looks like we'll have a good harvest. There will be plenty. You can hide in the storage cave when the gabbai comes."

Yoceph scoffed, "Right. And what happens when they suspect that you're keeping back some of the harvest, and they start looking a little harder? How many people have you told about that cave? You know when the tax man brings his wagons to collect his grain, he usually comes with a Roman escort. It won't go well for you."

David had no response. Yoceph was right. It was too much risk. The tax collectors could be brutal when they discovered hidden stores. He wondered, who *did* know about their cave? Perhaps it was time to look for another storage place.

Yoceph continued stoically, "Natan says it's a good time to learn the building trade. Opportunities are coming."

Yoceph was a half-head taller than David and broader in the shoulders. Like David, he had curly dark brown hair that he kept cut to a couple of inches in length. Yoceph always tried to put a good face on things. David loved that about him. The two were only a year and a half apart in age and had been through many hardships together, including the loss of five of their siblings, and most recently, their mother.

 Smiling, David said: "Well, with your good looks you'll probably become a rich merchant and end up supporting us all."

They made it back to the house. Mariamne had taken the children to the village well to fetch water for the evening meal. With Yoceph's help, David ambled to the courtyard where they found Mattanyah by the cistern, washing the road dust from his face. "David, you're hurt," he said with alarm.

"He can barely walk." Adlay was always overly worried whenever anyone stubbed a toe. "Sit. Sit. Let's take a look at this 'nothing'."

They undid the bandage. The entire foot was puffy and pink.

The inside of his heel where the root had jabbed him was swollen, and taking on a yellowish hue.

Adlay exclaimed, "Oh, Alilah Rapha, no! Just like your poor sister Devorah."

"Calm down Abbe. It's nothing like that. She crushed half of her foot with a grinding stone. I just need to keep off it for a day or two until it mends. Yoceph can help with the peas, and there are plenty of good feet around here for stomping grapes."

"Don't joke David. This is serious. We must pray. We must send for the rabbi from Sepphoris."

Mattanyah offered: "Yoceph and I met a healer in Sepphoris. What was his name, Yoceph?"

"Oh. Hmm. Taddai, I think."

"Yes, Taddai." Mattanyah continued excitedly, "He's a scholar. He talks to Romans *and* Greeks in their own tongues. A man told me that he makes potions in his shop that can cure anything. Maybe we can get him to come here."

Adlay scolded, "Hush, boy! No one asked your opinion. *Those* people are nothing but wickedness and tricks. Potions and magi are for gentiles. I will send for the rabbi from town. Perhaps if Natan puts in a word he will come."

Just then Mariamne entered the courtyard with Te'oma and Chunya. She was carrying a heavy water jug. The children were each holding one handle of an amphorae, and struggling with the weight of it. "What's this? What has happened?" said Mariamne.

"Please, *please*, stop this fuss," said David. "My dove, they are making beams out of splinters. Pay no attention to them. My foot is a bit sore. Give me some bread and wine and a good night's sleep, and I'll race Mattanyah to the ridge and back tomorrow."

Seeing the worried expression on the others' faces, Mariamne took charge. "Mattanyah please take Te'oma and Chunya inside and help them with the jug before they spill it." And then, turning to David, "Husband, let me see this splinter."

~

David awoke shivering the next morning and pulled the wool blanket tightly around him. Eerie light streamed in from the spaces between the roof beams and the ceiling. He wondered why the cavities were not stuffed with straw, as cold as it was. He opened his eyes and saw a gnarled man glaring at him from the center of the room. Blinking twice, he focused. Mariamne's father sat motionless in the chair. David lay back down and closed his eyes.

I am dreaming again. Old Yeshua passed on to Sheol more than three years ago. "You are not here," he said to reassure himself.

"What did you say, my love?" Mariamne entered the room carrying a lamp in one hand and a cup of barley tea in the other. "You have been shivering, my hart. Drink this. It will give you strength. Mattanyah has gone to fetch the healer he spoke of. With luck they will return by noon."

David sat up and focused again on the image in the center of the room – a robe draped over a chair, a trick of the light, nothing more. "But, I thought abbe wanted to send for the rabbi." David couldn't remember all of the conversation from the previous night. There had been a disagreement between his father and Mariamne. He swung his feet to the floor, wincing when his left foot made contact with the cold ground.

"Is it very painful?" She helped him rise. He could not put any weight on his bandaged foot. With difficulty they made their way to the courtyard. Chunya was playing with one of the cats, running about with a small bone tied to an old piece of yarn. She skipped over when she saw David.

"David! Mattanyah said you are sick today and that a *healer* is going to come to make you better." The cat followed her, pawing at the bone as it dragged along the ground.

"Good morning monkey. It looks like you've already been eating blueberries today."

She looked down at the front of her purple-stained tunic. "Te'oma bar Sabah picked me some. Te'oma says we're all going to his house today and make wine. You have to come too!"

"Of course I will." Mariamne had gone back into the house to

fetch bread and olives. The cat rubbed against his leg. He reached
down to scratch it on the neck. "This one's name is 'Jeaps', right?"

"No! Jeaps is gray. This is Tiki. She has white paws and a big
brown patch on her back, see?" Chunya sat down and started patting
the cat on the back, a little too hard. It trotted away and jumped
onto the stone fence at the edge of the courtyard. There it turned its
back to them and began licking its paws.

Mariamne returned with a plate of food. "Sabah brought over
the crutch he used last winter when he hurt his leg. You can use it as
long as you need. Chunya, can you go in and bring David his
crutch?"

The little girl ran into the house. Mariamne knelt before David,
"Shall I change the wrapping on your foot before we go to Sabah's?"

"No, leave it. Let's wait and hear what this healer says."

A little while later, the three made the short walk down the hill.
It was slow going for David on the rocky path. Mariamne and
Chunya both carried baskets for the grapes. Mariamne carried an
empty amphora with which to collect new wine for immediate use.

They arrived at Sabah's house and entered the courtyard. David
sat at the table with Adlay and Sabah in the shade.

Behind Sabah's house was a gently sloping shelf of limestone.
They had dug two wine presses directly into the soft rock. At the
uphill side, each press started with a bowl-shaped indentation about
knee deep and as wide as a man was tall. At the lower edge of the
bowl, a channel ran into a deep cavity, like a cistern. Tahmid had just
now finished filling one of the bowls with grapes from the cart.
Te'oma and another neighboring girl had been standing to the side
and now began holding hands and jumping on the grapes.

Chunya hurriedly took her sandals off and washed her feet.
Mariamne cinched up her robe to mid-thigh. She ran to join the
other children.

The other wine press had been filled with grape juice a week ago.
The bubbly dark mixture gave off a yeasty stench. Presently Sabah
came forth with a jug. Bending down, he brushed away some sticks
and leaves floating on the top and dipped the jug into the brew. He

drew it out, filled with warm wine. He sniffed at it tentatively and flicked a bug from the surface.

"It's a bit early in the day for that, isn't it Sabah?" chided David as he brought the jug back to the table.

Sabah grinned. "Son, these are the privileges of age, yes, the privileges of age." He poured a full cup and handed it to David. "Tell me what you think."

David took a small sip. "Not bad. Still too sweet. Another day or two and it will be perfect."

Sabah shrugged and looked at him sternly. "You don't look well, David. Your father here is worried about you."

David waved a fly from his nose. "Everyone's making a fuss. They even sent my brother into town to fetch some magi he met this week. I just hope they don't pay too much. What a waste."

Sabah scowled. "This was your wife's idea?"

"Actually I think it was Mattanyah's. He and Yoceph were very impressed with this fellow."

Sabah grunted and stood up, mumbling something about "bad business." He and Adlay exchanged a look. David thought he saw them nod to each other.

Sabah said, "This sun is too bright for us. We will be in the house. Enjoy the wine. Come in if you get too warm." Leaving the cup, Adlay and Sabah retreated indoors with the jug.

Everyone was sweating in the heat as the wine making progressed, but David simply could not get warm. They tried to get him to eat some bread and hard cheese at midday, but he had no appetite. Finally, Mariamne helped him hobble back up the hill to their own home to rest.

~

David awoke in the side room, not knowing how long he had slept. It was midafternoon judging by the light from the rafters. Mariamne sat against the wall to his left, dozing. He reached over and took her hand.

He heard voices in the house – Mattanyah's, and someone else.

Mariamne stirred and arose. She drew back the curtain from the doorway. She took two steps back as a girl entered the room followed by Mattanyah. The girl looked to be in her early teens, thin and very pale. She hefted a voluminous leather satchel over her shoulder.

Mattanyah busied himself lighting lamps while the strange girl looked about the room and took a step toward Mariamne. She dropped to her knees, and bowed low. "Dearest lady, I am to understand you are called Mariamne," she said with her face toward the floor. "I am Nura, daughter to Taddai the scholar. My father is saddened to hear of your distress, and regrets that he is not to be with you in flesh. I am come in his stead. I have now fourteen winters. I am the apprentice since I have eight years. The master entrusts me with his powerful secrets. I am to be your servant."

David watched silently from the bed. It sounded to him as if the girl had memorized this little speech so as to allay concerns her clients might have as to her abilities. She was slight. Her skin was whiter than anyone he had ever seen, her hair as black as a raven. Her voice was soft and soothing, which had the curious affect of commanding more attention, not less.

Mariamne spoke. "Please, child ... Nura, rise. Do not bow. You embarrass me. I myself am only seventeen. We are equals."

The girl arose and turned toward David. She had arresting deep-green eyes. Her full red lips stood out against her white complexion. It was obvious she was foreign, likely from some land far to the north. She stood still, meeting David's gaze with a pleasant half smile.

Mattanyah had gone to tend Nura's donkey, leaving the three alone. After an awkward silence, Mariamne said, "Forgive me. This is my husband, David. We are grateful to you for coming. May I offer you refreshment? It is a long way from Sepphoris."

Nura turned to Mariamne and took her right hand, holding it in both of hers. "Dearest Mariamne. There is no need. Mattanyah is very kind to me in our walk. I understand you are worried for the husband. To ease your mind is for what Taddai the scholar is training me."

She stood so close, her speech almost a whisper. Something about the warmth of her touch or the tone of her voice melted Mariamne's composure. Her eyes filled with water, and she began to sob. She put her arms around Nura, who held her quietly for several moments. At length Nura asked, "How far along are you?"

Mariamne looked up in surprise. "How did you know?"

"I told you. The master gives me his secrets. I see it in your eyes, your color, your scent. I guess you are three months since last blood?"

"Almost four."

"Then you must take care. Eat well. This is to be important for your child. Plenty of vetch, and meat when you can."

Calmed, Mariamne nodded and wiped her eyes.

Nura nodded. "Now we are to help your husband."

David rolled over onto his side, facing the wall. "I only need rest. Leave me in peace."

Nura knelt at the side of the bed. He rolled again onto his back. She took his hand in both of hers and pressed it to her breast. Leaning inches from his face, she whispered softly, "Dearest David." He was unable to look away from her piercing eyes. "In truth you are not angry. Fear shows in many ways." He was conscious of the flowery scent of her breath. "The wife worries for you. The unborn child is needing a father. I am come from Sepphoris for those who love you. My master, Taddai, learns healing arts of the Greeks, the Egyptians, the Gauls. Do the family a kindness. I am to be allowed to do my work?"

He looked up to see his beloved Mariamne gazing at him with deep worry. Mattanyah and Yoceph now stood watching from the doorway. Nura released his hand and reached into her satchel, removing a wineskin embroidered with strange symbols in colored threads. She asked Mariamne for a goblet. When it was brought, she filled it with a deep reddish-brown liquid. The smell reminded David of the spice racks in the marketplace in Sepphoris.

"Dearest David" began the mesmerizing voice again. "I am to

unwrap your foot. But first, take this cup and drink."

"I'm not thirsty" David waved the cup away.

"David, it is not for thirst. I regret for what I now am now to do. It is to be painful."

"It is nothing. I am not afraid." He said obstinately.

Knowing her husband's capacity for stubbornness, Mariamne added, "Please David, do as she asks."

"Tell me what it is." David took the cup. He gave it a sniff and wrinkled his nose.

"Strong wine, honey, hemp oil, some ground roots, and herbs. It is meant to take away pain. It also is having garlic and frankincense. These are good for healing."

David did as he had been asked. He drank the full goblet. He lay back and felt a strange warmth engulf his mind. After a time, his shivering stopped.

Nura produced a long wooden flute from somewhere in her satchel. She began to play. It started out as one long, sustained low tone growing in intensity. It dipped slightly and then bent upward. After an ascending flourish, it metamorphosed into a slow, plaintive melody. The tune was at once familiar and otherworldly, something like the tunes that he and Mariamne had danced to at their wedding, except slower. It was light and lilting, yet it spoke of sadness and loss. All around were transfixed. After several minutes the playing stopped. David gazed through glassy, unfocused eyes.

Nura put the flute away and deftly unwrapped David's foot. The inner layers of cloth were stuck to his foot with a dried crust. She produced a vial of fragrant oil and worked it into the wrapping until it loosened. She washed David's foot with cold water and wiped it with a white linen cloth. She washed her own hands and wiped them with the same cloth. She massaged more of the oil into David's ankle and foot for several minutes. David breathed quietly, watching all of this with detached interest, as if it were being done to someone else.

Nura looked up at Yoceph in the doorway. "You also are brother to David?"

He nodded, unable to find his voice.

"Sit at the side of your brother. Hold him firmly. He is to be trying to move."

David acknowledged Yoceph with a nod as he sat. He watched Nura pull a short knife from her satchel. It looked like a pruning hook, but smaller. Next she produced a small burlap parcel tied with an oily string. She undid the knot and opened the bundle to reveal a black pasty resin. A pungent smell filled the air.

Seeing the quizzical looks, Nura said to Mariamne, "Hold this. Taddai makes this poultice from an ancient recipe passed down by my people in the north. The master is learning it from my flesh father before he is with his ancestors. Some ingredients I can tell you: pine turpentine from Yerushalayim, sulfur, the same herbs and roots that are in the wine. With the help of your Alilah, David is to heal in three days."

Nura once again took the wineskin. She dribbled some directly on the wound, and then onto her own hands, first left, then right. It seemed like a ritual. She motioned for Mattanyah to hold the lamp close. She held the point of her curved blade in the flame for a moment. Then, nodding to Yoceph, she plunged the point into David's heel, exactly at the spot of greatest swelling.

David felt a white-hot stab of pain and tried to withdraw his leg, but Yoceph held him in place. He heard Nura's distant voice cooing, "Hush, dearest David, this is to be finished soon." After a moment the pain receded and it seemed to David that he was floating above the others as they worked on his own inert body. He watched from high above as the point of the knife went in deeply, well into the muscle of the heel. His heel? It sliced toward the center of his foot, about an inch. Blood and copious amounts of yellowish pus poured forth. When the flow subsided, Nura spread the cut wide with the index finger and thumb of her left hand. She dipped her right fingers into the poultice held by Mariamne and worked some directly into the wound.

The last thing he remembered was Nura turning her head toward the ceiling. She looked up into David's incorporeal eyes. "Sleep now, dearest David."

~

Somber music plays in the distance. A flute. The sun beats pleasantly on his face as he lay in the tall grass. A white-skinned girl touches him lightly on the hand. He raises heavy eyelids. 'Come', says she. David is running. He follows the girl as she prances through the meadow. She moves quickly, long black hair bouncing in the wind. The grass is soft and cool beneath his bare feet. He tries to keep up. Sometimes she has the appearance of a girl. Other times he follows a white-tailed doe. At the bank of a stream now, the girl removes her tunic and faces David, spreading her arms. With no shame she stands before him, smiling. David feels embarrassment to see the black bush of her sex. The girl repeats, 'come', and plunges into the stream. David follows, but the water is deeper and colder than he expects. She swims away from him. His robe heavy with water, he can no longer follow. He stands now in the sunshine on the opposite bank. A familiar gravelly voice calls, "Where is my son?" It is Mariamne's father. Old Yeshua. David is once again a small boy, clothed in a clean robe for shabbat meeting. He runs toward the voice of the old man. Happiness like the warmth of the sun. David sits on the man's bony lap. On a boulder at the edge of a meadow, they watch the wind making waves in the long grass. Old Yeshua asks again, 'Where is my son?'. David wants to tell the old man about his daughter – that she is with child. But when he tries, he discovers that he is unable to speak. He has no breath in him – no ruah. This frightens him. He tries to yell. The old man now asks, 'David, why are you here?' and, not getting an answer, he repeats: 'David, why?' Panic grips David but he is still unable to make a sound. Old Yeshua questions him more insistently: 'David, answer me . . . David . . . David . . .'

"David!"

His mind was a fog, his mouth dry and pasty. He tried to focus his eyes.

"David!" Again barked the grating voice. "Finally. You are awake. Sit up. Take some water."

David was handed a cup. He sat up and took a tentative sip.

"I am Eleazar, priest of the temple. I was in the city when your father's summons came. You are blessed that I am here. Do you understand?"

David drained the cup and rubbed his eyes. It was night. He was in his home, in the side room. Dim light was provided by a single lamp. A strange man stood in front of him, his head covered by a turban. An elaborate ephod was fastened with a sash around his waist.

Gradually, David's mind cleared. He realized his hair and clothing were wet. He had been sweating. He felt pleasantly cool. His headache was gone and the pain in his foot had been replaced by a welcome numbness. He realized that the priest was still glaring at him. "May I have some more water?" He asked weakly.

"Reuel! Get David more water with NO wine. It is evident he has had plenty to drink today already." The priest had addressed this to a boy, whom David now noticed for the first time. He looked to be about twelve, the same age as Mattanyah. He also wore a white robe and an ephod, although his was a plain dark color, perhaps red. It was hard to tell in the dim light. The boy bowed his head obsequiously and backed out of the room.

Again the shrill voice barked, "I asked you if you understand!"

"Yes, ... yes of course, sir. You are welcome in our home." David noticed his father cowering in the far corner of the room with Yoceph.

The priest sighed. "Child, I do not ask for your hospitality. I have many important duties to attend to in the city. Your father *begged* me to come here. I came out of charity."

The strange boy returned with a full cup of water and handed it to David. After he had taken a few sips, David looked up again at the Priest. "Yes sir. I ... I only meant that I am honored that you are here."

"Hm," grunted the priest. "Reuel! Fetch that stool. And more lamps – I will need better light."

David thought it odd that the boy had not yet spoken, and that he spent most of his time in a bow of exaggerated humility, or more likely, fear.

"David!" His attention snapped back. "According to the law I must examine your sickness and declare whether you are clean or *unclean.*" The last word was spoken slowly, with emphasis. "Place your foot on the stool."

This was all happening too fast. Like most people, David held pharisees in a mixture of awe and fear. They had real power, especially over poor folk. A rabbi could demand all sorts of payments and punishments: monetary fines, a portion of the harvest, or even prison. David also shared the opinion that many were in league with the Romans. If a man disobeyed a rabbi, it was rumored, he could get a visit from a soldier, which was never a welcome thing.

But this was no mere rabbi. Here was a priest of the temple. David had no experience with such, but he suspected that what was true for pharisees was doubly so for levites. Moreover, to be declared unclean could mean he would be ostracized. He might have to leave his home until he either recovered, or died.

"Sir." David demurred with exaggerated respect, "I am sorry that my father has wasted your time by summoning you." He cast a scornful glance at Adlay in the corner. "But, I believe I am healed now. I feel no pain at all."

The priest glared for a moment. "I am well aware that a sorceress visited you earlier today. That was ill advised. Your brother Mattanyah should be chastised for his lapse in judgment."

"Lapse in judgment?" David was starting to get angry. "He is twelve."

The priest snapped, "Do not interrupt me! I know how old the boy is." After a pause the priest continued in a calmer voice, "It is written that you shall not practice divination. Now the magi may seem effective, especially to you unlearned folk, but it is fleeting. The only true healing comes from ... Alilah Rapha." As he spoke these last words, he widened his arms and raised his face toward the ceiling, closing his eyes. He remained this way for a moment. David saw Adlay in the corner parroting the gesture. Finally the priest turned again to David. "Do you agree?"

David thought quickly. To disagree would be deemed a sacrilege. To agree would be to discount any good done by the healer. He tried a diplomatic approach, "Of course you are right sir, but Alilah Rapha can heal in unknown ways. If it be his will, he can even work through the hands of a healer."

The priest scowled. "I do not have time for this nonsense. Reuel! Lift David's foot onto the stool and unwrap it." The boy did so. The priest leaned close, peering at the wound without touching it. "What is that dark substance smeared into the wound?"

Yoceph exchanged a glance with Adlay and said, "It is from the healer. She said it would cure the wound. She left us with more for later."

"Bring it to me!" Came the shrill command. Yoceph hesitated but Adlay nudged him toward the door. He went into the back room and returned a moment later with the small burlap bundle. He handed it toward the priest. Eleazar waved him off and backed away, not wanting to touch the vile thing.

The boy came forward, took the package and unwrapped it. He held it toward the priest, who inclined his head to sniff the substance. Wrinkling his nose, he leaned away in disgust.

"I have warned *those two* about their vile concoctions. Reuel! Throw that poison into the fire." When Reuel complied, the brazier sputtered and flared up with a bluish-green flame. The priest's eyes widened in horror. "Sorcery indeed!"

"David! I will ask you some questions. You must be truthful to me in all things."

The priest went on with his inquisition for several minutes, asking David many question, some quite embarrassing. He asked if David had touched the dead body of an animal, if he had come into contact with any reptile, if he had taken any oaths, if he had lain with his wife during her monthly bleeding, if he had spilled his seed on the ground, if he had touched any human feces, if he had eaten anything with blood in it, and even if he had had relations with his sheep. David grew increasingly exasperated, but to each question he answered with an emphatic "No."

Satisfied, Eleazar pointed to a pile of dirty cleaning rags by the door. "Reuel, bring those rags. Fetch water from the cistern. Wipe that foulness off of David's wound."

Reuel started to work. In turns, he would spill some of the filthy water on David's foot and then wipe forcefully with the rag.

"Faster!" barked the priest. "You will have to reopen the cut. It is evident that the sorceress has worked the poison deep into the wound."

Reuel spread the cut and poured more water. He continued to wipe vigorously with the dirty rag. David felt a stab of pain and cried out.

"Silence!" shouted the priest. "Reuel, hold him still so I can see."

Freshly opened, the wound once again flowed with blood and a clear liquid. The priest leaned close, squinting his eyes. After a moment he said, "It is hard to say, because of the sorcerer's poison, but I do see a whitening of the hair, and swelling of the skin. I must rule for the protection of the family. This wound is *unclean*."

Turning to Adlay and Yoceph, Eleazar continued, "What I say now is very important, for it is written: In the case of a virulent skin disease, take care that you carry out everything the priest directs you to do." He went on with specific instructions for the rite of expiation. It was obvious to him that David was being punished for some sin, although the nature of the sin was proving difficult to determine.

They were to pitch a tent outside the small village, a little way into the wheat field. Eleazar had brought his own tent and would have Reuel pitch it nearby. Reuel and the priest were going to sacrifice a young lamb that Adlay had provided as payment. Some of the blood would be dabbed onto David's right ear, his right thumb, and his right big toe. For good measure, they would smear some into the wound.

They did everything exactly as Eleazar commanded.

~

In the dark of the night, David awoke and called out, "Mariamne!"

Adlay entered the tent and sat on the ground at his side. "Your wife is not here. She tried to come, but the priest will not allow her to visit yet. Is there anything I can do?"

"Abbe" was all David said. He lay quiet, breathing unevenly. Adlay thought he had fallen asleep and was about to exit the tent. "Abbe?" David said again.

"Yes son, I am here."

"Abbe ... a little water?" His father held the water-skin to David's lips. He took a sip. "Thank you for staying with me."

"Son, I will not lose you. I cannot bear it."

David asked, "Abbe, tell me about Mariamne's father."

"Old Yeshua? An odd request." Adlay scratched his chin and thought for a moment. "He was quite a bit older than me – already a grown man when I was born. When you and Mariamne were both very young, we met and decided on the shidduch between you."

David raised an eyebrow. "Really? I never knew! I always thought the marriage was our own idea."

Adlay chuckled. "Funny how Hashem works. You two became inseparable by your own choosing. I decided to say nothing. Let nature take its course."

David thought about this a moment. "Why did old Yeshua want the shidduch?"

"It was because ..." Adlay paused and swallowed. "It was because he had no sons to inherit his land. He didn't want it to go to some landholder in the city."

David took another sip from the water skin. "Abbe, I had a dream earlier ... of old Yeshua. He asked me where his son was. I never knew he had a son. Mariamne has never spoken of a brother."

"He had three. The oldest took his own name. Then there was Malachi and ... I don't remember the youngest one's name. They were much older than Mariamne. As you know, she was born of old Yeshua's second wife when he was already an elder. His sons were born to his first wife long before."

"What happened to them?"

Adlay replied slowly, "It happened when they were boys. The three brothers were playing in the field by the road that leads to the city. A Roman patrol came marching by. Who knows? Boys can be foolish. Maybe they taunted the soldiers and tried to run away. Maybe they threw stones. The Romans hacked them up with their swords and marched on their way."

Adlay wiped a tear from his eye. "It was old Yeshua who found them. He came looking for them when they didn't come home at sundown. His wife had already passed to Sheol, which was a merciful thing. He was never the same. It was many months before he would speak to anyone."

David pondered the senselessness of cutting down three boys. He wondered if Mariamne even knew about her brothers. "Abbe, in my dream, old Yeshua wants something from me, but I don't know what."

"Hmm ... Dreams are difficult. Watch and listen. It may become clear in time."

~

David was awoken in the morning by muted voices outside the tent. Mariamne and Yoceph were speaking with the priest. His wife seemed to be apologizing for some infraction. "Sir, I am gravely sorry for my behavior last night. Please pardon the foolishness of a wife afraid for her husband's life. I beg you to intercede on my behalf and to ask for Alilah's forgiveness."

David wondered what it was she had said or done the previous night. He worried that she might be 'putting too much honey in the milk', but Eleazar seemed pleased with her demeanor. He said, "Child, it is good that you have found wisdom. I will do as you ask. Now arise. You may accompany me as we speak to your husband."

The tent flap opened. Reuel and Yoceph entered and picked up the litter on which David was resting. They brought him out and set him beside the fire. He was shivering under his blankets, his face red. He squinted, adjusting his eyes to the morning light.

"David!" Mariamne started toward him, but the priest grabbed her hand.

"Do not touch him, child. He is not clean. Let us examine the wound in the light. Reuel! Remove the blanket from his leg."

Using a small stick so as not to come directly into contact with David's skin, Reuel pushed the blanket aside and slid David's robe up above his knee.

David sat up with difficulty. He saw the side of his foot covered with crusted blood. A small amount of whitish pus oozed from the jagged cut. But more striking than the wound were the bright red streaks on his skin. They were about as wide as a finger, and puffy. They started at the wound and proceeded up the inside of his leg. He reached down and traced one with his finger. It was hot to the touch.

"This is not a good sign," muttered the priest. "The streaks are from Hashem's whip. David has been flogged by the spirit. He is still in sin. My judgment last night was correct. David, do you now have anything you wish to confess? Perhaps you were not truthful with me last night?"

David shook his head and lay back down.

The priest sounded disappointed. "Take him back into the tent then, and cover him up."

Again using the stick, Reuel adjusted David's robe and blanket. He and Yoceph carried him into the tent. He could still hear the priest giving orders outside. "Reuel! Go prepare for our final rites."

"But sir," spoke Mariamne's strident voice, "I did not speak with my husband. I ..."

She was cut off by the priest. "Child, go back to your house. Prepare a light meal for your husband. If you bring bread, make sure it has no leavening. Bring water to quench his thirst. Yoceph, you shall accompany her. I have need to speak with David alone. He may still recover if it is the will of Hashem. We will do what we can for him this morning, but we must return to the city for the start of Shabbat."

~

After the others left, Eleazar brought in a cushioned stool and set it next to David's litter. He seated himself and waited for David to open his eyes. "Child," he began, "Hashem has decreed that everything that lives must also die. There is a time for every son of man. Your time may soon be here."

"Mariamne," muttered David.

"Yes – your wife. It is fitting that you call for her. A good wife is a gift from Hashem. Yours is high-spirited, although a bit disrespectful. Still, she may grow into a fine woman someday."

"She ... she is with child."

Eleazar's eyes grew wide. "Indeed." He sat, thoughtfully stroking his beard while looking out the flap of the tent. A gentle rain had started falling, filling the tent with a delicate pattering sound. "Do you know of our tradition called Yibbum?"

"Yibbum. Yes sir, but ..."

"It is seldom done these days. The tradition goes back to the earliest days. It was required by the ancient law." The priest cleared his throat and recited from memory. "When brothers are living together, and one dies without an heir, his widow must not marry outside the family. Her husband's brother must fulfill his duty and make her his wife; by this means his name will not be forgotten in the land."

David said nothing. The priest continued, "It is the proper thing, David. You must think about the welfare of your wife and your child. If you die, she will have no husband and will no longer be marriageable. Her lot will not be happy if she moves to the city. The child will become an orphan like so many others." He let that thought linger and then added, "Your brother, Yoceph, will take over the family farm. He will be in need of a wife."

David remained silent, his eyes closed, breathing shallowly. Eleazar was not even sure the young man had heard him. "I do not ask you to decide this matter now. But consider: Hashem may be calling you to him even now. Pray about these matters as you rest." The priest arose and exited the tent.

~

In Sepphoris, Mattanyah awoke with a start. He sat up abruptly and bumped his head on a wooden beam. Cursing, he remembered where he was: the hayloft of Taddai's barn. Disturbed by the sudden noise, a donkey brayed in the stables below.

He lay back and savored memories from the previous evening. After accompanying her back to the city, he and Nura had stayed up late, talking in the house next door. Mattanyah tried to recall all the conversation in his mind. He was enchanted by the sound of her voice, the curious way she used words. Although only two years apart in age, in terms of experience Nura was by far his senior. She had arrived in Sepphoris with her father when she was eight years old. Her father never told her why they had taken this journey, or even the name of her birthplace, except that it was some wild land far to the north. Her earliest memories were vague – stick houses covered in thatch with constant rain.

Sadly, she had no memories at all of her mother. But she did describe her father vividly: his bushy black beard and his bright smile, the funny stories he would tell with characters that were talking animals. She described her father playing the flute – the same one that Nura herself now played. She told Mattanyah how her father would close his eyes and enter a trance when he played, variously causing his listeners to fall asleep, weep, or dance with joy. He began teaching Nura to play when she was barely old enough to hold the instrument.

Her father had been known as a great healer in his own land. So when he arrived in Sepphoris it was natural that he and Taddai became friends. They both considered themselves scholars and could read and even write in several languages. After a time they trusted each other enough to share their healing secrets.

They had been in Sepphoris little more than a year when a tragic event ended her father's life. Taddai never told her all the details, except that her father had been drinking and had insulted some influential man. Such an offense could easily get a person killed.

Since that time Taddai had raised her as his own daughter.

Taddai had taught Nura to read and write, a rare skill for boys and unheard of for a girl. Last night, Nura had offered to teach Mattanyah letters if he wanted. He eagerly said he would like that very much, hoping for the chance to come back and visit again soon.

Ending his reverie, Mattanyah arose and scratched his side where he had lain on the straw. He descended the ladder to the barn floor and exited to the street.

A man pushed passed him carrying a heavy basket and barked, "Watch where you're going!" The sun was high in the sky. It was later than he had thought.

He walked the short distance up the lane to the front of Taddai's house. He called in through the doorway, "Taddai! Nura! Is anyone here?" Receiving no answer, he entered the house and saw that bread and dried figs had been left out for him on the table. He sat and began to eat.

He heard faint singing: a high-pitched girl's voice, from somewhere within the house. He arose and followed the sound to the back portal. He looked out into an enclosed courtyard and saw Nura with her back to him against the far wall. She had hung her robe on a peg. As she sang to herself, she bent low and dipped a huge sponge into a bucket of water. Mattanyah, mesmerized by the little tufts of black hair at her armpits, was unable to move as he watched her wash her shoulders, sides and legs.

Nura started to turn. Mattanyah quickly ducked back into the house, relieved that he had not been observed, but ashamed that he had taken such a lingering look. He decided to return to the barn until later. He stepped into the street and closed the front door behind him.

"Young Mattanyah! You have had quite a long rest. I trust that you found the hayloft comfortable?"

"Master Taddai – yes sir." The old man was walking up the lane. "Oh, here. Mariamne said that I was to pay you a sesterce for the service Nura provided yesterday." He found the coin in his pocket and offered it to the old man.

"Very well. Send her my thanks. I would have liked to come myself, but I was detained. A centurion's mare was having a difficult birth, and apparently to a Roman, a horse is more precious than a man. I trust Nura was able to do some good?"

"Oh, yes sir, she was wonderful!" Mattanyah proceeded to describe Nura's actions during the previous afternoon, lingering on a description of her flute music.

"Hmm, the flute, yes. She has tried to teach me to play that thing, but I simply don't have it in me. It is more relaxing than poppy oil." He continued, "And now, if you'll assist me, I have a cart down the lane that is stuck. I was hoping you'd help me bring it home."

Since the Romans had recently paved the streets, the narrow wheels common on hand carts were forever getting wedged between the paving stones. Taddai's cart was laden with grain sacks and was too heavy for the old man. Mattanyah lifted as Taddai pulled. The wheel popped loose. Together they pushed the cart back to the house.

They backed the cart into the front room and Taddai began putting things away. Nura now sat at the table running a wooden comb through her wet black hair. "Mattanyah, are you not hungry?" She looked up with a coy smile as she gestured to the hardly-touched plate of food on the table.

Mattanyah realized that she had seen him in the doorway. He turned as red as a pomegranate.

She added with a wink, "I hope you like what you are seeing in our city?"

"Eh?" Taddai turned to face the boy. "Yes. Sit. Eat. And if you can spare the day, I could use someone with a strong back for a few chores. Nura is not much use for heavy work."

"Yes. I would like to. I just have to be back before the start of Shabbat tonight."

~

The rest of the day was a blur. David remembered Mariamne and Yoceph helping him make the agonizing climb up the hill to their house after the priest had departed. People came and went as he lay in the sweltering back room. Chunya came in with some goat's rue she had picked. Pieces of conversations jumbled together in his head. At one point he heard a heated argument between his wife and his father. But afterward he wasn't sure if it had happened or if he had dreamt it.

He felt a coolness and opened his eyes to find Mariamne sitting beside him, patting his head with a damp rag.

"Rest, my love," she said. "The priest has gone. Even your father now admits that he did you great ill."

"Mariamne ..."

"Yes, my hart."

"You like Yoceph. He will be a good man when he is older. Will he not?"

Mariamne was confused by the question. "Of course, my love. Your brother is very reliable. If not for his cool head, I may well have struck the priest last night. Then where would we be?" She laughed ruefully.

"Tell him to feed my sheep," said David.

"Hush my love, you can feed your own sheep when you are up. Your brother Mattanyah should have been home by now. As soon as he arrives we will send him to bring the healer back. Even Adlay has agreed. The healer said you would be well in three days."

"Tell him to feed my sheep," repeated David before lapsing back into fitful sleep.

~

It was an hour before sundown. David was feeling stronger and sat by the brazier in the front room. Mariamne had kept an anxious eye on the lane throughout the afternoon as she made preparations for Shabbat. "Finally! I think I see him coming now."

Mariamne began scolding immediately when Mattanyah entered through the front door. "We expected you this morning! Where have you been? Your father has been ..." She realized he was holding his hand over the left side of his face. His clothes were scuffed and torn and he was missing one sandal. "Mattanyah! What happened?"

He lowered his hand. There was a large scrape and some swelling on his left cheek. It looked like it was in the process of developing into a capacious purple bruise. "Bandits," he said. "Hiding in the hills. I need to sit down."

Yoceph emerged from the back room with Chunya on his shoulders. "Brother you're hurt!"

"He was attacked. Let him sit down. Get him something to drink." Mariamne produced a clean rag and a basin of water to wash his face.

They sat around the table. Chunya crawled onto the bench next to Mattanyah. After he was settled, Mattanyah told his story. "You know that place just as you go over the hill and the road bends to the left?"

Yoceph nodded. "I know the spot."

"Well, as I was passing, the bandits came out from behind the boulders and attacked me."

Chunya gave a sharp intake of breath, her eyes wide. "How many?"

"There were two. They had ..."

"Were they very big?" Chunya interrupted.

"They were about the same age as David. They were kind of scrawny and dirty. They had ..."

"Horses?"

"Chunya, hush now and let Mattanyah tell his story," scolded Yoceph.

Mattanyah continued, "No, no horses. Big sticks. One of them whacked me right here on my cheek." His left eye was swollen half shut now. "I tried to ..."

Another sharp intake of breath from Chunya, "Did you fight back?"

"Well, yes. I punched and punched. That's why my knuckles are scraped." He paused to show Chunya the backs of his hands. She ran her tiny fingers over the abrasions. "I gave one of them a bloody nose, but then the other one ..."

"Did they have on masks?" Chunya interrupted again.

"Masks?" Mattanyah smiled and turned to the little girl. "Yes! How did you know? Metal masks, just like the Romans wear. And do you know what else?"

"What!?" Chunya's attention was rapt.

"One of the bandits was huge. He ..."

"What was his name?"

"Uh ... I think his name was Goliath. At least that's what the other one called him."

"Really?"

"Yes. He said 'Goliath, take your sword and chop off Mattanyah's head'."

"They had swords!" Chunya exclaimed.

Yoceph added, "And apparently they knew Mattanyah's name."

"Yes, and yes," Mattanyah went on. "I think it was some kind of magi's trick. One of them had a long staff just like old Moses that he was waving around and ..."

"Did it turn into a snake?" Chunya was giggling.

"Stop! Enough questions, Chunya." said Mariamne. "Bandits are no joking matter."

It was then that they all heard David chuckling. He had been sitting on his chair in the corner listening to the exchange. "I think," he said, "Chunya wins this round, as usual. But now Mattanyah, tell us, aside from your beautiful face, are you hurt?"

"No, I'll be fine, David. But Mariamne, they took your coin purse. It was the only thing I had of any value."

"Don't worry about the purse. You did give the sesterce to Taddai, didn't you?" Mariamne had resumed her preparations for the meal, in some haste now because it was almost sundown.

"Of course. And he got as much out of me in labor too. He had me clean his barn and help him rearrange his shop. That's why I am so late in returning."

At this point, David, who was trying to get up from his chair with the aid of his crutch, slipped and crashed to the floor. Mattanyah and Yoceph rushed to his aid. They picked him up, put him back in his chair and brushed the dirt off his robe.

"I don't know what happened. I lost my balance. Yoceph, would you help me into the back room. I think I will lie down."

"Husband, we are about to start our Shabbat meal."

"I am just so tired. I will eat something later."

~

The clouds had cleared by the next morning. It looked like the oppressive heat would return. The village and fields were quiet. It was Shabbat. No work would be done today.

Mariamne explained their plan to David. Mattanyah had jumped at the chance to travel back to Sepphoris to ask either Taddai or Nura to return. Yoceph would go with him this time in case they had further encounters with bandits, and to prevent Mattanyah from dallying. They would time their departure so as to arrive in the city when most people would be in synagogue. They didn't want to chance running into the priest or a rabbi. Adlay agreed that this was a matter of life and death and therefore traveling on Shabbat was justified.

After breakfast, Mariamne and Chunya had left for their own synagogue meeting with the neighbors. Mattanyah was preparing for the walk to the city. Yoceph went into the side room to talk to David, who was finally awake and sitting up in his bed. "Brother, how are you feeling?"

David stared at nothing in particular in the corner of the room. He looked up at Yoceph with bloodshot eyes. "Not well. Come. Sit. Talk with me."

Yoceph pulled the chair close to the bed and seated himself. "You must remain strong. Drink and eat something."

"Yes. I received the same lecture from Mariamne. Believe me, I want to, but I feel so weak." His voice was barely a whisper, his eyes half open. His head wobbled as if he was having trouble holding it up. "Brother, I am sorry that you are forced to leave your home.

You have borne this burden without complaint."

Yoceph shrugged stoically. "Alilah made you the elder."

After another silence David said, "Eleazar said something to me yesterday. It was the one thing he said that made sense."

Yoceph shook his head with disgust. "If that priest said *anything* of value I'd ..."

"He talked about something from the Torah. Yibbum, the old tradition – goes back to Moses, who knows? It says if a man dies with no sons, his brother must marry his wife."

David paused to let that sink in before continuing. "Mariamne is with child. It is early yet, not even four months."

"David, that's good news! You're going to be a father."

"I hope what you say is true, with all my heart. But ... I am sick ... more sick than I have ever been. We have both seen what can happen when someone gets the fever."

"David, don't despair. Mattanyah and I will bring the healer back today. The last time she came, she said you would recover. You *did* recover."

David waved him to silence. "I hope what you say will happen. But, think about this Yibbum tradition. If it happens that I am called to Sheol, I fear for my wife. She will be a widow with a child. You will inherit Adlay's farm. You know the Roman laws. She cannot continue to live here. Where will she go?"

Yoceph was deeply uncomfortable. He tried unsuccessfully to think of something to say to change the subject, but remained silent.

David spared him the burden. "Don't say anything now. Go. Bring the healer. Hurry back. I will force myself to eat. I will recover and we can forget this conversation." David pursed his lips. "But when you have quiet times today – while you are walking, think about this. Pray to Alilah for wisdom."

~

Yoceph, Mattanyah and Nura arrived back at the village mid-afternoon, and without delay Mariamne led them into the side room where David was resting. He had been slipping in and out of consciousness all day. Even when he was awake, he was unsure of his surroundings. He would mutter incoherently, occasionally calling out Mariamne's name, or curiously, the name of her father.

Nura took charge. "Mattanyah, fetch more lamps from the front room." She lifted up the hem of David's robe and spent several moments examining the wound and the red streaks. She did her best to clean the wound the same way she had on her first visit, but she did not reopen it this time.

David stirred. "Mariamne, is that you?"

Nura looked up. "Dearest David. Peace, peace."

Recognition dawned on David slowly. "The healer – you have returned."

"David, are you in much pain?"

David did not respond. His eyes were closed. It seemed that he had not heard the question.

Nura turned to Mattanyah once again. "Bring a cup. Fill half with wine – no water." She opened her satchel and dug around until she found a small vial. When Mattanyah returned, she carefully counted four drops from the vial into the goblet and swished it around. "Mariamne, help me raise David's head for him to drink."

They propped David up and helped him drink until the goblet was empty. This seemed to revive him somewhat. He looked around the room and noticed Yoceph, Mattanyah, and the two women. "How long have I slept? I am so tired."

Nura responded, "Dearest David, peace. Your family loves you. I am come to help you once again. Do you know where you are?"

He looked confused by the question. "Of course. The pain is ... I feel ... nothing."

Nura handed the vial to Mariamne. "It is from Mekone. Poppies. Very powerful. If he is needing more after time, do as you see me: four drops. No more. Too much and he will sleep."

"I understand."

"Good. Now Mattanyah and Yoceph, stay here with David. I have need to speak with Mariamne."

The two women retreated to the front room. Mariamne offered

Nura a glass of fresh water, which she accepted. They sat across from each other at the table. Nura took Mariamne's hands in hers and held her gaze. "Mariamne. David needs you to be strong now. He is on the edge."

"But, you can help him, can't you?"

"Dearest Mariamne," the soothing voice said. "David is beyond our skills. I take his pain. Nothing more. Now he is in the hands of your god."

Mariamne became agitated. "But you cured him before! Do what you did then. Reopen the wound. I will help you. Heal my husband. You must ..." She broke off, sobbing. Nura came around the table and embraced her.

"Shhhh, Shlomo, Mariamne, peace. These kinds of wounds have a process. Taddai is studying them many years. If we are to find them early, the poultice is good. But now ... the red lines appear. We have tried balms, herbs, powders, soaks. The Roman medicus would remove the leg, but we cannot."

After a moment, Mariamne gathered her strength and sat up straight. "What must I do?"

"Pray to your god. Stay near. Talk to your husband. Talk even when you think he is sleeping. He may still come back. But prepare yourself, dearest Mariamne. The end could be near."

Nura stayed the rest of that day, making plans to return to Sepphoris the following morning, once again to be escorted by Mattanyah. Mariamne and Nura took turns sitting with David through the evening as he slipped in and out of awareness.

~

David squints in the sunlight. He lies in a grassy field, wet with morning dew. A cricket alights on his face. He brushes it off and sits up. Cool breeze on his cheek. Sounds of water. He sits on a rock by a stream. Has he been here before? He is standing now. Mariamne will be waiting for him to return. Hurry. A white-tailed doe stands very still at the edge of the forest, observing him. David slowly approaches – close now and still the deer does not move. He blinks and the deer is gone.

'David?' came the gravelly voice of old Yeshua, standing at David's side. He is a small boy now. The two walk hand in hand into the field. They are sitting on a fallen log, watching the stream. A fire crackles. A lamb is roasting on a spit. The old man cuts a piece of meat and offers it to him, saying 'Eat Yeshua.' David chews in silence. He is walking by the stream. Alone now. He must hurry. The white-tailed deer watches him from the far bank. 'Come' says the deer. He replies, 'how?' The white-skinned girl beckons and repeats, 'Come.' He enters the icy water.

$$\sim$$

David awoke late at night. A single oil lamp burned on the stand in the corner of the room. Mariamne lay sleeping silently beside him. David was happy.

Mariamne stirred and noticed that he was awake. "Husband," she said, and rolled onto her side facing him, placing her hand on his chest. His shivering had subsided. He was breathing shallowly but clearly. "Do you want more of Nura's potion?"

"No, Mariamne. It makes me too sleepy. I want to be awake with you for a while. I believe that Alilah Sabtai is calling me."

Mariamne was amazed at what had happened to her husband. Only a week ago he was as strong as an ox.

They talked for a long time. They spoke of their childhood together. He recounted to her his memories of the first kiss she had given him and how deeply it had affected him. He told her about his recent dreams. How they were more vivid than any dreams he had ever had. He was sure that they were some kind of sign from Alilah – something that needed to be done for old Yeshua. Finally, he broached the difficult topic of Yibbum. He told her about the ancient custom and about his conversations with Yoceph. They lay silent as she absorbed the meaning of all this. Finally, she said, "Husband, I have always obeyed you."

∽

In the morning David's fever was again very high. He was confused and only half conscious. Occasionally he would shake violently. His breathing was shallow and rapid. Often he would open his eyes and try to speak, but he spoke in tongues that none could understand.

David died at noon. After a particularly strong bout of shaking, his face screwed up in a mask of pain and then gradually relaxed, becoming serene.

Nura had not left in the morning. She stayed and helped with the burial rituals. They cleansed David's body and wrapped it in a linen cloth. They anointed his body with oils and spices kept for this purpose. They placed his body in a long cart and processed down the hill to the base of the cliff where they had their burial caves. The entire village was in attendance.

After they laid him on the shelf in the cave, they rolled the stone into its place. Sabah, the village elder, chanted the mourner's prayer:

"Yit'gadal v'yit'kadash sh'mei raba ..."

After he finished they all replied "Amein."

Exodus

Yom Chamishi, the 5th Day of the Month of Elul in the 3774th Year of Creation
- Sepphoris -

C lopas the architect felt a flush of pride as he squinted in the morning sun. His eyes panned lovingly over the product of his labor during the past two years. The structure of the new basilica was all but complete, save for sealing the roof and installing a sculpted relief into the triangular pediment. Work was now proceeding on the interior: tile mosaics, wood trim and ceilings, carved moldings, and eventually, abundant frescoes.

The building was like a palace. Five fluted columns standing thirty feet high supported a triangular pediment into which a sculpted marble facing was to be installed. This carved facing stone had arrived late yesterday and now lay across two long wagons. It was enormous. Clopas marveled that they been able to haul this thing here all the way from the port at Caesarea.

He walked the length of the wagons, running his hand along the smooth edge of the stone. It was beautiful workmanship indeed, carved from white marble quarried in Greece, and transported by ship to the Yudaean port. There was only one problem: everyone had expected it to be shipped in sections, not a single block. The architect worried that it would be too heavy and unwieldy for the crane.

Clopas was a Jew in the employ of Herod Antipas. Ten years

ago, as a young man, he had been given the opportunity to travel to Rome to study with the famous architect, Vitruvius. It was a life-changing experience. Subsequently he had proven himself to be capable and hard working. Herod had lately entrusted him with oversight of the remaining construction in the city.

This present undertaking was a new government basilica to house the tetrarch's offices for revenue administration. All the gabbais will gather here, Clopas reflected. Out of sight they will work, counting the taxes they manage to squeeze out of the townspeople and surrounding farms. The head gabbai for Galilee was Ba'asha, a ruthless man and one of Herod's main advisers. Clopas had learned firsthand that he was not a man to be crossed.

It was a common problem for an architect: a patron with no sense of taste, and who knows nothing of building or design. Yet Ba'asha insisted on being involved in every decision, no matter how trivial. He had given detailed direction on floor plans, selection of materials, construction techniques, even the hiring of building labor. Clopas resisted at first, but after being summoned to the palace and humiliated in front of Antipas himself, he decided that he should let Ba'asha have his way. There would be other projects in the future where Clopas would leave his mark.

The architect retraced his steps along the length of the carved marble. It depicted scenes from the life of Moses: Pharaoh's daughter finding a baby among the reeds, an Egyptian master whipping Israelite slaves, and finally, Moses killing the Egyptian and hiding the body in the sand. The irony is lost on Ba'asha, thought Clopas. Every day slaves were whipped on this very site for the slightest infraction or hesitancy.

It was early yet, and the construction workers were just now arriving. Clopas frowned as he did his calculations on a wax tablet. He had taken measurements of the marble's dimensions and had estimated the weight. Next he considered the crane.

The Roman crane here had two tall masts on a platform ten feet above the ground level. It was capable of lifting a load to the top of the building. They had used it to stack the columns and the facing stones for the walls. They had used it to hoist loads of concrete and ballast to fill the walls, and then to form the pediment. The final task scheduled for today was to install the relief.

Clopas completed his calculations. The crane had two ropes, each with five pulleys. The winch was turned by a squirrel cage in which three workers could walk forward or backward inside a gigantic wheel, depending on the need to raise or lower the burden.

He had just decided that it was too risky when he looked up and groaned. Ba'asha's litter was being carried onto the construction site by his four Numidian slaves. His two bodyguards followed close behind, whips and swords fixed to their leather gear.

Clopas straightened his mantel and strode purposefully to meet his patron. He waited for Ba'asha to draw aside the curtains and emerge. "My lord, this is an unexpected pleasure. I thought you were traveling to the east today."

"I am. I am." Ba'asha climbed from the litter and brushed imaginary dirt from his white tunic. "I plan to leave within the hour. I heard that the sculpture arrived. Let's give it a look."

"Of course, my lord, it is right over here." Clopas led him to the stone, lying across the carts. "It is quite beautiful, my lord. Your idea for the subjects was brilliant."

Ba'asha ignored the flattery and walked the length of the stone. He made a comment about the relative sizes of the sculpted figures not being right. "I guess it will have to do," he concluded.

Clopas felt a tug on his sleeve. A worker had been standing behind him with a message. "Master, the stone cutter is here. He wants to talk to you about how this is to be done."

Ba'asha looked up from the sculpture. "What is left to be cut? All the facing stones are already in place."

"Well, my lord ..." Clopas gestured at the length of sculpted marble. "The problem is that *this* is too large for the crane. If you recall, we ordered that it should be delivered in sections that could be fitted together once lifted into place."

"Nonsense," said Ba'asha. "You cannot possibly be thinking of cutting my beautiful work of art into *pieces*."

Clopas sighed. He had worried this would happen, which was why he had directed the stone cutter to meet him early. He had not counted on Ba'asha's arrival. "I am afraid it will *have* to be cut, my lord, if we are to lift it atop those columns. I promise you – you will not notice the seams once we have it in place."

Ba'asha gave him a hard look. "Do not argue with me, architect. Do you want another meeting with Herod?"

"No, my lord. I meant no offense. It is just that I have done the calculations and ..."

Ba'asha was no longer listening. He turned and stomped off in the direction of the crane. Clopas hurried to keep up.

The crane crew was now assembling for the day's work. Clopas was normally amused at their motley appearance, but today he was wary in the presence of the master. The only respectable-looking one was the foreman. Clopas was not good at remembering names and struggled for a moment – Mattanyah, that was it. He was likely the same age as Clopas, but, living the hard life of a peasant, looked much older. He wore a dirty brown tunic and a roughly cropped graying beard. Clopas liked him. He was a careful, hard worker, if a bit slow.

With him were six slaves that Ba'asha had provided for the crew. Two were small-framed Africans, wearing only loincloths and turbans even in the chilly morning air. Another was obviously a Gaul, a tall light-skinned man with long blond braids and unkempt beard. From the appearance, Clopas doubted that his hair had ever been washed. Even now he saw leaves and sticks embedded in it. The final three were obviously from somewhere far to the east. Like the Africans, they were dark skinned and of small stature, but more muscular. They wore loose-fitting pants with their torsos bare.

Then he noticed the boy – some relation of Mattanyah's, a nephew or cousin. He would show up occasionally and do odd jobs. Clopas had the notion that he was dim witted. He seemed to spend a lot of time as he was now: sitting cross-legged on the ground, spitting in the dirt and stirring it with a stick. Clopas couldn't remember ever hearing him speak. But he was obedient. He would do whatever Mattanyah asked of him without hesitation.

When Ba'asha arrived at the group, they all stood up straight for their masters. All except the boy, who continued playing in the dirt. Ba'asha pointed at the foreman. "You! Come here."

The man looked from side to side and then said, "Me sir?"

"Yes *you*. Come here. Your name?"

"Mattanyah, master." And, not knowing what else to say, he then gestured toward the men standing around him. "And this is my crew, Alph…"

Ba'asha was not interested in pleasantries. "You are the leader of this team?"

"Uh, yes sir. I have worked this site since the beginning of the sum…"

Ba'asha cut him off again. "This crane – will it lift that stone?" He gestured toward the marble.

Mattanyah glanced toward Clopas questioningly, but the architect's face remained blank. "Well sir, I am not usually the one to make those decisions. Clopas here. He tells us what …"

"I asked you the question, *Mattanyah*, and I am waiting for an answer."

The poor man looked confused and afraid. Again he sought out Clopas' face for an answer, but found none. Curiously, it was the dim-witted boy who broke the tension. He had gotten up, and now stood behind Mattanyah to one side, scratching his ear with his muddy stick. He stole a shy glance toward Ba'asha and said in a calm voice, "My uncle wants to know what the correct opinion is. Then he will give it to you." Then, as an afterthought, he added, "my lord."

This surprised Ba'asha so much he didn't know how to respond. Was the boy mocking him, or was he just stupid? From his appearance, he decided to assume the latter. "Enough of this nonsense. You will at least *try* to lift the stone before we resort to cutting it."

Clopas rubbed his chin, which was shaved bare in the Roman fashion. "My lord, we *could* do that. But there is a risk that we will damage the crane. And then repairing it would cause delay – especially if one of the mast timbers is cracked. We would have to wait for a new one to arrive from the port. It could take weeks. We are already behind schedule. Also, there is the issue of the danger ... if the crane fails while the stone is in the air, who knows? It could ..."

Ba'asha rolled his eyes toward the sky. "You just said the crane could not lift it. Now you're telling me about the danger we will have when it does. Which is it? You can't have it both ways."

"My lord, it is ... My calculations show that ..."

"Again with the calculations! Architect, I do not have time for this. I have clients petitioning me this afternoon in the east. I have a long way to ride, and *you* are making me late. Cart the stone over there, fix it to the crane, and let us give it a try, shall we?"

Clopas could see he was beaten. "Yes, my lord. But this is against my judgment." He walked off before Ba'asha could chastise him further.

Using two of the oxen and several men, they pushed the wagons until the sculpture was directly beneath the crane pulleys. Several men climbed into the bed and set the stone upright. They affixed lifting tongs to each of the crane's hooks and set the ends into the specially designed indentations on the front and back of the stone.

Mattanyah directed three of his men to enter the squirrel cage and turn the winch until the ropes were taut on both sides. These were the easterners. Since most of his crew didn't speak Aramaic, Mattanyah had developed a system of hand gestures that they all understood.

Clopas told Mattanyah to try a test lift first. Just get the stone off the cart a few inches so they could examine the strain it was exerting on the various ropes and mechanisms.

Mattanyah gave the signal. The three slaves slowly walked forward inside the wheel, turning the winch. The ropes creaked as they became taut. "Stand back!" he called to a man who had ventured very close. Seeing that it was Ba'asha, he added in a more deferential tone, "Forgive me my lord, but if a rope breaks, the recoil could snap your neck." Ba'asha quickly retreated to observe from a safe distance.

In spite of this danger, Mattanyah's nephew had volunteered to stand atop the wagon holding the tongs in place until they held the load. It was a dangerous but necessary job. Clopas recalled this about the boy – he seemed oblivious to fear, a trait that would likely get the fool killed one day.

The ropes continued to strain. Creaks and pops came from the crane's structure as it absorbed the load. The three men in the wheel continued to walk slowly forward. Very gradually, the stone rose.

When it was just a hand's breadth above the bed, Mattanyah gave the 'stop' signal with his fist. The wheelmen stayed in place while the Gaul fastened the locking mechanism. "Get yourself down too now," he called to the boy, who leaped off of the wagon and rolled in the dirt for good measure.

Clopas carefully examined the timbers of the crane. It was a heavy load, but he thought it would hold. He had a ladder brought forth and climbed up to examine the pulleys. Everything looked sound. He motioned to the two Africans to bring water jugs to pour out onto the ropes. "We will do the lift, but slowly." He called instructions to several other men, who climbed the scaffolding on the side of the basilica to prepare to accept the stone and move it into place when it reached the top.

Clopas was startled to hear Ba'asha in his ear, who had decided the danger was past, and had sidled up to join them. "So much for your calculations, eh Clopas? You worry too much." The architect gritted his teeth, deciding it was not prudent to respond. They stood in silence, watching the stone recede upward.

All was well until it was nearly to the top. The three wheelmen were having increasing difficulty turning the winch. One of them signaled to one of the Africans to join them in the wheel.

Clopas now understood why: the tongs were inserted into holes in the stone that were about fifteen feet apart. Thus, as it rose closer to the top of the crane, the ropes from the pulleys were drawn apart at an increasing angle. This reduced the mechanical efficiency and greatly increased the strain on the ropes.

He heard cracking and popping, and then a sickening whistle as the rope on the right side failed and started to unravel. Finally it snapped altogether and the stone fell in an arc as the severed rope was drawn through the pulleys. Now suspended only on the left side, the long sculpture swung back and forth, the lower edge barely missing the wheel house.

The swinging caused the whole crane mechanism to rock back and forth unnervingly. The Gaul who was holding the locking mechanism panicked and bolted. Unfortunately, he tripped on his initial step, falling over the lever and releasing the lock.

As the giant wheel started to roll backward, two of the men inside were able to jump out quickly. The third was high up on one side and couldn't get free before the wheel started to spin. The weight of the stone continued to pull down, turning the wheel backward with increasing speed. The slave ran to stay upright, his eyes and voice full of panic.

Finally, he tried to dive out of the wheel as it spun. He didn't make it. His thighs were scissored between one of the wheel spokes and a vertical beam supporting the axle. The wooden spoke cracked and then broke, slowing the wheel. The next one held. The wheel jolted to a stop. The man's thighs were pinned tightly. He screamed in agony.

The stone stopped its fall. The trapped man was acting as a brake. The lower edge of the sculpture rested on the dirt. It leaned at a precarious angle, the upper edge suspended ten feet above the ground.

The slave continued to scream. Mattanyah and his nephew ran to him while Clopas went to the locking mechanism, hoping to be able to engage it and thus release the strain. He tried several times but couldn't budge the lever. "No good," Clopas called out, "We have to cut it loose!"

Ba'asha called out, "Are you crazy! That stone cost me a fortune."

"There is no other way," Clopas insisted. "If we do not get him out soon that thing will sever his legs."

Mattanyah and two from his crew were now supporting the upper body of the trapped slave, who continued to scream in an incomprehensible language. Mattanyah's nephew had gone inside the wheel now, examining the man's trapped legs. "Uncle, his left leg is broken above his knee. The right looks unbroken but is turning dark. We have to get him out."

Ba'asha approached. "Well then, cut his legs off if you have to. It's my loss anyway. The stone is worth a lot more than a lame slave. The idiot should have gotten out of the way more quickly and he ..."

In a quick motion, the boy reached out from the wheel and grabbed the dagger that Ba'asha kept sheathed on his belt. Turning, he reached out over the winch and severed the taught rope where it wrapped around the axle. With a 'twang' the rope shot upward and the stone fell onto the hillside, breaking into several pieces.

The boy turned and helped the others lift the injured man to safety. Mattanyah called to one in his crew, "Bring the stretcher. Take him to Nura in the city. She will know what to do."

Ba'asha was accustomed to being obeyed. It took him a moment to recover from the shock of what had just happened. He looked at the ruined sculpture shattered on the hillside. He looked at the men attending to the injured slave. Finally he turned to see the boy standing before him, holding the dagger by the point, offering Ba'asha the bejeweled ivory hilt.

Ba'asha grabbed the dagger and brandished it menacingly. "Boy, do you know what you have done?"

"Yes." The nephew stood before Ba'asha with a neutral expression. His calm demeanor was unnerving.

"You," Ba'asha fumed. "You have cost me ... a lot of money." His face was red with rage. Ba'asha expected some excuse or explanation, but the boy just stood before him. He even appeared to be smiling now. "Your name!" Ba'asha demanded.

"Yeshua," the young man answered simply.

"Five hundred denarii," Ba'asha bellowed. "I hope you or your uncle has it." He knew, of course, that neither would be in possession of such a fortune.

The boy stood silently, seemingly without a care.

Ba'asha called to his two bodyguards. "Take him to my villa and confine him in the work yard." And to Mattanyah he said: "Your nephew will be held until you can pay off this debt. Come to me tomorrow and we will talk about a settlement."

He stormed up the hill, climbed into his litter, and was borne off by his slaves.

~

Magdala Nunayya, on the coast of Lake Chinnereth, the Eastern Sea

Naomi surveyed the room for the seventieth time and considered her options. *The old fool cannot be serious, can he?* He had said terrible things before, but she had always assumed they were nothing more than drunken ramblings. This time was different. When she awoke this morning, her door had been bolted from the outside. She had yelled and pounded on the wood but eventually realized that no one was in the house.

She sat down on the mat and fumed. *This* is the fish that breaks the net. Her father was obviously bent on self-destruction, but she would not let him destroy her in the process. When he returned, she would just ... what? Leave? She savored the idea of flight in spite of its impracticality. She imagined herself walking out the door without saying a word to her flummoxed father. She would go into the hills and find Te'oma. He had told her to wait here, but he would not be angry. He had promised to take her to the south – to a new life.

Naomi sighed heavily. Her eyes alighted on two small windows set high in the stone wall. They faced east toward the water, letting in the morning light. She got up and stood on her toes to peer out at the docks in the distance. She heard the familiar mid-morning activity – fishermen at their boats, haggling with the fishmongers on the docks. She stretched a bit higher so she could look down at the road. The window was too small to squeeze through, and even if she could, she was on the upper floor of the house. It would be a long drop to the ground.

Abandoning the window, she lay back again and stared at the ceiling: exposed thatch and sticks, supported by heavy wooden beams. If only she had the strength of Samson, she would be able to rip the thatch apart and get through the layer of clay to the roof.

But she didn't. She would just have to wait for her father to return. She shook her head in disgust. What kind of man wants his own daughter to start whoring? If her mother were still here, she would not let this happen.

The thought of her mother brought fresh tears to her eyes. How could she have ever married someone like Achyan? Naomi had once asked her mother this very question. Her mother had said that Achyan was different when he was young. He was strong and handsome – a successful fisherman who even owned his own boat. Her mother said that at nineteen she was getting old for marriage, and thought herself lucky that her father had arranged such a sensible match. Achyan kept his penchant for drink well hidden in those days.

When Naomi was ten, Achyan's accident happened. He was out on the water stone drunk when a freak storm blew in and drove his boat into the rocks south of town. The mast crashed down on his left arm. He managed to crawl to the shore but his boat was ruined. The local healer amputated the arm the next day.

Since then, Naomi's mother held the family together. She took work as a cook and barmaid at a tavern in the center of town. Her mother told Naomi all about the tavern owner – a stingy miser named Lebbaeus who never paid a decent wage if he could avoid it. He was always finding ways to withhold part of her mother's pay if she broke a cup or ate a meal, or even paused for a minute's rest. Her mother said that Lebbaeus was constantly fondling her and asking her to become one of his whores.

Life used to be tolerable with her mother around. Then, near the beginning of this past summer, after eating a meal at the tavern, her mother became violently ill. She died in the course of two days. It was a messy, miserable way to go. Naomi winced as she remembered her mother's final hours.

That was only four months ago, Naomi reflected. That was when Achyan *really* changed. His eyes became distant and rheumy. He took constant solace in strong drink. Then the beatings started.

At fifteen, Naomi was old enough to take over her mother's chores at the tavern. She worked from dawn until late at night doing all sorts of unpleasant jobs – cleaning vomit from the floors, fetching water, emptying chamber pots, washing laundry and dishes. Lebbaeus was just as stingy (and twice as lewd) with Naomi as he had been with her mother.

But no matter how much she worked, the money wasn't enough. Since Achyan spent his days drinking, they could no longer even afford rent. The landlord was threatening to put them out on the street before the start of Tishrei.

And now he actually wanted her to start whoring! Achyan had first mentioned the idea last week. Naomi suspected that Lebbaeus had put the thought in his mind. And how persistent her father was! Every day he urged Naomi to be an obedient daughter, saying that her mother would have wanted her to do whatever she could for her family.

She sniffed and wiped her eyes, rolling onto her side on the mat. She wondered what it would be like – whoring. She had watched the whores with fascination in the tavern. The free ones would at least talk to her. The slaves though – she winced as she thought of the life they led. Naomi could not imagine how they survived such beatings and shameful acts every day.

Even the free ones had a hardness to them. They were so used to dissembling for their clients that lying became natural. You could never tell when one was telling the truth or playing you for a fool. And they treated Naomi as an outsider – accusing her of thinking she was better than they were. Naomi didn't know what she had done to give them that impression.

She shuddered and looked around the room again. When was Achyan going to return? It must be almost noon. She was hungry and thirsty now. She had not been able to empty the pot in the corner and now it stank in here. Flies buzzed in through the window.

She sat on the floor with her back to the wall and let her mind wander.

She closed her eyes and smiled as she remembered four weeks ago when Te'oma first appeared in town. When she first saw him she had thought him beautiful. He was tall and thin with unusually light hair and striking gray eyes. His beard was short but thick against his sun-darkened face.

She had been cleaning the bar in the tavern the afternoon when he came in for a meal, wearing his threadbare green vest. His hair was wet, pulled straight back revealing a high forehead with a strange red birthmark, shaped like a fishhook. He had been bathing in the sea, he said, to wash off the dust of the road.

There was no one else in the tavern at the time. The master was away in the west. So they were able to talk. Te'oma told her of his travels all over Yudaea. He had just arrived after a long walk from the south. He had been living in the camp of Yochanan at the cliffs near the dead sea. As he spoke, Te'oma mentioned the prophet in every sentence as if he could not form a thought in his head that did not include his teacher. He told her of swimming in the Dead Sea – that it was even bigger than Lake Chinnereth, but you could not drink from it.

At length, after Te'oma had fallen silent, Naomi began to tell him of her own joyless life, and of her desire to escape. Instead of berating her, he listened. He spoke to her like she was someone of value. He looked into her eyes and seemed to actually be interested in what she had to say. No one but her mother had ever treated her this way.

That was when Te'oma mentioned that some of Yochanan's followers were women – even *unmarried* women.

~

The construction site was an ants' nest of activity throughout the morning. It seemed that Ba'asha had left some threat over Clopas before leaving, because the architect worked at a furious pace. There was ample to do in the interior of the building that was not affected by the disaster outside: Walls were being plastered, painted, and prepared for elaborate frescoes. Tiling and woodwork were ongoing. The heated spa in the lower level had not been big enough to please Ba'asha, so now it was being ripped out and enlarged.

Outside, the main task was to clean up the mess and assess the damage. After a thorough examination, Clopas determined that the crane was salvageable. Some of the wheel spokes and the locking mechanism would have to be replaced, along with some bracing beams. The important thing is that the long masts were unharmed.

The pediment facing was a different matter. When it fell, it broke into three large pieces. Just as it should have been delivered, mused Clopas. Unfortunately it fell face down onto rocks and other debris. The beautiful sculpture was crushed in many places. Clopas didn't think it could be mended, but he would leave that for others to decide.

Mattanyah came to Clopas shortly before noon. He said with bowed head, "My lord, I ask your leave until this afternoon. My nephew – I want to go see how he is being treated."

Clopas had borne the brunt of Ba'asha's boorishness for months, so he was not without sympathy. "I suppose. We will have to wait until the master's return to see what he wants to do about the carving. For your nephew's sake, I hope it can be saved."

Mattanyah wasted no time in hurrying to the north side of the acropolis. He eventually found Ba'asha's villa part way down the slope at the end of some twisty streets. The front door was blocked by a surly guard, who barked at him to go away. But Mattanyah knew the law regarding imprisonment of debtors, which Ba'asha claimed that Yeshua now was. Most Galileans had firsthand experience in these matters. They could not lawfully refuse Yeshua's visitors, at least not for the first thirty days. After a lengthy negotiation and a payment of five denarii (two whole days' pay), Mattanyah was told to go around to a service yard at the back of the villa.

He found the pathway that ran behind the house. He sidled past a foul-smelling pit that opened to the underground sewer. There, a manservant wearing a pale green tunic was doing some sort of repair work. Mattanyah hurried alongside a high stone fence and came to an arched entryway into the yard behind the house.

The guard post at the gate was presently unmanned. Mattanyah entered and spotted Yeshua against the back of the house. He sat on the ground with his back against the wall, exposed to the full midday sun. His arms were stretched to either side. When Mattanyah drew closer he could see Yeshua's wrists tightly bound to iron rings set into the stone wall. There were four such sets of rings fixed to the wall in a row. Judging from the well-worn ropes and stains on the wall, these rings were used often.

Before he could reach Yeshua he was intercepted by the guard. Mattanyah tried to push past him. "Great cauldron of plenty! Have mercy on the boy. He has not committed any violence. Why should you treat him this way?"

The guard responded impassively, "We were told to keep him here until the master returns tomorrow."

"So keep him. But you do not have to torture him. Let me give the boy some water and loosen his ropes."

The guard did not move out of the way, but seemed to be considering what Mattanyah said. "Talk to the head steward in the house. If he agrees, then you can attend to the boy."

Mattanyah was ushered to the back door of the villa by the guard. There he was greeted by a young serving girl. Her skin was dark, almost black. She was very short, practically a dwarf. She had to crane her neck to look up at him. She had an ugly scar on one side of her face from her chin to the edge of her left eye, which didn't open completely. Mattanyah wondered if this had been given to her by Ba'asha's dagger.

Mattanyah explained that he needed to speak to the head steward. The girl told him that he should follow her through the house. As she led him, Mattanyah marveled at the richness he saw. The floors were made of smooth white stone interspersed with braided tile sections. Polished black pillars supported the paneled ceiling. Everything was painted with rich colors – red, gold, the color of the sky. Some of the walls were covered with expensive-looking draperies. Others were painted or tiled in ornate patterns of bright green and yellow. At one point, they went through a kind of interior courtyard – the room had a shallow pool in the center below an opening in the roof. Mattanyah was amazed at so much space and luxury to house a single man and his family.

At length they arrived in a large vestibule by the front door. She told him to wait and left him alone. The space was devoid of furniture save for two potted plants. Mattanyah stood for a long time. After what seemed like an hour, he decided they must have forgotten him. He was about to set off in search of someone, when suddenly the wall behind him opened to reveal a hidden doorway.

A man entered and said, "I am told you wish to speak to me. Hmm?"

Mattanyah was taken aback by the man's appearance. He was very tall, with a shaved head. The dark eye makeup made him look Egyptian, except for his light complexion. He wore the same pale green, knee-length tunic, cinched with a rope around the waist, that the other servants wore. It seemed to be a kind of uniform for the house.

"Hmm?" the man coaxed, with a flourish of his hands. "As you can see, I am busy. Speak your mind."

"Yes, I'm sorry. I wanted to … I am here about … about the boy – the one you have confined in the work yard. He is my nephew." He paused, expecting some response. The steward simply raised a painted eyebrow inquiringly. Mattanyah wished he had thought more about what to say. "I … I am Mattanyah. I have lived in town for twelve years with my wife, Nura. The boy lives …"

The steward interrupted, "Your wife is Nura? The witch?"

"Why … Some call her that. Do you know of her?"

The tension melted from the steward's expression and he smiled warmly. "Yes! Yes, I know her. If it weren't for her attention three years ago, I would be a one-armed man now, or worse. You see here?" The steward held up his left arm and pulled back the loose-fitting sleeve. Mattanyah saw a jagged scar around the outside of his upper arm. "The bone was broken in two. The lower half was sticking completely through, right here."

Mattanyah nodded appreciatively at the fully healed wound. He did not know what to say.

"Your wife is Nura, the witch." The man said again. "Everyone said I was a dead man, but she put me back together. The gods have favored you, sir. I am deeply in her debt." The steward took both of Mattanyah's hands in his own and looked him in the eye. "Tell me now, how can I help you? Hmm?"

Mattanyah smiled at his change of fortune. "Thank you. Yes, I *am* a blessed man. Um, my nephew ... the boy you have tied up in the yard. It is just that ... well he is tied so tightly, against the wall like that. I give you my oath that he is not violent. Can anything be done?"

The steward frowned. He let go of Mattanyah's hands and brushed the folds of his tunic in a prissy manner. He buried his chin and his mouth in his right hand. "Hmm. The master left orders that the boy remain confined. He will have to be tied in some fashion, but I see no reason why he could not be made more comfortable for the time being. It will be done. Come with me."

Back out in the work yard, the steward spoke to the guard. They untied Yeshua's hands and brought him to a bench in the shade at the side of the building. They tied one ankle with a loose rope to the bench.

The steward lifted Yeshua's chin and met his eye. Lifting one eyebrow, he said, "I am doing this for you because of my debt to your aunt. I am promised by your uncle that you are not dangerous. Do I have your oath that you will not do anything harmful, or try to escape, hmm?"

Yeshua licked his parched lips and nodded.

"Then we have an understanding. I do not know what you did, but the guards who brought you here tell me that the master was very angry." As an aside to Mattanyah, he said with a mischievous glint in his eyes, "I would have liked to have seen that." Then to Yeshua, he resumed his stern tone, "I will have to put you back on the iron rings before the master returns tomorrow. After that, he will likely have me whip you. For that I apologize in advance."

Before leaving the steward once again addressed Mattanyah, "Please convey my blessing to your wife. Tell her that Yidrah once again thanks her with his whole heart."

When the steward had left, Mattanyah joined Yeshua on the bench and handed him a water skin. The boy drank greedily.

"You have done it this time," said Mattanyah. "That carving is probably ruined. Ba'asha seems determined to get payment of some form – probably demand you become his slave to work off the debt."

"Impossible," said Yeshua between gulps. "It is unlawful for a Jew to own another Jew."

Mattanyah grunted. "Unlawful? We are talking about Ba'asha here – one of Herod's men. It makes no difference whether you are talking about Levitical law or Roman law. Either way, they bend the law all the time to suit their whims. I wish you had thought before you cut that rope. So impulsive."

"But the man was trapped."

"We would have freed him before long. All we had to do was back the wheel up a few inches. Did you think of that?"

"No," admitted Yeshua. "I'm sorry." He rubbed his wrists where the ropes had left nasty abrasions.

"You're sorry. Tell that to Ba'asha when he returns."

They sat for a while in silence. The autumn sun was high in the sky. Mattanyah said, "I have to get back to the building site. I will send word to Nura about your predicament. Between the two of you connivers, somebody will come up with an idea."

"Thank you uncle."

~

Naomi must have dozed off. She was jolted awake by the sound of footsteps and talking on the floor below. Father – with someone else. Who has he brought with him? He could not be bringing men *here*, could he? Is he making his own home a brothel?

She quickly decided she would plead with whomever he was

bringing into the house. Hopefully, they will have more sense than her foolish father. She stood in the center of the room with her head defiantly high and waited.

The bolt was withdrawn. The door thrust open. Achyan walked in, followed by Lebbaeus, her master at the local tavern. She started to speak when two more men entered the room. She recognized them as the ruffians who kept order at the tavern. She had never spoken to either of them. When they weren't running some errand for Lebbaeus, they usually sat at their table in the corner, silently eyeing the crowds. What would they be doing here?

She focused her attention on Lebbaeus. "Sir, I know I am late for my chores. My father has kept me locked in this room. I will work late tonight for you. I ..."

Lebbaeus held up his palm indicating that she should be silent. She had seen him make this gesture to his clients a hundred times. She stood waiting, her eyes lowered. Lebbaeus walked behind her, looking her up and down. "Not bad. A bit skinny."

Naomi started to speak again when realization dawned on her. He is ... *selling* me? My father is *selling* me to Lebbaeus? I am to be one of the tavern slaves?

Achyan preened in his whiny voice. "She is very healthy. I am sure you can fatten her up if you believe that is what she needs." Then he added, "and keep in mind – she is a virgin. That ought to be worth something extra."

Lebbaeus snorted. "You would think that, wouldn't you Achyan? And how many times will I be able to tell that to her clients?" He shook his head in disgust as he continued his inspection. "Open your mouth girl. I need to see your teeth."

Naomi hesitated a moment, considering resistance. Then she noticed the two goons standing by the doorway glaring at her. She had seen them in action and did not want to be the recipient of their services. Now was not her moment. She opened her mouth.

Lebbaeus pinched her cheek hard and turned her head toward the light streaming in from the two windows. He clucked his tongue as he examined her teeth. "Lift your arms up," he commanded.

After another moment of hesitation, Lebbaeus nodded to the taller of his two men. Naomi wasn't sure, but she thought his name was Mak'ka. Without hesitation, the man walked behind her and roughly grabbed Naomi's wrists, holding them above her head.

In one quick motion, Lebbaeus lifted Naomi's robe up above her breasts. She struggled, but Mak'ka held her firmly while Lebbaeus undid her loincloth and examined every inch of her. Her face grew red with embarrassment and fury.

"She has spirit," said Lebbaeus. "Looks nice enough. A few rotten teeth. What are these marks on her back and buttocks?"

Achyan had been averting his eyes. It took him a moment to realize that the question was directed to him. He had not been sure what to expect in this meeting, and he was startled at the brutal efficiency in which this transaction was proceeding. He cleared his throat. "Well ... as you say, she has spirit. Occasionally I have to whip her with a cane."

Lebbaeus shook his head. "You must learn how to mete out discipline without leaving a mark. Those scars reduce the price that I can charge for her. And then of course, she's never done this kind of work before, so no one knows how well she'll perform."

Lebbaeus dropped the hem of Naomi's robe and nodded to Mak'ka, who released her and once again took his place by the door. Naomi quickly adjusted her robe, covering herself. She stood with her head down, shaking with shame.

Achyan sensed correctly that Lebbaeus was saying these things solely to reduce his expectations of getting a good price for his daughter. Secretly, Lebbaeus was delighted. He had always thought that Naomi was quite fetching. She would be the star of his collection after she learned how to behave.

"I'll tell you what, Achyan. We'll take her to the tavern and see how she works out. I'll give you half the profits on her earnings for the first six months. After that, I'll own her outright. That will leave me at a loss after I provide a bunk, clothes, and food. But I'm willing to do this since we are old friends. What do you say?"

Achyan was flabbergasted. He expected Lebbaeus to drive a hard bargain but this was insulting. "To tell you the truth, old friend, I was really hoping to have some money up front."

Lebbaeus expected this. "Of course, of course, I can give you an advance on her earnings. What do you suggest?"

Achyan screwed up his courage. "I was thinking of an up-front *payment*, not an advance. How about thirty shekels? Since we are indeed old friends."

"Thirty shekels! That's more than Mak'ka here earns in three months. No, no, that won't do."

The negotiations went on for a long time. They finally settled on five shekels plus one third of Naomi's earnings for the first six months. Each man spat on his right palm and they shook. Lebbaeus concealed his delight. He knew that the old fool would have no way of knowing what Naomi was actually earning. He also knew that before the week was out, Achyan would likely spend his five shekels on overpriced drink in his own tavern.

What happened next surprised both Achyan and Naomi in its suddenness. Lebbaeus nodded to the two ruffians, who approached the cowering girl. Mak'ka grabbed her hands and held them in front of her with his vice-like grip. She looked up into his scarred face but saw no mercy in his cold eyes. The other one produced a set of manacles and fastened them over Naomi's wrists.

They were so tight! She tested the chain by trying to jerk her arms apart and then cried out as the metal bit painfully into the bones of her wrists.

Lebbaeus stepped in front of her. He grabbed her chin and turned her face toward his, waiting until her eyes met his own. "Behave, slave. You are my property now. I am your master. In time you *will* learn obedience."

She spat in his face. "You have made a bad investment. I am not a slave ... not a whore."

Lebbaeus stepped back. He produced a clean white cloth from within the folds of his robe and wiped his face. The one called Mak'ka stepped forward and clapped her on the side of the head, hard. She felt dazed and would have fallen if he had not then reached out, holding her upright by her hair.

Lebbaeus said, "I don't make bad investments. And in the future, you will speak only when you are asked a question, and then you will address me as *my lord* or *master*." With that he turned and left the room. Mak'ka grabbed the chain between the manacles and pulled her roughly along.

Naomi called to Achyan, "Father! Wait! No, please!"

Achyan stood in the center of the room and kept his eyes low. Perhaps even he was feeling some shame now.

~

Selah was having a fun day. She had taken advantage of her father being abroad by dismissing her Latin tutor, and then inviting her two best friends, Zilpah and Eliysheba, for a visit. They had spent the last hour playing knucklebones in her chambers. Now bored, they decided to go out to the work yard for a picnic.

The three children first visited the kitchen and collected a pitcher of pomegranate juice, three cups, a fresh loaf of flatbread, and a bunch of black grapes. Zilpah carried these items on a tray as they walked out into the sunshine. Eliysheba led the old gray dog, Chup, on a leash, who followed hesitantly, wagging his tail.

They walked to the shaded area in the yard and found a strange boy sitting on the ground, staring idly at the sky. When they drew close, Selah started when she saw that his ankle was tied with a length of rope to the bench. She motioned the other girls to stand back.

"You are the bandit that my father caught this morning!" She accused.

The boy smiled at Selah and her friends. "Bandit?"

"Keep back Zilpah. I'm sure he is dangerous," Selah warned. She was a little afraid, but also enthralled to be so close to a criminal. The boy was older than he looked at first glance. He had patches of whiskers here and there on his face. "How old are you?" She asked.

He turned and sat cross-legged on the ground, still smiling. "Sixteen. And how old are you?"

"I'm almost ten," she replied reflexively. But then she frowned and scolded herself internally for answering the question of an inferior, and an outlaw at that. "You didn't answer my first question." She said sharply.

"I don't think you asked another one."

She sighed. "You heard me. Are you the bandit my father caught? Yes or no!"

"Oh ... then no, and no. Not a bandit. Didn't run away. So ... you must be Ba'asha's daughter?"

This time Selah ignored the impertinent inquiry. "So you deny being a bandit. Then are you some kind of rebel?"

The boy seemed to consider this. "Some kind, perhaps."

Selah gave her companions a knowing glance. "You see how he evades my question? My father tells me this is how guilty men behave. He is hiding the truth," she said smugly.

The boy laughed. "You are indeed Ba'asha's daughter. Now you even sound like him."

"Enough of your insolence, boy! What is your name then?"

"My name is Yeshua." He gave a little bow with his head. Turning to the girl on the left he said, "I gather that your name is Zilpah. I am pleased to meet you."

Zilpah giggled. "I think he's making fun of you, Selah."

Yeshua turned, "Ah, *Selah* – rock. That's a hard name for such a pretty girl. But I take your meaning. No, I don't think I am what your father would call a rebel."

Selah persisted, "Well then, what? Did you kill someone? Are you dangerous?"

"Again, no and no, at least not to you, but both of those things are different from each other, and different from being a rebel."

Selah was confused. She seemed to have initiated a game of wits, which everyone was enjoying but her. Even the guard ventured close now to listen to the exchange. She thought for a moment and then said, "I think that you must have stolen something from my father."

Yeshua said, "That bread smells good. Fresh from the hearth."

"Ah, you see again how he ignores my questions?" Selah said

triumphantly.

The third girl now spoke. "But Selah, you didn't ask a question. This one is clever. You have to be careful how you word things." And then she turned to Yeshua and said with a curtsy, "And my name is Eliysheba."

Selah was catching on. "No more games, boy. Did you steal something from my father?"

Yeshua began doodling in the ground with his finger. "Your father pretended to value something. It was lost. I had a part in it."

Selah stabbed the air with her finger. "There – do you see? He answers with nonsense!" She turned back to Yeshua and said, "My father is one of the most important men in the city. What did you steal?"

Yeshua shrugged. "I did borrow something ... his dagger."

"His dagger!" Said Selah. "The one with the pearl handle and jewels? He never lets anyone touch that!" Then she thought another moment and added, "You said 'borrow'. So ... you gave it back."

Again after a silence Zilpah nudged her in the side. "Ask him a question."

"Oh, wait. My father would be angry about the dagger, but he wouldn't imprison you if you gave it back. Maybe just have you whipped. So you must have done something else. Maybe you stabbed someone with it." And then, after receiving no reply, she sighed heavily and added, "Why did you borrow the dagger?"

"I sliced through a rope," replied Yeshua.

Selah now felt she was getting somewhere. She pressed on. "A *rope*? Why would my father care so much about a rope? He can buy seven times seventy ropes."

The guard who had been observing now spoke: "Don't listen to him young miss, I heard about the whole thing. He cut the rope to the crane that was holding up a sculpture for the new basilica. It fell and shattered when ..."

"I don't believe I gave you permission to speak!" Selah said sharply. "Go back to your post at once."

The guard replied sheepishly, "Uh ... yes miss. Forgive me." He returned to the gate and watched from a distance.

Selah continued, "So ... you smashed my father's sculpture. That's what you meant when you said something he valued was lost." Again she remembered that she had not phrased it as a question, so she added, "Is that right?"

Yeshua looked up and smiled once again. "I said something he *pretended to* value was lost. No doubt he will buy another stone, another rock, another 'selah'. After all, it was just a stone."

Eliysheba now spoke again, "Selah, let's have our picnic here. This bandit is interesting."

Zilpah set the tray down on a small table. Eliysheba released Chup to roam the yard, but the old dog remained seated before them with his tongue hanging out the side of his mouth. The three girls sat on the bench and began eating grapes.

Selah asked her friends, "Dare I continue the interrogation?" They both giggled and nodded. Selah asked Yeshua, "So, you cut a rope and smashed my father's statue. Can you tell us why you did that?"

Yeshua responded, "If I answer, may I have some grapes?"

Selah smiled slyly. "First he evades, and now he bargains. But let's play along. Zilpah, give him three grapes. No more."

Yeshua got up on his knees. He took the proffered grapes and, to the delight of the girls, started to juggle them. After several seconds he threw each up high and caught them in turn with his right hand. He waved his hand high in the air, and then to his side. He brought his right fist before them and opened it, palm up. No grapes.

The girls were delighted. "Where did they go?" Eliysheba asked.

Yeshua said, "Well ... one is here." He opened is left hand revealing a grape. "Another is here." He reached behind old Chup's ear and retrieved a grape. "And finely there is one here." He opened his mouth to show a grape between his front teeth. He chomped down. "Delicious," he said.

The girls clapped and giggled with amazement. "How did you do that?" Selah asked.

"You just have to pay attention." Yeshua set the pitcher to one side and took the tray into his lap. He upended the three ceramic cups on the tray. "Now watch!" He raised each cup, one at a time, showing that there was nothing underneath, and then asked. "Where are the other two grapes you gave me? I seem to have lost them." He made a show of looking on the ground to either side, and under the bench. Finally he raised each of the three cups. They all now had grapes underneath.

Their jaws dropped. Selah said, "but you ate one!"

Yeshua continued by removing the grapes from the cups on either side, but he left the grape under the middle one. "Are you paying attention?" he asked.

They all nodded. He started to slide the cups rapidly about on the tray. After a moment he stopped and looked up at Selah. "Did you follow the grape?"

"I think so," she said pointing to the cup on Yeshua's right.

"Very good!" he said, turning the right cup over to reveal a grape.

Eliysheba said, "Huh! I thought it was the middle one."

"Very good to you too!" Said Yeshua, lifting the middle cup to reveal a second grape.

Zilpah reached over to the left cup, lifting it to reveal a third grape.

Again they all clapped. Selah said, "You *have* to teach me that."

Yeshua frowned, "Magis are supposed to keep their art secret, except to other magis. Are you a magi?"

Selah replied, "No. Well, I don't know. I never tried ..." And then seeing the circular logic in Yeshua's question, she said, "I mean, yes. I am a magi too."

Yeshua laughed. "Very well – I thought maybe you were. I can teach you, but it will take practice. And remember, once you learn, keep it secret."

Selah called to the guard that she had scolded before. "Fetch another chair and a cup for Yeshua, right away!"

~

Ba'asha was not accustomed to waiting. After traveling through the morning and midday he had now been sitting in this tavern for over an hour. Did Lebbaeus not *want* his his advocacy? He had better get here soon.

The barmaid came over once again and asked if there was anything he desired. She said something about a lovely lamb stew they have today. He shoved his empty goblet toward her and and waved her away. He did not want to wait in this dump one minute longer than necessary. Perhaps he had made a mistake in coming.

As he fumed, his mind wandered. He was still upset about the events in Sepphoris this morning – the impudence of that boy! There was no way he could make the idiot or his uncle pay. They obviously had no money. But he *would* exact his revenge. He could derive some enjoyment from that.

He took a deep breath and calmed himself. If things worked out as planned, it would be well worth a little inconvenience. He had the ear of Antipas as much as anyone, and more than most. Lebbaeus and the other hucksters in this town would pay handsomely for his patronage.

The barmaid brought him another goblet of wine and then withdrew wordlessly. Ba'asha sipped and idly stared at the mosaic floor. It was a strange collection of images done in white, sky, and rose-colored tiles. The boat and fish made sense – this was a fishing town after all. The kantheros, or two handled drinking goblet, made sense, he supposed, because this was a tavern. The ball-and-two-cups also seemed fitting. Indeed, he had seen young men betting their wages over that very game just a little while ago. The image in the upper left was harder to understand. It looked like two strigili, with something round in between – an aryballos maybe?

His thoughts strayed back to the political maneuvering that he was currently engaged in. Nobody knew why Antipas wanted a new capital city. To Ba'asha, it seemed a childish whim. The concrete wasn't yet cured on half the buildings in Sepphoris. It now had a spacious theater, a palace, a temple sanctuary, basilicas, and even a Roman bathhouse. The underground plumbing from the cisterns on the hilltop brought fresh water throughout the city. It was a thing of beauty.

 He sighed and reminded himself of his station. What Herod wants, Herod gets. He wants a new city by the inland sea, then that's what he'll have. Perhaps Antipas has some of his father in him. Whenever one project is finished he wants to start an even bigger one.

Ba'asha had been Antipas' advisor and chief tax collector for Galilee since shortly after Herod the Great died. Had it really been seventeen years? Antipas was always on the move, dividing his time between Sepphoris, Caesarea on the coast, and Yerushalayim. And now he wants to build another city here on Lake Chinnereth. Why?

Ba'asha's current task was to assist with the selection of a location for the new capital. They had narrowed the choice to two locations: here at Magdala, and another site a few miles down the shore – a tiny village named Rakkat. Wherever it was, Antipas had told him privately that he planned to name it 'Augustus' after the Roman emperor. Typical Antipas, thought Ba'asha, always pandering to the Romans. It would be amusing to see how *that* name would go over with the locals.

Ba'asha had considerable interest in seeing the capital built here in Magdala. Besides owning a good bit of the land here and in the surrounding hills, he was making alliances with other landholders here, like Lebbaeus. With a little luck, this would end up being very lucrative indeed.

He had to think of a way to outflank Antipas' other advisor, Abiyram, who was advocating for Rakkat. What an absurd choice that would be. There's nothing there, and the steep hills go right to the shore. Magdala was clearly the sensible choice.

One of Ba'asha's servants had recently given him some useful information. Apparently, Abiyram had an appetite for young boys. He considered how to set a trap to have a rabbi catch him in some sordid act. He needed a way to shame him thoroughly, so that even

Antipas would feel compelled to shun him.

The noise at the front door brought him out of his ruminations. He looked up to see the two tavern thugs dragging in a manacled girl, followed by Lebbaeus. The girl was putting up a good fight. As they reached the foot of the steps and pushed her up, she bent forward and kicked back, slamming her right heel into the shorter man's testicles.

The man roared with pain and was about to slam her with his fist when Lebbaeus grabbed his arm. "Fool! Don't damage my property. Take her upstairs to the back room and chain her to the post." Then turning to the girl, he said, "You *will* behave. Someone will be up to attend to you shortly."

Ba'asha laughed and called out, "Lebbaeus, it's good to see that you still provide quality entertainment in this establishment."

Lebbaeus noticed his visitor for the first time. "Ba'asha! What are you doing here? I mean, of course it's always a pleasure to see you. My lord, I trust that they've been taking good care of you?"

Ba'asha grunted, making it clear that he was displeased at the waste of his precious time. "I had other business in town and I thought I would stop in to check on my investments. It looks like you've had your hands full."

"I am sorry to make you wait. I have had to deal with a new ... acquisition, which took longer than I expected." Lebbaeus turned to the barmaid. "Send Sheraga to clean her up and put a dress on her. She can't continue wearing those smelly rags."

"Yes, master." The barmaid bowed and retreated to a back room.

Lebbaeus walked behind the bar and brought out a jug of wine and two fresh goblets. He joined Ba'asha at his table, poured the wine and raised his glass. "To success."

"Whatever Lebbaeus, whatever." Both men drank. "We have a problem."

Ba'asha took a few moments telling Lebbaeus about Abiyram, and that Antipas was seriously considering an alternate location for his new capital.

"Rakkat? You can't be serious. It's a latrine! Steep cliffs, and a few shacks. Here we have ...”

Ba'asha cut him off. “Save it. You don't need to convince me. I have a plan you can help with. I need you to find me a boy, about eight or nine years – someone who won't be missed.”

~

Yeduthun's mother told him to bring the basket of food straight to his cousin, but he had gotten distracted along the way. Just after passing the market he came upon three of his friends, shooting rocks at broken amphorae with their slings. Yedu always carried his with him and was easily persuaded to join the others in a contest. Thus the afternoon was waning when he finally ascended the hill to the acropolis.

His mother had given him directions to Ba'asha's villa and told him to walk around back to the servant's entrance. He entered the yard and spied his cousin dozing on richly colored cushions in the shade. No one else was around except for the guard, who sat in a chair by the entrance. The guard looked up as Yedu entered, but seeing that he was not a threat, waved him through.

His mother told him that Yeshua was imprisoned, but it looked more like he was being treated as an honored guest. He was in the cool shade and had a soft place to rest. A pitcher of water and a bowl of dates had even been placed on a table nearby.

“Yeshua?”

His cousin stirred and opened his eyes. “Yedu!” He arose from the cushions and yawned. “What brings you here?” He started toward the boy, but tripped and fell flat when the rope around his ankle became taut. He picked himself up and dusted himself off. “You will have to come closer to embrace me.”

Yedu approached. “My mother told me you were imprisoned – that you would be hungry, but ... you have plenty here already.”

“Nonsense. Let's see what my good Aunt Ruth has sent.” Yedu handed him the basket. He raised the cloth cover and inhaled the aroma of fresh bread. “Mmmm. How did she learn of my misfortune?”

"Nura stopped by our house a couple of hours ago. She said she could not visit you until tonight. So my mother sent me. What happened?"

"First eat, then talk. Help me drag this table to the bench, would you?"

They set the basket down and together slid the heavy oak table. They seated themselves and unpacked the food. Yedu's mother, Ruth, had sent a fresh loaf of oat bread, some olives in a wax-sealed jar, two boiled eggs, and a few brined parsnips. "A feast!" pronounced Yeshua. "Let's eat!"

Yeshua told the story of the crane disaster and the ruined sculpture. Then he had questions of his own. "Now Yedu, my aunt told me that there is going to be a wedding. Who is this man who is taking your lovely sister away from me?"

Yedu frowned. "You know my father does not like it when you joke like that." He paused to spit out a date pit. "His name is Ephrayim. He's young, but he already owns a farm in Cana. He comes to town on market days. He is some relation to my father – second cousin, I think."

"Cana? I went there once – a half day's walk up the old north road. Not much of a town – a few huts surrounded by farms – kind of like where I grew up. Years ago Yoceph sent me there to trade for an ox."

"I didn't know your father had an ox."

"The ox? It died the year after. Bad luck for Yoceph. And he's not my father."

Yedu looked at him quizzically.

"You didn't know that? I thought everyone did. I am Yeshua bar David," he said with pride. "David was my mother's *first* husband. He died before I was born."

"Oh." Yedu considered this. "But ... your brothers, Ya'aqob and Shimown, and your sisters?"

"Those are indeed Yoceph's children. You can tell, especially with Ya'aqob. He has Yoceph's height and ill temper."

Yedu put it together. "That's why you live here with Nura and

Mattanyah."

Yeshua spoke through a mouthful of bread. "Truly. Ya'aqob is to inherit. He is Yoceph's first born, not I. I came here when I was about your age, twelve is it?"

"Truly," echoed Yedu. He liked the way Yeshua spoke. "Twelve this past summer – not yet the 'age of majority,' as Rabbi Eyphah constantly reminds me."

Yeshua spat out a half-chewed olive. "Not that haughty old fool! Your father is sending you to *him* for instruction?"

Yedu was dismayed by the scorn in Yeshua's voice. "But Rabbi told me that you once studied with him. And your brother Ya'aqob does now too."

"Eyphah wouldn't stop for me and my brother if we were dying on the side of the road. But we are nephews of *your* father – the powerful Natan, master of the grain. So, yes. He taught me for a little while. Then I quit. Never listen to people who have all the answers. You'll never ask the right questions."

They sat for a while in silence, dipping their bread in olive oil and chewing pensively. Yedu felt compelled to defend his teacher. "Ya'aqob likes him. I don't think he's so bad. He says I can take part in the Yom Kippur fast this year. He says we must all expiate for our sins." His voice adopted a solemn tone.

Yeshua laughed. "And I'm sure your sins are grievous indeed."

Yedu said, "There are four of us in the group. He asked each boy what we most desired. I said I wanted a horse. One of the other boys in the group has one. His father is rich."

"Coveting," interrupted Yeshua.

"That's what Rabbi said. Then he asked what we thought about girls. One of the other boys said he dreamt about seeing his sister naked. Rabbi said that was very shameful."

Yeshua said, "Ah ... let me guess. He quoted the passage about how Onan spilled his seed on the ground and it was offensive to Hashem?"

Yedu looked up in surprise. "Yes!"

"Oh, but wait. You said the boy dreamt about his own sister. So he must have quoted the law about how you shall not have intercourse with your sister, whether she lives in the same house as you or not."

"That one too. How did you know?"

Yeshua shook his head in disgust. "I was once in one of his little groups. He makes all his boys tell their secrets and then finds some Torah passage to shame them."

"But ... if it is in the law, it *is* shameful, isn't it? He said that thinking about a sin was just as bad as actually committing it."

Yeshua sighed and shook his head. "After my sessions with Rabbi, I used to talk to old Onesicritus – you know, the cynic in town."

"My father told me to stay away from him," said Yedu.

"Yes. Natan would. But let me tell you what he once told me. That proverb you just said – thinking about a sin is as bad as doing it – the cynic said that proverb can either expand your heart or shrink it."

"What does that mean?"

"I'll tell you the way the cynic told me." Yeshua paused and cleared his throat. "Imagine you are a vendor in the market. On your grill you are roasting lamb skewers to sell. Meat is scarce and you paid a high price. The wood cost you dearly, and you also had to pay the market tax. You worry about making a profit. Now, along comes a dirty street orphan who tries to steal one of your skewers. How do you feel?"

Yedu replied without hesitation. "Angry I guess. My father always talks about how bad it is to steal. The boy should be punished."

Yeshua continued, "Now expand your heart. Suppose *you* are the dirty orphan. You haven't eaten since yesterday, and that was only a stale crust of bread. You're standing in the crowded market in front of a grill filled with succulent lamb skewers. The smell is tying your stomach in knots. The busy merchant doesn't notice you. He has so much and you have nothing. You don't think he will mind if one disappears. Now how do you feel?"

Yedu considered this perspective. "Well, I guess taking just one skewer wouldn't be so bad. The vendor should give him one. But ... what does that have to do with the proverb?

"We've all *thought* about stealing at one time or another. Maybe we shouldn't judge the boy who does steal, because we don't know the trials he is going through."

Yedu thought for a moment. "Then what's the way where it shrinks your heart?"

"That's the way your Rabbi Eyphah means it. He wants you to feel shame ... hatred turned inward. And why? So he can offer you forgiveness for a price."

Yedu sat in silence thinking about this.

"Don't worry too much about the rabbi," said Yeshua. "You haven't done or thought anything that every other boy hasn't, me included." Then with a mischievous grin he added, "*Your* sister Channah is rather pretty isn't she?"

"Yeshua!"

~

Mak'ka dragged Naomi up the stairs to one of the back rooms of the tavern. These rooms were where the whores lived and did their business. The other brute was keeping his distance, still limping and holding his groin. Mak'ka threw her down on a mattress on the floor, which consisted of a dirty linen covering a mound of coarse straw. At the head was a heavy wooden post rising through the room to support the ceiling.

Mak'ka knelt at her side and undid the manacle on her right wrist. What relief to have a hand free! Naomi sat up and flexed her hand. She rubbed her sore wrist against her side.

Mak'ka pushed her back down roughly on her back. He grabbed her free hand and dragged her toward the post. He looped the chain around the post and once again fastened the manacle to her wrist. It was even tighter than before.

"You might as well try to get some rest. It may be a busy night for you." He nodded to the other man and together they left the room, closing the door behind them. She heard a heavy latch being pushed into place on the outside of the door. *As if the chain isn't enough to hold me,* she thought.

As she lay on her back, she raised her head and looked around the room. Windows on two walls provided light and air. She could smell the fishy scent of boats bringing in their catches for the afternoon. She also smelled bread baking in the kitchen below. Her stomach grumbled as she realized that it was now quite late in the day. She hadn't had anything to eat or drink the whole day. Her throat was parched.

Some time later, the bolt was released and the door opened. Sheraga, the headmistress, walked into the room. She was an old woman, perhaps thirty-five. Naomi knew that she had been a whore in her younger years. It was hard to imagine men paying her to take her clothes off now. She was quite heavy with stringy gray hair. She had a pock-marked face with a big hairy mole on her left cheek.

"Oh, if it isn't pretty young Naomi. I thought that was you I saw dragged in. Not so proud now are you? Welcome to our brothel." She made an exaggerated bow.

"Sheraga, why are you mocking me? I was never disrespectful to you."

Sheraga snorted. "Oh, you didn't have to be, *sweet* Naomi. We could all tell from the way you looked at us what you thought of our business. What you thought of us."

"Sheraga, I never ..."

"Save it!" came the sharp retort. "The master tells me to come up here – get you cleaned up, ready for business. So that's what I plan to do."

"Sheraga, No. Please. Listen." Naomi's voice became a whisper. "You can just let me go. Tell him the room was empty when you came up. Tell him ..."

By the pitiless look in Sheraga's eyes, Naomi could tell she was wasting her breath. There would be no help here. She closed her eyes and awaited the next indignity.

Sheraga grabbed her chin and forced Naomi to meet her gaze.

"Now listen, we can do this easy, or we can do it hard. I'm going to have to undo one of the manacles. Before you think of giving me any trouble, know that Mak'ka is standing right outside the door, AREN'T YOU MAK'KA?"

In reply, a muffled grunt came from the hall.

"Now, I'm going to be *real* gentle. But, if I have to call for help, well then ... then things won't go so nice. First, I'm going to help you make your toilet. You smell. We'll get you nice and clean, and we'll put on this pretty red dress. Then I'm going to put a little makeup on that plain face of yours. You've probably never worn make-up have you?"

Naomi shook her head.

"I'm told it comes from Egypt. The men do seem to like their girls painted."

Sheraga squatted behind the post to unfasten one manacle. "Remember what I said. You behave – I'll even get you something to eat and drink. Life here isn't so bad, we just need to get to know each other better." She cackled as if she had said something hilarious.

Naomi did not resist. She breathed deeply and tried to calm herself. She would need patience. She would also need strength. Her mouth watered at the thought of food and drink.

She did everything Sheraga asked of her without complaint. True to her word, Sheraga had a bowl of runny stew brought up from the kitchen along with some water. Naomi wolfed it down hungrily while the headmistress watched her with an amused expression.

"Now girl, listen good. I'm going to chain you to that post again. Remember what we said about giving me trouble. You'll be on your back, so it won't be so bad. There *are* less comfortable ways to be chained. Soon, after the master trusts you more, the chain won't be necessary. But tonight, it is. You might have an easy night. I don't think the master has any clients for you just yet. He usually likes to break the girls in himself before he puts them in circulation." This was followed by another wicked cackle.

After Sheraga left, Naomi lay on her back with her arms stretched out above her head. Testing the chains, she noticed that the manacle on her right wrist wasn't as tight as before. In fact it was quite loose – not painful at all. She tried to make her hand as narrow as possible and pull it through the metal cuff. After several attempts she gave up. It was not quite loose enough, and now her hand was starting to swell where it was being squeezed painfully against the metal. She relaxed again on the straw mattress. Her mind wandered.

Her thoughts turned again to Te'oma.

Such a serious young man he was – so full of purpose. Te'oma boasted that he had been given his mission by Yochanan himself. He was to travel Galilee – to his home village and the surroundings. He was to tell Yochanan's sayings to whoever would listen, and bring them to the south to be washed in the river. There was some Greek word he used – baptize, that was it.

To Naomi, Yochanan sounded like a crazy man. Te'oma said he wore nothing but a burlap loincloth and ate nothing but crickets and bread. He even would take no wine. He preached that Alilah would come into the world very soon to restore the ancient kingdom. We would rule over the Romans, and the evil ones like Herod would be overthrown. He said that the priests and rabbis were in league with the Romans and that we must not to listen to them. When King David returned, there would be justice. The land would produce. There would be no tax and everyone would have plenty to eat.

Te'oma was so passionate. Naomi wanted to believe him, but his words were so foreign to everything she had experienced in life. Hardship and disappointment – these were real. Anything else was just a dream.

Te'oma had left Magdala five days ago, just after Shabbat. He went west toward Sepphoris. He said his childhood home was near there and he wanted to see his father again. Sabah – that was the name. He had promised to return within the week and take her with him to the south. He would be back any day now.

A scary thought occurred to Naomi: What would happen when Te'oma came looking? Her father might say that she had run off. Te'oma might leave for the south without her. She closed her eyes and concentrated, praying hard. She made a deal with Alilah that if he guided Te'oma to her, she would become an ardent follower of Yochanan. None would surpass her in zeal. Not even Te'oma.

~

It was late in the afternoon. It had been quiet in the work yard since Yedu left hours before. Yeshua idly watched a striped cat walk along a narrow dividing wall at the edge of the herb garden. It held its tail straight up, proudly displaying its hind parts.

Since Yidrah had spoken to him, the guard had been very accommodating to Yeshua, letting him walk around the yard occasionally to stretch his legs. He even let him untie his ankle and use the servant's latrine when he needed to. Still, he was restless. There was nothing to *do* here.

He was lost in his thoughts when three women entered the yard from the house. The one in front strode purposefully in a flowing white dress that accentuated her abundant figure. She had graying hair, done up in elaborate curls piled atop her head. Over her dress she wore a black lace shawl fringed with what looked like pearls. Her expression was sour as she stormed into the yard. Yeshua noticed the guard come to attention.

Following her was a much smaller woman wearing an Arabian dress with lavish gold jewelry ornamenting her ears, neck, and wrists. She walked several paces behind, keeping her head mostly toward the ground. She seemed frail – even dizzy – often leaning on the third woman for support. The third woman was the same black-skinned serving girl with the scar on her face he had seen earlier.

The three marched to where Yeshua sat. The fat one stood before him with a fierce glare. He looked up and smiled. But not knowing what was appropriate to say or do, he remained silent.

"Get up, boy. How dare you sit there like a toad in our presence." Her voice was low-pitched, almost masculine.

Yeshua complied. After arising he had a better view of the frail woman. She was much younger than the fat one. Indeed, Yeshua thought she might be about his own age, or maybe just a bit older.

She would have been pretty if not for her sunken, sad eyes. She looked up in short glances, but mostly kept her eyes to the ground.

Yeshua stammered, "Um, yes, ladies, I was just ..."

The fat woman rolled her eyes at the sky. "Do you even know who we are, boy?"

"Ma'am, I confess I do not."

The fat one clapped once and nodded to the serving girl, who stepped forward with a scared look. She cleared her throat and pronounced in a heavy accent, "This is Hadassah, wife of Ba'asha, mistress of this house." She folded her hands in front of her and lowered her eyes.

The fat one, Hadassah, sighed, turned, and then slapped the girl violently across the face. "Our guest. You must also announce our guest." And then, as an aside to the frail woman, she added, "If you don't strike them, they never learn."

"I am sorry, my lady," said the serving girl. Gesturing toward the sickly Arabian woman, she continued, "This is Phasaelis, princess of Nabatea and wife of the Tetrarch."

Yeshua looked sympathetically at the serving girl. What a lot of protocol these people demand, he thought.

Hadassah mistook this look for confusion. "The Tetrarch ... Herod, you fool. Mind your manners and give her a proper bow."

Again Yeshua complied by bowing low on one knee toward Phasaelis. When he arose he saw her briefly attempt a smile. Through purple lips, he caught a glimpse of graying teeth. She immediately lowered her eyes. Yeshua thought of the image of a trapped animal.

Hadassah said, "You are sure this is the one?"

The serving girl nodded profusely, not wanting to be slapped again.

Hadassah glared at Yeshua. "You are the boy that was brought here by the guards this morning. I am told that there is some debt involved, but I do not know nor care about the particulars."

Seeing that she was waiting for some reply, Yeshua said, "Yes ma'am."

Hadassah grunted and said to Phasaelis, "He looks harmless – so young." Turning back to Yeshua, she demanded, "Boy, I am told that you have been teaching sorcery to my daughter. Is this true?"

Yeshua widened his eyes. So that's what this was about. "You mean Selah? Oh. I wouldn't call it sorcery."

"What *would* you call it?"

"A trick ... with cups and grapes. Your daughter asked me to teach it to her."

She persisted: "So you admit that you teach the dark arts?"

Yeshua was alarmed at the direction of this inquiry. Sorcery was a serious charge. He hesitated, and then said, "Uh ... That is not what I said."

"You contradict me? How dare you, boy. I just heard you say it."

Yeshua sighed and looked at the ground. He mumbled, "Hear what you want to hear."

Hadassah wagged her finger accusingly. "I'm right here, boy. To whom are you talking?"

Yeshua glanced up briefly and then back at the ground. "To no one, because no one is listening."

The serving girl was aghast at Yeshua's impertinence. Hadassah was livid. She clapped her hands sharply and said, "Look here you little ..."

Just then Phasaelis widened her eyes in panic. Putting her hand over her mouth, she ran to the shrubs alongside the herb garden and began vomiting. Yeshua was, for the moment, forgotten. Hadassah and the serving girl ran to assist Phasaelis as she knelt at the bushes, heaving.

This went on for several minutes. The guard came over but no one knew what to do. Hadassah patted her on the back, trying to be comforting. "There, there, my lady. Get it out now, you'll feel better."

After a time the sickness passed, although Phasaelis continued to shake visibly. Yeshua appeared behind the guard, "Let us assist her to the bench, and bring those cushions over there." He then asked the serving girl to fetch her a cup of fresh water from the pitcher.

They made her comfortable on the bench. Phasaelis leaned back on the cushions and sipped the water, gradually becoming calm. At length she spoke: "We must take our medicine." Her voice was weak and high pitched, with a melodious accent. Sitting up, she untied a leather cord that had been around her neck. With the cord, she pulled from within her dress a wooden vial carved into the form of a woman with a very swollen belly. She unscrewed the head of the figure and pulled it off. Attached was a small ivory spoon. She upended the vial and measured two spoonfuls of a gray oily substance, stirring it into her cup of water.

Yeshua noticed a minty smell ... and something else. "My lady, may I ask what this potion is?" He saw that Hadassah was about to object to his effrontery, so he added hastily, "Ma'am, I am apprentice to a master healer in town."

Phasaelis answered, although she would not speak directly to Yeshua. To Hadassah she said, "Tell the boy this was prepared for us by the Roman Medicus. Why does he ask?"

Yeshua answered, "Ma'am, my master has taught me many recipes for potions. Even the Roman Medicus ... Macula I think his name is, comes to my master for advice from time to time. My master is Nura. Perhaps you have heard of her?"

Phasaelis looked up at him and actually smiled. "Indeed. Tell the boy to guess the ingredients from the smell." She held out the open vial for Yeshua to take a sniff. He recoiled at the strength of the odor.

All were waiting. He replied: "Cassia, something minty ... and something strong, like wild radish."

Phasaelis attempted a laugh, which ended in a coughing fit. When she recovered, she said, "Tell the boy he has a good nose. Macula told us the ingredients. We remember rhubarb, cassia, dead sea bitumen, pulegium, and ... croton oil. There were others that we do not remember."

Yeshua frowned thoughtfully. "Croton oil? My master uses that when someone has swallowed poison – to make them throw it up. That may be what is making you sick."

Hadassah objected: "Don't listen to him my lady. I think a medicus knows more about ..."

Yeshua interrupted her, "Macula is capable for the most part. But remember that he is, first and foremost, a Roman. And we are Jews."

Hadassah was about to reply but Phasaelis cut her off with a wave of her hand. "The boy speaks truth. Although we are not what you would call Jew, but rather daughter of the King of Nabatea." Then she turned to Yeshua and addressed him directly. "We would do well to have another opinion, as we have grown mistrustful of the medicus. Who are you?"

"My name is Yeshua."

"Yeshua ... The medicus prescribed to us because we are ... 'a field without crops.' We have been unable to produce an heir for the Tetrarch."

Yeshua nodded sympathetically.

Phasaelis continued in her sing-song voice: "Macula says our womb wanders about the body. This potion is meant to settle it down – to keep it between our legs."

Hadassah grew embarrassed by the intimacy of this exchange. She interjected, "My lady. I really think you're wasting your time talking to this common boy. We should ..."

"Pulegium?" asked Yeshua. "Pulegium regium – are you sure?"

Phasaelis dipped her head. "Yes. That is what he said. Why?"

"My lady, you should stop taking this potion. I believe that pulegium is taken by women who want to avoid having ... crops in their fields.

"What?" Again Hadassah exclaimed. "This is too much. Really. Macula has years of experience. He has served me well many times. Who are you to question his treatments? Don't listen to him my lady. Let us ... my queen?"

The frail young woman had begun weeping. She held up her hand to stop Hadassah's tirade. "Enough! Six months! We have endured this weakness for six long months. A curse on all foul Romans!" She lay back and put her hand over her eyes. Between sobs, she continued, "They tolerate our husband because he keeps order. But it is no secret that they despise him. They must think this a very funny joke."

Hadassah was still not convinced. "But ... why would they? What would they have to gain?" Then it hit her. She answered her own question. "An heir. They want to avoid any trouble with succession. They want to appoint their own praefectus to rule over Galilee as he does now over southern Yudaea. They don't want Antipas to have an heir."

Yeshua said, "This is what I meant about Macula. A Roman soldier does what he is told. We are to be used as needed."

After a while Phasaelis' weeping subsided. She sat for a while thinking, her expression unreadable. She abruptly threw the wooden vial on the ground. Her face became a mask of anger. "Our husband is a cruel man, but simple. This deviousness is beyond his guile. Romans are arrogant to no end. Such disdain they have for us. They don't even try to hide it. We have heard them speak openly: 'Herod is pain in the arse – always asking for more land, more power'. This is their way to ensure his blood line ends."

Hadassah consoled. "My lady, there must be some explanation ..."

"Silence!" Phasaelis' voice was gathering strength in her new-found rage. "Romans think they can use us howsoever they please, but in this instance they are mistaken. They shall pay for this insult. When our husband finds out about this, they will pay. They will learn what power Herod still has."

She abruptly rose. "We shall burn this foul idol of Tellus Mater." She picked up the vial and walked toward the brazier smoldering at the edge of the work yard, shaking with both weakness and anger.

"Wait!" It was Yeshua who spoke. "Do that, and they'll just look for another way to get to you. You can't beat the Romans directly. Instead, why don't we turn the game around?"

Phasaelis hesitated. "What do you mean?"

Yeshua thought for a moment and then said, "My master will visit here tonight. I can ask her to make a harmless potion that looks and smells like your poison. Whenever you visit Macula to refill the vial, send it to Nura to be discarded and replaced. In fact, Nura can probably find a formula that *will* help you conceive."

Phasaelis paused, considered this. "Again the boy speaks well. It may not be wise to tell our husband. He might start a war with the Romans. His hubris knows no bounds."

"Nura and I have sworn an oath as healers to keep our dealings secret with those whom we serve," said Yeshua solemnly.

Phasaelis looked up with scorn in her eyes. "But, what can we do with the original potion – the poison? It would be a pity to discard it. Let us find some way of feeding it to Macula. Or better – to his children. That would be justice."

Yeshua shook his head. "Neither Nura nor myself can be part of that. Our oath also prevents us from causing harm. Please, my lady, if you harm Macula's children, it will bring shame to you, not joy."

This was too much for Hadassah. "Boy, do not presume to lecture your superiors in how to behave. Remember your place."

"Friend Hadassah," said Phasaelis. "Our young healer is right. As much as we would like to see the Medicus suffer, it will be revenge enough to see the look in his face when we finally do conceive a child. His own superiors will find a suitable punishment for him then." She placed her palm on the side of Yeshua's face. "If this works, you will be rewarded."

She handed the carved vial to Yeshua. "Take this. Show it to your master. We will return tomorrow for the replacement." And then to Hadassah she said, "Friend, after his master visits tonight, you will let the boy go to sleep in his own home. He will promise to return in the morning to settle the debt with your husband."

Hadassah bowed. "Of course, my lady, whatever you think is best."

~

After hearing Ba'asha's plan, Lebbaeus laughed. "I think I know just the boy. He comes around here every morning asking for yesterday's bread. I'll have Mak'ka send him your way."

"Lebbaeus, you have been a faithful client. When it is decided that the capital is to be moved here, we will both prosper." Ba'asha lifted his goblet, clinked it against Lebbaeus' and drained his wine. "But we must be ready to move quickly. There will be many vultures trying to lay claim to land around here. We will lose some to the Romans of course – nothing can be done about that. But we will want to make sure everyone else pays a good price." He raised an eyebrow. "You may want to hire more muscle."

"I've already taken care of that. It's quite easy – so many men out of work in Galilee. They come streaming down from the hills all the time. Most will do anything for a sesterce."

The bar was quiet in the lull of the early evening. Now that their business was at an end, Lebbaeus bowed. "And now sir, may I offer you anything else? Some food perhaps? A room for the night?"

"I think I will stay in my usual room across the street. Maybe some of that stew a little later. But first ... a little entertainment perhaps?"

"Of course. Anything you like. What did you have in mind?"

Ba'asha stroked his beard. "How about that pretty girl you dragged in here earlier? I might enjoy spending a little time with her."

Lebbaeus frowned. "Sir, you may have anything you like of course, but that one is new – no discipline yet. She may be uncooperative, maybe even try to bite or kick you. How about Dinah over there? She's available."

Talk of resistance only excited Ba'asha more. "The young girl will do fine. I am sure I can persuade her to behave. By the way, you said she was new. Is she by any chance a virgin?"

"Her father claims that she is. He tried to get me to raise my price because of it." Lebbaeus chuckled at this but then grew serious: "Ba'asha, please, no scars – the last time you used one of my girls you knocked out three of her teeth. If she doesn't cooperate, call for Mak'ka. He'll be glad to hold her any way you like while you take your pleasure."

"I'm sure that won't be necessary." replied Ba'asha.

~

The sky was darkening when Nura made her way around to the back of the villa. She could hear boisterous conversation in the work yard. It sounded like a celebration.

She was burdened with a heavy sack strapped over her shoulder. She had brought food and wine for Yeshua, and because she did not know in what condition she would find him, she had also brought water for drinking and washing, along with cloths and a clean robe. She brought restorative herbs and a skin ointment in case he had been whipped, or if he had rope burns from his confinement.

She arrived at the back gate and saw a large bonfire burning in the yard. Several people sat around a table near the fire, eating and drinking. Nura's mouth watered at the unmistakable aroma of roasted chicken. The guard came to the gate and asked her what her business was. When she explained that she was here to care for the prisoner, the guard broke out laughing and told her to follow.

Nura drew near the table. Many servants in their green uniforms sat, evidently having some sort of feast. There was indeed a platter of roasted chickens on the table, along with bread, wine, pomegranates, boiled eggs, olives, and fresh greens. The center of attention seemed to be a man seated with his back to Nura. The guard tapped him on the shoulder.

Yeshua turned around. When he recognized his aunt, his face spread into a grin. "Nura! Join us!"

Nura set the sack near the side of the building. They made room for her at the table. Someone handed her a goblet of wine. She said, "I am confused. I am expecting you in a pitiful state. Mattanyah told me how he finds you this morning."

"Am I not pitiful?" Yeshua chided, between gulps of wine. The other revelers laughed and urged him to finish his story. He leaned toward Nura. "I was just telling them a tale I heard about a magic pearl. I heard it from a traveling pot seller who comes through town every month or so. Let's see, where was I?"

"He just buried the pearl in his field," called out one of the revelers, a young man.

"Well why don't I just start over for my aunt's sake? Let's see ... there was this rich fisherman. No, wait that's a different story. That one is about a serpent and an overly full net. We'll save that for another time. Hmm. So once, not too long ago, there lived a rich farmer with his son."

"What was his name?" Asked the same young man.

"His name? Who? The farmer or the son? Didn't I tell you that before? No? Then we'll call the farmer Barikar, because he too was the son of a farmer. So that would make the son Barbarikar, or a true barbarian, as our Roman lords would say. So, Barikar would travel with his slaves from time to time, selling his crops. And it was in a village by the sea. By the way, who here has been to the sea? I mean the real sea – to the west."

Several spoke up or raised their hands.

"Well, the man who told me this story lives in Caesarea, so he knows what he's talking about. Anyway, on this particular trip, Barikar traveled to a seaside village and was very successful. He sold all of his crops, so he was flush with coin. Before returning home he entered a shop and came across the most beautiful pearl he had ever seen. It was as big as a chicken's egg, and it glistened with many colors when you looked at it in the light." Yeshua picked up an egg from the bowl and showed it to everyone for emphasis. He tossed it from his right hand to his left, and then back. He waved his hand in the air and opened it. The egg had vanished. Everyone howled.

"I tell you truly that when he saw the pearl, nothing else in his life mattered. He knew he had to have it for himself. On the spot, he traded his two slaves, his cart, his donkeys and all the coins in his purse. He even had to throw half of his farmland into the bargain. It was a hefty price, but he was glad to pay it. He walked home alone with the pearl in his pocket, stopping from time to time to admire it in the sunlight." Yeshua's voice became quiet and intense. He looked from person to person as he spoke. "It was quite late when he finally arrived home. He thought about the pearl constantly, and the more he obsessed, the more he grew worried that something would happen to it. What would happen when he finally slept that night? Perhaps it would be stolen, or lost, or discarded. Then he got an idea. He found a small stone jar in his home, put the pearl in it, sealed it, and buried it in the one remaining field he hadn't sold."

Yeshua paused to take a long swallow of his wine and then belched loudly. Seeing that all were waiting for him to proceed, he continued. "As it happened, that night was his night to die. As Qoheleth says, 'that time will come for us all.' His son grieved for him as did all of his neighbors. Later when the new owners of the fields arrived, the son was surprised to find that he now owned only half a farm. He had no slaves to help with the work, no donkeys for the plow, no money to buy seed, and the harvest was already gone. He had no choice but to sell the remaining field. Then he moved away to live with his relatives in the south.

"Now, the new owner was a Gentile. He was out working his new field one day when the plow turned up the jar. He opened it and what do you think he found?" He picked up a serving bowl from the table and placed his hand on the lid, waiting.

"The pearl of course," replied a serving girl.

He lifted the lid and held out the bowl. The egg that had vanished now lay among brined olives and vetch.

"Of course it was the pearl! He was so happy to find something so beautiful! He decided to return to the house right away and give it to his wife as a present. When he showed it to her, they both danced with joy. She wanted to wear the pearl always, on a new necklace. So the next day she took the pearl into the city to a jeweler to drill a hole and fasten it on a silver chain.

"But something terrible happened. When the jeweler touched the pearl with the drill ..." – he paused for effect – "it shattered into a hundred pieces."

A collective cry arose from the listeners. One of the young men, getting into the spirit of the tale, grabbed the egg from the olive jar and popped it into his mouth. He chomped down on the shell, letting fragments fall here and there.

Seeing this, Yeshua said, "Oh, that's a good idea. Now I know a better ending. So, the Gentile's wife took the shards and fragments of the pearl home in a small sack. She was broken-hearted at the loss of something so beautiful. When her husband saw what had happened, he became angry. He grabbed the sack, ran outside, and upended it into the swine trough, scattering the fragments. The swine saw this and ... you all know that swine will truly eat anything don't you? The herd descended on the trough and gobbled everything up, pearls and all."

He paused, nibbling on a piece of bread.

"Is that it?" Asked one of the serving girls.

Yeshua held his finger up as he swallowed. "There's more! The swine became agitated. They broke through the gate and ran into the field making wild noises. It was as if they were possessed by a legion of demons. They ran up the hill and jumped off the cliff into the sea. And that was the end of the beautiful pearl."

There was a moment of silence, after which Nura said, "Oh, Yeshua, that is a terrible story."

"What's a 'legion'?" asked one of the girls.

"It's a handful of cohorts," responded the young man who had eaten the egg. He spoke authoritatively. "And a cohort is six centuries, each one with a hundred men in it, led by a centurion. So a legion is a great many Roman soldiers."

"Oh," responded the girl. "Well, what's the point? It seems rather jumbled."

Yeshua shrugged. "What do you think?"

The young man took on a solemn air. "How about – 'too much rich food can make you crazy' – get it, 'rich' food?" For this he was slapped playfully by the girl next to him.

The serving girl said, "I like the part in the beginning when he finds the pearl in the shop and trades everything he owns for it. I don't know why, but that seems romantic."

"Romantic?" Replied the young man. "It was totally irresponsible! It led to his ruin."

The girl persisted, "But did it? It was his time to die anyway. At least he found something of great value before he died."

The young man was more practical. "You can't eat a pearl. Even if you are a pig. He lost his farm. What is a farmer without his farm?"

"What makes him *just* a farmer? What makes you a lazy steward? Why is Ba'asha so rich that we all wait at his table?"

"Careful, love, it's best not to question some things."

A lively debate ensued. Yeshua and Nura listened, amazed that so much could be inferred from a silly tale. Finally Nura nudged Yeshua, "We need to talk. We can sit over by the house?"

The two excused themselves and retreated to the bench. Nura spoke: "Nephew, would you tell me what kind of confinement is this?"

Yeshua gave Nura an account of the day's events, particularly those concerning Phasaelis, the wife of the Tetrarch. He handed her the wooden vial carved in the shape of a mother goddess. Nura took a sniff of the potion and wrinkled her nose.

"She says pulegium and croton?"

Yeshua nodded.

Nura restoppered the vial and shook her head. "We are talking about Herod's wife – someone whom your people – *our* people, do not well love. I do not like to see any young woman abused this way – like a piece in some game. We must help. But ... we must keep our part in this hidden. Such people could have us killed with a glance."

Yeshua prodded, "So, you'll do it? You'll replace the potion?"

Nura shrugged. "We can replace pulegium with mint oil. For this awful gray color ... maybe ashes from a fire? I do have some herbs that may help her keep her husband's seed." She pursed her lips and added: "although they never are helping me."

"What do you mean?" Asked Yeshua.

"I desire to give Mattanyah a son or a daughter, but I am cursed by barrenness. I hear your people sometimes. They say your god punishes Mattanyah because he marries a foreigner."

Yeshua sat in silence. He had indeed heard other express this cruel sentiment, but did not know his aunt harbored this bitterness. Also, he had spent many hours with Mattanyah in the shop and on jobs, and knew that *he* did not feel any injury for the lack of children. Everyone knew what a perilous affair it was to have a baby.

At length Nura stood up and ruffled Yeshua's hair. "I need to be home for my husband. He will be wanting his evening meal."

Yeshua arose and lifted Nura's sack over his own shoulder. He started toward the gate.

Nura was perplexed. "Where are *you* going?"

"Didn't I tell you. The lady of the house said I am to go home tonight and to return in the morning. It's nice to have a powerful friend, eh?"

~

Ba'asha felt a flush of anticipation as he lumbered up the steps carrying an oil lamp. Lebbaeus had told him to go to the room all the way in the back. He found the door, threw back the bolt and entered. The room was dark. He found more lamps on a side table and lit them, placing them around the room. An orange glow filled the space.

The girl lay sprawled atop a mattress in the center of the room, her arms chained around a vertical post. How could she be any trouble? Lebbaeus, as usual, had been exaggerating.

He circled the room. The girl silently followed him with her eyes. He knelt and held the lamp close to her face. She was much prettier now than when he had seen her dragged through the front door. She was wearing a red sleeveless dress. Her hair had been combed and tied with a ribbon. Her cheeks had been dappled with blush. Her lips were now bright red, and some dark makeup had been applied to her beautiful eyes – eyes now steeped in apprehension.

His gaze continued lower. A little skinny, he thought. Young, maybe fourteen or fifteen? Not much in the way of breasts, but they had done what they could to make her alluring. He noted with approval that her armpits had been shaved.

"What is your name, girl?"

No answer. Was that fear or defiance in her eyes. He decided to find out.

He pulled his dagger from the sheath on his belt and played the sharp point across the girl's forehead, hard enough for her to feel, but not enough to cut – not yet. "You won't give me any trouble, will you, girl?" He traced the point lightly down the side of her face, the side of her neck and across her bare armpit. Her eyes followed the dagger. Finally, he placed the point in front of his own face. Her eyes met his. Fear. He felt a stirring in his loins.

"They tell me you are a virgin. Is it true?" Still no answer. He may have to use the dagger yet. "No matter, we will find out." He set the dagger aside and undid the clasps of the dress on her shoulders. He roughly pulled it down in a sudden motion. It slid under her legs and he tossed it aside. Startled, she tried ineffectually to hide herself by crossing her legs and turning to the side.

Once again, he picked up the dagger. He played the point across her breasts, lingering on her nipples. "Now you *do* want to be a good girl, don't you?" He brought the point again to her face and held it an inch above her left eye. "Lebbaeus says I am not to leave any scars, but ..." He shrugged. He wanted her to be submissive. He wanted to conquer her with fear alone. "Stop turning to the side. Lie flat. Uncross your legs!"

Gradually she relaxed. Surrender was clear in her eyes now. He had won. He sheathed his dagger and quickly removed his lower garment. Though he could feel some tension, she did not resist as he positioned himself between her legs. A tear slid down the side of her face, exciting him even more.

At the moment of penetration he saw her wince in pain. "Ah – so Lebbaeus wasn't lying for once – you are, or were, indeed a virgin!" He laughed. He was enjoying himself now. Still she did not resist. He quickened the rhythm of his thrusts. He saw pain and shame in her expression. *Good.* He continued, leaning his head back and shutting his eyes in ecstasy. He felt her struggling beneath him – a futile attempt at resistance. *Stupid girl, she doesn't know it only increases the pleasure.* He felt the familiar stirring in his loins and knew that he was about to reach his climax when suddenly there was a searing pain in his neck.

He tried to yell in surprise, but no sound came out except a sputtering. He looked down. The girl was covered in blood. *What?* He saw his own dagger in her right hand. Her eyes now contained pure hatred. No fear. So much blood. Everywhere. He felt dizzy. The realization dawned on him that the blood was his own. It was still spurting from the left side of his neck. He fell back on the floor and tried to stop the flow with his hands. *No good.* He tried again to yell. Again, only a gurgle emerged from his severed windpipe. He struggled to get to his feet. *To the door! So dizzy!* Again he fell back to the floor. *Weakness. Cannot get up.* His mind was going fuzzy – like a dream. *Haze everywhere – cannot see.* His eyes grew dim.

~

Naomi jumped up from the mattress and backed away from the writhing man until she felt the cold stone wall against her bare buttocks. She watched in horror as his struggling gradually slowed and then stopped altogether. Finally, he lay still. His face was toward her, his eyes staring accusingly. It took her a while to realize that though open, the eyes were sightless.

She hadn't meant to do this. As the old beast had thrust up and down, she had continued to struggle against the manacles. She did this without thinking, oblivious to the damage the sharp metal was inflicting on her wrists. Her right hand had become drenched in her own blood. Then she realized that the blood was making things slippery. She might actually be able to pull her hand through. She pulled as hard as she could. It scraped the sides of her hand badly but finally she was free! Still acting on instinct, she had grabbed the beast's dagger from the sheath at his belt and thrust it into his neck when he again leaned toward her.

She replayed the moment in her mind several times, still not believing it had happened. She had killed a man.

She looked down at herself. Her naked body was covered with the man's blood. Her right hand still clutched the dagger. She dropped it to the floor. Her hand throbbed with pain. The skin was torn on the back and inside, at the base of her thumb.

She picked up the dagger again and used it to rip a strip of cloth from the discarded red dress, tying it tightly around her right wrist. Her left wrist still had a tight manacle around it with the chain dangling to the floor. She sat next to the lamp and pried with the point of the knife until she worked the fastening pin free. The manacle fell to the floor.

She got up and surveyed the room. She found a basin in the corner by the door with a jug of water. Above the basin there was a looking glass and shelves with various jars of makeup, combs and other implements. In the opposite corner she saw a pile of dirty laundry. A glowing brazier on one side of the room provided meager heat. The night was getting chilly.

She went to the basin and began to wash off the blood. It was crusting over her chest, stomach and groin. It was in her hair and all over her face. She looked in the glass. She appeared ghoulish in that makeup. She continued to wash, roughly rubbing at her face with a wet cloth.

Reasonably clean now, she considered – I will need something to wear – anything but that red dress. She went to the laundry pile and found her own soiled robe on the top. She started to put it on and then had a thought. She continued to rifle through the pile until she found a rough colorless tunic, such as would be worn by a man or boy. She also found a rope belt and a short cloak. She quickly put them on.

She went to the brazier and took some cold spent coals from the periphery of the fire. She made dark smudges all over her face. I'll look like a dock boy covered in grease, she thought.

Next, she recovered the dagger and cut her hair in short jagged clumps, tossing the severed locks into the brazier. The acrid smell of burning hair filled the room.

She realized that she didn't have much time. The dagger will come in handy, she thought. She went back to the man's body. An ornate sheath was attached to his fine leather belt. She undid the belt and pulled it off of him, hearing a jangling as something fell to the floor. A coin purse! She grabbed it and took a quick look inside. She had never seen the like of some of these coins. Several looked to be made of gold.

She put the dagger with its sheath and the purse in an inside pocket of her cloak. She considered taking the leather belt, but it was very fancy and wouldn't match the rest of her outfit. She wouldn't want to have to explain where she got it.

Until that moment, the plan in the back of her mind was to sneak out the door, down the stairs, and then out back through the kitchen. But now she heard footsteps outside the door and Mak'ka's gruff voice. "Ba'asha, are you finished? You've been in there a long time. My boss told me to remind you not to rough her up too much."

She hurried to the window at the side of the room. It looked out over a narrow ally between the tavern and a stone building next to it. Too far to jump. She ran to the back window and couldn't believe her luck. The first floor, where the kitchen was, extended back about ten feet farther than the upper story.

Again, Mak'ka called from the hallway "Ba'asha – Is everything all right in there? What's that smell?"

She hoisted herself through the window and dropped to the flat roof over the kitchen. Trying to tread softly, she made her way to the back of the building. She swung out over the edge and dropped to the ground below, just as she heard a crash and a shout from the window above.

～

Naomi ran into the darkness – away from lights, noise, people. She kept to back alleys. She was vaguely aware that she was heading north – away from the docks. When she could run no more she found an alcove at the back of a building. She crouched in the blackness to collect her thoughts.

Until now she had thought only about *how* to escape. She now realized that she had given no consideration to what to do if she succeeded. Where to go? She knew that Te'oma would be returning from Sepphoris soon. She hoped she had not already missed him –

that he had not already come to her father's house.

Te'oma would return on the road that ran into the western hills from the farmland north of town. Good. So she was heading in the right direction. She needed to make it to the road and intercept him. Then they could turn around and go back into the hills. They would have to find another way south. Te'oma must know one.

But, what if she didn't find him? What if she continued into the hills and never crossed his path? She remembered that her aunt Taletha lived in a town called Cana. Naomi had no idea where Cana was – just that it was in the hills somewhere to the west. She had met her aunt only a few times in her life, most recently at the beginning of the summer. Taletha and her son Ephrayim had visited for about a week, just before her mother got sick.

Taletha was Achyan's sister, but they were *nothing* alike. In fact, when she visited she had spent most of her time upbraiding her brother. She knew what a lout he was – probably had *always* been. Naomi had the sense that Taletha would be sympathetic, and would help if she could.

But could she burden her aunt with this? Naomi had just ... (It was hard to think it!) She had just *killed* a man. And a rich man at that, judging from his clothes and his purse. The gravity of her situation settled on her. They will look for me! They won't give up. She had seen the lengths that Lebbaeus had gone to in the past in obtaining and keeping what he thought was his.

That's what he thinks of me, she thought. I am his property – an investment, nothing more. They will stone me if they catch me. I have killed a man.

She had stayed here long enough. She peeked out from the nook to be sure no one was about, and then resumed her flight. She walked briskly, staying in the shadows. She did not run, not wanting to attract attention. She made her way to the western edge of town, at the foot of the steep hills. She climbed a short way farther and then turned north, toward the farmland and the start of the road.

The ground here was rough. She had to scrape her way through brambles and scamper over an occasional boulder. But this was better than running the risk of being caught.

It was slow going. After an hour she came to a place where a cliff jutted out from the hills. At the base of the cliff, the flat expanse of land opened to the north. She would have to come down from the slope now, go around the base of the cliff, and walk across a half-mile of open grazing land. Then she would intercept the road.

The crisp, cool air eased her mind. She was feeling better and thinking clearly now. The open field would be the most dangerous. Would they be searching for her already? Would they guess the direction she had gone? They would probably first go to Achyan's house by the docks. When they didn't find her there, they would force Achyan to tell them where she would go. But what would Achyan tell them? She remembered his fury earlier this week when she had told her father of her plan to go south to join Yochanan. *That's* what he will say, she thought with satisfaction. He'll send them looking in the wrong direction.

It was late now. The stars were out with a full moon, so she could see quite clearly. She was halfway across the field when she saw a curious sight. Near the place where the road ascended to the hills, a bonfire sent flames and sparks high into the sky. Silhouetted in the light from the fire were five crosses in a row.

She knew about this spot. Everyone did. This was where the Romans did their horrid crucifixions. The bodies would hang here and rot as a warning to anyone entering the town. She had not heard about any crucifixions in the past few days, and she hoped there would be no Romans around so that she could slip by unnoticed.

She stayed well to the hillside, not wanting to go near the crosses. Her luck was holding! She didn't see anyone – not even a single guard. She was past the crosses now and making toward the road into the hills. As she passed the bonfire she noticed a small pile of half-burned garments. A flash of green caught her eye.

No! It couldn't be.

She approached the fire and pulled from the pile a singed green vest. Oh Alilah no, please, I can't bear it!

It was Te'oma's vest.

She steeled her nerves and turned toward the crosses, approaching slowly. The men were horribly disfigured. The Romans had nailed their heels into the wood on either side of the base. Their arms were tightly tied to the cross beams with coarse ropes. All five were slumped over, clearly dead – probably since this afternoon. Birds had already pecked their eyes out and had started on the flesh. On one, a leg had been ripped open, probably by a wolf.

She went to each one and forced herself to take a hard look. She got to the third. The face was slumped over but she could clearly see the mark on his forehead – a fishhook. She fell back hard on the ground. Te'oma. You never harmed anyone in your life. Why would they do this to you?

It was more than she could bear. Naomi turned over and lay prostrate on the ground heaving and sobbing. She beat the ground with her fists, her bandaged right hand freely dripping blood. She wailed at the world, cursing the Romans. She cursed Alilah for allowing this to happen.

She cried until her lungs burned. Her bruised fists eventually ceased their pounding. Her cries subsided to gentle sobbing. She was oblivious to her surroundings. She was not aware of the night air, which had become quite cold. She also did not hear the approaching footsteps or the harsh braying of the mule until she felt a gentle touch on her shoulder.

"Child – get up! You can't stay here. It isn't safe. This is *not* a good place."

She shuddered and looked up to see an old man with a braided gray beard and turban leaning over her.

"Come boy – this is no good. Where are your people?"

When he reached for her arm, she shrank from his touch, crouching in fear.

"What's the matter with you, boy? Can't you talk? What are you doing out at this evil place in the middle of the night?"

Without meaning to, her gaze was drawn to the hideous cross bearing the body of Te'oma – her hope for a new life. She wailed anew.

"Oh, I see – this was someone dear to you, wasn't it? Your brother perhaps? There, there …"

He tried to pat her head – meant as a comforting gesture. He wanted to persuade this youth that it wasn't safe to be out here at the foot of these crosses. There were bandits about that would slit your throat if they thought you had anything of value. Also the Roman patrol would be around again in an hour.

This time Naomi got up and backed away several steps. From somewhere in the folds of her vest she produced a dagger and brandished it menacingly toward the old man.

"Oh Alilah save us! I'm not trying to attack you, boy. Look – I'm harmless." He held his open hands in front of him. "Let me start again. My name is Bustan." He gestured toward the two mules pulling his heavy cart. "And these are my companions Deliylah and Yezebel." At the sound of her name, Yezebel nodded her head up and down making a spluttering sound with her lips. "I'm now on my way to Sepphoris, and from there to Caesarea on the sea. Look – my cart is full of citrons, figs, salted fish, and clay pots from Kefar Hananya. I'm just a merchant. I'm not looking to hurt you."

Naomi relaxed a little but stood her ground defiantly.

"Come, child, let us be friends. Put the knife away and we'll have something to eat?"

Except for the little bit of stew in the afternoon, Naomi had not eaten anything that day. The mention of food, and the smell of the salted fish, was enticing. She put her dagger away in its sheath in her inside pocket. "I … I am sorry. Forgive me."

"That's better. That's better. Come. You can sit up on the seat. You look like you've had a rough day. What did you do to your hand?" He gestured toward the cart. "Don't worry – I won't come near you." He stayed several paces back.

She climbed up onto the seat, keeping her eyes warily on the old man.

"If you reach behind you there, you'll find a wineskin and an open sack of figs. Help yourself."

Naomi did. Her throat was raw from crying. She held the

wineskin up and took a long drink.

"Easy, easy, lad! I only water it a little bit." He winked – a useless gesture in the dark. "It's pretty strong stuff."

Naomi continued to drink.

"Maybe you've had a worse day than I thought! By the way, what is your name, *boy?*"

By the way he said this last word, Naomi knew that he had easily seen through her simple disguise, even in the dark of the night. It must have been her voice. She must remember to try to disguise it – maybe speaking in a hoarse whisper would work better.

She was feeling more relaxed now, perhaps from the wine. Perhaps it was that she had cried all the tears she had. "My name, sir, is Naomi. Thank you for your kindness." And after a moment's hesitation, she added, "Can you take me with you to Sepphoris? I can pay you."

"Whoa, slow down. First of all, Naomi, I am very glad that Alilah has caused our paths to cross. Let's get away from this evil place first, and then we can talk about where we are going and why. Let's head up the road into the hills and talk while we go. You can sit there and ride. Don't worry – I won't come close to you. I'll walk alongside Deliylah for a while." And then, seeing her shiver, he added, "There's a blanket on the bench beside you. Feel free to use it if you are cold."

Naomi had grown unaccustomed to being treated with kindness since her mother had died. She was having a hard time trusting that this man's motives were pure. Several thoughts ran through her mind: Will he turn me over to the authorities? There might be a reward. Will he rape me, or kill me and steal my coins? I already told him that I could pay him, so he knows I have money. Stupid – why did I say that?

They started up into the hills. The road was rough but not steep. Sensing his guest's fatigue, Bustan did most of the talking. He told her about his wife in Caesarea. He told her about the port with the big ships that came in from Egypt, Greece, Rome, and other places even more distant, with names that Naomi did not recognize and could not begin to pronounce. He told her about the immense storehouses for grain, wine, olive oil and other goods.

Listening to Bustan made her realize how sheltered and pathetic her own life had been. Bustan apparently spent most of his time traveling. From his home in Caesarea he would take a load of foreign goods that had been shipped in – textiles, fancy furniture, and amphorae of various wines and oils. Once he had transported a load of glass tiles to be used in the many mosaics in Sepphoris. From there he would continue down to the towns on the northwest side of Lake Chinnereth, load up on different cargo, and then return. He was on his way back to Sepphoris now with salted fish, figs, and pots.

"I used to be able to make a pretty good living when I was younger and could move faster. Sepphoris was new and booming – construction projects everywhere. Now things seem to be pretty much done. Rumor has it that Antipas is bored – he wants to build another city somewhere. That could be good for business too, who knows? Of course I probably won't be around long enough to see it happen. In spite of my youthful appearance I'm getting old." He chuckled at his little joke – he looked anything but young.

"Yes – the old knees are giving out. Did I tell you that next month is my birthday? I'm going to be sixty. Not many men live to that age, you know, not even rich men. I tell you – I'm blessed that I didn't inherit any land. Farmers used to make a good living, but not anymore. Now they can barely make enough to live on. I know. I see the same thing everywhere I go. And now they have new schemes. They tax you more than you can pay and then lend you the difference. Before you know it, you're in debt up to your ears and then they take your land. Now you're a tenant farmer paying tax *and* rent."

Bustan prattled on and on. After a while he realized that he was receiving no replies. He glanced up to see that Naomi was reclining on the bench and had fallen asleep. It was all right with him. He was used to conversing solely with his mules. Yezebel had become a pretty fair conversationalist.

~

Yeshua returned to the work yard at first light. He took his spot on the bench, and because he was not sure when Ba'asha would return, he looped the rope around his leg to show that he was, indeed, a prisoner.

Despite the early hour, the work yard was abuzz with activity. Apparently this was laundry day. Halphaios the fuller was here. Yeshua had labored for him from time to time at his fullonica in the city center. He was a well-natured Greek man of middle age. He was short and well fed. Today he wore his customary spotless white tunic. He had told Yeshua once about the importance of a fuller always being seen in clean clothes.

At this moment, Halphaios was directing his three workers – all boys of about ten years of age. One was hauling in a full urine pot through the back gate. He was struggling with the rope handle, trying unsuccessfully not to spill the contents on his feet.

Another boy was filling vats with water from the fountain. One vat would be used to soak the clothes in the urine. The other would be used for rinsing. The third boy was preparing wooden racks on which to stretch and brush the cleaned cloth. They also had a pot of powdered chalk for whitening Ba'asha's formal togas.

Nearer to the stables Yeshua saw one of the household servants, a young girl, milking goats. Still another was working a churn for butter. Near the entrance to the villa, a manservant was sweeping the paving stones. The cook had set a huge pot of water over a bonfire and was now sharpening knives on a small stone wheel.

Yeshua sat idly and watched the activity. His mind turned to his own troubles: Ba'asha was going to try to make him work off the cost of the ruined pediment. He had named a ridiculously large sum of five hundred denarii.

He was mulling over the possibilities when he heard a voice from behind. "What are you doing here my young friend?" Yeshua squinted up to see Halphaios the fuller standing over him. "Just that little rope around your ankle? Ba'asha doesn't usually treat his prisoners so nice."

Halphaios sat on the bench and Yeshua told him about his predicament. Halphaios had already heard some of it. Gossip of the construction disaster was all over the streets. Yeshua asked the fuller what he thought he could do to defend himself.

Halphaios scratched his beard. "I've seen how these things go in this town. The Romans want everything nice and legal, so there will probably be some kind of trial. Lots of scribe-work." He thought some more. "So ... he's not accusing you of a crime really, rather just causing him a loss – his precious statue. Then your Torah-law is not involved, so you won't see any Levites. Probably just a judge."

"A judge? Who will it be?" Asked Yeshua.

"Most likely one of Herod's delegates. There are several. The Romans call it 'holding the Imperium.' They can't judge you unless they hold the Imperium."

"The Romans have so many rules," said Yeshua. "Even Herod has to follow them?"

"Indeed, indeed," echoed the fuller.

"But I was just trying to free the trapped slave. Do you think it would help if we *did* get a Levite involved? After all, if I hadn't tried to save the man, he could have died. Wasn't I obligated to help?"

The fuller laughed, "You are grasping at straws now, young friend. Stick to building. Leave law to the professional liars. And since when does Yeshua ever want to have anything to do with the Levites?" He tousled the young man's hair.

Yeshua was still trying to find a way out. "What about the sabbatical year? It's four years away, but won't Ba'asha have to forgive my debt then?"

The fuller considered this. "You know your Jewish customs better than an old Greek. I suppose if you are still here in Yudaea, and if you are still alive, then you can try to make that case. But neither of those is a certainty. Ba'asha is a powerful man. If he hasn't forgotten about you by then he will find a way to keep you under his thumb."

"You're not filling me with hope, Halphaios."

"Well, I've had a lot of experience with the legal system here. Every time a garment is lost or damaged, someone wants to sue the fuller. The trouble with the Roman system is that only the most serious laws are actually written down and applied consistently. Everything else is ... well, the city judge can handle it in any manner he sees fit."

"And the city judge will probably be one of Ba'asha's many clients," added Yeshua.

"Ah, he starts to understand," Halphaios said to the sky.

This was all very disheartening. It appeared his only hope was Phasaelis. She could make the whole thing go away with a wave of her hand. Even Ba'asha wouldn't cross her.

~

At the window in the upper room of my home. Dusk, waning light. Torches on the docks in the distance. A figure at the edge of the yard. Baggy hood covering a darkened face. It looks at me. I feel its gaze. Silent. Accusing. Cold. Alone. A hardness in my throat. Difficult to swallow. Something terrible I have to do – something already done. The one in the yard knows. I must leave here. A lamp in the corner of the room. Where is the door? Only stone walls. Dampness under my feet. Back at the window. The figure is closer now. Pale chin visible beneath the hood. A ladder in the corner of the room, not there before. Climb. I pull apart sticks and thatch. Dirt, chunks of hardened clay fall in my hair from the widening hole. Squeeze free. I stand on the roof. Darkness. Where are the stars? The one is here, white chin glowing at the far edge of the roof. A chill in the air and something else – a smell, like fish rotting in the sun. The figure is close now. Speak. Only a muffled humming comes from my hardened throat. Panic. Back to the edge of the roof. Move to the side – the figure follows my every move. Very close now. Again I try to scream but only a whisper comes out. Harder. Force air through my paralyzed throat!

"Aaaaah!" Naomi awoke with a start, the rancid stench still in her nose. She sat up and looked around. It took her a moment to realize where she was. She had been lying across the bench of Bustan's cart. The moon had set and the stars were dazzling in the crisp autumn air. The sky was beginning to soften in the east. She guessed it was about an hour before dawn.

She smelled smoke. The cart was in the middle of a clearing surrounded by woods. A campfire smoldered at the edge of the clearing. There Bustan lay, wrapped in blankets, snoring. The mules were near him, apparently enjoying the warmth of the fire. They were awake, staring curiously at Naomi, their ears straight up. Bustan apparently trusted them not to run off, because they were free to roam.

The mules soon lost interest in her and resumed grazing the lush grass. How long have I been asleep? It couldn't be more than a couple of hours, maybe three. The horrific events of the previous day began to encroach on her mind. She willfully blocked them for now. Now she must think about the present.

She got down from the cart and took her time stretching. Her legs were cramped from the way she had lain on her side. Her throat was parched. At the back of the cart she found a skin containing fresh water. She also helped herself to more figs. She decided to do a little exploring.

Bustan had made camp in a gently sloped clearing surrounded by thick woods. The grass was tall and slightly damp with morning dew. The old man continued to snore. She walked downhill to the other end of the clearing and found that the woods thinned out here. She ventured in amongst the trees. After only a few feet, the ground dropped off into a steep, rocky ravine. She could hear water rushing below. She returned to the campfire.

The sky was now bluish gray and turning orange in the east. She found a path near the cart leading uphill. She followed it into the woods. After a few minutes she emerged onto the paved east-west road. Bustan had chosen the spot well. The way the path was angled, it was difficult to see unless you were looking for it.

The road was fairly steep here. They were near the crest of a long hill. She faced east and looked down the long slope. She could see dozens of hills, miles distant, silhouetted in the brightening sky. It was a stunning view. She stood still, enjoying it for several minutes.

Then she saw movement in the distance – on the crest of the closest hill to the east. She quickly ducked out of sight. She couldn't be sure because of the back lighting, but it looked like men on horses.

She hurried back to the clearing and shook Bustan on the shoulder. He reached back and swatted, thinking that it was one of his mules nudging him. She shook harder. "Wake up!"

"Huh, what? Who? Oh." He sat up, yawned, and rubbed his eyes. "You. Why are we up so early? It's not even light yet. We only made camp a while ago."

Naomi was agitated. "On the road to the east. Men on horses. I cannot tell how many. They are looking for me. You must hide me! Now!"

"Huh? Calm yourself. You're imagining things. Why would men on horses be looking for a girl like you?"

She was frantic. "Please! You must believe me. They are looking for me. Tell me where to hide until they are gone. I will pay you money."

Bustan slowly got to his feet and grunted. "Again the offer of money. There is more to you than meets the eye. Odds are they won't even notice the path to this little clearing. But all right, if you insist. You go down to the other end. Go through the trees and a little way down the slope. You'll see a clump of large boulders on the left. Just past them, look under a rock ledge. You'll see the entrance to a cave I use for storage. Don't open any of my jars. Just stay there until I come for you." Bustan ambled toward his cart and grumbled, "I don't know why I'm doing this for you, but when this danger is past I will want some answers."

Naomi did as she was told. When she was out of sight, Bustan got a metal pot from his cart and filled it with water and oats. He gathered more wood and perked up the fire. He was cooking his breakfast when three Romans on horseback entered the clearing from the path. He could tell from the uniforms that the one in the lead held the rank of Optio; the other two were cavalrymen. Bustan was astonished. He whispered, "Yezebel, what has our new friend gotten us into?"

The Roman in front dismounted and led his horse to Bustan's fire. "Surge! Loquerisne Latine?"

Bustan could speak Latin very well. It was necessary for any merchant living in Caesarea. He was being commanded to rise and asked if he could speak Latin. He slowly got to his feet making exaggerated gestures of feebleness. "Etiam, etiam, modicum. Ego tantum videtur." (Yes, a little, I'm just an old man.)

The Optio continued in Latin. "How long have you been here?"

"Hmm... Here in Galilee, or here in this clearing?"

"Don't trifle with me, Jew. We are looking for someone who would be traveling west on the road since last night. How long have you been *in this clearing*?"

"Well, since shortly after sunset last night. I made my camp here with my mules. That one is Deliylah and this one here is Yezebel. I am Bustan. I am just a traveling merchant. I have some lovely pots I can sell you, over here, I'll show you." He started to walk toward the cart.

"Silence! Be still. Just answer the questions. Did you see anyone on the road last night or this morning?"

"No one last night, and as you can see, I am just starting my day. So ... no one this morning either, except for your honors of course. Would you like to share some oats with me? I have plenty. I also have some lovely pots you can eat from." He again started toward the cart.

"Idiot. Do we look like horses?"

"No sir. Well, I mean, your horses look like horses. I do know a horse when I see one."

The Optio gave him a hard look. "Stand still! You say your name is Bustan. Where are you coming from and where are you going?"

"Very good sir. I see that you're not hungry. I am coming from Gennesaret. They sell fine pots there from Kefar Hananya. I can show you. Very good workmanship. Strong and beautiful too." Bustan could see the Optio getting exasperated. "I'm going to Sepphoris and then on to my home in Caesarea. My wife is there.

She makes clothing for the shipmates. She made my vest, see ...”

"We are looking for a girl, about fifteen years old. She is a runaway slave. Have you seen her or not?”

Bustan's eyes widened. “Oh, a *girl*, and a slave at that! Her master must be very important for your honors to be chasing her. I've met slave hunters before, but I've never seen Roman masters such as yourselves doing that work.” By the angry expression growing on the Optio's face, Bustan could tell he was pushing his luck. “No, sir, no. As I told you I've been asleep here since last night. I haven't seen anyone except Deliylah and Yezebel.” Yezebel nodded and spluttered in agreement. “I'm just getting started this morning. I move pretty slowly, you know. Next month I am going to be *sixty*. When I get home ...”

The Optio had stopped listening and was conferring with his men. He turned back to Bustan. “We will search the area. If we find that you're hiding someone, it will not be good for you. This is your last chance to confess.”

Bustan feigned confusion. “Sir, of course, search. I don't know what or whom I would be hiding. Oh yes – you said you were looking for a runaway slave. A girl was it?”

"Silence, old man. Sit and eat your *oats*,” the Optio said with disgust. The two infantrymen thoroughly explored the clearing and the surrounding woods. They returned to their commander having turned up nothing.

As he remounted his horse, the Optio said, “If you see a girl on the road today, do not go near her. She is known to be dangerous. Also, do not tell her we are looking for her. When you get to Sepphoris, contact me. I am Optio Gnaeus Mocius. Can you remember that, old man?”

Bustan once again feigned confusion. “Optio Gnae ... I am sorry sir. Your Roman names are so melodious, but they are hard for an old Jew to pronounce. Can you say it again?”

"Just ask at the garrison for the Optio from the seventh. They will find me.” And with that, the three mounted soldiers trotted out of the clearing.

Bustan sat for a long time. He cooked and ate his oatmeal. He wanted to be sure that the Romans were really gone and not playing a ruse on him. After he finished his breakfast, he walked out to the road. They were, indeed, gone.

~

Bustan descended the hill to his storage cave. "Girl! What have you *done?*" He found Naomi crouching behind several amphorae. She was hiding her head in her hands and appeared to be weeping. "Come now girl, no blubbering. Let's get you out of this cave. We'll go back to the fire and get warm. I shall cook you some lovely oats. You can eat with Deliylah and Yezebel."

Naomi followed Bustan back to the clearing.

After she and the mules had eaten, Bustan looked at her sternly. "I just spoke with three Roman soldiers in this very camp. They were looking for a runaway slave girl, about fifteen years old. They went through the motions of conducting a search, and it's a good thing they didn't venture too far down the slope, or we would both be on crosses before the day is out." He saw her alarmed expression. "Don't worry. I told them I hadn't seen anyone. The Romans believe us to be inferior to them, so they are quick to believe it when we act stupid. Remember that."

Naomi looked up with bloodshot eyes and nodded.

"They have gone on to Sepphoris – so it won't be safe for you there, if that's what you were planning. Is it true what they said – you are a runaway slave?"

Naomi steeled her nerves and told him about some of her difficulties yesterday. She told about her father selling her into slavery to the brothel. She described her escape and her discovery of the body of her beloved Te'oma on the cross. She did not talk about the rape or the ... murder.

"I have met many slave hunters in my life," said Bustan. "Usually nasty, dirty, young men with no other way to earn their bread. I have never before seen Roman soldiers, an officer no less, searching for a runaway Jewish child. Your brothel owner must have some very important connections. Either that or there is more to this tale than you are telling me."

Naomi sat silently staring at the fire.

"Very well then ... It's probably best that I not know too much. Knowing would just put me in the middle of it. I've already gone too far in hiding you. My wife would be very upset with me for taking this risk. But let me ask you this: If you do get captured, can I count on you to keep your mouth shut about me?"

"Yes, of course – I would never say anything to get you in trouble, but ... I must ask you for one more favor."

Bustan sighed and got up. He started packing his things for the day's journey. "Well, what is it?"

"I need to go to my aunt's house in Cana, but I don't know the way. I can pay you money for your trouble." As she said this she reached into her tunic for the coin purse. As she did so the dagger in its sheath fell out onto the ground.

This was the first time Naomi had seen it in the clear light of day. It had a polished ivory handle that was encrusted with jewels. The sheath was made of fancy engraved leather. It looked very expensive. But the most striking thing about it was this: both the dagger and the sheath were covered in dried, brown blood.

They both stared at the weapon as it lay on the ground. After a moment, Naomi retrieved it and hid it once again in her clothing.

Bustan said, "Hm! Now I am sure that there is more to your story, and I am doubly sure that I don't want to know about it. That now makes three times you have insulted me by offering me money. I do not help you for money but for the law. When a stranger travels with you, you shall do him, or I guess her in your case, no harm."

"I am sorry. I only meant ..."

"I'll tell you what I will do – I'll take you as far as the crossroads, about 12 miles from here. If we hurry, and if Deliylah and Yezebel cooperate, we'll get there before dusk. Shabbat starts tonight, you know, so we must be off the road by then. At the crossroads, I turn south to Sepphoris. If you follow the north road, you'll get to Cana in about an hour, maybe two, depending on how fast you walk."

They packed the cart and started on their way – both walking this time. When they got to the road and started up the hill, Bustan stopped again and looked at her sternly. "One more thing, child. I don't know what you have done, and I won't condemn you for it, but the Romans will. I suggest you get rid of that … thing as soon as possible. A blade like that is easily recognizable and may be known to many people. I suggest that you not be caught with that on your person."

~

Yeshua awoke with a start. He had fallen asleep in the midday heat. He sat up and rubbed the drowsiness from his eyes. He thought he had heard a noise – like pottery being smashed.

Yeshua wondered at the profound lack of activity in the work yard. The place had been bustling all morning with everyone preparing for the master's return. No one wanted to be punished for some trivial infraction in case Ba'asha was in a bad mood.

But now, not even the guard was at his post. This was the first time Yeshua had seen the gate unwatched. In fact, he was completely alone in the yard.

He heard the sound again, unmistakable this time – something being broken inside the villa. And then again, closer – like some heavy piece of furniture being upended. Then a woman screamed.

A serving girl ran out the back door of the villa. Without stopping, she crossed the yard and escaped through the open gate.

Another girl came out at a full run. This time Yeshua was able to get her attention. He asked her in Latin what was going on, making a questioning shrug with his shoulders. She looked confused and frightened, but managed to say "Dominus … homicidii." She used her finger to make a slicing motion across her throat for emphasis. Then she pointed toward the house and said, "Latro domo … Abi. Cito!" She fled out into the street.

A moment later Hadassah, Ba'asha's wife, ran into the work yard. She was disheveled, her makeup smeared. Being a large woman, she couldn't move very fast. She noticed Yeshua and ran to him. "My daughter! Have you seen Selah?"

"No, ma'am," replied Yeshua. "I just just now awoke. Is she not about?"

"Oh you're useless!" She shoved Yeshua and started for the exit. "We're being robbed, you dolt. Find my daughter. There are terrorists in the house!" Just then another servant ran out of the house, a boy this time. "You!" Hadassah called, "Come here. You know the Roman barracks near the gate, don't you?"

"Yes ma'am," the boy replied.

"Go there immediately. Tell them that my husband has been murdered and there is a riot going on in our house. I'm going to my sister's villa down in the town." The boy nodded and ran off. Then Hadassah herself followed him out the gate and was gone, leaving Yeshua once again alone.

~

Esau was breathing so hard he became dizzy. He adjusted the black cloth mask in order to see better. He looked down at his shaking hand, still holding the bloody short sword. I must calm myself, he thought. *I made my sin known to you, did not conceal my guilt. I said, I shall confess my offense to YHWH.* His breathing slowed. Just moments ago, he had been utterly consumed with rage. Holy rage! But it seemed to have melted away the moment he saw the blood – so much blood. Now he felt ... shame. Had he really expected to get through this without using his blade? *And you, for my part took away my guilt, forgave my sin.*

Once again he felt a wave of anger. Why did that tall strange-looking man have to stand in his way? Esau hated him the moment he saw him, the shaved head, the earrings, the eyes painted in that effeminate manner. *The man who has intercourse with a man has done a hateful thing. He will be put to death and his blood will be on his own head.* That is it. The blood was on that man's own head, not Esau's.

This thought eased his shame. His hand shook less. His mind flashed back to his initiation into the Brotherhood. In his youth, he also had entertained sinful thoughts about other boys. He said a prayer of thanksgiving that he had never acted upon these unlawful desires. *How blessed are those who keep to what is just, whose conduct is always upright!*

Nachor had warned him that he must be ready to do battle – that there would be wicked men standing in his way. He must not hesitate to strike them down. *Everyone will be awestruck, proclaim what YHWH has done and understand why he has done it.*

The mission – focus! Nachor had drilled this into him a hundred times. He must not fail. He resumed his search from room to room in the villa. But his thoughts kept straying back to his youth, to when Nachor had found him begging on the streets after he had been abandoned by his miserable father, a drunkard and a brute who always favored Esau's younger brother.

Esau was large and strong. He towered a half head over most other men. But he was clumsy and walked with a limp. His mother told him that, when he was six, he had a fever that almost killed him. His father said it would have been better if it had, because now his left leg was shorter than the other due to a misshapen ankle and foot. His father told him he was useless. *You make us the butt of our neighbors, the mockery and scorn of those around us.*

Nachor brought Esau into his own home. He fed him and clothed him. He saw promise and capability in Esau. He personally saw to Esau's induction and training in the Brotherhood. He taught Esau how to memorize the holy words and their secret meaning. *Arrogant men are attacking me, bullies hounding me to death, no room in their thoughts for YHWH!*

Shame on all who serve images, who pride themselves on their idols. The master of this house was obviously one of those. In every room Esau entered, he saw frescoes on the walls and ceilings, statues on pedestals, tile mosaics of human forms on the floors. *Fire goes before him, sets ablaze his enemies all around.* Ablaze – yes! He would report to Nachor everything he saw. Nachor would be grateful. Perhaps they would plan a new mission to burn this abomination to the ground. Esau could lead this mission after having proved his worth!

All fled before Esau. He felt powerful. *You will not abandon me to*

Sheol, for you cannot allow your faithful servant to see the abyss. The small African servant girl had seen him kill the tall man and had run off screaming. Apparently the word had gone out to flee because he now saw no one, although he heard activity and yelling elsewhere in the house. *I pursued my enemies and destroyed them, and I did not turn back until they were consumed.*

Remember the mission: You must find the girl and bring her to the Brotherhood! He knew her name – Selah – and what she looked like. He repeated the description he had been given in his head: Nine years old. Well fed. Light skin. Curly brown hair. He had also been warned that these rich Jews painted their faces and dyed their hair just like Roman whores.

Take pity on me, YHWH, for I am in trouble. They had timed the mission for when the master of this house was known to be away. The Brotherhood had sentries posted down the street and would blast a horn if they saw the master returning, no doubt with his retinue of well armed guards. Esau's task was to get in quickly, find the girl and bring her back.

My strength gives way under my misery. The strange thing was that when he entered the front room, he found a group of hysterical women, already pining away about some tragedy. There was an old fat woman being attended by several servants, who were all wailing sympathetically. They didn't even notice Esau until the tall, effeminate one entered with refreshments. He immediately saw Esau, dropped his tray and ordered him out. *All he says is malicious and deceitful, he has turned his back on wisdom.* That's when Esau drew his short sword. Then the women noticed him. Yes. *Vexation is gnawing away my eyes, my soul deep within me.*

While they were keening, he had eyed each of the women and determined that none fit the description of the girl – his mission. Therefore he didn't follow when all but the African girl fled the room, leaving the ridiculous bald man to face Esau's sword. The man had yelled at him to leave, which only inflamed Esau's rage. *You hate evildoers, liars you destroy; the violent and deceitful YHWH detests.*

Esau shuddered as he relived the moment when he swung the

sword and slashed deeply into the man's neck. *There they have fallen, the evildoers, flung down, never to rise again.*

Concentrate! Find the girl, half-wit. *When people see me in the street they take to their heels. I have no more place in their hearts than a corpse.* He turned a corner in an atrium and saw a bright light coming from an open door at the back of the house. That's where they must have all fled. He hurried down the hallway. *Let YHWH arise, let his enemies scatter, let his opponents flee before him.*

He stopped abruptly upon entering the work yard. He brought his left hand to his forehead. Slowly, his eyes adjusted to the midday sun. The yard was empty except ... at the far corner stood a young man and ... yes! A fat curly-haired girl cowered behind him. *The upright rejoice in the presence of YHWH, crying out for joy.* He rushed to them before they could escape.

As he drew near he saw that the man was really just a boy about the same age as himself. He obviously wasn't one of the rich inhabitants of this villa, and he wasn't dressed as the other servants. He wore a plain linen robe, torn in several places and badly in need of washing. His hair was long, dirty, and unkempt. Esau had seen this boy on the streets of the city. He lived with that carpenter and his witch wife.

Esau stopped before the other boy, brandishing his weapon, but he could think of no words to say. The two eyed each other curiously. The boy should be afraid, thought Esau. I am large. I am wearing a mask. I am carrying a sword. But Esau saw no fear in the other's eyes.

Finally his tongue worked. "The girl," he said. "I will take the girl."

The girl shrank behind the other boy, not wanting even to look at Esau. *I am loathsome to my neighbors. My friends shrink from me in horror.*

The boy stood there, eyeing Esau thoughtfully. At last he said, "I know you – the way you walk."

Confusion! Does he not see my blade? Will he make me act again? *I am a worm, not a man.* Esau's courage was failing. He should strike, but his hand would not move. *My strength is trickling away. My heart has turned to wax, melting inside me.*

Esau felt feverish inside his robe and hood. He longed to take his mask off. "I will take the girl. My mission. She will bring a great ransom." Then he added half-heartedly, "you can join us."

"I have seen you," The boy said. "Nachor has been filling your head with lies. What is your name?"

Esau took a step back, unsure of what to do. *My mouth is dry as earthenware, my tongue sticks to my jaw.*

The boy continued in his calm voice, "Your mission was over before you arrived. Ba'asha is dead. His son will inherit his fortune and his burdens. His son is from Ba'asha's first wife and cares nothing for Hadassah or Selah. He is more wicked than even Ba'asha. No one will ransom the girl."

Esau became aware of a horn sounding in the distance. How long had it been sounding? But it was not Nachor's horn. This was the trumpet of Roman soldiers. Why would they be coming here? *A pack of dogs surrounds me, a gang of villains is closing in on me.* Esau stood frozen with fear.

The boy reached out and touched Esau on the shoulder, slowly pushing down the arm that brandished the weapon. He leaned close, looking directly into Esau's eyes and said, "Throw away your weapon. Take the south road until you come to a village. Ask for the house of Yoceph. Tell them Yeshua sent you. His harvest is plentiful and he needs more laborers. He will let you work for food and sleep in the caves. I will see you again soon."

Esau was confused. For once the voices in his head offered him no guidance. He was alone. He looked down again at the sword, unsure of what to do. He heard another blast from the trumpet, nearer this time, rousing him from his thoughts. He tossed the sword into the bushes, pulled off his mask, and ran out through the open gate.

There was a large cart laden with washings from the fullers near the gate. Yeshua hoisted Selah up on top of the garments. "Stay low now. Let's go find your mother." He pushed the cart through the abandoned gate and out into the alleyway.

~

Bustan made several attempts at conversation while they walked through the day. Each time, Naomi either responded with a single word or a shrug of her shoulders. She mostly stared toward the ground with bloodshot eyes. Eventually he gave up and passed the rest of the day talking to his mules. They arrived at the crossroads just before sunset.

Bustan pointed to the north fork. "If you follow that road, in a few miles it will bring you to Cana. Here, take this water skin with you. Stay alert. Keep to the side of the road and hide if you see anyone."

Naomi nodded in reply.

"Remember girl, those soldiers were looking for you *specifically*. They probably know your name and any relations you have in the area. They may have already visited your aunt. Be careful of walking into a trap. They may even be there now, waiting for you."

"Thank you." Seeing his concerned look, she added, "and I promise I will never mention your name."

"Very well. Whatever it is you have done will pass soon enough. They will stop looking for you. Until then, I will pray that Alilah watch over you."

Naomi had no reply to this. She had cursed Alilah the previous night. Alilah had abandoned her. She turned and started down the road.

When Bustan was out of sight she scolded herself: I must get my wits back. I have been relying on a stranger to watch over me, but now I am on my own again. Think!

She went to the side of the road and muddied her face. She was wearing a boy's short tunic. She wore no veil, so with her chopped hair in the fading light she could easily be mistaken for a young laborer returning from the city.

She made her way northward cautiously. She saw no one.

It took her almost two hours to cover the distance. This was not a paved Roman road, rather a beaten path through fields and hills. A couple of times she almost lost the trail, and she would have too, if not for the nearly full moon. At last she came to a cluster of houses with steep hills rising behind them. She could see feeble lamplight and bonfires at the houses.

They will have finished their Shabbat meal, she thought. They will be preparing for the night. The women will be indoors. The men will be out feeding the animals or …

"Who's there?" called a voice, startlingly close.

Naomi spun around to see a man walking toward her from a path leading out of the hills. She froze.

The man approached until he was quite close. Naomi backed up several paces. "Can I be of service to you?" asked the man warily.

He was young – about her own age, or perhaps a little older. Her wits returned. She spoke in a hoarse whisper. "Shabbat Shalom. I am looking for someone. Do you know a woman named Taletha?"

The man became guarded. "Who are you? We've been bothered enough for one day. First the soldiers, then a bounty hunter, and now you! Tell me what it is you want and be off with you," he demanded.

Something was wrong. Naomi again spoke hoarsely, "Taletha lives in this village, does she not?"

The young man studied her, keeping his distance. "Yes, she does. I am her son. Now tell me who you are and what it is you want!"

"Ephrayim?" Naomi said in her own clear voice.

"What?" He stepped closer and peered into her face. "Who – Naomi? Is that you?"

"Yes cousin."

Instead of embracing her, he immediately became alarmed. "Let's get you out of sight. Come with me, now!" He tried to take her hand but she shrunk from his touch. "Follow me, quickly, and keep silent!" He led her off the road, back up the path from which he had emerged. They went behind several houses and approached her aunt's house from the hills.

"Stay here by the stables. Neighbors are in our house. You must not be seen. I'll bring my mother when it is safe." He went back to the lane and entered through the courtyard.

Naomi crouched quietly in the dirt and waited. After what seemed a long time, she heard several people departing the house. Ephrayim and a woman whom she presumed to be her aunt were thanking the visitors for their help.

After the last of the villagers disappeared down the lane, Ephrayim and Taletha appeared. Taletha addressed her in hushed tones: "Oh, my dear Naomi, I thought they would never leave. You must be frozen to death. Come in and get warm by the fire."

Naomi suffered Taletha to put her arms around her and guide her into the house. Taletha continued her fussing. "Look at you child! What have you done to yourself? What happened to your beautiful hair? No matter. It will grow back. Oh you're filthy! Ephrayim, fetch a pail of water and a clean cloth."

Naomi allowed her aunt to wash the mud from her face and hair. She sat by the fire and they brought her a blanket, food and drink. While she ate she told them the same abbreviated story she had given to Bustan. She could not bring herself to even think about being defiled and the killing yet – let alone tell someone else. She told them about the kindness of Bustan, but without mentioning his name.

Taletha shook her head toward the ceiling. "My brother, I knew he was wicked. But this ... this is *unspeakable!* When your mother died I thought about bringing you here to live with us. I wish now that I had done so, and none of this would have come to pass. You poor child!"

Naomi didn't know what to say to this. She wished that Taletha *had* said something then. She would have jumped at the chance to get away from Achyan. After an awkward silence, Naomi told them about the incident in the morning when the Romans came looking for her. They sat curiously silent, looking at each other. "What?" she asked.

Ephrayim answered, "Three Romans on horseback came here this afternoon. They were looking for you by name. We told the truth – we hadn't seen you and didn't know where you were."

"Achyan," said Naomi bitterly, "He must have told them to look here. I hope they had to torture it out of him."

"Well, if it's any consolation, they said that they did indeed," replied Ephrayim.

"Good! I hope they kill him."

"Dear, we must not say things like that on Shabbat," said Taletha.

"I do not care!" Naomi felt a wave of emotion. She sniffed and wiped her eyes. "So, the Romans ... they are gone now?"

"Yes, but they didn't just take our word for it," Ephrayim explained. "They interrogated everybody here in the village. They beat up a dim-witted boy down the lane, hoping that either he or his parents would confess to seeing you."

Seeing Naomi's look of horror Taletha added, "Don't worry. He will be all right – strong as an ox – just bruises and a couple of missing teeth."

Ephrayim continued, "They searched every house in the village and made quite a mess. I think they were a little angry."

Naomi was despondent. "What am I to do? Do you think they will be back?"

Ephrayim nodded. "They *promised* they would. They threatened everyone in the village that if they saw you or heard any news, they were to alert the authorities. I'm sorry Naomi, but you can't stay here. Too many eyes. It won't be safe for you, or for us."

Naomi's situation was bleak. "Well then ... where?"

They sat in silence, staring at the fire. At last Taletha said, "I know a woman in Sepphoris who might take you in for a while. A good woman, runs a house for destitute women – always strangers coming and going. You only need to hide for a week or two. They will eventually give up looking."

"In Sepphoris? Herod's city? All of his men are there, and the Romans too. And they know my name."

Ephrayim rubbed his chin as he considered this idea. "My mother's idea might work. They won't expect you to hide there. And you've already taken the first steps to disguise your looks with that lovely haircut."

Taletha smacked her son on the shoulder. "Don't tease the poor girl. Now, Naomi, this woman, Nura is her name. A healer of great renown. Many people in this area owe their lives to her. The poor woman has no children – lives with her husband and his crazy nephew. She has a shop with all kinds of potions and powders. She'll disguise you so that even your own mother would be fooled."

"My mother ..."

"I'm sorry dear, it's just an expression. I didn't mean to bring up bitter memories. I just ..."

"No, I was thinking. My name – you said they are looking for me by name. I can go by my mother's name."

"What? Oh. Well, I hadn't thought of that. That's a good idea – I always liked your mother's name, Miryam. We used to call her Miri when she was young."

"Miri," Naomi repeated. "I like that. Just like in the old story – the one about Ruth."

"Who?" asked Ephrayim.

Naomi wagged her finger. "Cousin – did you sleep through all your synagogues? In the story, the old woman, Naomi, which means sweetness, changed her name to Miri, after tragedy befell her and her family. Miri means bitterness."

"Ooo, son, isn't she the smart one." Taletha was enjoying the budding conspiracy. "So then, it's settled. Now Naom ... I mean Miri – we have to get used to calling you that, and we might as well start now. Miri, Miri, Miri. We'll need a story for you. Who are you, where did you come from, and why are you in town? We'll get Nura to help us make up something that sounds right."

Naomi, now Miri, replied: "You are sure you can trust this Nura? How about her husband and ... nephew did you say?"

"Her husband's nephew – no relation to her. Stay away from that one – a born troublemaker. Her husband is nice enough – works as a builder. He has a wood shop and does odd jobs when he can find them. Makes very nice tables. We'll leave it to Nura to decide if he should be brought into the confidence."

Ephrayim stood up. "It's getting late. I plan to go into Sepphoris tomorrow morning to visit with Channah's family. I can stop by and see Nura. If she agrees, we'll figure out a way to smuggle you into the city."

"Who is Channah?" asked Miri.

Taletha beamed. "Oh, you haven't heard ... my boy is getting married." She pinched Ephrayim on the cheek. He rolled his eyes and blushed. "Channah is a lovely girl. Let's see, ah, you wouldn't know Natan, would you?"

Miri shook her head.

"Well I don't know if you remember my husband, Hozai. You would have been very young when he died. I think he did see you once. You were about three – such a precocious toddler you were – always running away, talking to strangers. I remember once when ..."

"Mother, you were telling her about Channah's family," said Ephrayim.

"Oh yes. How my mind wanders! Now, my husband, may Hashem watch over him, had a cousin on his mother's side. Yes, that's it. His mother's sister is Natan's mother. Natan is her second ... no, her third son. The second one died as a baby. I heard it from her own lips in this very house not long after Hozai and I were married." Having concluded her story, she smiled and folded her hands in her lap.

Miri was confused. "But what does that have to do with Ephrayim getting married to ... Channah is it?"

"Oh yes, that's what I was talking about. Natan, you see, is Channah's father. He made a shidduch with my husband for his daughter and our son. Natan has become a very important man in Sepphoris. He's in charge of all the grain shipments – even the ones that go to *Rome*. All the farmers have to deal with him. Don't get me wrong. He's a fair man, but he drives a hard bargain. This is a good match for my Ephrayim." She tried to pinch his cheek again but he batted her hand away. "Natan will be a powerful patron. And now, what else ... his wife is named Ruth. Ah! Just like in your story. Channah is their first born, and they have a son too."

Ephrayim nodded, "Yeduthun. He's twelve. Everyone calls him Yedu."

"That's right, Yedu. Handsome boy. Oh Naomi, I mean *Miri* – that's going to take some getting-used-to – I hope you have a chance to meet them. The wedding is very soon, just two weeks! It would be grand if you can come!"

Ephrayim placed his hand over his mother's. "Let's take one step at a time, mother. Let's get ... Miri safely hidden in the city. Channah's mother is already worried that the guest list is out of hand. There seem to be so few happy occasions these days."

~

A whisper in my ear: "Take by force that which was stolen. Let your anger rise within you. Then will you understand."

A naked man lies before me on his side. Wrists tied to ankles. A lamb waiting for slaughter. A black hood covers his face. Hundreds of candles burn, like the synagogue during Festival of Lights. A woman kneels to the side, weeping, praying. Whisper speaks from within the hood: "Do you desire to slay a powerful man?" I approach. Sword heavy in my hand. I am unsure. I test the blade by pushing it into the wall. It penetrates the stone easily.

More wailing from the woman. Silence! I raise the blade to strike. Again whisper speaks: "Now you understand the world. You have found a corpse. Are you better than a corpse?" The hood is gone. Stringy gray hair. I see his face. Achyan. Abbe. Tears fall from his eyes. Tears of weakness, regret, loss. More whining from the woman. The long blade still in my hand. I raise my arm. I strike.

Miri awoke in a black room. Faint moonlight shone through cracks where the stone walls met the ceiling beams. She heard the braying of a donkey outside. She remembered then. She lay in the back room of her aunt's house in Cana. The events of the past two days came crashing back to her. She closed her eyes and tried not to think – to empty her mind. She needed sleep.

But sleep would not come. Getting up, she felt her way along the wall until she found the arched doorway leading to the front room.

All was quiet. The remains of the fire glowed in the brazier in the corner. She grabbed a blanket and went out. In the courtyard, she lay on a wooden bench looking up into the night sky. The moon was just above the western horizon. It would be setting soon. She could see a dull glow starting in the east. The cock would crow and others would be up soon. She dared to think that the new day would bring a glimmer of hope.

She still felt exhausted even though she reckoned that she must have slept most of the night. She pondered the meaning of her recent dreams but could not make any sense of them. She tried to rationalize her fears – to think her way through them. But her fears were visceral, not rational. What kind of life will I have now, she wondered. Where am I to go? What will I do?

The idea came to her that she should do what Te'oma wanted of her. She should go south and find the camp of Yochanan. Maybe there she could find a purpose for her life. She could be like Te'oma, traveling the land spreading Yochanan's message: King David back from Sheol, the Romans gone. It was a nice dream, but was it anything more?

~

The day went as planned. Ephrayim left early for Sepphoris. Miri stayed in the house, unseen by anyone in the village. Taletha tried to pamper her – telling her to sit, rest, and eat. Miri insisted on taking part in the household chores. In the morning they sat spinning yarn from new wool while Taletha prattled endlessly, mostly about the plans for the upcoming wedding. More than once, she warned Miri to stay away from Nura's nephew, the troublemaker. Miri resolved to do so. She did not need any more trouble in her life.

And so the day passed. In the mid-afternoon, they heard the braying of a donkey. They arose and came to the front room just as Ephrayim entered followed by a strange-looking woman. She was slight, a little taller than Miri, but with a thinner frame. Her skin was pale, practically white. Her hair was very long and almost pure silver, with just a few streaks of black. It was tied with a ribbon behind her back. But, despite her white hair, she did not look old. Her face was free of wrinkles. The pale skin made her deep-green eyes more arresting.

"Dearest Miri, I am Nura," she said, giving a deep bow. "I am told that you are in need of lodgings. My home will be your home for as long as you desire."

It seemed that some response was required. "Thank you, ma'am. My aunt has told me many good things about you."

"She is kind." Nura smiled toward Taletha, who was now busy with the fire. "Taletha, it has been too long since our last visit. How is your arm, my dearest?"

Taletha arose and rubbed her left elbow. "Much better with that oil you left me. You are an angel, Nura. Sit down now. Let me get you some refreshment."

"Don't worry about me, dear. I rode most of the way." She then turned her full attention to Miri. "Ephrayim has told me some of your story. You should know that there is quite a stir in Sepphoris right now. It seems that one of Herod's advisors, a very wealthy man named Ba'asha, is now killed in a town to the east. They are looking for a slave – a prostitute from that town named Naomi, who is believed to have committed the murder."

Miri sat down heavily on the bench and looked at her hands. Taletha stopped what she was doing and looked up in alarm. Her jaw dropped.

Nura continued, "Ephrayim tells me that you come from that same town and that your name was once Naomi." Nura paused to let this sink in. "Now this is a striking coincidence, don't you think? But we know that this girl they are looking for cannot be you. You are neither a slave nor a prostitute. You are Taletha's niece."

Miri looked up with tears welling in her eyes.

"However, others might mistake you for this runaway slave. We must be careful. Your name from now forward will be Miryam, or Miri, as you prefer. You must practice this. Never use the name Naomi again, even among those whom you trust. Even among your family." Nura looked toward Taletha and Ephrayim, who both nodded their assent.

"Don't worry dearest Miri, this will pass. They do not know where this other Naomi is. They will not be looking for her in Sepphoris. We will say that you are my father's niece. You and I are cousins."

Miri looked confused. "But I do not look anything like you. People can see we are not related, you are ..."

"Yes – I am not from here. Anyone can see that. I speak of my adoptive father, who took me in as a child. His name was Taddai. In life he is well respected, but mysterious. He would travel often and nobody knew exactly where. Not even me. We will say that you are his niece, and that you have just become an orphan. You are coming to the city to find him. You did not know that he no longer walks the earth."

Ephrayim asked, "Will people believe that?"

"Why not?" Answered Nura. "The city is filled with orphans. No one pays any attention to them. If anyone asks, go ahead and tell them that you are from Magdala."

Ephrayim was doubtful. "Wouldn't it be better to say she was from some place far away – like maybe Yerushalayim?"

Nura had considered this already. "Many people make trips to Yerushalayim to see the temple. What if people ask details about this street, or that market ... she will not have answers, and they will grow suspicious. No. Tell them you are from Magdala and that you don't know this slave girl named Naomi."

Nura sat down on the bench across from Miri and accepted a cup from Taletha. From the jug on the table, she filled it with water and drank. "Still, dearest Miri – we will take precautions. I love your dark, straight hair. It must have been beautiful before you chopped it like that. I used to have dark hair myself." She smiled demurely. "But we should disguise you when we get back to my home. I have dyes that we can use to lighten the color and to give it some curl. Would that be acceptable to you, dearest?"

"Of course, but ... would it not be better for me to continue dressing like a boy?"

Nura laughed – a welcome, cheerful sound in their situation. "My dear, do you have any idea how beautiful you are?"

And so, early that evening, just after sundown, one could have seen Nura leaving Cana just as she arrived, riding on a donkey with a boy walking alongside. They continued southward, past the crossroads, and entered Sepphoris, which was now coming alive as Shabbat was ending.

Samuel

M iri sat up abruptly in bed. Breathless and soaked with sweat, she felt for a moment like she was going to be sick. She forced herself to breathe slowly. Gradually, she calmed.

The dream had been like the others – so strange, so vivid. She tried now to remember it, but it was rapidly fading, becoming increasingly vague. She had been carrying a lamb for sacrifice. But when she had set it down and tied it in order to tend the fire, the lamb became a boy. At one point she was sure it was Te'oma, but now she couldn't remember why she thought that – it didn't look anything like him. The lamb told her that she needed to become a corpse and be eaten. That's when she realized that it was now holding a knife. Then she had awoken.

She shivered, remembering where she was. When Nura had shown her to this room the previous night she could not see well in the meager lamplight, but she remembered a musty smell. Now she sat up and took in her surroundings in the morning sun.

The window shutters had been left open in the mild weather, and from the light streaming in she guessed it was mid-morning. She was sitting on a straw mattress covered by a coarse linen sheet in the center of a large room. In every direction she looked she saw floor-to-ceiling shelves, stacked with documents of all sizes and shapes. She got up, stretched her legs and circled the room.

Most of the shelves held scrolls, although one contained stacks of wooden tablets that Miri guessed were either clay or wax. Another contained rows of the new codex-style books with brightly colored wood or leather covers. Many of the scrolls looked very old and worn.

She came to an inclined table at the far end of the room. It had hooks fixed to the lower and upper edges, obviously designed to hold a scroll open. To the side she saw a variety of writing implements and jars of ink. Tallow candles were set on stands to either side of the table.

Miri had never seen so many documents collected in one place, not even in the synagogue at Magdala. Her brother, Rapha, had taken her there when she was younger. The rabbi had taken an interest in him and was teaching him letters. She remembered the rabbi telling Achyan that the boy had a natural facility that was rare. Her father had scoffed at this. He couldn't see how having a scribe for a son would profit him.

Rapha would bring home his wax tablet every night and show Miri how to make the letters, how to form the words, how to sound them out. She found that she could learn quickly – more quickly than Rapha. Soon she was the one tutoring her brother.

Emotion welled in her chest at the memory. She felt guilty when she realized she hadn't given any thought to Rapha in a long time. She had now lost every person whom she had ever loved – even Te'oma. She had at first been attracted to Te'oma but she did not really love him. He was too aloof, too driven. She saw him rather as a means of escape. To what, she did not know.

The image of the eyeless face of Te'oma on the cross flashed into her mind. When she closed her eyes tightly, the image was replaced by the accusing eyes of the rich man who had raped her as he lay on the floor clutching at his neck. She sobbed aloud and wiped a tear from her cheek. She had to steel herself – to stay in the present. She was not yet safe.

She approached a shelf at random, pulled out an old scroll, and blew the dust off. She brought it to the table and unfurled it, latching the wooden handles on the hooks. It looked very old. There were rips here and there, and a few holes where worms had eaten the papyrus. It was discolored and brittle. She was pleased to see that it was written in Torah language. She would be able to read this, albeit slowly. The title was at the top of the first page in bold letters: *The Testament of Michal.*

A loud creak from the heavy wooden door made Miri jump. She had not even seen the door in the far corner. Nura backed into the room carrying a tray of food. "Ah, dearest Miri you are awake. I hope that you have a restful time. I put you up here that it would be quiet for you. We frequently have visitors at all hours, and I do not want that you be disturbed."

"I am grateful, ma'am. I just awoke a little while ago. I hope you do not mind me looking at this." Miri gestured at the open scroll. "I was curious."

Nura approached the table and examined the scroll over Miri's shoulder. She reached out and cradled Miri's chin in her palm, turning the girl's face toward her own. Their eyes met. "You can *read*, Miri?"

Miri saw that Nura was surprised, but not upset. She blushed. "I learned to read Torah from my brother."

Nura beamed. "My dear, I believe you and I are the only women who read in this whole city! We will have much to share. Now what is this? Oh yes, the rabbi gives this and two other scrolls to my husband to be burned. I guess the scribe makes new copies. Mattanyah brings them here instead. No one here reads them yet. How far are you?"

"Just the title so far."

Nura leaned over Miri and read the title. She shook her head. "History. It is something you Jews have. In my tribe, the wise ones are forbidden to write about the gods. It is considered ... I don't know a good word for it ... dishonorable."

This didn't make much sense to Miri. She had loved reading the old stories with her younger brother.

Nura said, "Please – read all the scrolls in the room. It will give you something to do. Taddai collects many of these over his life. We have Greek scrolls on philosophy and medicine. We have many of your Torah scrolls. We have some tiresome Roman stories about warriors, gods, and their exploits. My nephew tells me about those. I do not read them."

"Thank you ma'am, I would like that."

Nura looked at her sternly. "We are talking about this last night. You are to be Miri, the niece of Taddai, who adopts me. So we are kin! Call me 'cousin,' or call me by name. But no more *ma'am*."

"Yes ... cousin." Miri was uneasy about relying so completely on someone she had only just met. She looked idly at the beginning of the scroll and ran her fingers along the first line, right to left: *I am Michal. I am the daughter of Saul, the true King of Israel. I write what I myself have witnessed. If YHWH wills it, the truth will be known to future generations.*

Nura stroked the younger girl's hair, or what remained of it. "I have much to do today so I am leaving you alone. Eat. Drink." She gestured toward the tray of food she had brought. "Use the pot in the corner there when you feel the need. It is best that you not go downstairs today, dearest. We have all sorts of people coming and going. We will show you the city tomorrow."

Miri nodded but did not look up. From somewhere deep inside her a fresh wave of sadness came up. A tear dropped onto the brittle parchment.

Nura placed her hand on Miri's shoulder. "Mattanyah will look in on you when he comes back at midday. Perhaps tonight we will do something about your hair. What a pity. We can at least cut it more evenly, maybe a little curl? Or perhaps a touch of reddish color." Nura leaned down and kissed Miri on the temple and then started to the door.

She was almost out when Miri called, "Cousin?"

"Yes dearest?"

"Hashem has blessed me to deliver me into your hands."

Nura smiled and said, "In every house where I come I will enter only for the good of those who live there, be they free or slaves." With that, she slipped through the door and pulled it closed behind her.

~

Having consumed the bread and tea, Miri sat down on the stool in front of the scroll table. She hadn't had the opportunity to do any reading for more than two years – since her brother had passed to Sheol. The idea of spending the day deciphering a scroll was appealing. At least it would keep her morose thoughts at bay.

Being out of practice, the reading was laborious at first. But after a while it came back to her. She started from the beginning.

The Testament of Michal

I am Michal. I am the daughter of Saul, the true King of Israel. I write what I myself have witnessed. If YHWH wills it, the truth will be known to future generations. Many are the lies being told in these evil days. I commit my memories to papyrus lest the truth go unknown.

Beware! The clan of Jesse and David are trampling the good memory of King Saul into the dust. Do not believe their lies!

You have been told that David is my husband. False! My father gave me in marriage to Paltiel. That was long before David abducted me. Paltiel was my beloved. David's soldiers said they would kill my husband and my children if I did not go with them. I still do not know what became of my children.

I call David by his common name. I will not call him king. My father was the rightful king. David is usurper, thief, and murderer.

Miri paused and rubbed her eyes. She was puzzled. She knew the basic history of her people from going to synagogue meetings and from reading with her brother. She tried to remember if she had ever heard of this Michal before. She didn't think so.

Everyone knew that Saul was the first king of all Israel, followed by David and then wise Solomon. But this scroll was written from a strange point of view. David — a thief and murderer? She read on.

I will tell you of my childhood. My father worked the land at Gibea, as his father had before him. The land provided abundance.

In those days, all of Israel lived under Philistine rule. Our masters allowed us to work our own land. They did not enslave us. They took a portion of the produce of our labors. The one thing the Philistines forbade us was to work iron. My father told me they were worried we would make weapons. They were right!

You know the names of my brothers and my sister. They are listed in the chronicles. I am the youngest of Saul's six children by his only wife, Ahinoam. I was the favorite of my father. He took me with him wherever he went.

I remember the day my father met the man of god. I was eight years of age. Everything changed on that day.

My brother fell asleep one night when he should have kept watch. He allowed six donkeys to wander away. We could not afford to lose them. My father left the next morning to find them and bring them home. I went with him, riding on the foal.

We walked all over the lands of Benyamin. We walked into the lands of Yudah before turning back. The danger there was great for Benyaminites in that time. We came at last to the town of Ramah. We approached the well to refresh ourselves and water the foal. There we encountered a very old man. His eyes were dim. He stood by the well leaning on his staff. My father greeted him. We did not know that this was a man of god. He was not having fits of rapture and visions as those men do. We did not know that this was Samuel, high judge for the twelve tribes.

We asked the man if he had seen our donkeys. He laughed. He said he could barely see what was in front of his face. He treated us kindly. We stayed the night in his home. Samuel took a liking to my father.

Samuel told my father his woes. They thought I was asleep but I heard every word. I will tell it to you!

Samuel was the high judge for all Israel. All came to him for guidance. His yoke was heavy. The people had grown disheartened. Enemies attacked them from all directions. They were tired of paying homage to Philistine masters who did nothing to defend them. They wanted a strong king who could lead them to glory.

Samuel did not want to appoint a king. He told my father how he replied to the elders of Israel. I remember exactly what Samuel said. I will write it down for you:

This is what a king will do: He will take your sons and send them to war. He will make them plow his fields and reap his harvest. They will make weapons for his chariots. He will take your daughters to be concubines and cooks. He will take the best of your fields, vineyards, orchards, and grazing lands. He will take your grain to feed his soldiers. He will take the best of your oxen, your cattle, your donkeys, your sheep, and your flocks. He will use them for his own purposes. The king will take everything, and you will be his slaves.

Samuel told my father that he needed to find a man without guile or ambition. YHWH had revealed to him that only such a man should be king. He had not been able to find such a man in all of Israel.

Samuel must be talking about *other* kings. Miri had heard many stories about King David and wise Solomon. These two at least were good and just – not despots. Jews were taught to pray every morning for the return of the ancient kingdom.

Feeling a stirring in her gut, she got up and went to the corner of the room to squat over the pot. As she pulled up her tunic she realized that she still had Ba'asha's coin purse and dagger hidden inside the folds of her mantle. She finished her ablutions, thinking about what to do with these items: I might need the dagger yet if trouble comes my way. I should keep it close. The purse though ... I can hide it here in this room. She went to the shelf of tablets, pulled out a few on the second row from the top, pushed the purse to the back and replaced the tablets.

Satisfied that the row looked exactly as before, she returned to the table. She wanted to read more about Saul and the man of god.

My father and I left early the next morning. Samuel revealed where we could find our stray donkeys. We were filled with joy! My father insisted on paying the man of god. He did not want an unpaid debt to YHWH.

Many weeks passed. Harvest came. One day, a messenger from Samuel arrived. He said that my father must return to Ramah at once. He did not say why. I went with my father once again. We arrived in Ramah the next day.

Samuel had assembled elders from every tribe of Israel. My father was confused. He asked me: Why did Samuel summon him to such a prestigious assembly? My father was a simple farmer. He was unschooled and unlettered. He was not even an elder in our own town yet!

Samuel stood before the throng. He spoke about kings. He repeated his warning, which I have already written down for you. He began to pray. He lay quaking on the ground a long time.

Samuel arose. He said: Saul of Benyamin, come forth! My father was troubled. He set me aside and told me to stay in my place. He went before the man of god. Samuel anointed my father with precious oil. He presented my father to the twelve tribes as their king.

Many yelled in outrage. How could Samuel anoint a farmer with dirt in his hair and mud on his feet? He was not a soldier. He was not a priest. How can he be king?

There was a rich man named Jesse who complained the loudest. He came from a town in Yudah called Bethlehem. He demanded that Samuel anoint his eldest son, Eliab. Samuel refused. Jesse cursed the man of god and swore an evil oath: May YHWH bring terrible ills and worse ills too upon me if my son is not anointed king. This oath was to be fulfilled, but not in the way Jesse expected.

Samuel told the crowd that my father was the guileless man he had sought. He warned what an ambitious man would do with great power. The northern tribes accepted Samuel's judgment. Only the houses of Yudah and Simeon went away in disgust.

My father never desired to be king. After these events, we returned to our farm. We continued to work the land. My father warned me not to tell anyone.

Some months later, a messenger arrived from Ramah. He demanded that my father travel north to Samaria. A war council had been called. The Ammonites had laid siege to a town in the east. My father was to lead an army. He could not escape his duty. It was dangerous, so I did not go with him.

This was the first of many wars.

I will tell you of my father. In the first five years of his rule, he aged before my eyes. By the time I became a woman and had my first blood, Saul looked like an old man. His eyes became sunken. His cheeks were hollow. I often heard him cry out in his sleep. He was haunted by innumerable spirits. He had seen many slain by his own hands and by the hands of our enemies.

~

Miri looked up from the scroll when she heard noises in the kitchen below followed by the shuffle of sandals climbing a ladder. A soft knock sounded on the door.

"Forgive me miss, I don't wish to disturb." Mattanyah, Nura's husband, peeked his head in.

Miri had met him briefly the previous night when they arrived from Cana. She had thought his large stature belied an agreeable, shy nature. She was surprised at the manner in which he deferred to

Nura. The woman seemed to have that affect on those around her.

Mattanyah backed into the room carrying another tray laden with food. Miri got up quickly to help him. "Sir, let me take that. You are the master in this house. It is not right for you to be serving me." She took the tray from him and set it on a table by the door.

Mattanyah stood, de-trayed, scratching his head. "It is no bother, miss. Sit, rest. Nura was quite mysterious about your condition but she told me that we are to take good care of you. Are you well enough to be up and about?"

"Oh yes, sir. I am not injured."

"Not injured, eh? So, I guess your difficulty was of a different kind. Nura did say that you'll be staying indoors today. I wonder what she's worried about."

Miri frowned. "I think she wants me to stay out of sight. There may be ... well, there were some men looking for me yesterday."

"Oh, *that* kind of trouble. We're used to that in this house," Mattanyah mused. "You should meet my nephew. He excels at trouble." Getting no response to this, he looked about the room and sought a way to change the subject. "I see you are reading. I never learned more than a few letters myself. My wife tried to teach me, but it's just not in me. A new world – women who read. Next you'll be owning property and divorcing your husbands." Mattanyah laughed nervously, seeming to feel a need to fill the silence. He gestured to the corner. "I'll take that pot for you and come back with some fresh water later."

"Oh sir, no. Allow me to do some chores. You and Nura have been too kind. As I said, I am not injured. There is no need for me to keep still."

Mattanyah looked uncertain and sighed. "Nura gave me instructions that you are to rest. Why don't you sit here and eat? I'll take care of ..."

"Look," Miri said, "I will wrap this shawl around my head and keep my eyes down. No one will recognize me."

Mattanyah shrugged. "If you insist. But you look scandalous in that short tunic." Miri noticed that Mattanyah had been keeping his

eyes to the side, not wanting to look at her bare knees and shins. "I'll
wait downstairs while you change. There is plenty to do today and I
could do with another pair of hands. Bring that pot with you when
you come."

Miri wrapped a tan shawl around her face, covering her hair and
chin. She put on the tunic and mantle that Nura had given her the
previous night. They were plain, old and worn – just the thing to
blend in. She would look like any woman in town. She found an
inside pocket in the mantle into which she stuffed Ba'asha's dagger.
She felt safer with it on her person even though she doubted that
she would be able to use it if the need arose.

A short time later Mattanyah and Miri set off to fetch water, each
laden with a shoulder pole and two empty buckets. Mattanyah led
them through narrow, curvy streets. He narrated as they walked.
"We live in the oldest section of the city. This is all that remains
from the great destruction that happened years ago, probably before
you were born."

"Oh, yes. I heard about that. You are talking about Varus."

Mattanyah cringed. "That is not a name we speak aloud." Under
his breath, he added, "But yes. It was him. That one was the Roman
governor in Syria at the time of the troubles. There was a drought
that summer and most of the crops failed. There was very little food
– no apples, wheat. Even the grape vines withered. The cattle and
goats stopped giving milk. People were starving. And here in
Sepphoris ... here Herod had plenty – warehouses full of grain, oil
and wine. And the hill up there with cisterns as big as a house! Filled
with water. I've seen them. Did he feed his people? Did he give us
water? Of course not. He kept his stores shut and guarded. Said
there wasn't enough to go around. Whole warehouses!"

It was obvious that this was something Mattanyah, and probably
any townspeople old enough to remember, still felt bitter about.
"Were you living here when this happened?"

"Watch your feet," said Mattanyah, pointing at a pile of fresh
dung. He led them around a broken cart blocking the street. The
owner had tied his donkeys to a railing while he tried to mend an

axle. "Me, no. Nura was here with her father, but not me. I was still a boy. I lived with my father in a small village to the south. My oldest brother was a crafty one. We had storage caves that we kept hidden from the tax collectors. We had enough. This city though ..." Mattanyah shook his head.

"What happened?" Asked Miri.

"It started as a riot over food. A group of men tried to break into the barley stores. Herod held them off for days. It was a stalemate until the Romans arrived from Syria."

Miri looked up in alarm.

"It was a slaughter. The ones that they didn't hack down in the streets they took to the hillside on the north side of town, near the crossroads. All those crosses, hundreds of them. Then they came through with clubs, axes, and torches and destroyed and burned everything. This little corner of town ..." Mattanyah gestured around him. "This is all that remains."

They walked on in silence through the curving streets. She heard the sound of splashing water ahead. They turned a final corner and found themselves on the side of a modern paved road.

"This is what the Romans call the 'decumanus maximus.'" said Mattanyah. "Most of the city has been rebuilt in the past dozen years." Mattanyah spread his arms. "The Romans like their streets straight and orderly."

Miri took in her surroundings. To the southeast, the wide street continued up until it disappeared over the crest of a hill. To the northwest, she looked downhill a short distance and saw bustling activity at an outdoor market. In the distance rose a steep hill – almost a cliff face. At the crest was a huge building made of white marble fringed at the top with gold and blue.

Mattanyah saw where she was looking. "Herod's new palace," he said. "They call that hill the Acropolis. Up there is where the important people stay, looking down on the rest of us. We live to serve them," he added.

Miri stared open-mouthed at the splendor of the buildings atop the hill.

"I helped build that palace with my own hands," said Mattanyah. "There is some of me in most of the buildings up there. Yeshua and I were up there just a few days ago working on the basilica. You can see it just behind the palace to the left." Miri saw the scaffolded structure. "Building stopped yesterday after the overseer, a man named Ba'asha, was murdered – guess you've heard about that?" Miri remained silent, her eyes turned to the ground. "Anyway, they'll start again in a day or two, and I'll be back up there."

Miri felt a splash of water on her face. Her attention was drawn to two children playing in a shallow pool next to a well. Their mother quickly came over and scolded them, leading them away by the hand.

"There's plenty of water in town most times – wells like this one." Mattanyah continued his narration. "There's even a fountain down by the market when they release water from the hill."

Miri observed two slave boys working a rope and pulley suspended above the well. It looked like hard work. They were filling a shallow pool from which townspeople waited in a line to draw water. Miri and Mattanyah joined the queue.

After they filled their buckets, Mattanyah helped Miri lift her pole onto her shoulders. Then he hoisted his own. As they crossed back over the street, Miri tripped, but managed to recover her footing before spilling the water. Looking back she saw a deep gutter set into the stonework on the side of the street.

"Drainage channel," said Mattanyah. "Romans put them on all their streets."

Miri was accustomed to heavy lifting and managed to carry the water all the way back to the house. But she was glad when they arrived and Mattanyah relieved her of her burden.

"Let's leave one here at the house. The other three go to the shelter. I'll show you."

They continued down the street past a fenced-in courtyard. They came to a long, squat building facing the street. It looked like a barn for livestock. Mattanyah opened one of the double doors and led Miri into the gloom. When her eyes adjusted, what she saw did indeed resemble a barn. There were long rows of stables on either side of a central aisle. But not for animals – these were obviously intended for people. Each living area was about a ten-foot square, cordoned off with shoulder-height wooden fencing. As she and Mattanyah walked down the aisle, Miri saw straw mattresses, chairs and an assortment of other furniture. The spaces looked lived-in, although it appeared that most occupants were out for the day. Strewn about were garments, combs, brushes, cups, oil lamps, bowls, and spare sandals.

"Apulia! Great cauldron of plenty – cover yourself." Mattanyah shut his eyes tightly and turned to the side. When Miri reached his side she saw what was offending his vision. A woman sat at the back of one of the stalls, naked. She held two babies, a boy and a girl, also naked, who nursed hungrily on her abundant bosom.

The woman observed the two visitors with an amused expression. "What's the matter, master-of-the house? You've seen breasts before, no? This is what they do when men aren't playing with them. If that lovely wife of yours doesn't take care of you then come see Apulia sometime, no?" She laughed and then noticed Miri. "Hi honey. I'd get up to greet you but as you see ..." She nodded toward the babies. "My name's Apulia. It's Roman. Isn't it a pretty name?"

It took Miri a moment to recover her voice. "Oh, hello. My name is Nao ... I mean Miri. I am Nura's cousin." Miri entered the living space. "What beautiful children!"

"Well, thank you, 'Nao-I-mean-Miri'. This one's mine." She jostled the boy on her left breast. "The girl belongs to my friend, Zibiah. She's gone into town. She'll be back before long. Could you take her from me for a moment?"

Miri sat next to the other woman and took the girl, who instantly fell asleep in Miri's arms.

"Look at that, great lord," said Apulia "She has a gift. And what a pretty young lady she is. Doesn't look much like your wife, does she, master-of-the-realm?"

"Apulia, stop calling me that. You know my name." Mattanyah

kept his face turned and his eyes shut, causing both Miri and Apulia to giggle. "She's not a blood relation. Anyone can see that. She's old Taddai's niece from ... where was it, Miri?"

After a brief hesitation, Miri responded, "Magdala Nunayya. On Lake Chinnereth."

"Hmm, Magdala," said Mattanyah. "But I thought Taddai was from ..."

"My father was a fisherman. I did not know my uncle well."

This seemed to satisfy Mattanyah's curiosity. He glanced and then quickly covered his eyes again. "Please Apulia, cover yourself. If you need a new tunic, I think I saw Yeshua with a stack of them from somewhere."

"No need, my lord, no need." She pulled a blanket from the floor and draped it loosely over her torso. "And where is that handsome nephew of yours? He was supposed to take the baby for a few hours this morning."

Ah, Miri thought, so that's how it is. The baby belongs to the troublemaker.

Mattanyah, seeing that it was safe to do so, lowered his hand and opened his eyes. "Yeshua left yesterday to visit his mother. He didn't say when he would return."

The baby in Miri's arms awoke and smiled brightly. "Aren't you a charmer," said Apulia. "You've had practice with babies haven't you?"

Miri blushed. "I used to take care of my youngest sister while my mother worked at the tavern. She died though."

"Who, your mother or your baby sister?" Apulia said flippantly.

After a moment's hesitation, Miri replied flatly: "Both."

"Oh honey, I'm sorry. I'm so crass sometimes. That must have been terrible for you." Apulia placed her hand on Miri's back. After an awkward silence, Apulia continued: "Your mother worked in a tavern, eh? That's what I do. Or did until ..." She nodded to her still-sucking baby. "So was she a, you know ... a *working* woman?"

It took Miri a moment to realize what she was being asked. She said abruptly, "Oh. No. She was not. I mean she did not. Not that ...

well if that is what you do, I do not mean that there is any shame in it, but ... she did cooking and cleaning. That is all."

Apulia seemed to enjoy making other people uncomfortable, as she had with Mattanyah moments ago. She laughed. "It's fine love, you can say it. A prostitute, a whore, harlot, concubine, tramp, fallen woman. Yes – that's what I am. Isn't it funny how men have so many names for it? What do you think master?"

Mattanyah shook his head. "Why do you tease me so?"

Apulia turned once again to Miri. "I had the bad luck of getting pregnant. Bad timing. I'll be working again as soon as I get my figure back. Come by and see me sometime at the tavern on the west side of town."

Miri didn't know how to respond to this invitation. She got up and handed the baby girl back to the woman. "Is there anything I can get for you, Apulia?"

Apulia glanced at Mattanyah. "I like this one, lord-of-the-palace. What proper manners she has." And then to Miri: "Why yes dear, if I could get a cup of that fresh water, it would be grand. My cup is there in the corner."

Miri smiled and obliged the woman. She filled the cup and handed it to her new friend.

~

After saying goodbye, they continued down the row of stalls. They came to an open area that served as a kind of kitchen. "We call this our 'triclinium,'" Mattanyah said with a chuckle. "That's what the Romans call their formal dining rooms. You wouldn't believe the way they eat. They lie on their sides. They have these long couches set around the room. I've seen them up at Herod's palace. Always trying to adopt the Roman ways, he is. It's the most ridiculous thing I've ever seen. Had to pinch myself to keep from laughing. You can set your water bucket over there." He indicated a space against the wall next to a smoldering ceramic brazier.

Unburdened, Miri took in the room. Against the wall were several shelves holding a variety of pots and dishes. On the floor were several sacks of grain and an amphora of oil. "So is this a kind of inn?"

"I suppose you could call it that, although few pay to stay here. Come, this last bucket is for the animals." Mattanyah led them back through the structure. "This all used to be stables. A few years back, Nura converted it into kind of a charity house for the poor. Anyone is welcome to come and take shelter. We provide food when we can. This time of year it's not usually a problem – harvest time you know, and a good year too. Local farmers know about this place and most are generous when they have extra food. They all know they might need a place like this themselves one day."

They came to an adjacent building, a two-story barn. It had pens with sheep, goats and a few chickens. There was a loft in the back accessible via a ladder.

Since Miri was anxious to help, Mattanyah asked her to water the animals and sweep out the barn. Then he said goodbye. He had a paying job in the town fixing some equipment at the community olive press.

After doing these chores, Miri settled back into her upstairs room to continue her reading. She lit the tallow candles and sat at the table. She had been thinking about what she read that morning. She recognized the name Jesse. It took her a while to remember that Jesse was King David's father. It sounded like Jesse was going to cause trouble for King Saul.

> After battle, you know the normal practice: When a tribe is conquered, the men are killed, the boys are enslaved, the women and girls are divided among the soldiers. This had been done since the days of Aaron.
>
> King Saul did not do this! My father was merciful. The mercenaries from the south did not like my father's ways. They wanted blood. They wanted the spoils of war.
>
> Jesse's clan spread a rumor that Samuel had rejected my father as king. False! They said that King Saul failed to follow YHWH's command to put the Amalekites under

the curse of destruction.

I will tell you the truth. Samuel ordered no such curse. Samuel always counseled my father to show restraint. He told my father to kill only when there was no other way.

Today the lie stands unopposed. Neither my father nor Samuel walk the earth. I must tell the truth for them. May YHWH protect these words!

I will tell you about war. War will drive sane men mad. Only men who are already mad with ambition will thrive. Beware a man who loves war!

Over time, my father was driven mad. He was overcome by the endless battles thrust upon him.

One summer my father was afflicted with the terrors. Jesse sent his youngest son to serve him. This was the first time I laid eyes on David. I admit I thought him fair. He was the same age as me. His youthful face had only a hint of stubble. But even then his deep-set eyes were dark and full of purpose.

David played the harp and sang for my father. He brought gifts, wine and food. Saul accepted him with gratitude. David's music calmed my father's spirit. Saul allowed David to stay by his side, even when he met with his war council. My father assumed Jesse sent his son as a peace offering. He did not know that David was reporting back about my father's every weakness.

This went on through the summer. When autumn came, David said he needed to return to Yudah to help with the harvest.

Miri had to stop and think at this point. David had just entered the story as a spy, reporting to the wicked Jesse. This was not David the hero of Israel that all children were taught about. This was not the David that the rabbis spoke of, the righteous king beloved by Hashem.

Miri would like to have discussed this with Te'oma. He would have had an explanation.

~

The next morning, Miri found Nura in the front room and joined her for a small breakfast. Miri asked why she ran the shelter. Nura explained that the synagogue on the north side of town hosted a charity house where men or boys could get a meal twice a day and possibly a place to sleep if they did work for the rabbis. Women, however, were not welcome. Many stayed on the streets, which left them susceptible to the weather, bandits, ruffians and drunk soldiers. Nura's stable house was of little use, so five years ago she had converted it to an open dormitory, mostly for women.

"If you're finished, let's see if we can do something about your hair," Nura cleared the dishes and stood behind Miri, examining the uneven shearing she had given herself four days ago. Nura got out a pair of bronze scissors and went to work. "It will still be very short. You should wear a shawl in town in any case. The sight of a woman's hair tends to make men wild. Especially such lovely hair as yours. It curls nicely when it is longer, no?"

Nura found some powdered makeup and applied it to Miri's face, making her skin several shades lighter. "There, now we might even pass for real cousins." At last Nura helped Miri wrap a long beige shawl around her head with the ends draped under her chin. She held up a tin mirror so Miri could see herself. "I doubt even your kin would recognize you if they met you on the street. Which they might, you know. Your cousin, Ephrayim, comes to town often. He is using any reason to be near his lovely Channah."

"I would like to meet this Channah."

"I am sure you will, soon. But this morning I have an errand to do. I am to deliver something to the palace – up the big hill across town. I am hoping you will come with me? You would like to get out and look around, I think."

Miri beamed at the suggestion. "I would love to! I am sure it will be safe enough."

And so it was decided. Nura pulled out a stool and placed it before a row of shelves in the kitchen. She reached up to the top shelf and took down a small statuette of a fat woman. She unscrewed the head of the figure and handed it to Miri. It was hollow inside – a kind of vial. She asked Miri to hold it while she lifted the trap door and descended into a cellar storage area. She returned with a brown glass bottle with a wooden stopper.

"Hold the vial steady while I fill it."

Miri did so. A strong smell filled the air making Miri's eyes water. She almost sneezed. "What is *this* for?"

Nura frowned, unsure how or if she should explain this. "It is … complicated. Actually, this is for Herod's wife. It is a plan hatched by my nephew."

"Herod's wife! Your nephew? My aunt warned me about him – that he is a troublemaker."

Nura laughed at this. "I do not think that he *makes* trouble, but it is true that trouble is good at finding him. He should be back tomorrow or the next day. You can ask him yourself. I do not know all the details – just that this potion is a substitute for some poison the queen is given. We are switching it with my own recipe. Strong smelling but harmless."

"But … Herod's wife! I have heard stories. Are you afraid?"

Nura thought about this while she stoppered the bottle and put it away. "To tell you the truth, I *am*. It is best to avoid such people altogether. You do not want to be standing nearby when one of them needs – you Jews have a good term for it – a scapegoat. Here, I will take that." She took the little statue from Miri and screwed the cap back on tightly. She then fastened it inside her mantle. "But we have to agree to this. It is the only way to get Yeshua free. You see, he was being held prisoner by a rich man at his villa."

Miri pursed her lips and nodded, but said nothing. This confirmed for her what her aunt had told her: stay away from the troublemaker. She resolved to take this advice.

~

A short time later the two women set out. Nura followed the same alleyways that Mattanyah had on the previous day until they emerged in the new section of town. They turned left and walked down the decumanus. There had been a brief rain earlier in the morning, and now the mid-morning sun was becoming hot. The air was sticky as the remaining puddles evaporated.

They continued downhill, toward the center of the city. The wide street was lined on both sides by stone buildings fronted by numerous merchants. Miri was surprised that the street was not more crowded. Nura explained that market days were Shlishi and Chamishi, or Martis and Jovis as the Romans would say. Tomorrow the town would be packed.

At most corners stood a Roman soldier. The one they passed now seemed to be no more than a boy. His face was drenched with sweat as he shifted his weight uncomfortably from foot to foot trying to stay alert. Nura had warned Miri to walk quickly past and never make eye contact. She leaned her head down and pulled her shawl around her head.

The next block was taken up entirely with a large ornate stone building. The facade had pillars and weird-looking statues protruding from the sides just below the roofline. One was a woman's head with snakes for hair. Another was a man's head, except that he had horns like a stag. Nura told her that this building held the communal baths. "Jews tend to stay away from this place," she said. "In the courtyard of our house, we have a bath – a mikveh. My husband fills it every week on the morning before Shabbat."

They were about to cross the next street when a toothless and shirtless man approached them. "Gentle ladies, would you have any coin for an elder in need?" He was half bent over and squinted up at them in the morning sun. He wobbled back and forth, swatting imaginary flies from his face. The smell of strong drink accosted Miri's nostrils.

Nura said: "Shemer, you know I do not carry coin. If you seek a meal, the hospitality house at the synagogue is open today. Or soon Chasidah will prepare midday meal at our shelter. You know the way, no?"

The old man's eyes widened in recognition. "Nura! It is you.

Fine then. Food, no coin." He then noticed Miri, who stood at Nura's side with her shawl covering her face. "And who is this fine old woman? Madam, I am Shemer." He attempted an elaborate bow but lost his balance and ended up sprawled on the side of the street.

Miri let go of her shawl and knelt at Shemer's side to help him up. "Sir, are you hurt?"

He shrunk back. "Why ... so white! A ghost! Nura, save me!" He batted away Miri's attempts to help him and continued to flail on the ground. Passers-by had to veer around.

Nura spoke with some urgency. "Dearest Shemer, this is my cousin, not a ghost. Now, Miri," she said, giving a quick nod down the street in the direction from which they had come. "Help me get Shemer off the street. Hurry, if we can."

Miri stole a glance in the direction indicated to see the Roman guard they had just passed. He had noticed the commotion and appeared to be taking an interest in Shemer's antics.

The two women each took one of Shemer's shoulders. They physically lifted him off the street and walked him down a side alley behind the baths.

The old man was oblivious to the danger. "Leave off now ladies. I'm not lame you know. Where are we going? I wanted to ..."

They got to the next intersection behind the baths and waited just out of view. Nura stared anxiously back. They were not being followed. Apparently, the young guard had found someone more interesting to molest, or he had gone back to his daydreaming.

Shemer was now eyeing Miri appreciatively. "Cousin, eh? Strong you are. Ah – younger and prettier than at first. A shapeshifter then? Did Nura conjure you with one of her spells?"

"Shemer," Nura scolded, "do not say such things. And I am warning you many times about taking strong drink. Do you see the guard back there?"

The old man looked confused. "Guard? Where? I was just ..."

"Tssst! We need no trouble today! Now look." Nura pointed down the side street. "Follow this street as it is bending to the left. Pass by the old south road and come to our shelter. Go in, find an empty space and sleep. I am back to see you later. Promise me you are to do this?"

Nura stood directly in front of Shemer, holding both of his hands. He was forced to meet her gaze. "I'm sorry Nura. I'll do as you say. It's just …"

"Dearest Shemer, there is no need to explain. I know you are a good man. Go. I am back this afternoon." The old man walked off dejectedly. Nura and Miri made their way back to the decumanus and proceeded on their way.

They came to a potter's shop on their left. An old woman sat at a wheel, kicking the heavy stone disk with her feet as she expertly shaped a tall vase with gnarled hands. A much younger woman sat behind the shop counter and beckoned to Miri as she walked by. "Phausteer eueidees mageuma – Lukhnomanteia?" She held up an elaborately carved lamp. It had the tail of a fish and the body of a woman. The wick emanated from the woman's mouth.

Miri marveled at the details and the brightly colored paint. "Nura, what did she say?"

The girl noticed Nura and quickly put the lamp away. "Tumbas, pharmakis – Apobaino!" She kept her eyes to the side, not wanting to even glance at Nura. She made hissing sounds and waved dismissively with her hands.

The two left the counter and continued down the street. "What was that about?" asked Miri.

Nura shook her head. "First she wants to tell your fortune with a magic lamp. Then she accuses *me* of being a sorceress." She laughed. "Maybe she does not like competition."

The next corner was a wide street perpendicular to the decumanus. "They call this the 'cardo,'" said Nura. "And that," pointing across the decumanus, "is the open market." It was a huge fenced area with gates opening to the street. They couldn't see much inside the market except that it was divided into numerous tent-like stalls. "Come here for market day tomorrow – food, musicians, jugglers. Taletha and Ephrayim may be here. Perhaps my nephew, Yeshua, will be back and can accompany you."

They walked on. The buildings thinned out as the road continued up the hill of the acropolis. After a while, the road angled to the right and plunged into a thick sycamore forest. Some of the trees were quite old – tall and straight with papery bark. A thick carpet of ferns and vines covered the ground between the trees.

The road was steep in places. A small stream ran down the hill on the left side of the path. Miri noticed clay pipes here and there emerging from the hillside, emptying into the stream. Nura explained about the plumbing on the hilltop. Every drop of rain was channeled into huge underground cisterns hewn into the limestone. From there they kept a steady stream of water flowing down into the town to run the sewers under the streets.

The road ascended to the left, skirting the north side of the hill. The forest ended abruptly, revealing an impressive view into the northern valley. Green fields lay far in the distance as far as Miri could see. At the base of the hill below them, and extending for about a mile, sprawled a Roman military camp. In one long field, soldiers in full armor were now marching back and forth in formation.

They continued up the road and soon arrived at the flat hilltop surrounded by a high stone wall. They entered through an arched gateway flanked on both sides by guards in their Herodian uniforms. Once through, Miri gasped.

She was looking down the length of an immense forum with stone colonnades on both sides. At the end of the forum, a quarter mile distant, was an enormous building made from sparkling white stone. The roof was lined with turrets painted blue and gold. "That must be Herod's palace," Miri guessed. "You can see the other side from the town."

"A bit daunting at first, is it not, cousin?"

Miri shivered. "Yes, but, is it safe?"

"Safe?" Repeated Nura. "I think not. But we are bound to our task. Servants and delivery people come here all the time. That is what we are today – delivery people."

Miri nodded. They were standing just within the forum. She

turned completely around, taking in the splendor evident on all sides. She noticed a series of fancy villas on the northwest side of the hilltop. "Who lives there?"

Nura saw where Miri was looking. "Important people – or so they think of themselves. Advisers to Herod, officials, the big tax collectors, a couple of Levites." Nura pointed to one villa partway down the hill at left edge. "That house belongs to the man who is killed – the one named Ba'asha."

Nura observed Miri and saw her wince at the mention of the name. "Don't worry, cousin, we are not going near that place. It is good that you see it. That is where my nephew is held last week – where he met the queen."

This surprised Miri. "Your nephew was held by Ba'asha? But ... why?"

Nura shrugged. "A building accident. He can tell you about it when you meet. It is not important now. Ba'asha is gone. The debt is forgotten."

Miri felt an overwhelming mixture of dark emotions. She was glad the wicked man was dead. She straightened herself and turned away. She did not want to break down now. She would be strong.

They started down the right side of the forum under the shadows of the pillars and arches. When they got near the southern end, Miri saw an unfinished building through the colonnade to her right. Scaffolding covered much of the facade.

Nura saw the direction of Miri's gaze. "That is where my husband and nephew are working last week when the accident happened. My husband is to be back working here soon, I am sure."

"What about Yeshua?"

Nura laughed at this. "You see there on the ground – broken white rocks? *That* is Yeshua's work. I do not think the foreman wants him back."

"But why ..."

"Come," coaxed Nura "We must not be late."

They came to the end of the colonnade, turned left, and walked past the front of Herod's palace. Two lone guards loitered in front of the structure. "Do you notice how casual the guards are?" Nura spoke in hushed tones. "Herod is not here now, or they would be in fear of their lives. He is traveling in Rome for two months now. They expect him to return before the high holidays with many important visitors. I hear that he is planning a great feast."

"That is what kings do," answered Miri. "He will take everything you have and you will be his slaves."

Nura eyed her quizzically.

They passed the far corner of the palace and turned down a well-worn paved stone walkway. There was room for a small cart to pass but not much more. To their right rose the high stone walls of the palace, to their left, a sheer drop to the forest floor. They came to a heavy wooden door leading to a cellar under the main level.

~

"This is how Yeshua describes it." Nura descended three stone steps and banged loudly on the door. From within they heard a heavy bolt being withdrawn. The door opened with a gush of warm moist air. They entered into a bustling kitchen, their eyes adjusting slowly to the orange light from many candles and torches. The air was stifling. Numerous cooking fires blazed, heating a variety of hanging kettles, grates, and spits. Many sweating servants busied themselves with peeling, chopping, grinding, rolling, mixing, and other culinary activities. All were women except for one: a muscular guard stood to the side eyeing the activity suspiciously. Miri guessed that his job was to ensure no poison found its way into the fare.

The woman who had answered the door gestured angrily at their clothing. "Ha! Mayd? Mayd? Kmin talqumin takuzinit gulu?" Seeing the blank looks on Nura's and Miri's faces, she sighed heavily and said in broken common language, "You ... new ... cook girls, to be here, no? Late. We wait. You ... not cook in dressing like that, ha?" With the back of her hand she flicked a lock of damp hair from her face and waited expectantly.

"Oh – no. Not cooks. We are here to deliver something," said Nura. "We are told to ask for someone – Afra. Is Afra here?"

The woman rolled her eyes and exclaimed, "Afra! Ha? Diq! Wahi anbyi daddg! Tamara!" She leaned in close to Nura's face, eyeing her with a grimace. "We work here. No guests." She shook her head in disgust and retreated the length of the kitchen muttering something that sounded like "pickles, pickles." She yelled something unintelligible into a back room. "Pickles," she mumbled again as she went back to her labor at the cauldrons.

They waited patiently, watching the well-choreographed activities. A girl peeling some darkly-colored tubers slid them down the table to another girl who hammered them with a stone to a fine mush. Another girl scooped the mush into a large bowl and mixed it with ingredients prepared on another table. The result apparently was destined to become some kind of stew.

At length, a large light-haired woman entered, wiping her hands on an apron. Her cheeks were beet red and her eyes squinted in a scowl. She seemed of middle age, although it was difficult to tell in the faltering light. She was rotund, which was unusual except among the very rich. Perhaps working around food afforded her ample opportunity to sample her own wares.

Afra's apron was stained red. She used it now to wipe copious blood from her hands and fingernails. Obviously, she had been engaged in some manner of butchery in the back room. She approached and eyed Nura doubtfully, completely ignoring Miri. Her voice was piercing: "Kmin asrdunt, iyyah?"

Nura hesitated, again unsure what she was being asked.

"Asrdunt – ha ... you bring, for lady. Iyyah?" She made a gesture as if she were holding something small between her thumb and forefinger. "Iyyah? Hurru. Ur sala!"

Nura responded, "Yes ... yes. I have something for the queen."

Afra motioned Nura and Miri to the corner where they were out of earshot of the guard. She held out her hand discretely. "Lady say ... taymust tmswit ... pooshna, ha? Pooshna, iyyah?"

Miri whispered under her breath: "I think she is asking about the potion."

Afra nodded and continued: "Ha, hdu s'srf. Lady give." She

extracted a gold coin from her pocket. She bit into it and held it inches from Nura's face to demonstrate the teeth marks. For the first time, her scowl disappeared and her entire face grinned. She laughed and nodded enthusiastically. "Ha! Argaz'nm awj'jim q'qar i s'simanas mantur sksw aya, iyyah?" She nudged Nura's arm playfully. One of the other cooks in the room overheard and began giggling.

This Nura could not decipher, so she smiled and nodded her head in response. She reached inside her tunic and extracted the vial, quickly exchanging it for the coin.

When Afra saw the female form of the carved vial, her eyes grew wide. "Mayd, Taweret, ha? G'gan - Wait!" She went to a table where another cook was cutting vegetables. She grabbed something from the table and returned. "Daddg ... here – tilkmin. You need," she said earnestly.

Nura saw that she was being handed a large turnip. Not understanding, but not wanting to offend, she accepted it solemnly, placing it in her inside pocket. The business now concluded, Afra unceremoniously motioned Nura and Miri toward the door. They had just stepped back onto the sunny walkway when suddenly the kitchen became dead silent.

Nura peeked her head back into the room to see if anything further was required of her. To her surprise and puzzlement, she saw that all of the servants, including Afra, now lay prostrate on the floor. The room was silent except for the bubbling of the cauldrons. Fearing that something was wrong, she re-entered the room and saw the reason for the change.

An extravagantly dressed woman stood in the center of the kitchen. She wore a complicated green-dyed garment with white lace fringe. Her abundant black hair was braided on one side with gold bangles fastened on the ends. On the other side, her hair hung loose, but was carefully combed and placed. She was a small woman, but her expression was haughty as she waited expectantly, her eyes toward the ceiling.

Miri followed Nura into the room. "Cousin, is there anything ..." Nura waved her to silence.

Belatedly, they realized that they were committing an indiscretion. Nura averted her eyes and fell to the floor in imitation of the other servants. Miri did likewise.

The queen relaxed. "You may rise, woman." Nura did so, being careful to keep her eyes toward the floor. The other servants remained prostrate. "We are to understand that you are the powerful witch?"

Nura felt flustered. "I am a healer. I do no sorcery. My name is Nura. Yeshua is nephew to me. I prepare the draught that he brings to you last Shabbat. May it ..." The queen raised her hand indicating that she desired silence.

"Servant Nura then. We wanted to see you face to face. We ... have gratitude. As you can see, we are much improved. We have not been sick since the evening before last. We can now eat again."

Nura felt relief that she wasn't being reprimanded. "Thank you, my queen. I shall give thanks to Belenos."

The queen eyed her curiously. "Belenos? Of course ... you are not a Jew. You are not from this part of the world. But from a different place than these slaves." She gestured to the still-prostrate cooks.

After a moment of silence, Nura realized that this was a question. "Yes, my queen. My father brought me here when I am a small girl. I am born in the north. In life my father is a healer among his people."

"A foreigner then. We have that in common with you. And who is this? Rise child." Miri got to her feet. "Hmm, also so pale, but this one is a ruse, no?" Phasaelis reached out and lifted Miri's chin until their eyes met. She laughed. "It would fool someone from a distance but ..." She rubbed her fingers together. "This is makeup."

"My queen," began Nura. "This is my cousin, Miryam, but as you observe, not by blood. She has ... a skin rash. That is why she wears powder."

The queen looked alarmed. She picked up a nearby towel and began wiping her hands vigorously.

Nura quickly added, "Do not worry, my queen. It is not

something to make you unclean by touching."

The queen looked relieved but continued wiping until all trace of the makeup was removed. "Enough. We see that you have mysteries surrounding you. Yeshua, the boy – also not a blood relative?"

"He is my husband's nephew."

"An intelligent boy. But naive, no? He does not know to keep his place around superiors. You must train him better. We do not think it would go well for him if he were to meet our husband."

Nura frowned. She didn't know whether this was an idle comment or some kind of threat. "Yes, my queen. I try to teach him, but he ... has his own mind about things."

"Then he is destined for many sorrows. He shall not come here again. You shall bring us the next potion, yes?"

"Yes, my queen. Today I bring enough for one week. I can make more as you are in need. Send word through my husband. His name is Mattanyah. He is working on your new basilica. Send for me when you receive a new vial from Macula."

"Macula – yes." The queen adopted a cruel smile. "He is to visit on Mercury's day. We hope to disappoint him."

"My queen, forgive me for speaking. I know Macula. He is not a bad man. He is not even a bad medicus. He is being told what to do by someone higher."

"Don't worry servant Nura, we shall not have him harmed. That would give away the game, no? We will let him keep his testicles."

Nura winced. "I mean that ... perhaps my queen, when you see him you can feign illness? Let him think his treatment is working a little longer?"

Phasaelis pouted. "What's the fun in that? He is but a worm. But do not fear for him ... yet. Now, that is all we require of you today. We shall send word when you are needed again." With that, she abruptly turned on her heel and departed.

~

After Nura and Miri returned home, they shared a meal of apple slices, goat cheese, figs, and limon water. Nura had two more visits to make that day, so Miri returned to the upstairs room. She was looking forward to spending the afternoon once again in solitude, reading the scroll.

After a few moments, she found where she had left off. David had just returned to help with the harvest. This was after he had been spying on King Saul for his father, Jesse.

In spite of his afflictions, King Saul was successful in battle. He kept the enemies to the north and to the east at bay. In time, our Philistine masters grew alarmed by my father's increasing reputation.

One day, a messenger arrived from the Philistine King. He demanded that King Saul meet them in the valley of Terebinth. My father did not want to fight the Philistines. It was one thing to fight the Moabites or the Aramaeans. But the Philistine army was too strong. It was renowned for its discipline and ruthlessness. My father worried that they would annihilate all of Israel.

And so King Saul went to parlay with the Philistines. He did not expect battle. He wanted only to barter for peace. I was permitted to go with him. My father believed that I brought him the peace of YHWH. I kept away the terrors.

Saul went to the appointed place. Each of the twelve tribes sent two elders and fifty men. We set camp on the eastern ridge overlooking the valley. The Philistines arrived the next day and set camp on the western ridge.

For the next seven days, the parlay went on. Each morning my father sent messengers into the valley to meet the Philistine delegation. Each afternoon the messengers returned. My father would then discuss with the elders of the twelve tribes how to respond.

My father sought a truce which would allow us to throw off the yoke of oppression. He was close to success when he was betrayed by Jesse.

Much has been told of the size and ferocity of the Philistine delegate named Goliath. I was there. I saw him with my own eyes, so you can know this is the truth! He was large for a man, perhaps a head taller, but no more. It has always amused me how stories improve with age like wine. I have heard it said recently that he was a one-eyed giant, larger than a horse and swifter than a chariot. False!

Jesse started a rumor that my father was so afraid of the Philistines that he offered his daughter in marriage to anyone who could slay Goliath. False! Jesse told these lies to justify my abduction. I will tell that tale soon. But first I will tell you what really happened in the valley of Terebinth. It is not what you have heard.

Each day, David would arrive with other boys to bring provisions and messages. David tended to the needs of his three oldest brothers. They were soldiers for the tribe of Yudah.

My father once caught me staring at David. He admonished me to keep my eyes lowered. He said that soldiers are lusty and cannot be trusted, even with the daughter of a king. At that time I had newly become a woman. My father had begun looking for a suitable match for me.

Early on the seventh morning since our arrival, I walked through the camp. I saw David arguing with his brothers. I could not hear what the dispute was or who prevailed. In the end, David broke off and started toward me. I straightened as he approached, thinking that he wished to talk to me. I was a fool. He did not even notice me standing in the path. I followed him to where my father sat by the fire, conferring with the elders.

David did not understand that this was a negotiation, not a battle. He stood before my father and volunteered to fight Goliath. Saul was amused by his young servant. The elders laughed. My father pointed to his armor and spear hanging on a rack. David could barely lift such heavy implements. He told David to stick to song and harp play.

David was haughty. He stamped on the ground. He

kicked dirt into the fire. He said that someone must fight this unwashed Philistine. The elders laughed. My father grew angry and sent him away.

Now I know: one does not laugh at David of Yudah. His face grew red. He marched straight down into the valley past the front line of archers. He ignored their commands to return. The Philistine delegation was just coming onto the field, led by Goliath.

I am sure you have heard the story. I will tell you what I saw. David approached the Philistines. Perhaps they thought him a messenger boy, coming to delay the parlay. This very thing had happened the previous day. David fell on his knees at Goliath's feet as if paying him a tribute. The Philistine pushed him away and gestured for him to return to his camp on the ridge. David was but a few paces away when he put a rock in his sling and sent it directly into the large man's eye. Goliath fell down dead.

When this happened, all the soldiers from Yudah and Simeon gave a yell and ran into the valley. There was great confusion. Eventually soldiers from the other tribes of Israel joined the rout.

The Philistines were not girded for battle. They had expected this to be the final day of negotiation. Then they would return to their lands in the west. Instead they were attacked and chased away. They left their armaments, their provisions, their women, and their idols.

My father should have punished David that day, but he could not. The boy was being treated like a hero. Now I understand why. Most soldiers love violence. They were restless at my father's efforts at peacemaking. They were glad to be killing and taking booty once more.

Miri sat back from the scroll and closed her eyes. This was not the story that every child was told. In this version, rather than being a boy hero, David had been spying on his king. He also thwarted

Saul's attempts at peace. From the tone of the writing it was plain that this Michal did not hold David in high regard at all – quite the opposite.

A mosquito landed on Miri's arm. She swatted at it, but it was too quick, and darted toward the window. She heard sounds from the courtyard below and arose to take a look. From the window, she saw an elderly man she did not recognize. He was tending a bonfire in the courtyard behind the house. Soon they would cook an evening meal. The man noticed her, smiled a toothless grin, and waved. She smiled meekly and waved back.

She returned to her table, wanting to read more about David while there was ample light.

My father was apprehensive. He knew the Philistines would soon regroup. Then there would be war on a scale he had never seen. He had no choice but to begin preparations. He traveled from town to town, urging all of Israel to muster.

I went with him when he traveled south into the lands of Yudah. We stopped in Bethlehem and met with Jesse. Jesse said he would not call Yudah to war unless Saul fulfilled his promise. He demanded riches. He also demanded that Saul's daughter be given to the one who had vanquished Goliath.

You know from the chronicles that I have two sisters. Merab is three years older than me. At that time she was already married with a son. My half sister, Naomi, is the same age as me. She has gone from this earth now. Naomi was born of my father's only concubine, Rizpah. At that time my father had already promised Naomi to the King of Geshur. This meant that if one of Saul's daughters were to be given to David, it would be me.

My father was troubled. I have already told you that he had made no such promise! He had no intention of giving any of his daughters to the house of Jesse. He told Jesse this. He only promised a relief from taxes for the clan of Jesse if they would agree to muster and fight alongside the other tribes.

Saul summoned David forth. The boy came before the king. Saul spoke harshly. He told him that killing the Philistine was brave but foolish. He told him that killing his enemy did not make him a man.

David took the scolding sullenly. He did not understand my father. David thought my father was chastising him for only killing one man. He thought Saul was challenging him to kill more!

We returned to Ramah. Three years passed. Despite our worries, war did not come. This puzzled my father greatly.

When the time came, my father gave me in marriage to Paltiel. My father chose well. Paltiel was a good man. We began our lives together in the lands of Gallim. There we had fertile fields to the west, but not far from Ramah. Thus, I could visit my father to ease his spirit.

I was visiting my father when David returned. He came with his brothers and five hundred armed men of Yudah. It was not the fighting season so my father's army had returned to their homes. We were defenseless.

Jesse's sons and their mercenaries had been raiding the lands far to the south of Yudah and Simeon. They had been taking booty and using it to bribe the elders of the southern tribes. Despite his young age, David had taken charge of the clan.

Now I must tell you something horrible! Killing two hundred Philistines and taking their foreskins was David's idea. My father never demanded such a grisly brideprice! He was sickened when David presented him with a sack containing the shriveled members.

David once again demanded that I be delivered to him as wife. He said if Saul did not give his blessing, he would burn the city. My father wanted to refuse. I persuaded him to hand me over. He promised me that he would rescue me in time. I was taken away!

David was never interested in me. He simply wanted it to be known that he was the king's son-in-law. It gave him a legitimate claim to the throne.

David feared that my father would seek a speedy revenge. So we did not stay in Bethlehem. David secretly took me far to the south, to a town called Ziklag on the border with the territory of Simeon.

It had never occurred to Miri to question the veracity of the old stories. But here was a personal account from one who witnessed the events. The point of view was totally different from the tales she had heard in synagogue. Those stories heaped praise on the ancient heroes, none more so than David. Miri wondered if the rabbis were aware of Michal and her testament. Questions flooded her mind.

The light had failed. She heard Nura in the house below. She descended the ladder and spent an enjoyable evening with her hosts and neighbors.

~

Floating on the surface of an immense lake. Gentle waves lap about my sides, my feet. Tepid water undulates beneath me, in the small of my back. The sun shines directly overhead, but it does not hurt my eyes. Its warmth is on my face, on my breasts, my stomach, loins, thighs. The taste of salt on my tongue. Why am I not afraid? Not far is the shore, a narrow beach, then a cliff face. Someone sits halfway up on a rock outcropping. A man watches me with wistful eyes. He is far away, but I see him clearly. Strong chin with tenuous brown beard. I do not mind his gaze. I feel warmth, anticipation. He watches, contemplates. I return his longing stare. A breeze passes. In it, I hear the soft peaceful cacophony of many birds in the distance. I close my eyes, lean back and roll to the side, pulling the light blanket under my chin. Voices now add to the chirping. I cannot tell what they are saying. A distant sound of a hammer on wood.

Miri felt refreshed as she opened her eyes in the scroll room. She folded her hands behind her head and gazed at the ceiling in the half light. She reflected on how pleasant her time here had been thus far. Last night, she had shared a meal of turnips, roasted almonds, and bread with Nura's family. They were joined by Mattanyah's sister, Chunya, who was in the city for some kind of legal proceeding. Miri enjoyed the way this family behaved toward one another – good-natured teasing, inside jokes, lots of laughter, the obvious unspoken affection and unquestioned support they shared.

The mysterious Yeshua had still not appeared. Mattanyah mentioned that his brother in the south was blessed with a huge harvest, and thus may have need of Yeshua's assistance for a few more days.

She cleaned herself and dressed. Her plan today was to explore the city. Nura had urged her to do this, saying that the market crowds would keep her anonymous if she kept her face veiled. She retrieved a few coins from Ba'asha's purse, secured the dagger in the inner folds of her tunic, and set out on her way.

She tried a different route than Nura had taken the previous day. In the old part of the city the streets and alleyways were curved and unmarked, with several dead ends. But between the houses she could see the palace on the hill in the distance, so she knew the general direction that she needed to go.

Finally, she came to a familiar site. She was behind a woodyard just off the decumanus. This seemed to be the boundary between the old and new cities. The streets became straight and wider here.

As she walked, she passed a group of children sitting in the yard, drawing pictures in the dirt with sticks. Most were between five and ten years, but one seemed older. His back was to her and he was wearing a green tunic that looked oddly new and clean. Perhaps he is one of Nura's many charity cases, she thought. Most likely he is a simpleton, unable to play with children his own age.

The street noise grew loud as she approached the city center. This was very different from yesterday. Throngs of people milled about on both sides of the wide street. A long line of carts waited to enter the market yard through tolled gates. She was fascinated by the people – people of many races in all kinds of strange and colorful clothes. This was nothing like Magdala.

She had to step out in the street to go around someone who had a fire going in a bronze pot. He was roasting and selling some kind of meat, and doing quite a good business. The smell made Miri's mouth water until she looked closer and realized that the animals roasting were snakes. She felt a wave of revulsion that went beyond the fact that this was trayf – unclean food. She had once been bitten by a snake and had been sick for weeks.

She returned to the sidewalk and continued toward the market. One shop had an awning extending out over the sidewalk. As she passed under it, a black-hooded woman hurried from a dark doorway and grabbed both of her arms. She held Miri fast and examined her face carefully with an expression deep with worry.

"What is it, ma'am? Can I be of service to you?" Miri tried to shake her arms loose but the woman's grip was firm. An image of a rat held in the claws of an eagle popped into Miri's mind.

"Augur," said the woman in a breathy, low-pitched voice. "Tu videntis, somnianti. Ita est?"

"I do not understand," protested Miri. "Please, let go of my arms, you are hurting me."

"Forgive me child." She let go and brushed the sleeves of Miri's tunic. "I saw you and I knew. The goddess has given me inner eyes to see many things." Miri saw that her actual eyes were cloudy with cataracts. A few oily strands of gray hair protruded from a tight black shawl covering her head. The old woman said, "You are a seer. One knows another. Isis has given me this gift. You are troubled, child. It is my gift to help you. Come. Come inside." She motioned toward the dark interior of the shop.

Miri was wary, but she yielded to her curiosity. The woman led her behind a heavy curtain, which she drew closed behind them, snuffing out the light and much of the noise from the street.

The entire room was lined with curtains. Tallow candles burned on tables set around the perimeter of the space. The floor was littered with potted plants, several of which were blooming. Miri wondered how she was able to get flowers to bloom indoors. There was a pungent smell – incense, perfume from the flowers, and something else – possibly the stench of burning fat from the candles. The subdued light and odd smells had a calming effect. Miri felt the tension and energy of the busy street melt away. The crone motioned for her to sit on a cushion on the floor.

In the center of the room stood a low altar supporting a life-sized statue of a woman wearing a strange headdress. Noticing the direction of Miri's gaze, the woman said, "It is the goddess. She goes by many names. You have heard of Isis, no?"

"Isis," repeated Miri. "An idol."

"Ah. You are a Jew. I could not tell, but now, yes, I hear it in your voice. You have been told to worship only your god, jayvewuh, is this not so?"

"Jayvewuh? Oh! You mean Yeh ... but, you know, we do not speak that name except in prayer. Say 'hashem.'"

"Haysheem, Jayvewuh, the burning bush, the pillar of fire. Yes, yes. I know your god well. Your god is an angry war god, not suitable for a woman. You must come to know the goddess. I call her Usat. She has much to teach us. Now sit." She pointed to a cushion on the floor.

Miri started to retort but the woman hushed her with a gesture. With old painful joints, she slowly sat on the cushion facing Miri. She took both of Miri's hands and held them shoulder height. Raising her head to the dark ceiling, she closed her eyes and intoned: "Goddess of life and love. Goddess of mothers and daughters. Goddess of sorrow, of loss, of tears. Goddess of joy, of redemption, of second chances, of renewal. Goddess of young lovers, of longing, of passion, of tenderness. Come. We shall be your hands doing your work. We shall be your lips speaking truth. We shall be your eyes seeing the sorrow of life. Come now and dwell within our hearts."

She paused after this, sitting in silence. Miri was aware of her breathing, of the muffled sounds in the street outside, and the calmness enveloping her mind.

The woman took a deep breath, lowered her hands and opened her eyes. "Tell me your name, child."

After a moment's hesitation she responded, "Miryam."

The woman frowned. "Did I not tell you, child, that I am seer for the goddess. You must never lie to a seer. It is like lying to your ... haysheem. It must not be done. Your true name then?"

Miri didn't see any harm in telling this old woman. "Naomi. But you must never call me that."

The woman relaxed at this. There was another lengthy pause. The woman seemed to be listening to something, her eyes tightly shut in deep concentration, almost as if in pain. She still held Miri's hands in her own. Miri noticed she had rings on every finger, including her thumbs. The woman began to hum, softly at first, then with growing intensity. Miri began to feel lightheaded.

At length the humming stopped. The woman opened her eyes. "You are a dreamer. Tell the seer your dreams."

And so Miri did. The woman closed her eyes and listened. She continued to hold Miri's hands gently. Miri told of the fearful dreams, of the confusing dreams, of the shifting dreams that seemed to be going in one direction and then suddenly took off in another. She spoke every detail she could remember – and in the telling, things came back to her that she had forgotten – a silver brush lying in the straw in her bedroom in Magdala, the leather lashings on the cage that held the sacrifice, a black goat with long horns and intelligent eyes. The whole time Miri spoke, the woman sat motionless with eyes closed. At one point Miri thought the woman had fallen asleep and stopped talking. The seer gently squeezed Miri's hand and nodded for her to continue. Miri finished by relating the peaceful dream she had had this very morning. She vividly remembered the puffy clouds in the impossibly blue sky above the lake.

The seer rose and turned her back to Miri, facing the altar and the statue of Usat. She was mumbling something under her breath. At length she returned to the floor, taking Miri's hands.

"The goddess of abundance has spoken to me. She has allowed

her seer to know the true meaning of your dreams. But first you must make a small offering." She gestured to a box of coins in front of the altar that Miri now noticed for the first time.

Miri hesitated. Of course this was the woman's plan – to draw her along this far and then demand payment. I am so gullible, she thought. But then ... she *had* gone this far. She might as well part with a coin. If nothing else, the woman had provided some respite from the chaos outside. She fumbled in her inside pocket and tossed a coin into the box.

The old woman retrieved it and held it close to her cloudy eyes. With a look of bemusement she showed it to Miri. "Divini Filius – Son of God. It is the face of our emperor, Augustus. Why does a Jewess carry Roman coin? Another mystery ... but no matter, I will leave you your secrets."

The seer pulled open the collar of her tunic and untied a leather cord that had been around her neck. A small bauble slid off the end as she handed it to Miri, who reached out and saved it from falling to the floor. In Miri's hand was a piece of polished bone carved into the shape of a cross with an oval on the top. Miri looked at the woman quizzically.

"It is called Ankh," said the seer. "You see the goddess wears one too." She gestured to the statue. There was indeed a similar figure carved over its heart. "Keep this with you always. It means life." She carefully rethreaded the leather cord through the oval and tied it around Miri's neck, tucking the ankh under Miri's tunic.

She looked at Miri with sudden intensity. "Pay close attention. The goddess has shown me that you have suffered great harm. But if you are strong, and if you have help, you will not be consumed. You are at a crossroads. Honor demands revenge, but life abjures it. Men heed honor and vengeance. Women heed life. You must soon choose a path, and it will determine your fate. The goddess beseeches you: reject the rage you feel toward those who harmed you. Remember: even your war god is not in the storm winds, nor in the earthquake, nor in the fire, but rather in the gentle whisper. You cannot hear the gentle whisper if your heart is full of rage.

"At last, the goddess told me that your soothing dream this morning is her gift to you. It is a sign of good things to come. Although you are a dreamer, you are awake – more so than most. Most live within illusions. You do not. Your eyes are open. You cannot live a lie. This may bring you great joy in your life, but it will also bring you sadness. The demons of the world do not like seers. They do not want to be recognized."

~

Miri emerged from the seer's shop and stumbled onto the street. She had to shield her eyes from the bright sunshine. After a moment, she walked slowly in the direction of the market. The line of carts waiting to enter was smaller now. It was almost midday and the market was in full swing.

She came to the main intersection at the cardo and crossed over. There was a paved open area here with a large pool in the center, fed by a fountain. Several children splashed in the water as adults sat on the stone benches surrounding the pool. Miri felt a little woozy and decided to do likewise. She splashed some water on her face and retreated to an unoccupied bench.

Adjacent to the open space was an imposing stone building. When they had passed this spot the previous day, Nura had explained that this was the old basilica – a kind of courthouse. Many of the administrative functions of the city took place here. Land records were kept. Taxes were collected from the market and counted. Herod's deputies would hear disputes here and administer justice – typically a flogging, which would take place at the back of the market just across the street.

Miri watched as a portly man in an oversized toga ascended the steps in front of the building. He moved with difficulty in the heat, panting and dabbing sweat from his forehead with a white cloth. He looked like an official of some sort. Under his left arm he held a heavy leather satchel bulging with documents.

As the man neared the top step, a boy approached him. She couldn't be sure, but it looked rather like the simpleton she had seen earlier, except that his green tunic was now completely soiled. The boy held forth a wooden-framed tablet. He seemed to be arguing with the official. The man tried to wave him off, but the boy was persistent. She strained to hear what they were saying, but they were too far away.

The man looked exasperated, but he apparently decided the quickest way to rid himself of this nuisance was to examine the proffered tablet and render a judgment. He set down his heavy satchel and accepted the tablet. As he read, Miri watched another boy, this one in a short black tunic, approach the official quietly from behind. This other boy grabbed the satchel and took off at a sprint into a side street, and then disappeared down an alleyway.

Such effrontery, thought Miri – banditry in front of the basilica on a busy market day. I shall have to take great care in this city.

The official realized that there was no way he could catch the youth. He looked up and down the street but the nearest soldier was at the other end of the block and wasn't even looking in this direction. Now red-faced and furious, the official threw the green-tunic'ed boy's tablet on the stone steps, shattering it. He pushed him out of the way, and stomped off into the building. The boy collected his broken tablet and walked away dejectedly.

Miri wanted to help but there was nothing she could do. She certainly wasn't about to approach any guards or soldiers to tell them what she had seen. She felt sorry for the official and the boy, but she decided to let it pass and go on with her day. She was now feeling refreshed. The incense haze in her mind had cleared.

The main gate to the market stood directly across the decumanus. Most of the merchants had already entered, so the line she had seen earlier was gone. As she got up and started across the street, she heard urgent yelling to her left. She turned and froze. Six leather-clad men with shaved heads were carrying a covered litter at quite a trot. They didn't look like they were going to stop or even slow down. Miri quickly jumped out of the way, being careful not to trip on the drainage ditch as she had before. She noticed that each slave wore a metal plaque bouncing on his chest as he ran. Miri had seen these plaques before. They would bear the name of the slave's owner, who was probably reclining in the litter at this moment.

She crossed the street and waited in line to enter the market. The toll for a non-merchant was a half sesterce. She found the appropriate coin and handed it to the man at the gate. He waved her through without bothering to look up.

The market occupied several city blocks. It was a large fenced-in area, crowded, and chaotic. Merchants were selling crops and wares directly out of ox or horse carts. The animals were unhitched and tied on evenly spaced posts. Bales of hay had been set out.

Some merchants had erected tents, booths, and tables. She passed a table laid out with pretty jewelry. Next to this was a cart with a delicate overhead structure, from which hung many colored glass bottles and vials. The next cart was filled with dried-up reddish-brown roots and little bundles of dried herbs. She liked the smell from this cart – it briefly overpowered the stench of dung that permeated the air.

She came to an area where short fences divided the space into pens. Many types of animals were being sold: sheep, goats, chickens, pigs, and some she didn't recognize. Someone had made the mistake of stacking a pen with pigeon cages next to a pen containing dogs. The birds were driving the poor dogs crazy as they leaped and barked in vain.

She stopped to gawk at one pen that held huge turtles. They were bigger than a man's head. A young boy stood in the next pen, tending a small flock of sheep. He couldn't have been more than four. He wore a striped robe that reached to his ankles and held a miniature shepherd's staff. Miri thought he was adorable.

Everywhere was the sound of commerce – yelling, haggling, arguing. She came to an area with braziers and bonfires. Merchants were cooking and selling food here, and she realized she was quite hungry. She purchased a flatbread and nibbled on it as she continued through the market.

The next area was for grain merchants. A man stood in front of a wagon filled with threshed wheat. His three daughters sat on a bench in front of the wagon. Each worked at a stone mortar, grinding the wheat into flour with wooden mallets.

In the very back of the market, she wrinkled her nose at the overpowering stench of human excrement. Here she saw rows of cages, each one large enough to accommodate five or six slaves. Miri felt a wave of revulsion and nausea. There were men, women, boys, and girls – all living in fetid conditions. Most ignored her as she walked by. Some looked up and stared at her with languid, hopeless eyes.

At the end of the row of cages, an auctioneer stood on a raised platform extolling the virtues of a pair of light-skinned men. Each man was naked and had his hands tied to a post behind his back. They both looked fearful as the auctioneer talked about their strength and how capable each would be behind a plow. Miri couldn't watch. She moved on.

She came to a crowd of people with their backs to her. Over the heads of some children she could see what was so interesting: A man tied to a post was being flogged. The man doing the whipping was wearing one of the uniforms she had seen on Herod's guards up on the Acropolis. He had a little table set up with implements of torture – ropes, leather whips, some with metal tips, nasty looking tongs, and an iron poker heating on a brazier.

Miri tapped one of the spectators, a woman, on the shoulder and asked why the man was being punished. "Tried to set some slaves free," the woman replied. "If he survives, he'll end up a slave himself. Fool." The woman clucked her tongue and shook her head, but her attention remained riveted on the whipping.

She had had enough of the market after that, and made her way back to the gate. As she was about to exit, she had to stand aside as a handcart was coming in. It was piled high with clothing, sheets, curtains and other linens. As it passed, she saw that it was being pushed by a boy in a dirty green tunic. It couldn't be the same boy, she thought. Her curiosity was aroused, so she followed at a distance.

It *was* the same boy. She was sure of it. At first she thought he was selling the items on the cart, but as she watched, he seemed to be simply *giving* them away to anyone he passed. Many people seemed to know him and gave him a friendly greeting or slap on the back. Some laughed and shook their heads, as if to say 'There goes the town fool playing another of his silly jokes.'

~

After leaving the market, Miri followed the cardo southwest into a different part of the town. She walked quickly as she passed a tanner and then a fuller's shop. Between the two, the stench made Miri's eye's water. She took a side street and ended up in front of a tavern. Two whores lounged on a bench in front. It reminded her strongly of Lebbaeus' place in Magdala, and she was filled with a sense of foreboding. She found herself involuntarily rubbing her wrists where the manacles had bitten into her flesh. She turned around and headed back the way she had come.

After a short distance, she decided to take a side alley to avoid the stench of the fullers, which really was quite awful. She quickly realized this was a mistake. The alleyways were narrow and shadow-dark. Every time she thought she would emerge back onto the cardo, the alley made a turn and went off in a new direction. Pretty soon, Miri became disoriented.

Finally she came to a long narrow courtyard behind several houses. She could see the cardo just beyond. She passed by two people tending a bonfire with their backs to her. She was almost to the street when realization dawned on her. She turned and looked again. Both figures were boys, one with a short black tunic, and one with a longer green one. They were obviously friends from the way they interacted – playfully punching each other on the shoulders, and laughing.

And they weren't just *tending* the fire. They were feeding it with scrolls and wax tablets that they pulled from a large leather satchel on the ground. So, she thought, they are together. Green-tunic accosted the lawyer and provided a diversion by pretending to ask a question about a tablet. When the moment was right, black-tunic snuck up and stole the documents. She shook her head in disgust and walked on.

She got to the decumanus across from the market and turned right, heading up the hill toward Nura's house. It was mid-afternoon, and a crowd had formed outside the ornate building housing the Roman baths. She thought it strange – men and women who have no relationship going into the building to bathe together in the nude. She wondered what the rabbis thought about this.

As she turned down the street that led to the old part of the city, she saw Mattanyah coming toward her pushing a cart laden with furniture. She was happy to see a familiar face.

"Ah, young Miri. Nura mentioned you had gone off exploring. A good day you had I hope?"

"Yes, sir – I am sorry I was not around to help with the chores. Is there anything I can do for you now?"

"Don't be worried about chores. I am glad to see you up and about. Staying in that musty old scroll room can't be healthy. Are you sure you wouldn't rather have us set you up in the shelter with the other women?"

"Oh no sir – I like it there. Nura said I could read the scrolls. I am greatly enjoying it."

"Reading." Mattanyah shook his head. "I enjoy working with my hands. I made these here." He gestured at the articles in the cart: two chairs and a small table. They were as fine as any Miri had seen. "A wedding gift for Channah – You've heard about the wedding?"

"Yes sir. Nura told me all about it. Do I have it right? ... Your brother, Yoceph, is married to a woman named Mariamne, who is the sister of Ruth. Ruth is married to Natan. And Channah is their daughter. Is that it?" Miri didn't mention *her* connection – that she was a cousin of the groom, Ephrayim. Nura was the only one privy to that secret.

Mattanyah laughed. "Your memory is much better than mine. Would you like to come and meet the bride and her family?"

Miri beamed. "Yes! I would love to."

It turned out to be only a short distance. They veered to the left in front of the woodyard and followed a side street for two blocks. Miri recognized the spot she had passed this morning – where children had been drawing in the dirt.

As was his habit, Mattanyah talked as they walked. "This is a fortunate match for the boy from Cana. Natan is an important man to have as a father. Been here a long time. He's been involved in just about any kind of shipping you can think of: spices, fancy foods, wood, jewels – whatever the rich people want. Now he runs the grain business. Gets a piece of all the wheat going out of the city."

They spent an hour or so visiting with Natan and Ruth. Miri took a liking to Ruth instantly. She was a vibrant, intelligent woman. At thirty-one, she still retained a youthful look – her hair was dark with only a couple of streaks of gray. Except for the few worry lines on her forehead, her skin was smooth and unblemished. She had a nice smile revealing a single missing tooth in the top front.

Natan seemed very serious. He was obviously much older than Ruth. He had arthritis and the gout, making it difficult for him to move around. He sat mostly in a cushioned chair, sipping a goblet of wine. He was cordial, but after the initial greetings, he said little.

Miri was disappointed that Channah was not at home. She had gone to the market to buy material for a wedding garment. Mattanyah and Miri were about to take their leave when a young boy came in from the street. Ruth introduced him: "This is our son, Yeduthun. Yedu, this is Miryam, Nura's cousin."

Yedu came close and bowed to Miri. When he straightened up, he eyed her curiously. "Nura's cousin? You don't look like her. You're *much* prettier."

"Yedu!" Scolded Ruth. "You insult your uncle Mattanyah. You are talking about his wife."

"Oh ... I'm sorry uncle. What I meant ... well you know ... Nura is, well she's *your* age. And Miryam is ..."

Mattanyah chuckled as the boy dug a deeper hole for himself.

Miri was charmed by Yedu's precocious nature. "Call me Miri. And you are right – I do not look like her because we are not related by blood. Did you ever meet the man who raised Nura? Taddai was his name."

Yedu looked questioningly at his mother. "I think I did. But I was young. I don't remember him."

"Well," explained Miri. "I am Taddai's niece. I used to live in a town by the eastern sea."

"Oh." Yedu thought about this. "So ... are your parents still there now? Why did you come here?"

"My parents are ... they are gone. I came to live with Nura for a time. I ..."

"Forgive my son." Natan broke his silence and gave Yedu a withering glare. "He asks too many questions."

Miri shrugged. "People used to say that about me. So I guess I am tasting my own potion."

Yedu took this as an invitation to continue his inquiry. "Hm ... the eastern sea. Have you been to the town where the murderess came from – what was it, mother? Magdala?"

Ruth confirmed the name of the town with a nod.

Miri said cautiously, "Yes. That is the very town where I lived. But I do not know anything about a murderess."

Yedu's eyes grew wide. "You haven't heard the news? *Everyone* is talking about it. There was a murderess – like an amazon, with muscles and beard like a man, as strong as Samson. She killed my father's patron and cut off his head."

"Your father's patron?" asked Miri.

Natan put his hand on Yedu's shoulder to quiet him. "*One* of my patrons. A man named Ba'asha. The city will get along well enough without him." Then to Yedu he added, "And don't believe everything you hear. People love a good story. I think it changes every time it is told."

Ruth frowned. "Your father is right, Yedu. I've heard the story several ways now. In one telling, she cut out his heart and ate it on the spot. You knew him too, didn't you Mattanyah?"

Mattanyah scratched his nose, "Ba'asha? I wouldn't say I knew him ... saw him once or twice. A pleasant man he was not. I haven't heard anything about a female Samson – just that he was killed by a woman. What was the name? Nataniela or Navah – something like that."

"Naomi, uncle – it was Naomi," corrected Yedu. Then, with sudden interest he turned to Miri. "Did you know her?"

Miri paused to consider how to answer this. She noticed that all eyes in the room were awaiting her reply. "I ... I do not know. Maybe. It is a common name."

They were disappointed by this response but politely accepted it. Miri was relieved when the conversation moved to a different topic. Yedu was excited about an upcoming event with a famous preacher named Hanina ben Dosa. He was to appear in one week's time on market day morning. It promised to be quite a show, complete with miracles and healings. After a while, Miri said that she was tired and wanted to return home to rest. Mattanyah offered to go with her, but she assured him that she knew the way. It was only a short distance.

As she walked up the hill of the decumanus, she found herself recounting the events of the day. The words of the seer haunted her: *Honor demands revenge, but life abjures it.* There was wisdom in this.

When she looked up, she realized that she had gone too far. She had missed the cutoff by the well that led into the old neighborhood. As she turned around, she saw a curious scene across the street. Three Roman soldiers lounged in wooden chairs with their helmets in their laps. They were drinking ale from large goblets. Next to them squatted a boy with his back to Miri. The boy had obviously been conscripted to sharpen their swords. He was working hard, honing one of the blades with a flat stone and a jar of oil.

They all were bantering amiably – even the boy. Miri thought the sound of the Roman language was rather feminine. The delicate tones seemed odd on the tongues of such ruffians.

Not wanting to be noticed, she started back down the hill and then it hit her. She stole another glance to make sure. Yes. It was indeed the mysterious green-tunic'ed boy she had seen all over the city. My, how that one gets around, she thought – even with the Romans.

~

Back in her room, Miri wanted to finish the next part of the scroll before night descended. She was anxious to find out what happened to Michal after David's soldiers abducted her. She was starting to feel a kinship with this ancient woman.

I hated every day living with David. He was cruel to me. He made me do things that I cannot write because there are no words. He beat me when I did not obey his every desire.

David did not trust me. He would send his servants to test me. They would try to lure me into a confidence against David. They would say: *tell us what you think of your husband,* or *wouldn't you like to escape? We can help you!*

Once I spoke ill of David. For this, I still have scars.

David had an idol that he would pray to. He called it YHWH but it was not! It was a crude statue of a man, almost as big as himself. It was fashioned from sheepskin stretched over a wicker frame. It was painted with human blood. It had ram's horns fixed to the head. Hideous!

One day David came to me and told me to put his idol in my bed and cover it with blankets. He told me to arrange a fleece of goat's hair over the head. I did what he said.

In the dim light the idol looked like David himself, lying on his side. He told me that soldiers would come looking for him. I was to show them the idol and tell them that David was ill and near death. I thought this was another test. I did everything exactly as he said. It wasn't until my father arrived and David had fled that I knew he had used me to help him escape.

I rejoiced in being reunited with my father! He brought me home and returned me to my beloved. My husband did not shun me even though I had been used by another man. My father declared that my marriage to David was invalid because I had been taken by force and never consented to the union. This is true!

After this, Philistines began raiding many towns of Israel. At times they marched deep into our territory. Saul suspected they had a guide who knew the land and the customs of our people. No towns in Yudah were ever raided. My father grew suspicious.

I learned later what happened. I will tell it to you. David had become an adviser to the Philistine king. The king treated David as a son. David had made a pact with him after spoiling my father's chance of doing so.

My father fought the raiders where he could. He could never catch them. They seemed to know his every move. My father became obsessed with David. He said that David was undermining him.

David's fame grew. He came to be feared among the people of the northern tribes. My father knew that soon David would make a grab for the throne.

My father was right! I was with my father in Ramah when a messenger arrived. The Philistine army was marching toward Samaria.

This was a trap set by David. I have since heard him boasting of the plot with my own ears. David persuaded the Philistine king to attack far to the north to draw King Saul away from Ramah. My father marched several days with his army to defend Samaria. David gave the Philistines an account of Saul's army and methods of attack. He lent him many mercenaries. My father was outmatched. The Philistines surrounded him on Mt. Gilboa. They killed my father along with my brothers. Thus ended the reign of the true King of Israel.

Miri wiped a tear from her cheek. She envied Michal for having a father worthy of devotion.

She thought about David. For this story to be true, history must have been rewritten. She remembered what Michal had written near the beginning of her scroll: *The clan of Jesse and David are trampling the memory of King Saul into the dust. Do not believe their lies!*

She read on:

We received word that David had declared himself king of all Israel. Absurd! He had the support only of the tribes of Yudah and Simeon. He had given many bribes to their elders. David also had the support of the Philistines. This gave him power but it did not enamor him to the northern tribes.

The general of our remaining army was a cruel and shrewd man named Abner. He betrayed us. He told our army to stand down. He told them to return to their homes. He stole the royal bracelet and crown and went south to offer these to David, along with his allegiance.

As a final insult to my father, Abner raped and abducted my father's only concubine, Rizpah. She was like a sister to me. We were the same age. She had given my father a daughter and three fine sons. She did not deserve to be used in this manner.

With the army gone, there was nothing to do. We went to our homes. We prayed to YHWH. We awaited what would come.

I will tell you of my tragedy! Abner's men came to my husband's house. They demanded that I come with them. My husband took up his sword to resist, but I pleaded with him not to. The soldiers would have killed him. Then who would provide for my children? I have not seen my husband or my children since that day. I do not know what became of them.

Later I learned that David had demanded I be returned to him. He thought having Saul's daughter as his wife would persuade the northern tribes to follow him.

I will tell you of my life in the house of David. I was treated like a slave. I slept with the slaves. I ate with the slaves. I was given demeaning tasks. In time I was given the task of taking care of David's many sons when they were young. David wanted his sons to be educated. Each day I would take them to the scribe. I listened as they were taught philosophy and letters. After many years, I myself managed to learn. Thus I took on the duty of teaching them myself. This is how I am able to write this scroll you now hold in your hands.

This revelation surprised Miri. She had assumed that Michal had dictated this scroll to a scribe. Apparently there were women who could read and write even in those times.

An amusing thought occurred to Miri. She wondered that if a book were to be written about her and the people she knew, how it might change over time. But this was silly. She was nobody. Why would anyone write about her?

~

The evening meal on market days was always a busy affair at Nura's compound. Those staying in the shelter would attend along with friends and relations who happened to be in town for the market.

This was harvest time, and it had been a good year. Vegetables and fruits were abundant. Wine was plentiful. Animals were fat. And despite the ever-increasing taxes, few were starving. Consequently, few needed to take advantage of Nura's hospitality on this evening.

The two mothers from the shelter, Apulia and Zibiah, were present with their babies. Also attending were two women whom Miri had not yet met named Basmat and Chasidah. Both were widows in their thirties – far past marriageable age. Both had the misfortune of lacking male offspring who survived childhood. Thus, although healthy and willing to work, they were destitute. They had lived at the shelter for well over a year now. They did most of the cleaning and cooking as well as providing meals for anyone in need.

The old man Miri had seen from her window approached and

introduced himself. His name was Amit. He seemed friendly – perhaps a bit too much so. After exchanging names, he held Miri's hand overlong. There was something lascivious in his toothless grin. Miri recovered her hand and looked away, not wanting to make eye contact.

Amit lived in the house behind Nura's, sharing the courtyard. His son, Zehavi, was in town with his wife and two daughters. They had come for the market and had joined the group for evening meal.

As they sat at the table Amit boasted of his son. "He is a very successful merchant, you know. There are few shipments that come into Caesarea that Zehavi does not have an interest in. You see those jewels my daughter-in-law is wearing on her arms and neck? Very rare. From *Spain*."

Miri didn't know where Spain was, but from Amit's tone, she gathered that it must be some place far away and exotic. She was seated at the table with Nura on her right and Zehavi on her left. Zehavi's wife, whose name was Ligeia, sat across from her.

Miri said to Zehavi: "So, you live in Caesarea?"

"Indeed I do, young miss. Have you ever been there?"

"No, not I. But I met someone recently who lives there. He is also a traveling merchant. Perhaps you know him? Bustan is his name."

"Bustan! Of course. Everyone knows Bustan. He's been around as long as I can remember. He must be nine hundred years old."

Miri smiled. "Actually, sixty next month. He was very proud about his coming birthday when he told me."

"Sixty," repeated Zehavi. "I would have thought older, although he still gets around through these hills. Odd man, Bustan. Everyone likes him. Never was much of a businessman though. I've tried to bring him into several opportunities that have come my way. He'd be a valuable ally, knowing everyone in Galilee as he does. But he always declines. Says he's happy as he is, hauling loads of trinkets over the hills with his wagon and those two silly mules."

"Yezebel and Deliylah – I met them too."

Zehavi chuckled. "The very ones. Treats them like children. Odd man Bustan, very odd. How did you come to know him. Is he here in town now?"

"I ..." Miri hesitated, remembering that she should not be giving away too much of her recent activities. The wine, pleasant surroundings, and good company had put her too much at ease. She resolved to be more careful. "I met him on the road and he was kind to me," she said obtusely.

"Kind – he is that. Indeed. Give you his last fig and the tunic off his back. Not much of a businessman though." Having nothing further to add, Zehavi bit into a crust of bread.

Finally, Mattanyah had finished at the spit. He brought forth a platter of meat and set it in the center of the table. He then took his place at the head, between Amit and Apulia.

Basmat inhaled the aroma from the platter. "Sir! I didn't know you could cook like that." The lamb pieces had been marinated in olive oil and wine vinegar, and then roasted over the bonfire. The scent of garlic, onions, mint, and peppercorns was also evident. "Nura, how did you catch such a man?"

Nura laughed. "I drugged him with hemp and married him on the spot before he can recover his senses."

"Really?" Asked Zehavi's older daughter, who had evidently taken the response seriously. She looked to be about eleven. "Can you teach me to make this potion?"

Ligeia replied: "Daughter, I think our hostess is joking. You are, aren't you?"

Nura took another sip from her wine glass but remained coyly silent.

"Of course she is!" answered Mattanyah. "It is I that got the better end of this match. Enough of this nonsense. Can we say a prayer and eat?" He raised his hands in the traditional gesture of supplication.

Zehavi put his bread down and joined the rest in adopting the appropriate pose.

Mattanyah continued: "Alilah, now at the start of the new day of Yom R'vi'i make our deepest desires your desires. We thank you for filling us with your breath another day, and for providing this food for us to eat. Please watch over our friends and kin who are absent, and see that they return to us another day."

Most of them had heard this simple prayer hundreds of times. They mumbled the standard response, "Alilah shemaya."

Ligeia said, "What a lovely prayer. Isn't it, husband? You Jews have such a nice way with words. So which god is this Alilah? What does he do?"

Chasidah, the widow at the end of the table opposite Mattanyah responded solemnly, "Alilah is not *a* god. Alilah simply means *the* god. We are not permitted to speak the name of our god outside of the synagogue."

"My wife is Greek. She doesn't understand these things," said Zehavi apologetically. "They have many gods, depending on the need at hand."

"There is but *one* god," pronounced Chasidah, effectively ending the conversation.

They began to pass the food around the table. Zehavi handed Miri a wooden bowl with small green balls in a fragrant dressing. Seeing her inquisitive look, Ligeia said: "Dumplings. My daughter made them. We get some exotic ingredients on the coast that you might not find here. Tell Miri how you made them, dear."

The daughter (Miri could not remember her name) recited proudly. "First you take barleycorns and you boil them in lamb's broth. You have to make almond paste in a mortar and then mix it into the barley. Then I added some yellow raisins. It makes a sticky, lumpy paste. Then you squish it into little balls with your hands, and wrap them with grape leaves. But first you have to soak the leaves in oil overnight. Then you put them in a kind of sweet dressing – I used citron juice, honey, and new wine. Oh, I also sprinkled some fennel seeds on the top." She smiled in a self-satisfied manner and continued eating.

Miri took a dumpling from the bowl and passed it on to Nura. She bit into it tentatively. It was indeed delicious.

Mattanyah saw that Amit was leering in an unsubtle manner at

Apulia, who was seated directly across from him. In an effort to distract him he said: "Good harvest this year, Amit. Have you ever seen better?"

The old man reluctantly withdrew his attention from Apulia and furrowed his brow. "I recall a particularly good year, hmm ... it must be twenty years ago because it was back in the time of Herod. The old Herod I mean, not this fool son of his that rules Galilee now. The harvest was so good we couldn't store it all. We had to leave some to rot in the fields."

"Fool son indeed," scoffed Zehavi. "He wants to raise the tax on shipping to finance some new building project he has planned in the east. He's too busy playing the catamite ... pardon my language. What I mean is that he's always making pointless trips to Rome with his expensive bribes. He cares not about the needs of his own people."

Mattanyah said: "I hear there's a new procurator of Yudaea. We'll see how he gets along with Antipas, eh?"

Zehavi made a dismissive gesture. "Annius Rufus is his name. Some bureaucrat they brought in from Tarsus. I hear his lamp is but half full. Antipas will ignore him like he did his predecessor. Antipas is a Herod. It rankles him that he doesn't get to be called king. He wants to rule the southern provinces as well as Galilee."

Miri thought this conversation was interesting, especially in light of the scroll she had been reading. It was intriguing to learn of the ambitions of the current king, even if he was officially called a tetrarch, or quarter king. She also found it curious that even after all these centuries the northern and southern lands still held antipathy for each other.

She was passed a plate of flatbreads and a large bowl of mixed fruits: apple slices, grapes, figs, and mango pieces. She had seen Nura enter the house earlier with parcels of fruit she had purchased at the market. She took some and passed it on.

"I don't think it's proper to discuss such things in front of women, husband." Ligeia admonished. "Perhaps you and Mattanyah can share a cup of wine later? So now, who can tell me about this wedding I've heard mentioned?"

Apulia had been trying to avoid eye contact with Amit. She took this opportunity to turn to her right to address Ligeia. "Natan's daughter, Channah, – you know Natan, don't you love? Everyone in this town does. I imagine your important husband here has dealings with him." She winked at Zehavi.

Zehavi nodded vigorously as he chewed a mouthful of lamb.

Apulia continued, "Channah is betrothed to some boy from out of town – a land owner."

Miri interjected, "Ephrayim. His name is Ephrayim. He's from Cana. I hear that he's very smart, and handsome too." Then, seeing the quizzical looks from several people she added, "I visited the family today with Mattanyah. I didn't meet Channah. She was out at the market, but her mother told me all about it."

Apulia picked up the thread again. "Mattanyah here is uncle to the bride. So we're all going to the celebration. Isn't that right my master?"

"Apulia, I've asked you seventy times not to call me that. There are no masters at this house – only hard workers."

"And some loafers," added Chasidah.

Another bowl was passed to Miri. This was a thick stew of lentils in a broth spiced with garlic, peppercorns, basil, cumin, and a little vinegar thrown in for some bite. Basmat had been working on this all afternoon and had explained the recipe to her just before they sat down. She spooned some onto her flatbread and passed the bowl to Nura.

"It was a good market day, I trust, father," said the unnamed daughter after a lengthy silence.

This perked Zehavi up. "Yes. It was quite a good day I should say. The price of wheat is very low this year – thanks to Natan. I'm arranging a large shipment to Rome. We can undercut the Egyptians for once. I don't usually come to the Sepphoris market myself – usually just send a servant with a slave or two. But the hills are beautiful this time of year and I was overdue to visit my father."

"Overdue indeed. I haven't seen my granddaughters since the

springtime," said Amit indignantly. "Such beautiful girls they are becoming."

"I did stop by to speak with Natan myself earlier this morning." Zehavi did not want to be deterred from talking shop. "He and I are going to do a deal on a shipment of ore from Syria."

"How will it be transported?" Asked Mattanyah.

"Gentlemen," chided Chasidah. "Can you discuss these things after our meal?"

Zehavi laughed and shrugged his shoulders. "Mattanyah, my friend. I see that you know what it is to live in a house ruled by women. We shall talk later."

From inside the house, they heard a door slam. A moment later a boy entered the courtyard burdened with a heavy satchel. He set the satchel by the bonfire and joined them at the table.

"Yeshua!" Mattanyah rose to embrace the youth. "We weren't sure when to expect you back. I trust my brother is doing well with his harvest?"

"Very well uncle. I returned this morning, but I had chores that needed to be done in town."

Miri's jaw dropped. It was the same boy with the green tunic that she had seen all over town, although the tunic looked black in the evening light. She also noticed the satchel. It was the same one he had stolen outside the basilica.

Nura introduced Yeshua to Miri, Ligeia and the two daughters. He had met Zehavi once before. Zibiah and Ligeia each moved to the side, opening a space at the table for Yeshua to sit. This put him directly across from Miri.

Miri wondered if the family knew the kinds of mischief that this one engaged in during his days. She resolved to behave cordially toward him during the meal. She would find time later to inform Nura of his antics she had witnessed today.

As food was passed to him, Yeshua tried to engaged Miri in conversation. "Miri, how do you come to be joining our family this evening?"

Miri kept her eyes on her food and mumbled simply, "visiting."

Nura asked Yeshua, "Nephew, what are these chores you speak of? Building is resumed on the hill. Your uncle may be able to get more work for you."

Mattanyah grimaced. "Ah ... That may not be a good idea. I did speak to Clopas today. He says he's in a lot of trouble over this business with the sculpture, and he doesn't want to see Yeshua anywhere near his building site."

"Chores," scoffed Miri under her breath as she shook her head.

"What?" asked Yeshua.

"Perhaps Clopas does not want his lumber to disappear," Miri suggested.

"Eh? No – I think you misunderstand, young Miri," said Mattanyah. "Yeshua here was not in trouble for thievery, but rather ... questionable judgment."

Miri said snidely, "He did not answer your question, Nura – about the chores."

There was an uncomfortable silence broken at length by Apulia. "Yeshua bar David, you haven't come to visit me lately. He's cute isn't he Zibiah?"

Zibiah had consumed quite a bit of wine. She turned to her right and looked Yeshua up and down, and then turned back to Apulia. "A bit scrawny don't you think, love?" She leaned in and kissed Apulia on the lips.

Miri picked up on the use of the patronymic title and assumed that it meant that Yeshua considered himself descended from the ancient house of King David. She had heard others make the same ludicrous boast. David the king lived a thousand years ago and likely had hundreds of children. Even if you *could* trace your lineage back to him, so what? Half of Yudaea could make the same claim.

Besides, having read the scroll up in her little room, she had other reasons to scoff at the claim. "*Bar David* indeed! It is not something to be proud of, is it? He cared only about his own kin, and only his male kin. Boys and their clans!" She rolled her eyes and continued eating.

Yeshua was befuddled. "But ... you couldn't have known David.

You're too young. And are we not supposed to honor our fathers?"

The image of her own wicked father popped into Miri's mind. It was less than a week since he had imprisoned her and then sold her into slavery. Her upper lip quivered as she said. "You are all the same. Talking about honor. How women and children suffer for the sake of honor!" Then remembering the words of the seer, she added, "Men value honor. Women value life."

There was an awkward silence. Everyone at the table was taken aback by the intensity of Miri's retort. No one knew what she was talking about.

Nura, who believed that one should listen ten times as much as one speaks, decided to intervene. "Dearest Miri, Yeshua speaks of his *actual* father. His name was David. He died before Yeshua is born."

Miri felt foolish at this revelation, but she was not about to apologize. She knew how Yeshua had spent his day, and so, for now she remained silent.

The rest of the meal passed in meaningless smalltalk. Afterwards, Zehavi left for his rented lodgings with Ligeia and his two daughters. Amit returned to his house. Apulia, Zibiah, Basmat and Chasidah all went back to the shelter to prepare for bed. This left Nura, Mattanyah, Miri, and Yeshua at the table.

Mattanyah turned to Yeshua and asked sharply, "What have you been doing this day?"

Before he could answer, Miri blurted out: "Thieving! I saw him and another boy attack an official at the basilica across from the market. They took a big satchel full of documents. It is that very one there by the fire. Later I saw them burning the documents down near the fuller's shop."

Yeshua was abashed. He had no idea he had been observed. "Attack? No one was attacked. No one was harmed."

Miri said triumphantly, "So you do not deny it. Who is your accomplice? The tall boy with the cropped hair?"

Mattanyah said, "Oh Yeshua, you are not spending your time with Baruch again? That boy is wicked."

Yeshua felt that they were ganging up on him. "Baruch is hot-headed but he's not bad, uncle. What I did was important, but I thought it best that you and Nura not know. It's ..."

"Go on," Miri challenged. "Try to save face. But have the decency to not lie."

"Decency? Who *are* you?" Asked Yeshua. He turned to Nura. "The man is a lawyer ... for the tax collector who is trying to turn Chunya and Tahmid out of their house. That weasel has been busy doing the same trick all through the hills. We stole his leases and burned them."

Mattanyah threw his hands up and shook his head. "You can't be taking such things into your own hands. Do you want to get locked up again or worse? How would you like working in an ore mine in Greece? You wouldn't last a month. There are ways to petition these things. We should talk to Natan. He knows many good lawyers."

"Uncle – the laws are designed by the rich to steal from everyone else. Natan has found a way to work things to his advantage, but he can't or won't change anything. If a law is found benefiting a poor man, they are quick to change it. This whole kingdom is rotten. Burning the leases will slow things down – maybe give Chunya and Tahmid a little more time."

"A little more *time*? But they would still be turned out eventually," rebutted Mattanyah.

"Time is all any of us has," answered Yeshua stoically.

Nura was concerned about the danger. "Yeshua, you put yourself and your family at such risk. It is reckless!"

"Onesicritus says that to avoid risk is to avoid life."

Mattanyah erupted, "Again with the blather of that cynic. Why do you listen to that disgusting man? You can smell him from miles away. Is that what you want to become? Will *you* start defecating in the streets now? What you need is a hard day's work."

Yeshua was resolute. "I did what I *had* to do."

"So you oppose the kingdom?" Miri asked sarcastically. "That is why I saw you with the Roman soldiers – happily sharpening their swords, prattling like old friends."

Yeshua grinned. "Oh, you saw that too? I wonder why I didn't see you. I was ..."

Miri turned abruptly to Nura and Mattanyah. "I am intruding on your family's business. Kindly excuse my behavior. I need my rest." She stomped off into the house.

After she had left, Yeshua asked, "How does she come by here?"

"You are to be treating her with respect," answered Nura curtly. "Now Yeshua, you are my apprentice. Sharpening implements of war goes against everything I am teaching you. This is ..."

Yeshua sat sullenly and said into his cup. "I have not broken my oath."

"But the swords?" Asked Mattanyah.

Yeshua shrugged. "Roman soldiers really should pay more attention. They won't be cutting anything harder than fresh cheese with those blades."

1 Kings

The next morning,
After Yom Revi'i the 10th day of Elul

Miri awoke to a crack of thunder. A brisk wind blew in through the unshuttered window. The air was heavy with the promise of a coming storm.

She had been dreaming again. This time, she had been with the seer. Or was it the seer? The old woman in her dream had glowed with internal light, like a goddess. She had told Miri that the time had come for her to make a choice. She grasped at the wispy outlines of the dream – of what exactly it was she was supposed to choose. An image of seed scattered on the ground stuck in her mind.

Miri arose and closed the shutters. This left the room in gloom, so she lit a lamp from the candle. Carrying this, she descended to the main floor of the house and found Mattanyah alone at the table. He was having a simple breakfast of bread, honey, and new wine.

"Join me, child." He pushed a flatbread toward her.

"Thank you sir. Have the others all left?"

Mattanyah chewed the day-old bread and swallowed. "Nura has gone off to the village in the south. One of my brother's laborers has injured himself with a plow."

"And Yeshua?" Miri asked sheepishly.

Mattanyah shook his head. "I sent him to the fuller's shop. Old Halphaios is always looking for laborers. He has a hard time keeping steady help."

Miri remembered the awful stench and was not surprised that nobody wanted to work there. "Sir, I want to ask for your pardon. I acted badly last night."

Mattanyah chuckled. "You were spirited indeed. Don't worry. We all speak our minds in this house, and we all have thick skins as a result." He paused and then continued more seriously, "You should know, though, about Yeshua, he's not a wicked boy. He's smart – too smart for his own good sometimes. He's just ... unfocused. We try to keep him busy."

Miri knew what she had seen the previous day, but she accepted this, and decided she would give the boy another chance if she met him again. "So where are you going today?"

"Me? Well, there won't be anything done at the building site up on the hill at least until this afternoon. The rain slows everything down and gives everyone a break. So I thought I'd tinker on a few projects in my workshop."

~

Later that morning Miri settled herself back in the scroll room. She adjusted the candles and found the spot where she had left off. Michal was now a captive in the house of David. She had taken on the job of educating David's many sons.

Most of David's sons are like David himself. They are interested only in competition and conquest. They have little patience for learning. All save for one: The runt, Solomon, excels at learning. Solomon is the son of the witch, Bathsheba. He is clever, but he is heartless and cruel.

When Solomon was very young, his brothers would torment him because of his small stature. Now he is becoming a man. Though he is still small, I have noticed that his brothers fear him. Solomon is not like his father. He is not filled with lust and sport. Solomon is cold. You can feel it when he stares at you. I pity the world if that one ever manages to claim the throne. May YHWH prevent it!

David is never satisfied. He enjoys the conquest of women just as he does killing men in battle. He now has seven wives for whom he has paid a dowry. I am numbered among his wives, but I told you that this is false! He also has untold concubines. Once he conquers her, he loses interest in a woman.

One day David held a grand celebration to bring the Ark into Yerushalayim. He paraded naked through the town collecting serving girls as he went. Afterward I told him that he disgraced himself in doing this. He gave me to his soldiers that night. I do not speak to him now.

I have written about Solomon. Now I will tell you about his mother, the witch. Bathsheba is the craftiest of David's women. She is his last and youngest wife. To this day, David believes he stole Bathsheba from her husband. This is false. Bathsheba once bragged to me how she arranged the whole thing.

David's manservant brought him to the roof of his palace one day when Bathsheba was bathing in the next yard. She put on quite a show, pretending she did not know he was watching.

The plan worked. After David took her, she pretended to be with child. She urged David to put her own husband on the front lines of battle, where he was killed.

Bathsheba to this day has David under a spell. The other wives are afraid of her, just as the other children are afraid of her son, Solomon. Beware these two! Their tongues are poison. Their deeds are full of destruction!

Miri stood up and stretched. The more she read the more fantastic it seemed. Solomon and David are the most revered among ancient kings. Solomon was supposed to be consummately wise. Didn't he write the proverbs and love songs that we all learned?

~

In the early afternoon, after a fitful nap, Miri made her way to the shelter to visit Apulia and Zibiah. She walked the length of the stalls and found the two at the table in the triclinium. Zibiah was attempting to nurse her baby, but the little girl kept fussing and pushing the proffered breast away. At length, Zibiah stood up and swung the baby over her shoulder. She bounced gently on her toes trying to elicit a burp.

By contrast, Apulia's boy slept soundly in a rocking cradle bundled with blankets. Apulia sat astride the bench, her outside foot gently rocking the child. She was working with a long knitting needle at a dark thick rope. Her hands and the table were wet. Miri noticed that the rope was being drawn from a bucket of water at the end of the table. Apulia pried the strands of the rope apart and a little piece of silver metal fell onto the table. She carefully picked it up and tossed it into a bowl where it jangled with similar shards.

"What are you doing?" Miri asked.

"Making sandals. Have a seat. My other helper here is useless." Apulia rolled her eyes in an exaggerated fashion.

"Some of us make better cows than others, my love," was Zibiah's retort. She was now walking around the table in circles, bouncing gently as she walked. The baby had stopped fussing, but was wide awake, her eyes following the lamp light as Zibiah turned.

Miri sat at the table. Apulia handed her a long needle and fished the end of another dark rope out of the bucket.

"Just unravel it like this." Apulia demonstrated, unwinding the thick strands that made up the rope. "Mind the little metal bits, some of them are sharp. When you finish, roll the laces around one of those spools there."

Miri started to work. The ropes were made from braided leather laces. Perhaps they were used for horses or some kind of livestock. Having grown up in a fishing town, Miri wasn't familiar with such things. But good leather was valuable and always being re-tasked.

Zibiah's baby became fussy again. She tried cradling her in her arms as she hummed a gentle tune, swaying from side to side.

Apulia gave Miri a wink. "A little wine on a rag usually does the trick for me."

In a soft voice, Zibiah countered: "You should give some to your baby too." Both mothers laughed.

They worked for a while in silence. Miri's fingers became stained brown by the wet leather. "Why do you soak them? I would think water will make the leather crack."

"Ah, we'll get them nice and dry and then oil them before we lash the sandals. They'll be fine. We had to wash them." Apulia unhitched another metal shard and tossed it into the bowl.

"But why? It looks like new leather."

"Blood," said Zibiah simply. "Won't do to have bloody sandals – not on my pretty feet."

"Blood? But why would ..." Miri examined the rope she was working on more carefully. With a jolt she understood. This was a whip, and a nasty looking one at that. Every foot or so, a looped piece of sharp metal was braided into the leather. "But where did ..." Then she noticed the satchel on the floor by the table – the same satchel Yeshua brought into the courtyard last night.

Apulia noticed the direction of her gaze. "Nice thick leather that. We'll cut it up for the soles. Double it up first. We'll be able to make five or six nice pairs. Do you need one dear?"

"Me?" Miri shook her head. "Oh. No. The sandals I am wearing are fine. But where did he ... Yeshua, I mean. I saw him bring that satchel home last night. He stole it, you know."

Apulia laughed. "Quick with his hands, that boy is. Told me he took the satchel to the slave stalls at the back of the market and stole the whips right under their noses. I don't know how he gets away with it."

Zibiah's baby at last seemed to have fallen asleep. She gingerly sat at the table with the other two women.

Miri remembered the cruel episode she had witnessed the previous day – the smell of sweat and blood, the cries of the poor man being flogged. She had wanted then to do something to help, to stop the torture. But she was powerless. She had been consumed by her own troubles.

As she continued to work in silence, she reconsidered what she heard Yeshua say at the meal last night – about the whole kingdom being rotten. She smiled as she thought of the heartless guard not being able to find his implements of torture today. Today the whips will become sandals.

She happily spent the afternoon with the two mothers. When they were finished, they had seven pairs of new sandals. The bowl of shards would be taken to the metalworking shop. Perhaps they would be reforged as jewelry or nails, or perhaps part of a plow.

~

Yeshua left early the next morning to wait with others in front of the city court where farmers and foremen would collect day laborers. He was still not allowed anywhere near Clopas' building site.

This was Yom Chamishi, the second market day of the week. It would not be as crowded today, being mostly limited to local merchants and nearby farmers. Taletha and Ephrayim had come to town to sell the produce from their farm in Cana.

Nura proposed to Taletha and Ruth that the women have a midday meal together in an open garden on the north side of the market. She suspected that Miri might like to see her aunt and asked her to join the group. Nura reminded her that, in her new identity as Taddai's niece, she must pretend to be meeting Taletha for the first time. Very likely there were still people looking for Ba'asha's killer, although they hoped it was far away from here.

The lunch was supposed to be strictly a women's affair. But unfortunately Yeshua returned to the house midmorning without finding any work. Nura asked him to accompany them.

They arrived at the market and purchased food from booths just off of the street. They went to the tables in the garden and unpacked their bounty. They had a jar of salted fish soaked in a thick chutney. Ruth unwrapped a cloth containing flatbreads that had just been fried in olive oil. Yeshua carried a jug of water and another of new wine. Nura had purchased a clay pot in which a pungent eggplant stew had been baked. When she opened the lid, the aroma of garlic and ginger filled the air. Miri carried a basket of fresh figs and raisins, and another with spicy meat skewers that Ruth had purchased.

They sat and began to eat.

"Nura dear," said Taletha with an officious air. "It must be a blessing to have a husband who is so hard working and resourceful. My husband, Alilah keep his soul, also had that admirable virtue. Never a minute would go by when he wouldn't find something that needed to be done. In the fields, in the barn, at the market, helping the neighbors. He was practically never at home. My son Ephrayim, young as he is, has inherited this desirable trait. Such a useful, busy person from morning to night. It is a gift from above indeed to stay busy bringing food home for the table." She gave a not-so-subtle glance at Yeshua, who, oblivious to the insinuations, was dipping a piece of bread into the chutney.

Miri had to smile at her aunt's manner, although she thought Taletha was being a bit unfair. Yeshua had tried to find work this very morning. Miri felt indifferent toward the boy now and resolved that this time she would *not* pick a fight with him. "Tell us more about your life in Cana, Aun ... um, Taletha," she prompted.

"Ah yes ... Miri, is it? Yes, thank you for asking. We have a good amount of land to be sure, although not as much as we could have had. My brother was quite prodigal and asked my father for his inheritance when he was still young. His name was Achyan."

Miri winced at the name. She raised a cloth to her mouth and pretended that she had bit into an olive pit.

Taletha continued: "So he took his portion of his inheritance and went off to Lake Chinnereth to try his luck as a fisherman. After that my father became ill, so when I married, my father, who was also quite elderly at the time, split the remaining lands and included them in the dowries for my sister and me. Unfortunately, my dear sister, Alilah keep *her* soul as well, passed on to Sheol from the fever. She had a sweet disposition, unlike my brother. You would have liked her, Miri. So now my son must work the land himself, with whatever hired hands, boys mostly, that he can find. Why, he was at the court this very morning looking for pickers. It's a pity that you didn't run into him, Yeshua. If you had been a bit earlier perhaps, but of course you need your rest."

Yeshua looked up at the mention of this name and smiled broadly with a mouthful of fruit. Juice dripped down the side of his mouth. "In fact I did see your son, and I will be working your land after Shabbat. I look forward to your legendary hospitality. I shall try not to break any pots this time."

Taletha smiled disingenuously and plowed on. "Anyway – we're all very excited about the wedding." She nodded toward Ruth. "Channah is a delightful young woman. Alilah willing, I hope she will produce many strong sons. She raised her glass and drank." At last, she fell silent and began nibbling at a flatbread.

Miri had forgotten this aspect of her aunt's personality – her habit of making endless, nervous chatter. As she glanced up, Miri spied two Roman soldiers coming out of a building across the street. One of them kicked an old beggar who had been sitting on the curb. The beggar hobbled off in the direction of the synagogue. The soldiers were stumbling. One of them punched the other playfully. Then they both started walking toward the market. "Romans!" Miri whispered sharply.

This had the unfortunate effect of causing the whole party to look up. Nura spoke. "Keep your heads down and speak only if asked a direct question. With luck they will leave us be."

They had no such luck. The Romans were drunk and hungry. One was tall and thin, the other of middling height and portly. Both were armed and looked capable of violence. After they arrived, they circled the table, eyeing each person in turn.

The tall one came to a stop behind Miri. "Cisseus, what have we here? Hmm, smells good." He reached rudely over Miri, leaning into her as he did so. He grabbed one of the pieces of meat from the platter and popped it into his mouth. "Jew-food." He made an exaggerated show of chewing, looking from one person to another, daring them to object.

The portly one was looking curiously at Nura. "Hey Glaucus, They're not all Jews – This one's got a Gallic look about her. White as a ghost, like Lo's tits." He grabbed his hefty chest and rubbed it as if he were fumblingly caressing a woman. Then, seeing Nura's cross look he grew wary and held his hand in front of him, index finger and pinky extended. "Don't you be cursing me, now. I'll put it right back on you."

Taletha, Miri, and Ruth could not understand a word that either soldier spoke. They heard only gibberish. As it turned out, these were conscripted soldiers from Thrace. They were speaking a heavily accented and vulgar mishmash of Latin and Greek. Nura and Yeshua were familiar with both of these tongues and could thus make out the gist of the taunting.

Nura considered a reply to this rudeness, but in the end she remembered her own advice and decided it wouldn't be prudent to endanger her companions. She lowered her eyes in a manner of humility and remained silent.

Yeshua, on the other hand, watched the soldiers' every move, calmly meeting their gaze.

The tall soldier noticed this. "Oh, I've seen *you* before. You're that simpleton that walks around here playing tricks." He tapped Yeshua hard on the forehead with his gloved finger. He spoke loudly and slowly, as if addressing a child. "Look at your Jew-friends. They have good manners." He slapped Yeshua on the top of the head. "Lower your head when your masters talk." Yeshua continued his stare.

"Say, Glaucus ... look at what we have here. I thoughts it was just hags and the half wit, but look at this sweet one." Cisseus, who had been standing behind Miri now noticed that she was much younger and prettier than the other women at the table. He reached out and drew back the veil which had been covering Miri's head and most of her face.

Miri appeared to be either seething with anger or petrified with fear. It was hard to tell which. Her eyes were wide open, her head tilted slightly down, staring at the bowl of figs on the table. Her hands fumbled with something in the folds of her robe.

Glaucus took an interest in her also. "Now *that* is a face. I tell you, Cisseus, some of these Jew bitches are quite fetching. I'd rather do her than the whores in the westside tavern any a day. Give me a kiss, pretty one." He grabbed his own crotch for emphasis.

Cisseus broke out laughing at the gesture. "Glaucus, that's the first good idea you've had. Say, there's a quiet alley over there, how about we go over and ..."

Yeshua stood up abruptly and placed himself between Miri and the soldiers. He remained silent but continued defiantly to meet their gaze.

Cisseus was annoyed. "What is this? Does our Jew-boy want to play?" He nodded to Glaucus and then pushed Yeshua on the shoulders. Glaucus had, at the signal, extended his foot. Yeshua fell backward and landed hard.

To the consternation of the soldiers, Yeshua quickly got to his feet and resumed his place, still blocking their path.

Glaucus said, "Oh, this one's got spirit. I thinks he does want to play." He grabbed Yeshua's arm and attempted to pull him away. But the boy made a twisting motion with his arm, a trick he had learned on the streets. The soldier lost his grip. His own momentum, aided by his drunkenness, caused him to lose his balance. He fell clumsily to the ground.

While this was happening Cisseus reached out and grabbed Miri's hair, pulling her head back violently. She cried out in alarm. Now free from the floundering Glaucus, Yeshua reached out and gave Cisseus' wrist a hard twist, causing him to let go.

To a Roman soldier, it was intolerable to allow a Jew to accost him in this manner. Glaucus got to his feet and brushed himself off. "Never mind the girl. We'll have fun with her later. Let's teach this sheep dung to mind his place." He drew his short sword and stepped forward.

Cisseus was rubbing his wrist. "That was a mistake, Jew-boy. Prepare to meet your no-name god."

As Glaucus raised his sword to strike, Yeshua continued to look him in the eye. There was no fear in his expression. He did not move to defend himself. It was unnerving.

"Hold!" shouted an angry voice. Both soldiers stopped what they were doing and looked in the direction of the command.

A Roman officer rode toward them on horseback, picking his way between the shrubs. "Legionnaires Glaucus and Cisseus – why am I not surprised? Aren't you in enough trouble already?"

The two soldiers immediately stood at attention. Yeshua nudged Miri, motioning her away. They ambled to the other side of the table and stood at a safe distance. Miri's hands remained inside her robe.

The soldiers remained silent. "Legionnaire Glaucus, don't you have to be on duty at the seventh hour? Are you planning to report drunk?"

The soldier's eyes remained forward while he barked his reply. "No Optio sir. We were reprimanding these Jews, sir."

Cisseus added helpfully: "That's right, sir. This boy was causing a disturbance."

The Optio turned on him sharply, "Legionnaire Cisseus, have I addressed you?"

"Ah, no sir."

"Then why are you talking?"

Cisseus now looked confused. He *had* been speaking out of turn, but now he was being asked a question. He hesitated before stammering, "Uh, it's, uh, sir ..."

The Optio shouted, "Are you also drunk, Legionnaire Cisseus? You've been disciplined for that before. Do you want to spend the next year digging latrines?"

Cisseus was defensive. "Well, sir, I've had a bit of wine, but I'm off duty until midnight."

The Optio had better things to do than waste his time with these two idiots. "I suggest you find a place to sleep it off before then. Now ..." He waved his hand toward Yeshua and Miri, who were standing with the other ladies now. "Are you trying to start a riot?"

The two soldiers eyed each other, not sure what they were being asked. At length Glaucus said, "No sir, of course not."

"If a Jew-dog causes a problem, you *arrest* him so he can be properly flogged and crucified. You don't slice him up in the street.

You know how excitable these peasants are."

"Yes sir. I didn't think of that. We'll arrest him then, sir."

At this point, Yeshua spoke to the Optio in Latin. "Do you treat your dogs with such cruelty?"

The Optio was surprised. He pivoted his horse toward the boy. "Hold a moment, legionnaires. This dog has learned how to speak real words. I'm so used to hearing 'barbarbar' that I forget that some of them can talk." He glanced at the soldiers. "Apparently he has understood everything we have said."

The Optio had been speaking Latin. Now he switched to Greek. "But a dog is still a dog, even though he fancies himself to be as smart as a Roman. And he looks like a dog too ... filthy. One of those cynics, I'll wager."

The two soldiers laughed in the forced manner that inferiors do when their master has attempted to say something witty.

In perfect Greek, Yeshua replied, "Would it not be demeaning, not being Roman, to myself not to think I am not as smart as a Roman?"

The Optio needed a moment to work this out. In the end he couldn't decide if he was being insulted or ... something else. A tense silence ensued.

Finally the Optio broke out in a hearty laugh. The two soldiers joined him. The Optio switched back to Latin. "Come closer, boy. Let me get a look at you. There may be some value to a Jew-dog after all." Yeshua complied, drawing within a few paces of the horse-mounted Optio. "You're quite scrawny. How old are you?"

Yeshua replied, "Sixteen, sir."

"There. You see legionnaires, he can speak respectfully. He called me sir. You could learn manners from this one." Then he turned back to Yeshua and said sternly, "Look here, Jew-dog. I don't care how smart you think you are. I can't have you causing trouble. I could have you and your women killed with a word. Is that what you want?"

Yeshua understood that the question was rhetorical, so he ignored it. Instead he asked a question of his own. "Why do you call us dogs? You take bread from the mouths of our children and feed it to your dogs. You also let them eat the scraps from your tables. You give them warm places to rest their heads. You give us nothing."

The Optio's eyes went wide at being addressed with such impudence. "Boy – you are either very brave or very foolish. Legionnaires – perhaps you were right. This one may need a good flogging. He needs to learn his place. Look at me boy!"

Yeshua complied and calmly met the Optio's gaze. The Optio switched to yet a different language. Yeshua had heard these hard consonants in the streets of Sepphoris. He recognized the language as Persian. Unfortunately he only knew a few words. The Optio went on at some length. It was obvious that the two soldiers were similarly in the dark.

At last the Optio fell silent and seemed to be waiting for some acknowledgment or reply from Yeshua. Not wanting to leave the women at the mercy of the soldiers, Yeshua decided that now was not the time for continued defiance. Adopting a manner of humility and surrender, he bowed low and waited for the Roman's verdict.

The Optio's jaw dropped in astonishment. He turned to his soldiers and switched back to Latin. "Legionnaires, here we have a diamond in the rough. I give him an ultimatum and tell him to bow his head or be arrested, and he understands." He turned back to Yeshua. "Stand up boy, look up at me. How do you come by such knowledge? Surely you have not been to Persia?"

Yeshua shook his head.

The Optio laughed. "Men – give the boy a denarius for his trouble and leave him be. Now listen boy, normally it would be necessary to have you flogged, but it would be a shame to mar such young skin. I could see as I rode up that you were *not* trying to cause trouble, but merely protecting the honor of your ... sister, is it?"

"She is my aunt's cousin," replied Yeshua. "She is from Mag..."

"Whatever boy, well done I say. Listen, I am normally stationed in Capernaum. There, my son and I maintain a household with a few servants. I know what it is to have people rely on me for protection. My name is Gnaeus Mocius. If you are ever in Capernaum, find me and we will talk further."

He turned back to the soldiers. "Now you two, since you seem to have so much time on your hands, hike up to the palace and help unload the supply carts. They seem to be short-handed today and Antipas is due to return soon. I hear he wants to throw another banquet in our honor."

At last, the soldiers left, escorted by the Optio on horseback. The women and Yeshua all looked at each other — each breathing a sigh of relief, not quite believing what had just happened. This was clearly Alilah's intervention.

Yeshua wanted to make sure Miri was uninjured, but she shrank from him warily as he approached. As she did so, something clattered to the paving stones. Yeshua picked it up. "I know this knife. But it's all dirty now. Is that …"

Miri quickly grabbed the dagger out of his hand and hid it once again within the folds of her tunic. No one else had seen it. She seemed cross with Yeshua. "You needn't have interfered. I can take care of myself."

Yeshua raised his palms in a gesture of surrender. "Of course. You did notice though, that the soldiers were wearing hardened leather armor? You would need more than a little dagger to get through that."

Miri had *not* noticed that. "Well I could have … never mind. At least I would have tried. What were *you* doing? You almost got yourself killed. How did you expect to beat them?"

Yeshua considered this. "I didn't expect to beat them. I guess I didn't think much about it."

Taletha had come near and she now joined in the scolding: "So then what? You were just going to stand there and let them kill you? *Then* who would there be to defend us?"

Yeshua was despondent. He shrugged and said under his breath, "Lucky is the lion that the human will eat, so that the lion becomes human. Foul is the human that the lion will eat. The lion will still become human."

Taletha rolled her eyes. "There he goes with another of his

riddles."

Miri felt a wave of relief wash over her. She sat down. A terrible tragedy had been averted. She was not really angry at Yeshua. Indeed, she was starting to have respect for this unwashed hooligan.

Lamentations

Near midnight, Yom Rishon the 14th day of Elul, the evening after the end of Shabbat.

I ncense vapor rose in delicate tendrils toward the arched stone ceiling high above the mosaic floor. Menorahs on tall iron pedestals were spaced around the perimeter, providing an eerie dancing light, and filling the synagogue with ghostly shadows. One huge candle, representing the presence of YHWH, burned in the corner.

The rabbi stood at the head of the gathered worshippers, his arms outstretched, eyes closed on his upturned face in a traditional pose of supplication. Men knelt or sat on cushions from the front to the back in order of social status, patrons before clients.

Miri had arrived late, and now stood in the back with the other women. Each covered her head and face with a black veil, leaving only eyes visible through a slit in the cloth.

Musicians had just started when Miri arrived. Straining to see over the shoulders of two taller women, she could glimpse them near the front. One plucked somber, deep arpeggios from a huge lyre. Another tapped with small sticks on the strings of a kuch'in, producing a soft, pulsating sustained tone. A flutist played a halting melody, punctuated with trills and ornaments. His style sounded like the eerie tones made by Nura when she practiced late in the evenings.

This was the lamentations service, enacted every week at

midnight after the end of Shabbat during the month of Elul. It was intended as a cleansing ceremony, done in preparation for the coming new year and day of atonement. Miri had learned of the service earlier this evening after returning to the city. The events of the last two days weighed heavily on her heart, and she hoped this ceremony might ease her black mood.

At length, the flute ceased its meandering melody, leaving only the rhythmic drone of the strings. The rabbi moved to one side and knelt on a cushion. The reader approached the lectern – a middle-aged man in a pristine white robe with black leather tefillin strapped to his forehead and hand. He adjusted the scroll, cleared his throat, and began in a sonorous bass voice.

The city now lies deserted, where people were once many. She is like a widow, who was once revered above all nations. She who was a princess among the lands has become a slave. Bitterly she weeps in the night. Tears roll down her cheeks. No one comforts her in her distress. Among all who once loved her, all have betrayed ...

Earlier this evening Miri had left the southern village shortly after sundown. Yeshua's family had all entreated her to stay another night. But she felt the need to return to the city to be alone, to mourn, to feel, to weep. She realized now that her flight through Galilee, and her subsequent experiences here in Sepphoris had not allowed her time to grieve. She felt that she indeed had much to grieve, and so she insisted on returning. Yeshua accompanied her despite her protestations. He said the hills were not safe at night. The boy had become her guardian since the terrifying events in the garden two days ago. Miri admitted to herself that she was glad to have his protection.

... harsh labor, she dwells among the nations. She can find no place to lay her head. Her pursuers overtake her in her distress. The roads of ...

Protection? Is that what Yeshua was doing with those Roman soldiers – protecting her? What kind of protection would it be if they had just cut him down? None at all. And why do I think of him as a boy, she wondered. He is more than a year older than me.

... has become unclean. All who once gave her honor now despise her. In her

nakedness she groans and turns away. Great uncleanness is in her skirts ...

Indeed. Miri felt a cramp in her gut and discretely felt between her legs to make sure the rags Nura had given her were securely bound in place. Her flow was not yet heavy, so she didn't think it would be a problem attending the service, especially in black garments at night.

She remembered arriving back at Nura's house earlier this evening and feeling the first pains of menstruation. It had been a great relief to her – knowing that Ba'asha had not planted his seed in her. She had been carrying this worry since the night of her rape. She was thankful that she would not yet become a mother ... not in this way.

My sins have become a heavy yoke around my neck. My strength fails. YHWH has given ...

Miri's thoughts turned to the previous morning. Yeshua's aunt, Chunya, had come to town because she had been summoned by a lawyer. It was something about collecting on her husband's debt. She had stopped by Nura's house on the way and shared refreshments with Miri and Yeshua. Yeshua told her to go home – that the records had been lost, and that she could stay with her family on the farm for the foreseeable future. Chunya was suspicious. She was wary of trusting her family's future to Yeshua's mischief.

Miri remembered that she had reached out and touched Chunya's wrist in a comforting gesture. "I know you are anxious, but Yeshua speaks the truth. I can assure you that the documents are indeed lost. Perhaps for good."

That was when Chunya had said it: "If you both say this then I will believe it. Sabah will be happy to stay in the house for another season. He's been slowing down these past years. This winter may be his last."

"Sabah?" Miri had asked. "Your husband's father is named Sabah? Did he have another son named ..." Miri had trouble speaking the name out loud. "Te'oma?"

She saw Chunya's eyes brighten at the mention of this name and knew immediately that Te'oma was someone dear to her. "Yes! He

does. Do you know ..." Then Miri's use of the past tense dawned on
Chunya. Her face darkened. "Why do you say '*did* he have'? What do
you know of Te'oma?"

*... virgin daughter of Yudah. I weep for these things. My eyes run with tears.
No comforter is near ...*

The memory brought fresh tears to Miri's eyes. She had the
unhappy task of relating Te'oma's death to Yeshua and Chunya.
They were stunned. Chunya wanted proof. Miri was forced to
describe how she saw the green vest in a discarded pile of garments,
and then (Miri shivered at the memory), on the cross, the corpse,
with Te'oma's distinctive birthmark. After that, Chunya was
inconsolable, weeping and keening freely. Miri was touched by the
depth of the woman's grief. Clearly Te'oma was someone she had
truly cherished.

*... am disturbed. I have been rebellious. In the streets, the sword takes life.
Inside there is death. People have heard me groan ...*

When she recovered from the initial shock, Chunya insisted that
Miri return with her to the village to tell Sabah this tale firsthand.
Miri would spend Shabbat and the next night there. Yeshua would
accompany them to the village and stay at his mother's house. It was
all decided very quickly.

*... women of Yerushalayim have bowed their heads low to the ground. My
eyes are filled with tears. My spirit grieves. My heart is poured out on the earth.
Children faint in the streets, calling to their mothers, "Where is grain and wine?"
Their life is poured out on their mother's breast.*

They walked southward, over the hills to the village. It took little
more than an hour. They arrived at Chunya's house to find Sabah
napping in the mid-afternoon sun. He awoke on their arrival.
Standing, he greeted them warmly. He seemed a kindly man – tall,
thin and wiry. He smiled brightly when Miri was introduced. She was
surprised to see a still-toothy grin in one so old.

Miri knelt before him, her face prostrate.

"What is it child? Get up, sit. Have some refreshment. Why do
you *kneel* before me?"

Miri looked up, her face a mask of pain. Sabah recoiled and

turned to Chunya. "Daughter, what evil omen is this. What dark spirit have you brought into my house?"

At last Miri spoke. "Father. I was a friend to your son, Te'oma."

Sabah was befuddled. "A friend to my son?" He shrugged and feigned indifference. "What is that to me? The boy left here in anger not two weeks ago. Vowed he would never ... Oh, I see what this is. *He* sent you here. Tell the truth! What is it he wants now? More money? Has he planted his seed in you? Is that why you are doing his ..."

Miri had started to weep at Sabah's feet. "No, father. Your son – he is gone to Sheol."

The old man stopped his tirade and stood in silence. At length he collapsed onto the bench heavily. Chunya and Yeshua moved to sit on either side. Slowly he dropped his head into his hands. "No," he said simply.

Miri's voice was barely a whisper. "Te'oma spoke of you often. He said you are a good man. He understood your need to give the land to your oldest son."

"Psha! The farm should have gone to Te'oma!" Sabah said angrily. "I was a fool to entrust it to Tahmid – the lout is good for nothing. Out there sleeping in the fields even now, no doubt with a skin of wine. Chunya – I'm sorry daughter. I know you always loved Te'oma."

Having seen Chunya's reaction in Sepphoris, Miri was not surprised by this revelation. Now Sabah was clearly wracked with guilt. "Sir," Miri said. "You should not punish yourself. I did not know your son long, but he told me that he was happy. He was full of purpose. He said he had found something worthy to dedicate himself to. He had become a follower of Yochanan and ..."

"Bah," the old man scoffed again. "A lunatic wandering naked in the desert teaching others how to get themselves killed."

Miri continued softly. "He was doing what he believed to be important. I do not fully understand it, but he said ..."

Sabah abruptly stood up, his face full of rage. "Look, whoever you are, I don't know why you are here or what you want. You say you were a *friend* to my son. Were you betrothed? No. Then why have you come? There will no brideprice if that's what you seek."

Miri, stung by the rebuke, did not know what to say.

Sabah slowly walked toward the house. All of a sudden he seemed a much older man. Chunya rose to help him, but he shook her off. Instead of entering the house, he left by the gate and walked toward the southwest, into the barley.

... visions of your prophets were false and foolish. They did not show you the truth. You remained captive by your sin. Their prophecies led you astray. All who pass by you extend their fingers and shake their heads in derision ...

Miri wondered, "false and foolish prophets" – is this what Yochanan is? What does he think he is doing, urging his followers, both men and women, to reject the temple and appeal to Hashem directly? And why does he think his vision of the creator is any better than the temple's?

... daughter of Zion, your tears run like a river, day and night. You allow yourself no relief; your eyes do not rest. Awaken! Cry out to the watches of the night. Let your heart flow like water in the presence ...

A vivid memory popped into her head unbidden: the act of killing Ba'asha. The feel of him thrusting inside her, his grunting, the smell of his sweat, his head arched back in pleasure at the act of defiling her, the redness of the blood that flowed from his neck onto her own face, the salty taste of it in her mouth. She shivered and heaved this memory from her brain in the same way she had heaved his sputtering body off of hers on that terrible night. No more. Do not think of these things. Never again.

She directed her mind once again to early on the previous morning, before Chunya had arrived. She had been sharing bread and tea with Yeshua in the courtyard. She had wanted to thank him for his act of bravery in standing up to the Roman soldiers. The boy shirked off the compliment and wanted to talk about the knife – Ba'asha's knife. He had seen it when it fell out of her tunic. He had picked it up and handed it back to her.

He told her of his own experience with that same dagger and how it had led to his own troubles. They shared a laugh when he imitated Ba'asha's bemused face when the rope from the crane had been cut and he saw the precious carving shatter on the hillside.

... blocked my way with hewn stones. He makes my path crooked. Like a bear stalking. Like a lion hiding he drags me from my way ...

Like a bear? Like a lion? Why is YHWH like this? Her thoughts returned to yesterday afternoon. They had let Sabah wander off into the fields. It was obvious that he needed time alone. The three started up the sloping lane toward the house of Yeshua's and Chunya's childhood. Chunya felt the need to retrieve her girls – to hug them close. Miri felt a stab of envy. She had never loved anyone the way Chunya had loved Te'oma.

They walked silently up the stone pathway, worn smooth by generations of foot, animal, and cart traffic. As they approached the house at the end of the lane they saw a boy of about ten in the courtyard. He was tending the fire in a tannur clay oven, probably preparing to bake challah for this evening's shabbat meal.

"That is my brother Shimown," said Yeshua. "And there," pointing to an even younger girl, "is my sister, Keziah. As you can see, playing in dirt runs in my family." The girl was filthy from head to toe. She was talking to a burlap doll in a soft singsong voice as she manipulated the toy's arms.

They entered the house through the front door. Yeshua's mother, Mariamne, had her back to them. She was perched on a stool, bringing down wooden bowls from a high shelf. She had not noticed them enter and now called through the unshuttered window to the courtyard: "Keziah – stop playing now and clean yourself. With water. Then come in – I need you."

She turned around and noticed the three standing in the entryway. "Chunya! What are you doing home so early? I didn't expect you back until tomorrow." She turned and called into the relative darkness of the back room of the house. "Sarah! If the babies are awake bring them out. Their mother is here."

"I'm not a baby!" Cried a squeaky voice. "I'm four!" A naked child ran giggling into the room at a full sprint, a long thin piece of cloth trailing behind her. "Hello, mother!" she called as she ran past

Chunya and out into the courtyard.

Sarah, a pale girl of about twelve, followed close on her heels. "Come back here you little ... oh, Chunya, when did you return?"

"Just now we ..."

"Brother!" Sarah abandoned her chase and gave Yeshua a hug. "I didn't expect to see you again until the wedding."

Mariamne interrupted, "Indeed. What brings you back again? I hope you haven't brought any more laborers. The ones up in the cave eat more than they pick!" She turned to the window and yelled once again, "Keziah – in here, *now.*"

"The baby is just waking. I'll go and get her for you," said Sarah to Chunya. She scurried into the back room. Chunya followed her.

Keziah came in finally, holding hands with Chunya's little girl, who was still naked but now had the gray cloth wrapped around her head like a turban. Keziah had washed her hands, but the rest of her was still filthy. Her bare feet were tracking in clods of mud.

Mariamne made a sigh of disgust. "I just swept. Get back out there and wash those feet – and your face too. Your father will be back soon with Ya'aqob. You don't want them to see you like that."

Miri had been watching this chaotic scene unfold with amusement. Mariamne had been blessed with a large vibrant family. She obviously had her hands full.

Mariamne faced Yeshua. "And who is this?" She said, nodding toward Miri. "We can't afford more help right now."

"Oh! I'm sorry mother. This is Miri. She is Nura's cousin. Don't worry she is not here to look for work."

Mariamne looked relieved. She wiped her hands on a cloth and took Miri's right hand in both of hers. "I'm sorry dear – as you can see, we are up to our necks in nonsense at the moment."

Keziah returned, her appearance much improved. She was a lively girl with dark eyes. She stopped in front of Miri. "Who is this, mother? She's pretty. Is she going to live with us now?"

Mariamne ignored the question. "Please take that broth back to Yehudah. He's awake now and he's hungry."

Yeshua asked his mother, "How is he today?"

Mariamne looked at her eldest son and frowned, worry lines creasing her forehead. "Today he's better. The fever seems to come every other day. But I don't know. He is getting so weak. I fear that Alilah will be calling him soon."

"Who? What is wrong with him?" Asked Miri.

Yeshua answered: "My brother, Yehudah. He's eight years old. He has hill fever."

"Oh. I am sorry." It was called marsh fever where Miri came from. It was usually very serious. "Does Nura have any remedies for ..."

Yeshua shook his head. "Just rest. Cold rags when the fever gets bad. He will recover if Alilah wills it." Yeshua then took Mariamne's hand. "Mother, Miri knew Sabah's son Te'oma. I'm afraid she has some bad news."

And so Miri told the story of Te'oma's demise to Mariamne as simply as she could, sparing the details. Mariamne was a strong woman and no stranger to tragedy. She sat down on the chair by the door. A look of pain crossed her face briefly and then was replaced with resolve. She stood again and took Miri in her arms, rocking her gently back and forth.

Miri had not expected this. At first she stiffened, but then accepted the older woman's embrace. Mariamne whispered in her ear, "Hush, dear. I know. I know what it is to lose your love at such a tender age."

Miri started to object. "No you misunderstand, I ..."

"Hush." Mariamne repeated and continued the embrace.

This triggered something in Miri. She found that she could no longer hold back her tears. She held Mariamne tightly, sobbing freely into her shoulder.

... and gave me gall to drink. My teeth are broken with gravel and I am trampled in the dust, deprived of all peace. I have forgotten what it is to be prosperous. So I proclaim ...

Miri grieved for so many things. Besides the loss of her friend, Te'oma, she had lost her innocence, and any chance of marriage and children of her own. Her mother and brother had been taken from her, not to mention the rejection of her father.

It had felt good to finally let go. Yeshua is lucky to have such a mother. The pain of loss was still fresh and raw in Miri's mind, but she felt now that she would be able to move on. Alilah would have more things in store for her. She silently gave thanks for her newly found friends.

... there may be hope. Let him offer his cheek to one who would strike him, filling his enemy with disgrace. No one is cast off from YHWH forever. As he brings ...

The words 'offer his cheek' stuck in her mind. That is what Te'oma did, no doubt. He wouldn't have tried to defend himself even if he had a weapon. She wondered if the soldiers who crucified him were 'filled with disgrace.' From what she had seen of Romans, she doubted it.

And then Yeshua had done the same thing three days ago. They struck him down once, so he got up and offered his other cheek. Yeshua had more luck than Te'oma. It was obvious what would have happened had not the officer come by.

... abundant compassion, his love is unceasing. he does not bring affliction willingly, or grief to the son of man ...

After visiting with Mariamne and her family, Miri and Chunya took the two babies back down the hill to await Sabah and Tahmid. The men had still not arrived at dusk when Mariamne sent Sarah down with fresh bread and stew. Thus they shared a simple Shabbat meal with the children.

Tahmid finally stumbled home about an hour after dark. He grunted a few times and then retired to his bed without eating. After the babies were put to bed, Miri sat up with Chunya drinking a cup of wine. The two women talked as they waited for old Sabah.

They shared stories about Te'oma. Miri told of the time they met in Magdala, and how they had planned to go south to join Yochanan. Chunya openly said that she had always loved Te'oma and wanted to marry him, but that circumstances would never allow it. Miri asked Chunya to tell her stories of Te'oma's childhood.

After a moment's thought, Chunya asked: "Did he ever tell you about his coming-of-age celebration?"

Miri smiled. "No. Tell me."

Chunya collected her memories and began. "It was a couple of weeks before Te'oma's thirteenth birthday. Let's see, I would have been eleven at the time. Yeshua was about six or seven, and was always hanging around the two of us. He would never leave us alone." She winked.

"Like this year, the harvest had been plenty, and Sabah wanted to show off his wealth. He went into town to talk to Natan for ideas. Natan convinced him to host a celebration, and to really impress, he should send out written invitations. Natan had his own scribe make them up, each on its own small piece of papyrus. He also had the scribe make up a suggested guest list – all the right people in town – potential patrons, men in a position to help Sabah. Sabah thought this was very crafty.

"Now Sabah never learned to read, but he was very proud of the invitations. He had Te'oma recite them to everyone who came by. I think there were about thirty of them. He packed them in a satchel. He gave them to Te'oma with the list and told him to go into town and deliver them. Of course Yeshua went with him.

"I had to stay home, but Te'oma told me afterward that they stopped to play a game with some other boys just outside the town. It started pouring rain, so they grabbed the satchel and ran for shelter. Now, the satchel was good quality and it kept the invitations dry, but Te'oma had the list stuffed inside his tunic. It was soaked and all the writing had run.

"So they had a dilemma. They had no idea where to make the deliveries. I think they were afraid of Sabah's anger if they were just to return. The old man has always had a fiery temper. So ... Te'oma told me that this was Yeshua's idea. It sounds like it. Watch out for that one, Miri. Even at that young age he had a crazy streak. They went to the decumanus outside the market and just handed out the invitations to anyone who happened by. Then they came home and never said a word."

Miri's jaw dropped. "But ... did anyone actually show up to the party? Sabah must have been furious."

Chunya laughed. "I thought the same thing when Te'oma told me what they had done. But two weeks later, on the appointed date, guests did indeed arrive. The house was full and Sabah was embarrassed when the wine ran out. My brother Yoceph had to go and fetch some of his own."

Seeing Miri's questioning look, Chunya continued. "Who, you are wondering, showed up? Well, each group arrived with one of the fine invitations, so Sabah had to accept them into his home. The first was a merchant whom Sabah had never met. He arrived with his wife and son and thanked Sabah profusely for the unexpected invitation. Then came a group of servants from Herod's palace – just common stablemen and their families. I remember that they wore filthy boots and took them off by the door when they entered. An elderly Rabbi showed up. Oh, and then ..." Chunya suppressed a laugh, "three prostitutes from the tavern arrived in colorful dresses and jewelry. They even brought some musicians with them.

"The room became silent when the gabbai arrived. Everyone knew the tax collector, and usually tried to stay well clear of him. Now here he was at a party where they were trying to enjoy themselves. Sabah thought he was here to levy some new tax on celebrations until he produced one of the invitations.

"Poor Sabah was growing more and more flabbergasted. These were not the people he had hoped to entertain!

"A shepherd from a town to the west showed up with his four sons. He had happened to be in town for the market on the day the invitations were handed out." Chunya pursed her lips in concentration. "Hmm. There were others too. There was a group of servants who worked in the grain mill in town. They had to get permission from their master. Oh, and the last to arrive, you won't believe. A Roman administrator with his young wife and daughter, all in fine white togas. I think he assumed from the rich invitation that this was some kind of official gathering."

"Such an odd group of people," Miri wondered aloud. "They had nothing in common. It must have been uncomfortable."

Chunya continued. "Te'oma, Yeshua and I watched the gathering, hoping that fights would not break out. It *was* uncomfortable for a while. But then the musicians started playing and the wine started flowing. I think even the gabbai had a good time. Everyone did, oh, except for the rabbi. He only stayed a short time, then he made an excuse and left."

... deprive the son of man of justice, before the holy one, to defraud a man in a lawsuit. YHWH sees these things. Who can speak and have it happen ...

Miri had been smiling as she remembered the story. But then she winced as a cramp tightened her gut. She had felt the start of the familiar monthly churning earlier this evening, just before the end of Shabbat at sundown. She had planned to stay another night with Chunya in the village, but she felt the need to be alone – to come to terms with the strong emotions laying siege to her mind. She insisted on returning to the city right away. Yeshua insisted on escorting her. They walked the distance in silence and parted ways when they reached Nura's house.

... of Zion, weighed against fine gold, are now but clay in the potter's hands. Even jackals offer the breast to nurse their young ...

Weighed against fine gold ... Miri could feel the weight of Ba'asha's dagger, fixed to the loop inside her tunic. She pictured the dagger in her mind, with its bejeweled ivory handle. The image brought many thoughts: I have carried this implement of violence since my defilement. Only a week and a day have passed, though it seems longer. Bustan urged me to get rid of it. Perhaps he is right. This thing would do me little good if I ever tried to use it. It would only worsen any trouble I found myself in, and if the wrong person were to see it ... that would just bring more trouble and not just to me. Nura also might be implicated. I came to this service hoping to clear my thoughts – to find peace. The dagger has become a symbol of my injury, my rage. I will cast it away – tonight.

... been given to strangers. Foreigners live in our houses. We are orphans, without a father. Our mothers are widows. We must pay for our water and our wood. Our pursuers are at our backs ...

Miri prayed fervently to YHWH or Usat. She was confused, not knowing to whom to pray, or if it mattered. She prayed for deliverance from her troubles. She prayed to know the reason why Te'oma had to die. Will there be redemption for Te'oma? He always spoke of a new life – of the return of the ancient kingdom. But after reading the sad scroll of Michal, Miri suspected that the return of *any* kingdom would be just as bad as the Romans.

The voice of the reader was rising in a closing cadence:

... do you forsake us for so long? Bring us back to your bosom that we may come home. Renew us, as in days of old, unless you have rejected us utterly and are angry beyond knowing.

$$\sim$$

The service ended with a prolonged period of silence. Finally, the men in attendance stood up and walked to the doors. They left, again in order of their prominence. The women standing against the back wall were the last to leave.

The stars were brilliant in the crisp autumn air. She walked toward the street and saw a group of people warming their hands on a bonfire outside the synagogue. The earthy smell of the burning logs and dung cakes filled her nostrils. A silhouetted figure detached itself from the group and walked toward her.

When he was quite near, she recognized the familiar face of Yeshua. He must have been standing out here this entire time. She admitted to herself that she was once again glad to have his company for the walk home. They started down the road together without exchanging a word. After a while she slipped her hand into his. They walked on silently.

She felt the weight of something knocking against her side – the dagger inside her tunic. They had just gone over a narrow bridge crossing a stream. She untied the dagger and showed it to Yeshua. She stood back and threw it as far as she could. They heard a faint splash as it hit the water many yards downstream.

She once again took Yeshua's hand and they continued their walk. "Ba'asha defiled me. He took my virginity," she said. When Yeshua made no reply she added. "I killed him."

"I know," said Yeshua simply.

After a moment, Miri asked, "do you forgive me?"

Yeshua seemed puzzled by the question. "Do *I* forgive you? You have done me no ill."

"I know," she said. "I have been thinking about something a woman said to me. She worshipped the goddess Usat. She prayed sincerely that her own hands would do the work of the goddess. I think that we must seek to do Hashem's work. So if I am to be forgiven, I suppose you will have to do it, since you are the only one I have told."

Yeshua smiled as he thought about this for a moment. He stopped, took Miri's two hands, and said solemnly, "I forgive you."

Miri couldn't say why exactly, but this filled her with a sense of comfort.

Nura's house was dark when they arrived, everyone having long since retired for the night. Before ascending the ladder to her chamber, on an impulse Miri reached behind Yeshua's neck. She drew him close and kissed him on the mouth. She lingered several seconds and then turned and scampered up the ladder, leaving Yeshua surprised and enticed.

Proverbs

*The day after the Lamentations service, Yom Rishon
the 14th day of Elul, early afternoon*

"Mine is a trireme with thirty rowers and a broad sail," boasted Tal.

"Then *mine* is a quinquireme with *seventy* rowers, a broad sail, *and* an iron ram," countered Bart.

Ichabod bar Shalmai stood at the edge of the stream and barked his command, "Captains! Take your places for the race! The winner shall battle my *undefeated* pentakontor!"

Ichabod, at twelve, was the oldest and largest of the three, and thus tended to be the organizer of the trio's activities. He was unnaturally thin and average height, with an unkempt mop of reddish hair. That, and his abundant freckles belied his half-Gallic heritage. His mother had been brought here from the north country as a slave when she was very young. She was purchased by a local merchant who fathered three children with her before granting her freedom and making her his third wife.

The boys had carved model ships from discarded wood scraps and decorated them with homemade dyes and small human figures formed from red clay. The rules of the game were simple: You had to lie flat on your stomach on the footbridge. From there you lowered your boat to the water, which, with all the rain of late, was only an arm's length below the bridge. The boats were taken by the current, and the one that traveled the farthest before either running aground or being caught up in the reeds was the winner.

Thus despite the one-upsmanship, the larger boat had the disadvantage.

Tal was very proud of his vessel. He was the youngest of the three. He was short, even for a seven year old, with straight black hair and dark skin. His tunic was cut too long so that when he was engaged in any outdoor activity the bottom hem tended to get stained with dark mud. His *trireme* was a model of simplicity and efficiency. It was essentially a long flat triangle of wood with a short rudder fixed to the stern. Using clay as a fixative, he had indeed attached fifteen 'oars' to both sides made of thin reeds, thus the claim of thirty rowers.

Bart was Tal's older brother and shared his skin and hair color. He was eleven, and in many ways the most mature of the three. He was starting to have the hint of whiskers on his chin and the sides of his cheeks. Of this he was abundantly proud. Girls were always telling him how fair he was.

Bart had attempted to make his boat larger and more elaborate than his brother's. But whereas Tal's was elegant, Bart's was haphazard and overdone. It had not fared well in the races thus far. So, before this race, he made some adjustments. He shortened the rudder and scraped off many of the rowers, which being made of heavy clay, tended to make the boat ride too low in the water.

They were about to start the race when the rabbi came walking along the road toward the synagogue just up the slope. Fearing a scolding, they cleared the bridge and stood to one side until he was gone.

"Once again captains – take your places." Ichabod resumed the ceremonies.

Tal lay on the right side of the bridge where the current was swifter. Bart lay just to his left. Tal's arms couldn't quite reach the surface of the water so he held his boat suspended several inches above the stream.

"Commence!" Shouted Ichabod.

Tal dropped his boat and Bart let his go, cheating only a little bit by giving it a slight shove downstream.

The boats were off! The thee boys got up and ran down the side of the stream, following the boats as they were taken by the swift current. Tal's boat ran straight and true. Bart's ran into some trouble right away as his shove had pushed it a bit too far to the side, into a patch of tall grass. But since it was still moving downstream in loping circles, the race was still on. Finally, the boat cleared the grass and continued on course into the center of the stream, although now it was sailing backwards.

Tal's boat was traveling a bit *too* fast. It smashed into a rock in a short section of rapids, and several of the oarsmen fell off. Finally it was washed to the starboard and continued downstream sideways.

"It's allowed as long as you still have *some* oarsmen," ruled Ichabod, playing the part of referee.

By this time, Bart's quinquireme had righted itself and sailed quickly past Tal's damaged vessel, which was now listing heavily to the port. After another short distance Tal's boat attempted to go over a waterfall between two large rocks and got wedged tight. It looked like the race belonged to Bart.

Ichabod and Tal waded out into the stream to recover the damaged ship while Bart continued to follow his. He wanted to see if he could beat Ichabod's distance record. "Go, go go!" He chanted.

The boat actually managed to navigate the bend in the stream and then some. He was now the undisputed champion! After the bend, the boat meandered into the shallows on the left side of the stream. There it abruptly stopped in the water, quivering – held tight by some unseen obstruction.

Bart waded across to the immobilized boat. Before picking it up he passed his hand below the ship to see what had impeded it. "Ow!" He drew his hand out of the water to see a clean cut in his palm start to bleed.

He picked up the boat and looked down into the clear water. There was something white and shiny just below the surface. He had cut himself on a blade that was sticking up. Using his left hand this time, he reached down and carefully pulled it out by the hilt.

It was a beautiful knife – very fine, very rich.

"What do you have?" Called Ichabod, as he and Tal sidled up to him to see the discovery.

"Whoa! You know what that is?" Ichabod asked rhetorically. "*That*," he said with awe "is ivory. It's made from an elephant's tusk."

Tal was incredulous. "An *elephant*! But those aren't real."

His brother corrected him. "Yes, they are Tal. I know a girl who saw one in Egypt. She said it was as big as a house!"

"Look at the jewels," said Tal. "I've never seen red and green jewels like that. Do all elephants have jewels in their tusks?"

Ichabod scratched his freckled cheek. "Who would throw such a thing away? It must be very valuable."

"We're rich!" exclaimed Bart, doing a little dance.

The three retreated to the side of the stream and sat in the tall grass to examine the discovery at length. It was beautifully made. The ivory handle had three jewels in it on each side: two red and one green. The blade was curved and very sharp without a spot of rust. It couldn't have been in the water very long. It must have been deliberately thrown away because if it had been dropped from the road it would have just sunk to the bottom beneath the bridge.

After much discussion they decided on a course of action. Ichabod's father had a booth in the market where he sold all kinds of trinkets. They would show it to him and see what price he thought he could get. Market day was the day after tomorrow, and this week it was supposed to be particularly crowded because of the visiting preacher. People with serious money would come to see the famous Hanina ben Dosa.

Bart agreed that they would split whatever money resulted. Ichabod was sure that his father would want to take a large cut. But with luck maybe the three would soon have some coin in their pockets!

~

Sweat drips from my face. I remember this time vividly. I am six. My mother sat with me half the summer until the white worm fully emerged from the blister on my heel.

"Calm child, it will soon be passed." My mother strokes my wet hair. She sets a basin of cool water next to my legs, lifts my foot and soaks the blister. A moment of intense stinging. Then ... nothing – blessed numbness.

"Easy, easy." It is no longer my mother, but the Seer, her oily gray hair wild, her eyes clouded with cataracts. She places a hand on my heart. "You have a female soul, child."

"A female soul," I repeat.

"We are empty vessels. We nurture that which is given. The female soul follows the Goddess. Sacred bearers, we protect the seed. Life. Seek. When you find, then you will be troubled. Then astonished."

Te'oma is here now, lying on another litter. Sightless bird-pecked eyes. Birthmark visible below shaggy locks. The old crone places her hand on Te'oma's chest. She whispers: "The male soul follows Jayvewuh, the war god. Blood. Honor. He creates the seed but cares not where it is sown."

Te'oma stands and removes his tunic. He is beautiful – hairless muscular chest, powerful thighs, circumcised sex protruding. He wants to speak but does not. Shaking his head from side to side, he walks out through the open door.

Miri felt a cool breeze on her cheek. She opened her eyes. This dream seemed to have a message. She went over the words in her mind so as to commit them to memory. She considered whether she should go to the seer to ask her what it meant, though it would surely cost her more coin, and she didn't have much left.

In her unclean state, she had stayed in this room all of the previous day. Now, seeing that her flow had subsided considerably, she decided to venture out.

She descended the ladder and entered the front room just as Mattanyah walked in from the street. He carried a pitcher of fresh goat's milk, which he set on the table. He started when he saw her standing in the shadows. "Ah! There you are. Up and about today I see. Good. Sit. Eat."

Miri sat down at the table. Mattanyah broke several crusts from yesterday's bread into a bowl, sprinkled in almonds and raisins, and covered the mixture with the milk. Finally he opened a jar, and drizzled honey on the top. He slid the bowl across the table to where Miri sat, and handed her a wooden spoon. "Give it a moment to get soft."

"Thank you, sir." She prodded the mixture with the spoon.

"You were out very late the night before last. We were becoming worried. I hope you do not mind that we asked Yeshua to follow and watch after you. But I think he had planned to do that anyway."

Miri took a bite of the porridge and wiped her mouth with the back of her hand. "I met him at the synagogue and we came back together. Where is he now?"

"You won't believe it. He actually found work this morning."

"Really! A miracle. How did you manage it?"

Mattanyah chuckled. "It wasn't me. There's a new pig herder at the Roman encampment. They have hundreds of pigs. Can you imagine! Since he is new in town he knows nothing of Yeshua's ... reputation. It will be interesting to see how this turns out."

"Pigs." Miri said between spoonfuls. "I guess there's no sin in minding an unclean animal."

"No, no sin. Not that it would matter much to Yeshua anyway. You have noticed that he tends to make his own rules."

Mattanyah set the lid over the pitcher containing the remaining milk. "Could you set this down in the storage cave when you are finished? Basmat says she will be making yogurt this afternoon. I have to be off to my workshop."

~

Miri spent the morning reading her scroll. The next passage continued the story of Michal's life with David.

I will make it plain how wicked David is. This happened when my father was still alive. It was battle season. Saul was away in the northern lands.

Now there is a town called Gibeon not far from my

father's house. David stole into the town with a hundred men in the middle of the night. They slaughtered everyone they could find. Only a few managed to flee with their lives. Then he spread the falsehood that my father's men had committed the attack. The men who survived never forgave my father.

But that is not the end of the story! Only last year, the people of Gibeon came to David. They claimed that the descendents of King Saul still owed them a blood debt. David was delighted to have an excuse to hand over the remaining descendants of Saul. David was afraid that the house of Saul would one day regroup and challenge him.

I have told you before of Rizpah, my father's only concubine. When the men of Gibeon demanded blood, David handed over Rizpah's two sons. They were dismembered and their remains strewn on the hill outside the palace. Thus Rizpah's sons paid the price for David's wickedness.

Rizpah mourned for her sons from springtime until harvest. It made David furious to hear her keening every day outside his dwelling. Soon other women joined Rizpah. I admit I did not have the courage. Eventually the mighty David was shamed into giving the bones a proper burial. These women did what the Philistine army could not.

Miri was impressed with Rizpah's courage. What was it that Yeshua had said the evening when she first met him? We must oppose the rotten kingdom. Apparently it was as rotten in the time of David as it was now. Poor Rizpah found a way to oppose it – perhaps the only way. And she had won – at least in a small way.

Miri read on. She was near the end of the scroll.

Now I will tell you the true story of David's son, Absalom. Do not believe the chronicles! I will make plain his lineage: My father, King Saul, begat Naomi by his only concubine, Rizpah. I have already told you this! Naomi begat a daughter, Maacah. Maacah was married to David, and they begat a son, Absalom. So Absalom was David's son, but he was also Saul's great grandson.

Absalom was enraged by the treatment given to Rizpah and her sons. He also feared for his own life. He knew that he was a descendant of King Saul. But he did not need to fear. David was unaware of Absalom's lineage. I have kept it secret!

Much has been written about how Absalom almost managed to take the throne of Israel away from David. Absalom was cut from the same cloth as his father. He was stubborn and arrogant. Neither man could admit to a fault or forgive one in another.

I was already an elderly woman when David fled Yerushalayim to escape from Absalom. David took me with him to watch over his young sons. He did not want to leave them behind for fear that Absalom would kill them. This was prudent. I believe Absalom would have done so.

We fled north and then west. We crossed the Jordan and marched into the hills. David laid a trap. We marched up a steep forested valley, leaving clear tracks. He told his archers to line the ridges on either side of the valley. When Absalom's men pursued us, burning arrows fell on them by the thousands. There had been a drought and the wood was dry. It burned quickly. The forest claimed more victims than the sword. Absalom was killed.

That was many years ago. No one has challenged David since then. But now he is becoming weak and careless. Adoniyah is the oldest of his sons. He will succeed David soon. Adoniyah is strong but not clever. He will not last long on the throne.

I pray to YHWH that someday a worthy man, such as was my father, will once again rule the tribes of Israel. I do not believe that such a man will spring from the line of David.

Soon I will also go the way of my ancestors. I have come to the end of this scroll. My faithful servant has promised to hide this testament in a jar and bury it beneath the palace. I pray that someday when David and his clan are but a distant memory, this scroll will be recovered and the truth may be finally known.

Miri sat in thought. Even though it ran counter to what she had always been taught, she believed this woman from so long ago. She felt an obligation to try to pass on this knowledge, but she did not know how. She suspected that the rabbis were unaware of this scroll. Or perhaps when they gave it to Mattanyah, they intended that it be destroyed with no remaining copies.

She wondered when it had been unearthed and how it had found its way to the old synagogue. This couldn't possibly be the original, could it? It must have been copied at some point. Perhaps the best thing Miri could do would be to bury it again. Or perhaps she should make a copy and bury that. Then, if this document was destroyed, the knowledge might live on.

And why is this important? What would be wrong with letting people continue to believe the stories about brave King David and wise old Solomon?

The only answer she could think of was that truth is important. It's better to have a hard truth than a pleasant lie. The sad plight of Michal gave Miri perspective on her own situation. Perhaps things weren't so bad.

~

Two days later, the morning after Yom Shlishi

Market day arrived. On this day, the famous holy man, Hanina ben Dosa, was to speak across from the square. Everyone had been talking about it with anticipation.

Yeshua had spent the last two nights tending the Roman pigs, returning home shortly after daybreak. This morning his plan was to go directly to the square. Miri set out early, hoping to meet up with him.

The streets near Nura's house were practically deserted. She enjoyed the crisp fall air. It was a good day for an outdoor event. It was warm enough, yet the sky was clouded over, which would save people from the harsh midday sunshine. The crowds increased as she strode through the town. By the time she was within a block of the square she could barely move through the throng. She thought she heard a voice calling her name. She looked all around but could not see anyone she knew.

"No – up! Up here!"

She scanned the rooftops and saw Yedu and Yeshua leaning over the edge of the potter's shop that overlooked the fountain square. Many pairs of legs dangled over the edge of the wall. She called back: "Is there room for me up there?"

"Yes, but hurry. Around to the back, then through the alley. You'll see a ladder."

Miri followed the instructions. She had to wait her turn to ascend onto the already-congested roof. More people were arriving constantly. She silently prayed that the structure would support the weight. She squeezed her way through to where Yedu and Yeshua sat. They had saved a spot between them on the very edge of the building.

She had not spoken to Yeshua since he had walked her home after the Lamentations service three nights ago. She felt embarrassed. She had been so vulnerable that evening, so overwrought. And also, because of the kiss. She wondered if Yeshua felt the same, because he seemed to be avoiding eye contact.

From where they sat, they had a perfect view of the square. A fancy stage had been erected in front of the fountain, which had been shut off for the event. She judged the stage to be thirty feet long and some twenty feet wide. It was shoulder-high with a flowing white curtain completely surrounding it.

Smoke momentarily got in her eyes and she fanned it away. Two large iron kettles containing smoldering fires sat on either side at the back of the stage. The smoke from the wood gave off an acrid, spicy smell – like incense. In the middle of the stage stood a table holding a huge wooden bowl. From their high vantage, they could see that the inside was completely inscribed with circular writing.

Yedu tapped Miri on the shoulder. "Settle this for us. Yeshua says that Hanina has people planted in the crowd, and he is trying to spot them. He thinks the miracles are not real. What do you think?"

Before she could answer, Yeshua leaned close and pointed. "Look. That woman there – front row – a little left of the center, the one with the striped shawl over her head?"

"What about her?"

"I've never seen her before. Now look three rows back and to the right a few seats. The boy – younger than Yedu – curly hair, swinging his feet back and forth."

Miri looked where he was pointing. "Yes. What about *him*?"

"The woman and the boy arrived together – quite early. Why did they choose to sit apart? Every now and then she glances back to him. There – just now she did it again."

Miri didn't understand what he was getting at. "A woman and a boy – so what?"

Yedu answered: "Yeshua thinks that Hanina is paying them – that they're going to take part in some trick."

"Ah, I see," said Miri. "Is *that* what you think?"

Yeshua nodded. "Wait and see. Maybe Hanina will guess something about her past – that her husband died two years ago and she has three sons and her ox died last night. Or maybe she'll just fall backwards in a swoon when he makes some gesture. The boy too – they're both part of the show."

Yedu argued, "But, how do you ..."

"And see the man two seats to her left – gray beard, dark gray vest, walking stick?"

"Yes ..."

"He also arrived early, carrying the stick over his shoulder. I'll wager that he will come forward, barely able to walk, and Hanina will cure him – a great sign from above."

"Yeshua talks to his cynic too much," said Yedu dryly. "I don't know why he even came."

"Ah, gullible cousin, I have a good reason for coming. Hanina is a master at illusions. I want to learn his tricks."

Miri pointed toward the back of the crowd. "Look! There are your brothers. It doesn't look like they have a very good spot."

Yedu said, "They arrived in the city early this morning. They stopped at my father's house before coming to the square. Ya'aqob kept trying to get everyone to hurry. He wants to bring Yehudah to Hanina. He wants Hanina to cure him."

Miri recognized Ya'aqob and Shimown pushing the crippled boy in a cart. They were behind the last row of benches, trying to maneuver forward into one of the aisles, but no one was giving way.

Yeshua shook his head. "It will be hard to get the great Hanina's attention from back there."

"Quiet! It's starting," hissed Yedu.

Miri heard them before she could see them – a trumpet blast, then drums, cymbals, high-pitched flutes, and some kind of plucked stringed instruments. A parade issued forth from the double doors on the side of the basilica opposite the park from where they sat.

First came the musicians. Many boys marched in rows four across – drums, cymbals, lyres, flutes, whistles, and other instruments Miri had never seen. Following them were two muscular guards walking single file. They wore leather skirts with curved swords at their belts. Their chests were bare except for a complicated lattice of leather straps that went up and around their shoulders. Each guard wore an Egyptian headdress with a golden cobra protruding from the crown.

A tall man in a full-length red robe followed the guards. His head was shaved and his face was devoid of hair. Perhaps he shaved as the Romans do, or more likely he was a eunuch.

Finally came Hanina himself. His full-length robe was as bright as the sun. His head was covered with a simple white skullcap. His curly brown hair flowed majestically over his shoulders. His long beard contained just a hint of gray, and his sideburns descended into curly locks that ended halfway down his chest. His head was uplifted in an angelic expression, his full lips stretched and parted in an inviting smile, his eyes half closed. He turned from side to side as he walked, hands outstretched, acknowledging people in the audience with a nod.

"He looks like he's been smoking poppies," said Yeshua.

Miri elbowed him in the side. "Just watch."

The parade made its way up the steps to the stage platform. The musicians continued to the other side and descended steps back onto the paving stones, taking their place on reserved benches at the front. The two guards took their places at the rear of the stage, standing next to the fire kettles. Hanina stepped forward with his beatific smile, his arms outstretched, palms facing the audience.

At length the boys stopped playing their instruments. Hanina stood motionless in his odd pose, allowing the tension to build for several moments. At last he began to speak.

~

"YIR-rah, YIR-rah," Hanina chanted slowly. The first syllable was strongly accented and high in pitch, the second almost a sigh. "Say it with me, my children. YIR-rah, YIR-rah ..." He repeated the phrase many times. It was gradually taken up by the crowd. After several minutes he raised his hands and stepped to the edge of the stage. All became silent.

"Hashem has heard you, my children. YIR-rah is the old word for fear — fear of the creator, the one who is. YIR-rah is the beginning of wisdom — of knowledge more valuable than silver or gold. YIR-rah will lengthen your life.

"I will give you another old word: SAY-mem, SAY-mem, ..." Again the mantra was taken up until it filled the space. Hanina raised his hands for silence. "You have spoken wisely. SAY-mem is to be astonished — to be in awe at the creator, the one who is.

"Close your eyes, my children. Imagine what it is to feel fear and astonishment together — YIR-rah and SAY-mem." He let them imagine for a moment. Then he went on at length, describing the myriad benefits his teaching would provide: happiness, long life, and treasures. He spoke with a perpetual smile. He looked from side to side, making eye contact with many in the crowd. His voice was strong, clear and inviting. Miri felt herself drawn in.

"My beloved, Listen! There are four creatures very small yet very wise on the earth: the ant, the coney, locusts, and the lizard. The ant is small and powerless, yet he stores up an abundance of food in the summer. The coney is a rat with no way to defend himself, yet he makes his home in the crags and hollows of a cliff face, exposed to the wind. Locusts have neither king nor commanders, but they advance in formation that would make the Roman army envious. The lizard is weak – small enough to fit in the palm of your hand. Yet he lives without fear in the palaces of kings.

"Fear and astonishment – the beginnings of wisdom. Are you afraid?" The crowd murmured. "I asked ARE YOU AFRAID?"

A stronger reply came as many yelled, "Yes!"

"ARE YOU ASTONISHED?"

The crowd replied without hesitation, "YES!"

Immediately the iron kettles erupted in spouts of flame. Many yelled in fear and attempted to back away from the stage, but the crowd was too thick.

"Did you see that?" Yeshua nudged Miri. "The guards – at the back of the stage."

"What about them?"

"They threw something into the fires. Let's watch more carefully."

Miri was puzzled "But what would make the fire do that?"

"I have heard of something called naphtha," answered Yeshua. "Romans use it for siege."

Miri noticed that Hanina was in constant motion as he talked, walking from one side of the platform to the other – his broad smile always present as he met the gaze of those in the throng. His arms were animated. When he spoke of Hashem, they would raise high, palms facing the sky.

"Quiet my children. Hashem is here. He does these little miracles as a sign to you that I am speaking truth – nothing more.

"YIR-rah, SAY-mem ... wisdom. But why, my beloved? Why do you want wisdom? It is something that the ant, the coney, the locust, and the lizard do *not* have. Yet they lack nothing they need. Why do you seek my wisdom? WHY ARE YOU HERE?"

People in the crowd looked at each other in confusion, unsure if the question was rhetorical or if they were supposed to attempt an answer. At length, the little boy whom Yeshua had pointed out previously yelled out: "We are not animals! We are Hashem's chosen people!" Several in the audience laughed.

"Do not laugh, my children. The young one is right!" Hanina closed his eyes and held his palm toward the boy who had spoken, rapidly intoned a blessing. Miri could not hear the words through the crowd noise.

Hanina raised his hand for silence and said to the eunuch, "Livianus, bring forth the child!" The man in the red robe descended from the stage and went into the crowd. The boy shrank from him as he drew near. Hanina called from the stage, "Do not fear my young servant. Hashem offers you a precious gift. Come."

Slowly the boy got to his feet and took the eunuch's hand. Miri saw him steal another nervous glance toward the woman in the front row, who nodded reassuringly. They made their way to the aisle and then to the front. The boy's left arm was curled tightly against his chest. His hand was stiff and fingers contorted.

Hanina watched with an affectionate smile as the two approached. "What do we have, Livianus?"

The eunuch pronounced, "A boy, master. His hand is withered."

Hanina dropped to one knee and gazed into the boy's face. "Boy, where are your parents?"

"They are gone to Sheol, wise master. I am but a poor orphan, all alone in the world." The boy's voice was loud and clear. Miri thought he sounded like he was reciting lines he had memorized.

"An orphan!" Repeated Hanina. "And why are you here, young orphan?"

The boy started to cry, which had an immediate effect on the audience. Hanina continued in a softer voice. "Do not be afraid my child. You have spoken well today. Hashem will reward you. Now tell me: why are you here?"

The boy looked up. "It is for my arm, wise master." He attempted to raise his stiff, malformed limb. "I had the withering disease, sir, when I was but four years old."

Hanina rose to his full height and put his hand on the boy's head. "Help me my people. Close your eyes. Pray for the orphan. Selfless prayers are beautiful to Hashem."

Everyone in the audience did as the preacher asked. At length he said, "Open your eyes now, my children. Hashem revealed to me that your prayer is worthy. Now, young orphan, GIVE ME YOUR WITHERED HAND!" The command startled the boy, who took a step back. Then he slowly outstretched his left arm. The hand and fingers gradually uncurled until they looked completely normal. Hanina picked the boy up by the waist and lifted him high, parading him from one side of the stage to the other. "SAY-mem, my friends! Are you astonished?"

The crowd cheered loud and long as the boy danced back to his seat. The drummers and cymbal players beat their instruments.

Hanina motioned the crowd to silence. "Who else here has an affliction and is in need of Hashem's healing power?"

Several in the crowed yelled out. The Eunuch came off the stage again and approached one, seemingly at random. They spoke for a moment with their heads bowed. Yeshua glanced at Yedu with a knowing smile. It was the man with the walking stick he had pointed out before the show.

"What do we have, Livianus?" Shouted Hanina.

The eunuch answered. "This man, Hanina, has a useless leg. It was run over by an ox cart when he was but six years old! He has hobbled ten miles to be here."

"Come forward! Help him, Livianus, help him. He has already walked ten miles." Several laughed in the audience as the lame man put his arm over the eunuch's shoulder and they slowly made their way to the stage. They came before Hanina. "Can you kneel, my son?"

"I cannot, wise master. My leg will not bend. It has been thus since I was but a boy." Again Miri had the impression that the cadence of the reply was stiff and unnatural. It sounded rehearsed.

Hanina turned toward the audience. "Once again my sons and daughters I ask for your help. Turn your eyes toward heaven. The sun is behind those clouds. We know the sun is there but sometimes we cannot see it. We know Hashem is there but sometimes we cannot hear him. Clear your minds, my people. Chant with me, SAY-mem, SAY-mem."

The crowed picked up the chant for several minutes, urged on by Hanina. "Keep going my beloved. See through the clouds. I feel the presence of Hashem. SAY-mem, SAY-mem. He comes, my children, he comes."

Yeshua nudged Miri and pointed toward the guards. She looked down just as they both subtly tossed something white into the bowls. The flames shot up at the same moment the drummers beat a sudden shot, instantly breaking the trance of the audience. Again several cried out.

"My son!" Hanina spoke in a strong voice. He placed his hands over the head of the old man. "Hashem demands that you WALK." The man fell backwards into the arms of the eunuch, who gently lowered him to the floor of the stage.

After a moment's hesitation the old man sat up as if waking from a nap. He arose gingerly, gradually placing weight on the bad leg. It held. He took a few tentative steps, and then a few more. He started walking and then running about the stage gleefully. Again, the crowd cheered long and loud.

Yeshua leaned close. "He's going to ask for money next."

When the crowd became silent, Hanina continued: "The wise are upright. How do you know them? Because Hashem is kind to them and they prosper! Let us rejoice when the upright prosper. There is no shame in prosperity. It is the wicked that will come to ruin."

Miri thought that this might be a risky message for people steeped in poverty. Certainly *they* were not prospering. But Hanina boldly continued in the same vein:

"My children, Hashem loves you and wants *all* of you to prosper. He will provide wealth for you if you have faith. Hashem will help those who help *his* servants. Bring forth your goods, your first fruits of your crops, your wealth. Give, and your barns will overflow. Your vats will be filled with new wine. Like the ant, the coney, the locust, and the lizard you will lack for nothing!"

The musicians began to play a tune from the side of the stage. Hanina stepped to the side and sat in a chair, lowering his head in contemplation. The two guards came forward, each with a large basket, and began circulating through the crowd. Livianus the eunuch gave a little speech during the collection, extolling the virtues of Hanina and urging the people to give generously.

After the baskets, now laden with gifts, had been brought to the stage, Hanina came out of his trance. "Sons and daughters, Hashem will grant you prosperity when you are generous. There is one here in the crowd who is living proof of this. Natan bar Talmai! My old friend, come forth!"

Miri looked in the direction that Hanina was pointing. She was surprised to see that Yedu's father was the person indicated. Natan sat with Ruth near the back. He was trying to wave off the attention.

Hanina persisted: "My children, everyone knows that Natan always deals honorably. He is patron to many of you. Because of his good works, Hashem allows him to prosper. Natan, come forth. We are waiting. My children, give him some encouragement." Everyone joined in with applause, finger snapping, and cheering. Eventually Natan ambled slowly to the front. His face was red with embarrassment.

Yedu leaned toward Miri. "My father didn't want to come today, but my mother insisted."

When he got to the stage, Hanina put his arm around Natan's shoulders and continued in his strong voice. "My children, good Natan bar Talmai is *always* generous. This is why Hashem blesses him with a wife, a family, a beautiful daughter who is to be married in only a few days, and *abundance*. It is said 'No one who gives to the poor will lack for any need. Close your eyes to the poor and you will be cursed.' My good friend, what will you give today to help us with Hashem's work?"

Natan was on the spot. The crowd waited expectantly.

Yedu whispered, "That's why he didn't want to come. He said Hanina bears him a grudge."

"But why?" asked Miri. Yedu shrugged his shoulders.

The crowd grew restless. Several called out, first with encouragement, and then after getting no response from Natan, with increasing derision.

Hanina moved behind Natan as he faced the crowd. He placed both hands atop Natan's head and gently pushed him down to a kneeling position. "No, my children, do not speak ill of Natan bar Talmai. He is a good man. Let us pray."

Natan saw that he was trapped. He wanted this to end quickly. Before the praying could start he blurted out: "Five hundred denarii! I will pledge five hundred denarii for your good work."

The crowd cheered. That was more money than most of them would ever see. Natan hastened back to his seat. He gave his wife a disgusted look and kept walking past, leaving the assembly. Ruth followed quickly after him.

"He'll be upset," said Yedu. "He has already been complaining about what the dowry and wedding celebration are costing him."

Hanina smiled triumphantly and moved back toward the center of the stage, standing behind the table with the large bowl.

Yeshua whispered: "Next there will be some miracle. Watch closely. See if we can guess the trick."

Hanina waved his hands to quiet the crowd. "You see, my children? A righteous man scatters his money and gains even more. A miserly man withholds his treasure and comes to poverty. Be like Natan bar Talmai."

The tone softened, almost a whisper. He gestured to the bowl in front of him. "Come, eat my bread and you will live. For Hashem will not let the upright go hungry."

The eunuch stepped forward to assist Hanina in hefting the

bowl. It was huge – three feet wide and flat on the bottom. They tilted it toward the audience and angled it right and left so that all could see inside. "This, my children, is an incantation bowl. It is very old. This writing inscribed within are the words of Solomon himself, the greatest and wisest of kings. I will use it to pray to Hashem for you."

They carefully placed the bowl back onto the table and covered it with a black cloth. Hanina stretch out his arms. "Hashem, I have faith and know that you always hear me when I pray. I speak aloud for the sake of my children here, so that they too will believe that it is you who acts today."

He paused for a moment and then pulled away the cloth. He reached into the bowl with both hands and pulled out several round loaves of bread. "Eat my bread and you will live!"

The crowd cheered boisterously. The guards stepped forward and carried the bowl into the crowd. The eunuch walked with them, withdrawing loaves, ripping them, and distributing a piece to each man.

Yeshua turned to Miri and Yedu, a knowing smile crossed his face. "Did you guess it?"

Yedu shook his head from side to side. "What? It's not a real miracle?"

"Of course it isn't. Ask yourself – why did he cover the bowl?"

"I don't know, why?"

"So that we here sitting on the roof could not see into it." Yeshua waited. Miri and Yedu both looked at him with blank faces. "When we do an illusion, we always hide what is happening. Whenever you see that something is being hidden, become suspicious."

Miri asked, "What do *you* think happened?"

Yeshua thought for a moment. "Look at the stage. What else is hidden?"

Miri got it. "Ah! The whole stage is shrouded by a curtain. And so is the table in the middle. You cannot see underneath."

"Good! And now look closely, Yedu." Yeshua pointed at the

table on the stage. "Do you see the circular outline where the bowl was?"

"What about it? That just holds the bowl in place so ..."

Miri interrupted: "Someone is inside the table. The bowl has a false bottom. They open the bowl from underneath and fill it with bread."

Yeshua remained aloof. "That could be."

"Then what do you think ..."

"Wait! They're coming back. The first bowl wasn't enough. He'll have to do it again. Watch the curtains on the side of the table."

The guards placed the bowl back on the table. Miri noticed that after they set it down, they adjusted it carefully to be in the exact center of the tabletop. Hanina repeated the ritual.

"There! Do you see?" Yeshua pointed. "The right edge of the curtain – see it move?"

"But," objected Yedu, "That could just be the wind."

"Do you feel any wind?"

"No but ..."

"He is right," concluded Miri. "Someone is in there."

Once again the bowl was miraculously filled with flatbreads. These were also distributed to the delighted crowd.

After this, Hanina called out for others who wanted to be healed. Many stood up, raised their hands, and called out. Repeatedly the eunuch would venture into the crowd with his hands folded in front of his chest. He would select one and then call back, "Hanina!"

Hanina would answer, "What do we have, Livianus?"

The eunuch would explain the affliction in a loud clear voice. The person would come forward and Hanina would pray over him. Without fail, each person was healed and walked away whole.

After numerous healings, Hanina began to preach again. "Sons and daughters, my wisdom is a fountain of life. Drink from this fountain and you will avoid the snares of death."

After a pause, he continued. "Some people ask me, Hanina, are you a prophet?"

The audience yelled. Miri heard people yelling things like

"Prophet Hanina!", "The righteous one!", "Elijah returned!"

Hanina allowed this to go on for a while before waving them to silence. Miri had the impression that he enjoyed the adulation. "My children, I tell you that I am *not* a prophet, nor the son of a prophet. But I do know the power of prayer. If I ask Hashem and my prayer flows sincerely from my lips, then it will be answered. Take my words to heart and you will have no lack of treasure."

Yeshua sighed heavily. "Don't you find this tiresome?"

Miri shrugged. "At least he is entertaining."

"And dangerous – look at how the crowd cheers him."

Hanina sounded like he was wrapping up. "Hashem's ways are *not* our ways. There are things beyond our comprehension: An eagle flying in the sky! The way of a snake slithering on a rock! The way of a ship plowing through the high seas! Who can know these things?"

He went on but Miri had stopped listening. Yeshua too had become bored and was idly looking through the crowd. She nudged him in the side with her elbow. "He is about to finish. Let us see if we can get a look under the stage and see if you are right."

~

The show had finished by the time they descended from the roof and worked their way through the crowd. They arrived at the edge of the stage just as the parade of musicians disappeared into the basilica, followed by Hanina and Livianus. Some adulatory crowd members waited by the aisle and attempted to touch Hanina's robe as he walked by.

The two guards had remained behind the stage. They had removed their elaborate headgear and now stood sullenly in front of the baskets containing donations collected during the service.

Yeshua pulled Yedu and Miri aside. "Don't look. Don't attract their attention. I have an idea, but ..." He looked at Yedu doubtfully.

"What?" asked Yedu.

"Your father will have me flogged if I get you in trouble. Especially after the soaking he just took from Hanina. You'd better go wait across the decumanus."

"No," Yedu complained. "What are you going to do? I want to be a part of it."

"Yedu," said Miri. "Yeshua is right. We are just going to have a peek under the table to see if Yeshua's theory is right. Nobody knows *us,* but if *Natan's son* were to get in trouble ... well, Hanina would have a good time with that, would he not?"

Yeshua added, "If anything happens, go back to your father's house. We'll meet you there and have a good laugh."

In the end, Yedu crossed the street dejectedly and stood by the entrance to the market. The crowd was still thick as many waited to get into the shops and stalls.

Miri and Yeshua came up with a quick plan. Miri's task was to distract the guards, and she had a good idea how to do it. From her time at the tavern in Magdala, she was well acquainted with the way whores spoke to their clients. She decided she would flirt with the guards to draw their attention away.

They separated. Yeshua went to the front of the stage, mingling with people in the crowd as he went. Miri headed back to where the guards stood at attention. She tried to strut and swing her hips the way the tavern ladies did. "Excuse me, lords, you are they who work for the wise Hanina, are you not?" She cooed this in a sultry low-pitched voice.

The nearest guard was the younger of the two. He had leered at Miri's every step. After a moment he nodded his head and said, "Yes, woman. We have the privilege of serving master Hanina. I can pass along your petition. How can I help you?" His words were courteous but his manner was not. He spoke mechanically as if reciting words he was taught to say.

Miri took a step nearer. "Oh, you must be very proud! Such an important man is your master. I think I could add something to your show. I could be in the crowd – you know, like the others who are in on the act."

The two guards looked at each other. The older one responded: "What do you mean, woman? There is no act."

Miri took a step toward him and touched his arm with her finger, playing with the leather straps surrounding his biceps. "Oh, do not worry. The secret is safe. Tell me – the woman in the front – you know the one with the bad back that Hanina cured? That was her son who spoke up at the beginning. Was it not?"

The guards exchanged another look before the elder answered. "Woman, we don't know what you ..."

"Fine." Miri winked. "But anyway, I want you to tell Hanina my idea. Can you pass it along for me?"

"Uh, I suppose," said the confused guard. Miri was still fingering the leatherwork that adorned his arms. He looked down at her delicate hand.

"Good! Here it is: I will sit in the audience just like the others. Then, when the master nods, I will become possessed by seven demons. I will make a big spectacle. And then when I come forward, Hanina can cast the demons out! I will thrash around like this." She flailed her limbs spastically. She had maneuvered herself so that the guards were now looking away from the stage as they interacted with her. "Or perhaps I will rip my clothes. I can show you that too." She ripped the bottom hem of her robe and started to pull it upward.

The elder guard reached down and grabbed her hand before she could disrobe further. "Not here, Woman, not here. But, perhaps when they're finished breaking down the stage you can go with us back to our inn and show us ... I mean, show us your *act*. If it's good, we'd be happy to take you to the master."

The other guard was practically drooling as he nodded his head in agreement.

As soon as the two guards had turned their backs, Yeshua ducked underneath the stage. He had to stoop low to move under the crossbeams. The air was hot and stagnant. He saw two sets of legs working near the middle of the stage and maneuvered toward them. When he got there, he was directly underneath the central table and could stand up. In the dim light he could see that the legs belonged to a boy and a girl, perhaps a few years younger than himself. They were busy piling unused flatbreads into covered baskets.

When the two saw him, Yeshua adopted an air of authority. "Hey, you two! Livianus sent me to take over. He said you weren't fast enough today. The nasty old fart is angry."

The boy and girl stopped what they were doing and looked at Yeshua with worried eyes. The boy pointed his finger accusingly, "It's her fault! She doesn't hand the bread up fast enough. I told her to load it onto the ladder ahead of time but she won't listen."

The girl countered, "I tried, but I can't reach that high!" She gestured toward the ladder, which extended up to the underside of the table top.

Yeshua understood the system. The boy would stand at the top of the ladder, just beneath the trap door in the table. The girl would hand up the bread so the boy could fill the bowl from underneath. There was a large shelf built into the underside of the table. He wondered why they didn't just hoist the full basket to the shelf.

The faces of the young servants appeared to be truly afraid. He said to the girl, "If he beats you, come back and find me. Now go. Livianus said to meet him at his inn. I'll finish this task and join you there – you know which inn, don't you?"

"Of course," answered the boy. "Malach's, across from the slave quarters where we are staying."

"Good – off you go now." He gestured toward the front – away from the guards. They headed in the indicated direction. They ducked under the curtain at the edge of the stage and were gone.

Slave children, Yeshua thought, the cheapest labor around. They didn't cost much to buy. They work hard out of fear, and they don't eat much. He hoped that they wouldn't be punished too severely for what he was about to do.

Yeshua took a basket of leftover bread and hoisted it up to the shelf he had seen. He climbed the ladder and opened the trap door in the table. He was looking at the underside of the wooden bowl. He saw two recessed latches. When he turned them, the bottom of the bowl fell painfully onto his head. He almost lost his balance as the heavy circular piece of wood clattered down the rungs of the ladder and broke into two pieces on the pavers below. Ah – he thought to himself – *that* is what the shelf is for.

Outside, Miri was still flirting with the guards. In spite of their protests, she was doing her best impression of a woman possessed of demons. She danced around and had hitched up her robe so that her knees and part of her thighs were scandalously bare. The guards were trying to get her to stop because people were beginning to take notice.

The guards' attention was suddenly diverted by a commotion in the crowd outside the market. They turned around to see several people yelling and laughing. They were pointing toward the center of the stage.

Miri's jaw dropped. The incantation bowl on the table seemed to contain the top half of ... Yeshua. At first it looked like a vision of magic – like a jinn coming out of a lamp. Then the illusion was spoiled as Yeshua repeatedly lowered himself to reach somewhere inside the table. Each time he came up, his arms were filled with round flatbreads, which he would fling, side-armed, to the amused onlookers. Several children were running with glee, trying to catch them as they flew.

"Hey!" The elder guard yelled as they both climbed up onto the stage. "What are you doing? Get down!"

Yeshua turned to see them running toward him. He whooped and threw the remaining breads all at once, and then ducked quickly down the ladder, disappearing underneath the stage.

Miri laughed so hard that she fell down. She noticed a small white parcel lying on the paver beside her. She picked it up and held it to her nose. It had a strong acrid odor. She guessed that this was the stuff they had thrown on to the fire. What had Yeshua called it? 'Naphtha' – that was it. One of the guards must have dropped it. She stuffed it into her inside pocket and got up.

The first guard to reach the table was the younger of the two. He decided to follow Yeshua into the trapdoor. He flung the bowl aside and climbed up onto the edge of the table. But, not being built to support so much weight, the table collapsed, sending the startled guard through the floor of the stage in a heap. The growing crowd roared with laughter. The older guard tried to guess which way Yeshua would flee and ran toward the front of the stage to head him off.

Yeshua quietly emerged at the back, took Miri's hand, and the two quickly scampered down an alleyway past the metalworking shop. Before they turned the corner, Miri stole a quick glance back. The elder guard was still looking under the curtain of the stage. He hadn't seen them escape.

~

The sun would be setting soon. It had been a slow day at the market. Shalmai the merchant was starting to pack up his trinkets into crates. Because he lived here in town he didn't have far to travel, and thus could afford to stay open a bit later than the competition. Hanina's show always attracted more people, but they were the wrong kind of people. They had no money – or what little they had they gave to the preacher.

He bent over to lift one of the heavy crates and felt a twinge of pain in his back. "I'm getting old," he mumbled to no one in particular. He looked forward to the day when Ichabod would take over and he could just sit here and watch him work. He set the crate down on top of another and sat in his chair. He decided to wait a bit longer to see if any stragglers came along.

He observed two rough-looking men walking down the aisle. The larger one, with dark unkempt hair, had his mouth set in a sneer, which would have been intimidating except that it showed off his two missing front teeth. Shalmai decided they were likely the personal guards of some wealthy man. "Perhaps the master, too, is close by," he said under his breath. He straightened up and put on his best shopkeeper's smile.

Although they stopped directly in front of Shalmai's booth, the men had not noticed him. The dark-haired one had turned back toward the gate.

"Huh?" Said dark-hair. "Is that ..."

"What?" Asked his companion. He was half a head shorter but

more muscular – too well fed for a common peasant. His hair was a shade lighter, cropped short. A jagged scar adorned his right cheek.

"Over there – near the gate. I thought I saw ..."

"What, Mak'ka? Spit it out."

"I don't see her now. You remember that girl – the one who killed Ba'asha at the tavern?"

Scar-face laughed. "The one that back-kicked you in the testicles? *That* was a hoot."

"Never mind that! I thought I saw her. Or someone that looks like her."

"You're seeing things. Have you been drinking again?"

"Forget it." Said the one named Mak'ka. "Lebbaeus says he needs wine. Let's see if we can ..."

He had turned and was staring at Shalmai's table. The shopkeeper was pleased to be finally noticed.

Scar-face gave a heavy sigh. "What now? Hey, is that ...?"

"Yes, I believe it is."

Shalmai's table was covered with an odd variety of jewelry and tools. Mak'ka reached down and picked up the bejeweled dagger, turning it over in his hands. "Where did you get this?" He asked gruffly.

"You have excellent taste, gentlemen. It's for sale of course," answered Shalmai.

"I didn't ask you whether it was *for sale*. I asked you where you got it."

Realizing that he had misjudged these two, Shalmai changed tactics. "Gentlemen, that fine piece was given to me by a visiting prince of Nabatea as a bonus for my good service, but of course if you like it ..."

"You're lying, old man." Mak'ka grabbed the merchant's hand and pulled it toward himself, twisting it so the wrist was upturned and exposed. He set the blade of the dagger against Shalmai's wrist. "Shall we test the sharpness? The truth – Now!"

"Mercy, good sir, the truth, yes. My son – my son found it and brought it to me. He was playing in a stream down by the synagogue with his friends. He told me he found it in the water."

Mak'ka met the man's gaze and held it for a minute. "If I find out you are lying I'm going to come back here and it won't just be your wrist I cut."

"Please sir, mercy, I meant no harm. Take it. Please – take it as a gift. I do not want to see it ever again. Evil – I told my son when he brought it to me. Nothing good can come from such a thing. Take it!"

Mak'ka quickly turned the merchant's hand over and gave it a quick cut across the back, just above the knuckles. Shalmai cried out in pain and jerked his hand back.

"As a warning," grumbled Mak'ka. He turned to his companion. "Come on. Lebbaeus will be very interested in this. I'd wager that girl is in town too. Keep your eyes open."

The two left toward the gate, leaving Shalmai cradling his injured hand in a cloth.

2 Kings

The morning after Yom Revi'i the 17ᵗʰ day of Elul

After Varus laid waste to Sepphoris some sixteen years ago, the Roman conquerors laid out a regular grid at the foot of the acropolis and then used the rubble from the destroyed buildings to make the roads. For three years, before Herod Antipas decided to make the city his Galilean capital, it served solely as a Roman military outpost.

And Romans needed their baths. The bathhouse in Sepphoris was one of the first structures built after the roads were laid. It occupied two full city blocks on the decumanus just a short walk up from the market square. It was an imposing edifice made from local concrete and decorated with numerous macabre gargoyles that overlooked the street. These, combined with the incessant noise and steam from the furnace, gave rise to the local belief that the place was inhabited by demons.

Numerous slaves worked in the bathhouse. In addition to stoking the furnaces, they provided massages and anointing of the patrons. Cooks were employed to prepare a variety of food and refreshments. Other slaves cleaned the perpetually damp surfaces, which were prone to being fouled with mold. Still others acted as personal attendants, providing whatever services a guest might require. These were mostly good-looking young boys and girls.

Zakkai was one of these.

Zakkai said a silent prayer that he would not be penetrated this day. He was still sore from yesterday and could not sit down without pain. He entered the caldarium carrying a tray of refreshments for the four lounging men. He was thirsty and hungry himself – he usually was. But it was not his place to eat during the day, and especially not food prepared for the guests – ripe plump grapes, apple slices, and goblets of wine. Zakkai had once been caught sampling the guest fare. He had lost one of his fingers in punishment.

Today was like any other day for Zakkai. He was told he looked to be about nine years old, but if you were to ask him, he wouldn't know his age, nor his birthday. These things were not important to a slave. The important thing – the only thing, was getting through another day. There once was a time when he would look forward to the evening – when he could cuddle up in his older sister's arms and fall asleep, enveloped in her warmth. Tammah was her name. He could still remember that. He didn't remember his mother's name nor what her face looked like. He had a vague recollection of her smell – clean, like lavender.

But now Tammah was gone too. Zakkai's evenings had become cold and lonely. Sometimes if it was quiet and he closed his eyes, he could still remember the sound of her voice – high and clear like a bell. She used to sing to him when he was restless or afraid. He knew the song by heart:

Arise, my beloved, my lovely one, come.
The winter is past, the rain is gone.
Flowers spring forth. It is the time for happy songs.
We will prune the vines to the cooing of the turtledove.
The fig tree gives its first fruits, the vines, their fragrance.
Arise, my beloved, my lovely one, come.

Zakkai tried to remember how long it had been since he last heard Tammah's sweet voice. Was it a season ago, a year ago, two years, more? Slave time is like that, Tammah used to tell him. One day is like any other, all of them dreary, with no hope for change.

Ever. The very young cry, but eventually they become numb to it, and time flows by in a kind of haze. Slave time. Soon Zakkai would be too old to work here and they would send him to the mines. He had heard bad stories about the mines. He did not wish to go there. He must always try to please his masters.

These four men in the caldarium looked peaceful. Perhaps today would be an easy day, in spite of the fact that he hated the hot room. Demons lived under this floor. You could hear them. Zakkai did not want to meet those demons. Guests stayed here for only a half hour, but Zakkai would be attending all day. The heat was unbearable sometimes. He was supposed to stand quietly just inside the door unless one of the men asked for something. He liked it when they asked for refreshments because then he could go to the kitchen for a few minutes. Sometimes he could get a sip of water for himself if the cook was in a good mood.

He knew the older man. Abiyram was his name. He was very old. He came here almost every day. He was kinder than most, or at least not openly cruel. Abiyram was now reclining in the hot pool with another man. This other man had been here before too, but not often. Was he here earlier in the summer, or had it been longer? Zakkai could not remember – slave time. This other man must live somewhere far away.

Abiyram and the other were serious men, talking in hushed tones about important things. Zakkai could hear them over the hissing of the steam and the gurgling of the fountain. They seemed busy. This was good. Zakkai knew that Abiyram did not mix business with pleasure.

"You needn't worry about your paltry possessions in Magdala," Abiyram was saying. "You will be more than fairly compensated – especially after what you and Ba'asha tried to pull." He laughed. "Did you really think there was a chance that the new city would be located there? It was always going to be Rakkat."

"I assure you, my lord. The scheme was Ba'asha's doing," the other man said. Zakkai recognized the deferential tone. Everyone spoke to Abiyram that way. The name of the man came to him –

Lebbaeus. He was still talking: "Can you imagine my plight. An important man like Ba'asha, Herod's man, comes to my town and tells me to buy properties for him – what am I to do? Believe me, my lord, I have no allegiance to his clan. It was simply a matter of rank."

"No matter," said Abiyram dismissively. "If you are to be *my* man now, see that you take care to never hide things like this again. I will be expecting great things from you in this town."

It was then that Zakkai glanced at the third man – a fat man. Zakkai saw that his eyes were not closed. In fact they were looking directly at *him*. The boy quickly lowered his head. A slave could be beaten for looking a guest in the eye. Zakkai still had the image of the man in his head: sitting on a bench, drenched in sweat and oil, hunched forward, rolls of belly fat occluding his genitals.

A rumbling came from the demons below. The stokers have the fire very hot today. Zakkai was thankful that his master allowed him to wear wooden sandals in here just like the guests.

Abiyram continued: "I believe you know a man named Natan who lives in this town? He will be disappointed that he is not being appointed to take over for Ba'asha. He will feel that he should be next in line, but I have doubts about his ..." He searched for the right word.

"Devotion?" offered Lebbaeus. "You will have no doubt about my commitment. I understand your needs, my lord. The farms *will* be consolidated. The taxes *will* be collected. The shipments *will* be made on time. You will have ample profits for yourself."

"For the tetrarch, you mean," corrected Abiyram.

"For the tetrarch," echoed Lebbaeus.

"I am impressed by your enthusiasm, and of course your reputation for ruthlessness precedes you."

Lebbaeus smiled demurely. "I look forward to many years in your clientage."

The fat man had gotten up and was splashing cold water on his face from the fountain. He turned to Zakkai. "Boy ... strigil!"

Zakkai collected the strigil, a fresh towel, and a tray. The fat man waddled to the massage table and sat upright on the edge. Zakkai started with the man's shoulder's. He scratched the curved strigil blade down the outside of the man's arms until it had collected a thick coating of muck. This he flicked onto the tray. He wiped the strigil clean and then continued to scrape the man's body. This man had not exercised very vigorously, so he did not not have much dirt on him, but he must not bathe regularly, or at least not recently, because he had a foul smell. Zakkai was careful to show no signs of disgust.

He was closer now and could hear Abiyram clearly. "We can compensate you for your failed investments in Magdala. I'm sure your income will be adequate. You can start by taking possession of Ba'asha's villa on the hilltop."

Lebbaeus was surprised. "My lord! That is generous indeed."

Abiyram chuckled. "You needn't thank me. You can do me the favor of evicting the present occupants of course?"

"You mean ... Ba'asha's widow."

"Widow, daughter, and several servants, I believe. Take your pick of the servants if any suit you, though I expect you have your own slaves."

Zakkai had finished with the strigil. He set the tray in the corner to be collected later.

"Boy ... massage!" The fat man said. He lay down on his back. When the folds of fat settled, Zakkai could see that the man had an erection. It looked like his prayer for a sex-free day may go unanswered. No matter, he thought. One day is like any other.

Zakkai began by massaging the man's flabby shoulders and arms. That was when the fourth man approached and lifted Zakkai's tunic from behind. "Gamal, what do you say to having some sport with this one?"

Gamal lifted his head and raised an eyebrow questioningly at Abiyram, who was just getting out of the hot pool. "By the tern's beak Kalev, you two and your nasty habits – he's a bath attendant, not a catamite. Go ahead if you must, but take him over there in the corner. We're trying to talk business here."

The fourth man was nasty and rough. His nose and jaw

protruded from his shaven face, giving him a dog-like appearance. "Over there, boy, now." He gave Zakkai a shove.

Zakkai had already noticed that the fat one's member was not very big. He hoped this was true of the one called Kalev also. He worried that they might become angry if he bled too much.

Kalev barked an order, "Turn around. Hands on the wall."

Zakkai did not want to do that. He was not afraid of being entered – that had happened to him hundreds of times. He was afraid because he knew there was a chimney vent here. The wall would be scaldingly hot. He ventured to speak: "But, master ..."

The backhand blow across the mouth took him by surprise. Zakkai had thought the fat one would be the gentler one, but it was he who had struck. "You were not asked to speak, boy! Do as you are told!"

Zakkai grimaced as he turned round, bent forward and placed his hands against the wall. He tried to ball up his hands to minimize the amount of skin touching the hot concrete.

After they commenced sexing him, Zakkai closed his eyes and ... went away. His sister had taught him how to do this. Tammah would say – when the master comes to do bad things, close your eyes and imagine you are home with me. It is nighttime and I am holding you in my arms.

Flowers spring forth. It is the time for happy songs.
We will prune the vines to the cooing of the turtledove.

Zakkai was far away in his sister's embrace when he heard a rumbling like a distant thunder. It grew louder. He felt the man inside him. The painful pounding from behind came back into his consciousness. He was back in the hot room. The demons under the floor must be very angry because the rumbling did not stop. It grew ever more violent. Now he could even feel the walls shaking through his burned palms.

The old man, Abiyram, called from across the room: "Earthquake – we should get out." His voice did not sound urgent. He slowly arose from the pool.

Zakkai then felt a great lurching. The floor under him gave way.

He was standing on a section of tile that was still attached to the wall. The floor buckled toward the center and he fell backward, on top of the dog-faced man who had been sexing him. The fat one, Gamal, had been standing to the side. He too fell in.

Zakkai felt the searing heat of the air around him. It hurt to breath, so he did not. The one called Kalev was screaming in agony. There was a sizzling sound as the man's back rested on the subfloor of the hypocaust. The demons were consuming him. Without thinking, Zakkai scrambled to his feet, stepping on the stomach of the screaming man. Only a small section of the floor had collapsed. Zakkai was able to hoist himself up onto the adjacent tiles that had held.

The caldarium rapidly filled with smoke. Zakkai's eyes stung and he could not see. Someone pushed past him, and he almost toppled back into the hole. He recovered by grabbing the edge of the fountain. The one called Lebbaeus had fled from the chamber. Abiyram had fallen back into the hot pool and was coughing. Zakkai ran to him and took his arm, pulling him upright. "Quick master. We must leave now!"

The old man appeared dazed. Zakkai propelled him toward the exit. They got through the door and into the central courtyard of the bathhouse. All around was mayhem. Other sections of the floor had collapsed. Naked bodies were screaming and running through the dimly lit corridors to the street. Zakkai put the old man's arm over his own shoulder, guiding him through the chaos.

When they were almost out, the old man straightened. He pulled a towel from a stack and wrapped it around his waist. He grabbed Zakkai by the shoulders. "Boy, hurry back now and help the others." He shoved Zakkai back toward the caldarium.

Zakkai did not want to go. The demons were very angry now. When he got to the door of the hot room he could not see because of the thick smoke. It hurt too much to open his eyes. All of his instincts told him to flee this room. He could feel his flesh wilting. *Be somewhere else. It is night. I am in Tammah's arms.*

It was dark. He knew where the collapsed corner was. He came to it by inching forward, tapping gingerly with the toe of his sandals until he arrived at the edge of the hole. He was trying to decide what to do next when a hand reached up and grabbed his ankle. *Demons, trying to drag me into the abyss!*

Suppressing these thoughts, he reached down and grabbed the hand, prying it from his ankle. With all his might he pulled. Another hand emerged. Zakkai heard it slap the tile floor. He got down on his knees and pulled the man's arm from under his shoulder. The smell of burning flesh came to him in his shallow gulps of air. It reminded him of pigs roasting on a spit at the banquets he sometimes had to serve. He ignored the burning on his knees as he lifted the man from beneath the floor and dragged him toward the exit.

They made it to the relative cool of the central courtyard. There were other servants here, who took the dog-faced man from Zakkai and carried him out to the street.

Zakkai had been told to go back and help the others. He knew that the fat one was still under the floor. The demons were feasting on his flesh. But still, he *must* obey the command or his master would punish him and send him to the mines. He once again overcame his revulsion and entered the caldarium.

He tried to repeat his motions from before, but the smoke was too thick, the heat too intense. He became confused. He inched toward where he thought the collapsed floor was. It seemed to take a long time to reach it. He felt the edge of the hot pool and he knew he was on the opposite side of the room from where he needed to be. He turned around and tried again. This time he bumped into the fountain, which had now stopped gurgling. Again and again he tried. The demons were playing tricks on him. At last he found himself once more at the door. He was blind. He could not breathe. He could not stand.

He had been given a command, but he could not remember what it was. Slave time. *The winter is past, the rain is gone.* Zakkai collapsed through the door into the courtyard and instinctively crawled toward the exit to the street. People were running past him in all directions, stepping over him. Somebody yelled something and kicked him to the side. He did not mind. Indeed, he felt a small splash of water on his back and thanked the gods for the blessed coolness.

No one noticed as the small boy, covered in soot, crawled out of the building. He crept on his knees and elbows, his burned palms facing upward. There was too much activity outside. A huge crowd had gathered. Smoke and steam poured from the exit. The small boy kept crawling as if blind. He eventually collapsed in the drainage ditch on the side of the street. He lay still.

~

Nura and Miri had been cleaning the house when the ground shook. Earthquakes were not uncommon, and this one seemed relatively mild. Still, they ran out to the street during the tremors.

After the rumbling subsided, they waited several minutes and then surveyed the house, shelter, and barn from the outside. Aside from a crack or two, there was no visible damage.

All the women who lived in the shelter were currently out about town. The only other person here would be Yeshua, who was sleeping in the barn loft. He had arrived home at dawn after spending the night tending the Roman pig herd, and had apparently slept through the entire incident.

They resumed their cleaning. After a short while there came a banging on the front door. Nura answered.

"Ma'am!" Two serving girls stood in the street. They wore short plain tunics and nothing else – a little scantily dressed for this time of year. Their feet were bare and their faces were covered with a blackish powder. The taller one spoke. "Ma'am! Come quickly. The bathhouse ma'am. My master is burned. They sent me to fetch you!"

"Who is hurt? How many?" Asked Nura.

"I don't know, ma'am. Many, I think. My master is hurt – burned. They told me to fetch the healer. Please come quickly ma'am." The two girls seemed frantic.

"Come inside for a moment." Nura held the door open and said to Miri: "I will gather the things I need. The earthquake must have started some kind of fire. Go and wake Yeshua. I may need his help."

Miri hurried off to the barn and started up the ladder to the loft. This was where Yeshua lived when he wasn't off day laboring, tending pigs, or getting into mischief. Miri had never been up here before. She got halfway up and called for him. "Yeshua! Are you there?" No answer came, but she could hear his heavy, deep breathing. She climbed the rest of the way. The air was warm and musty up here. In the dim light coming through the eaves, she saw Yeshua lying on his back on a bed of straw. He wore only a loincloth as he lay sleeping. Miri admired his form for a moment before remembering her task. She squatted at his side and shook him.

"Huh. Miri. What?"

"Get up! Nura needs you!"

Yeshua sat up and yawned. It took him a minute to collect his wits. Miri explained the situation. He pulled his tunic over his head and announced that he was ready.

Nura, Miri, and Yeshua were led by the two serving girls through the old town toward the city center. In the distance, they saw a crowd standing outside the bathhouse. Most just stood and watched. Clusters of people were here and there, tending to an injured person lying prone on the ground or in a litter.

When they arrived, Miri noticed the unmistakable smell of smoke in the air. Looking at the bathhouse she could see that the facade was stained with soot. Puffs of black smoke emanated from the front door of the building. Many people were coughing.

The serving girls dragged Nura to one of the litters. "My master is here. His name is Abiyram. Come quickly."

Abiyram sat on the edge of the waist-high litter. He looked up and squinted at Nura in the sun. "Ah, the healer is finally arrived. We sent for the medicus but he is *unavailable*. The soldier said we must rely on our own."

Nura ignored the slight. "Are you hurt, my lord?"

"Of course I am hurt. It's my feet!" Abiyram held up one foot and then the other so that Nura could see the soles. Both were red, and covered with blisters still in the process of forming. "I was in one of the pools when it happened. I had to hurry out without my sandals."

Nura said to Miri. "Take that bucket there. You are to go to the fountain up the street and fill it with as much cold water as you can carry. Yeshua, you are to go among the crowd and see who else is needing help." She turned back to Abiyram. "My lord, first we are to wash your feet. The cold water will feel good and keep the burn from deepening. Then I will wrap them with a healing balm. How is your breathing, my lord?"

Abiyram said that aside from some coughing he was fine. Nura pressed her ear to his chest for a moment and then nodded. He had been fortunate to not inhale much smoke.

Miri returned with the bucket. Nura directed her to wash the old man's feet while she prepared the balm and the wrappings.

The serving girls were still standing about. Nura said to the older one. "Do you see how Miri washes his feet? You are to do this every morning. Now watch what I do. After washing, you are to apply fresh ointment and bandages." The girl nodded.

When Miri had finished, Nura asked her to go find Yeshua and assist him. She scurried off.

Nura got Abiyram's attention and said in a stern voice. "My lord, I know that you are not used to being told what to do, but you are to take heed. Your feet are badly burned. It is to be painful for you for several days. This ointment is made from grape seed oil, snail mucous, poppy extract, honey, and a bit of powdered silver. It will take away some pain and quicken healing. It is important, my lord, that you not walk on open ground until your feet are healed."

"But, when I walked out here, the cold ground felt good."

"My lord, if you walk on the ground with an open wound you will get the tetanos. As it is, your feet may still become black. If that is happening, I may need the help of maggots to clean the dead skin. That is painful but it will save your feet. We do not want to call the medicus. We know how much Romans love to cut."

His servants had told him that Nura was a powerful healer, and so he had agreed to allow his servants to fetch her when the medicus had refused them. But still, Abiyram was aghast at this strange-looking woman talking to him as if she were his equal.

Nura applied the ointment and bandages. Almost immediately the pain subsided. Perhaps this woman knew a thing or two after all. "Snail mucous, did you say? I wonder how you collect that?"

Nura smiled at him. "It is a trade secret, my lord. It has amazing healing powers. You will see."

~

Yeshua circulated through the crowd looking for other injured people. There were many spectators. You could tell the ones who had been in the bathhouse because they were either wrapped in towels or the loose-fitting robes given to bathers. Yeshua examined several people who were coughing and a few who were vomiting. He advised them to drink lots of water. Few appeared to be seriously injured.

He came to a dense circle of people and pushed his way through. A man in the center of the circle lay on a stretcher. The air was thick with the sickly smell of burned meat and hair. They hadn't bothered to cover this one. He lay on his back, still naked. His sightless eyes were open but covered with a cloudy film. He was awake and muttering incoherently. Just then he turned his head and coughed up black mucous and blood.

Most of his skin was red and covered with blisters. Patches here and there were blackened and charred. Yeshua thought that maybe there was still hope until he attempted to roll him onto his side. The cloth of the litter stuck to his back at first, and then peeled away, taking patches of blackened skin with it. Much of his back was burned clear through to the muscle.

"What happened to him?" Asked Nura as she arrived at Yeshua's side.

One of the bystanders responded. "Looks like he jumped into the furnace."

A young man kneeling by the burned man's head said, "No. I was there when a slave boy brought him out. He was in the caldarium – where the floor collapsed. He is my father. His name is Kalev."

Nura and Yeshua took a step back and conferred with each other. Both agreed that there was no hope for this one. He would be dead within the hour. Also, in his delirium, he didn't appear to be in much pain. Indeed he seemed quite calm. They returned to the injured man's side.

"Where's the boy?" Asked Yeshua.

"Who?" Asked the son.

"The boy – you said a boy brought him out of the caldarium."

The young man was annoyed by the question. "I don't know. Who cares? It was a slave. What will you do to save my father?"

Nura placed her hand on the young man's shoulder. "Dearest son – your father is being called by his god today. See now, he is already on his way. He is in no pain. There is nothing we can do to keep him from his journey. Stay here and talk to him. Give him a drink of water if he asks. Be here in his final moments in this world."

Yeshua had already left the scene. He continued to look for the injured. By now a brigade of water bearers was streaming into the building. As they worked to extinguish the furnace and cool the stone surfaces, white steam flowed from doorway and upper windows. Yeshua recognized Clopas the architect directing the operation. He wore a bath tunic, so he must have been among the bathers when the earthquake occurred.

The stream of bucket bearers was interrupted by a commotion at the front door. Four men emerged from the building carrying a pallet. On the pallet was something blackened and still smoking. As they brought this out to the street, people who were near turned away in revulsion.

They set the pallet down very near where Yeshua stood. There was no need to examine this man. He had obviously been very fat. He looked like he had been charred over direct flames, which was likely, because the furnace vented directly into the hypocaust under the caldarium. What remained of his skin was blackened and split. His final moments had been agonizing indeed. Yeshua directed that he be covered with a cloth and taken to the synagogue.

~

After Nura told her to go find and assist Yeshua, Miri had bustled off. The crowd was loud and thick, and she could not find him anywhere. She remembered that there was a raised stone pedestal on the corner of the bathhouse. From that vantage point she would be able to see the whole area.

She headed uphill and started across the street. That was when she noticed the prone figure in the gutter on the far side of the street. In the pandemonium, people stepped over the figure as if it were a pile of garbage. Miri wiped the sweat from her face and refocused her eyes, thinking that perhaps she was seeing an apparition.

Miri ran and sat at the boy's side, rolling him onto his back. He was alive! The boy's eyes looked up at her and focused. "Tammah?" the boy said. Miri wiped the soot from his face with the hem of her tunic. "Tammah," the boy repeated, but this time it was not a question. He coughed up some black phlegm and then rolled so that his head rested in Miri's lap. He began to suck his thumb.

A young woman her own age stood by. Miri called to her, "You. Go fetch the healer. This boy needs help."

The woman actually laughed. "Why do you care? Is this *your* slave? I think not." She walked off shaking her head sardonically.

The boy crawled up further into Miri's lap. He curled his legs up as he lay on his side. "Tammah, I miss you. Where have you been?" The boy rocked himself back and forth. Again he had a fit of coughing. When it passed he lay still, sucking his thumb and humming quietly to himself.

Miri tried repeatedly to get others to fetch the healer but each time she was ignored. At length she gave up and turned her attention to the boy.

He was badly burned, but his face seemed unharmed. Indeed, it was beautiful. His clear brown eyes gazed up at her, shining with innocence. With his free hand he reached up and touched Miri's lips. After a while, he extracted his thumb and sang quietly, his voice barely a whisper. "Arise, my beloved, my lovely one, come. The winter is past, the rain is gone."

Miri knew the song. She began to weep at the memory of her mother singing it to her when she was young. She sang the next verse with the boy. "Flowers spring forth. It is the time for happy songs." The boy smiled and closed his eyes. His lips continued to move, but no sound came out. "Arise, my beloved, my lovely one, come." The boy shuddered once, and then again. He became silent. As he lay in her lap, Miri could feel the tension flow out of his body. He was gone.

It was some time later when Miri felt a hand on her back. She looked up to see Yeshua and Nura standing over her. The excitement was over now and the crowd was dispersing. She did not know how long she had been sitting here, cradling the boy like a baby in her lap.

"Dearest Miri, there is nothing more you can do for him."

~

Late in the afternoon, two hours before the start of the new day, Yeshua and Miri sat in the open park behind the market. Yeshua had brought a wineskin, which he now opened and offered to his companion.

Miri had said little since the events at the bathhouse earlier in the day. She hadn't known the boy, but something about his passing disturbed her deeply. Perhaps it was the song that reminded her so strongly of her own childhood. Perhaps it was the fact that no one else in the world cared about this boy, either in life or in death. He was just another nobody. She had been brooding all afternoon.

Miri accepted the wineskin and took a long pull. The liquid felt warm going down and she savored the feeling of calm enveloping her mind. She was grateful to Nura and Yeshua for their understanding. As healers, they must be accustomed to seeing the worst human situations.

Miri looked at her tunic, which was covered with soot. She had held the boy for more than an hour – until Nura persuaded her to let go, promising that the child would be given a burial with honor.

Yeshua once again handed her the skin, but she waved it off. She did not want her mind to be numb. She wanted to reflect on this sorrow, to see what wisdom it could bring. They sat in silence as people came and went around them.

Miri realized that they were sitting in the same garden where the Roman soldiers had accosted them the previous week. Reflexively, she looked toward the building where she had first seen them emerge from a tavern. There was no one there now.

Her gaze wandered up the cardo. In the distance she saw a man and four boys approaching from the direction of the synagogue. When they drew near, she recognized the man as the rabbi who had conducted the Lamentations service. She also recognized two of the boys: Ya'aqob and Yedu. Yedu waved to her and shook the rabbi's sleeve, pointing in their direction.

"Hello brother," said Yeshua when the three arrived. "Please join us." He did not get up, as would have been proper in the presence of an elder.

Ya'aqob answered, "Thank you, *brother*. If the teacher says it is permissible, we will do so." The rabbi nodded. Room was made for the newcomers.

It occurred to Miri that this was the first time she had seen Yeshua and Ya'aqob interact. She would not know they were kin to look at them. There was something strained about the way they spoke to each other – something overly formal.

Yeshua offered the wineskin to the rabbi, who waved it off in disgust. He offered it to Ya'aqob, who ignored it. He shrugged and took a drink himself.

After an uncomfortable silence, the rabbi addressed Yeshua. "You should be proud of your younger brother. He is doing very well with his torah studies. He has the same talent you had." As an afterthought he added, "and of course, Yedu, you also possess this talent, as I have mentioned to your father on numerous occasions." He patted Yedu on the head.

Yedu was embarrassed by this condescending gesture. He stole a quick glance toward Miri to see if she had noticed.

The rabbi again addressed Yeshua. "I have not seen you much since you dropped your studies. You rarely come to synagogue. I hope you have been prospering?" His voice rose, implying a question. "Remember, He who accepts guidance walks the way of life."

Yeshua took another pull from the wineskin and then re-stoppered it. "Teacher, since my studies with you ended, I have been walking the ways of life, taking guidance from what my eyes have seen. Is that what you mean?"

The rabbi tried to discern if there was some hidden slight in Yeshua's response. He couldn't. He reached out and placed his hand over Yeshua's. "My son, it is not sufficient merely to *see*. Even the eyes of the fool wander the ends of the earth. The intelligent person seeks wisdom. Perhaps you do not see as much as you think?"

Yeshua withdrew his hand. "So, if I do not see, then I am blind. But if I allow a blind man to lead me, will we not both fall into a pit?"

Miri sniggered.

The rabbi turned to Yedu on his left. "I am not accustomed to being laughed at. Young Yedu, do you know this rude girl, who thinks that something is funny."

"Yes, Rabbi Eyphah. This is Nura's cousin. She is staying at my uncle Mattanyah's house."

The rabbi cleared his throat. "Someone should teach her to mind her manners when men are talking." Turning quickly to Yeshua, he wagged his finger. "Child, now I remember how tedious our sessions were. You have a quick retort to everything I say without first listening. Would you not agree this is foolish?"

Yeshua sighed heavily. "Rabbi, I listened well to everything you said, as my brother does now. I drank from your trough, but it did not quench my thirst. The Greeks say there is truth in wine." He unstoppered the skin and took another gulp.

The rabbi shook his head and leaned toward Ya'aqob. "So little has changed. Your brother was always speaking in riddles. What do *you* say to him when he is like this?"

Ya'aqob adopted a scolding tone. "Brother! Humble yourself in the presence of the rabbi. Hashem abhors the arrogant heart. Did you learn nothing from Hanina's sermon yesterday?"

Miri interjected, "We understood Hanina very well."

Ya'aqob looked surprised. "You were there? We looked but did not see you."

Yedu explained, "I was with them. We were on the roof of the potter's shop, next to the stage. We saw you in the back of the crowd, near the market entrance."

The rabbi looked pleased at this news. "Good, Yedu. Tell us, what did you think of the speech?"

Yedu cast his eyes from Miri to Yeshua, hoping for support. At length he looked into his lap and said softly, "I don't know. It was fine, I guess."

Ya'aqob had never been one to pick up on nuance. "You are right, cousin. It was a *fine* sermon. We were all impressed by your father's generosity. We were near the back, but we could hear well. Hanina has a strong voice. The crowd was too big for us to get Yehuda very close, but I left Hanina a note and the rabbi says he can put in a word for us."

The rabbi patted Ya'aqob's hand. He started to add something but Yeshua cut him off. "Brother, your intentions are good, but in Hanina you have misplaced your hopes."

This angered Ya'aqob. "And what do you know? What is it that you *do* all day? You have no land. You do no work. You drink strong wine in the middle of the day. You congregate with filthy beggars. Yet you lecture me."

Yeshua kept his eyes downcast and said softly, "There was once a rich man who put his money to use sowing, reaping, and planting, so as to fill his storehouses with goods. But that night he died."

Ya'aqob rolled his eyes. "What is that? Did you get that from the town cynic?"

Miri got the impression that the two had been sniping at each other for years. But she had heard this saying too. "Te'oma," she said.

Yeshua raised his eyebrows. "Yes – that's where I heard it. From Te'oma. He said he heard it from Yochanan himself."

The rabbi pursed his lips. "Young Yeshua, it pains me that you have fallen astray. You are now repeating the abominable sayings of that wretch, Yochanan. Take care. He tells people they don't need priests, or sacrifice, or even rabbis."

Miri snorted, "So, it is a small wonder why *you* disapprove." Then, intending to look defiant, she grabbed the wineskin from Yeshua and upended it into her mouth. The flow was more than she expected and she gagged, spitting the liquid to the side in a fit of coughing.

The rabbi shook his head and said sharply to Yeshua. "I see you have found another fool who will listen to you. You should teach her that it is unseemly for a woman to speak in the presence of men. Take heed of the proverb – drunkards and gluttons will have poverty as their reward."

Miri wanted to retort to the rabbi's offensive remark, but she was still coughing.

Yeshua responded for her. "Rabbi, you misjudge my friend. She speaks from knowledge. We both witnessed Hanina speak and do his tricks. He told us that we must give to *him* in order to prosper. Do you think that is right?"

"Child, Hanina is a pillar of our faith. You must not mock him. He is like a father to us all, and the wise child heeds the father's instruction."

Miri had recovered now. "Unless the father is wrong."

The rabbi gave Miri a long, disapproving look. "Yeshua, your girl is comely, but ignorant. Like a golden ring in the snout of a pig is a beautiful woman without discretion."

The warm feeling that the wine had given Miri now fueled her anger. She noted that the rabbi had thus far avoided addressing her directly. She responded in kind. "Yedu, please ask the rabbi how much Hanina gives to the synagogue?"

Yedu looked to her, and then up at the rabbi. He did not want to be in the middle. Before he could speak the rabbi turned to him and said, "Yedu, tell the girl it is no matter. Hanina is generous to us. What of it?"

Miri snorted. "He pays the temple, the synagogues, the tax collectors. He tells everyone else to do likewise. He of course keeps the first share for himself. He acts as innocent as a dove but he is as sly as a snake."

Rabbi Eyphah said to the boys in his charge, "We should not have sat here. I did not know we would forced to hear the wheedling words of a confused and deceitful woman." Finally, he could contain himself no longer. He turned to Miri directly, his tone sharp. "Young woman, I will speak to you, for it appears there is no one else who will discipline you. The stroke of a rod would do you well."

Miri started to reply, but the rabbi held up his hand. "I am not finished! Your lips drip with honey as you say these silly things and you get *fools* to listen to you." He gestured toward Yeshua. "But do not pretend to correct *me*. You derogate the reputation of a fine man like Hanina, who preaches the wisdom of Solomon. What now? ... Why do you shake your head like that? Have you no respect?"

"The wisdom of Solomon," Miri repeated calmly. "That is what Hanina said yesterday. It is what all you *learned* men say. You pray for the return of the old kingdoms. Do you not remember Samuel's warning when the people first asked for a king?"

At this they all gave Miri a questioning look – even Yeshua.

Miri sighed. "Have you not read your own scrolls? Samuel warned the people about all the evil things that a king would do. And then every single one of the kings did those evil things – none more than David and Solomon. The king took their sons and daughters, their lands, their harvest, their gold. He used them with no mercy to support his endless wars."

After a moment of confused silence, the rabbi said, "Yeshua, have you been filling this poor girl's head with ridiculous notions?"

Yeshua was cut off by Miri. "He has not! I read for myself."

The rabbi laughed derisively. "As if *you* could read! David was faithful to Hashem throughout his life. Solomon took his direction straight from Hashem. Solomon was faithful almost to the end of his life. It is true that when he was very old he made the mistake of listening to a *woman* who lured him into idol worship."

Miri ignored the slight. "You are wrong. David was an idolator from the beginning."

The rabbi smiled triumphantly. "You say you have read the scrolls, but you are again lying. The text says very clearly that Hashem was his guide."

Miri thought for a moment. It was clear to her that the rabbi had not read the Testament of Michal. She wondered if he even knew of its existence. She decided to ask him about a thought that had occurred to her the previous night. "Wise teacher," she said, "allow me to ask you a question. Who wrote the Torah scrolls about David and Solomon?"

The rabbi looked puzzled. "What do you mean? The scribes of course. They ..."

"No, I mean, who told them what to write?"

The rabbi paused for a moment, trying to figure out where this was leading. "I suppose David and Solomon had priests and scholars, just as we do now."

"Just as we do now," Miri repeated. "And what do you think our tetrarch would do if one of your scholars wrote that he was an idolator and a coward who grovels to Rome."

The rabbi glanced around nervously to see if anyone outside their group had heard this. At length he said softly. "I don't think anyone who wrote that would live very long."

"Just so," Miri said. "The stories always praise the ones in power. Maybe what we read is not always true."

The rabbi shook his head. "I don't know what you are getting at but ..."

Yeshua interrupted, "Solomon had no prophets. Did you ever wonder why?"

"What?" The rabbi rolled his eyes. "No. I never *wondered* such a thing. I know the answer, as you would if you had any sense. It is because of his wisdom. He had no need of ..."

Yeshua interrupted, "Saul had Samuel. David had Natan. All the kings had prophets except for Solomon. He had no one to speak truth to him."

Miri picked up the thought. "Even his brothers were afraid to speak a cross word to him."

Yeshua added, "I have heard people speak of the emperor in Rome in the same manner – that he allows no dissent."

"Enough!" The rabbi spat this word out. "This is nonsense and blasphemy ... and dangerous!" He turned to the boys. "My students, I command you to ignore this drivel. The fool always thinks his way is right. The wise listen to advice. Put no faith in your own perception but trust in Hashem with your whole heart."

Yeshua mumbled something under his breath.

"What did you say?" Asked Yedu.

"Something else Te'oma used to say: Some people are full of light and illuminate everything around them. Some are full of darkness."

The rabbi was already up. "Come along, young ones. Ya'aqob, it is a pity that your brother seems to be born for adversity. And as for this haughty girl – I will hear no more of it. These two are caught in a trap spun from their own wicked thoughts and, most likely, deeds."

Ya'aqob sprang to his feet. "Rabbi, my father tried to talk sense into him but he would never listen, and he would never do a full day's work. My father used to say that those who work the land will have bread to spare. Those who chase fantasies have no sense."

"Your father is wise. Come, Yedu let us be off."

"Rabbi, I think I will sit here a while longer." Said Yedu.

Song of Songs

The morning of Yom Shishi the 18th day of Elul.
Shabbat will start this evening at sundown.

Miri enjoyed dressing in the fancy clothes Nura had loaned her. It was important for her to look her best. The white tunic was a bit long, but she was able to cinch it up with a black linen belt so that it wouldn't drag in the dirt. She wrapped the tan palla around her shoulders, under her arms and around her waist, fastening it in the front with a silver clasp. Nura said the image depicted on the clasp was the god Nemetona – a wide face with inlaid pearl eyes set atop a spiral pattern.

She covered her head with a light green scarf, wrapped under her chin and tied in the back. A bundle of extra cloth was fixed behind her head inside the scarf, giving the illusion of abundant hair tied in a bun. She decided to leave her face uncovered and without makeup this time, feeling more secure than when she and Nura had first visited the acropolis. She examined herself at length in Nura's mirror and decided she was ready.

Before leaving this morning, Nura said that she expected to be busy all day. Abiyram had sent for her again. Apparently he was still in a great deal of pain. He complained that his servants were not dressing his feet correctly, so he insisted that Nura come to his villa right away. After that, she needed to visit two women who were about to deliver babies in outlying farms. She did not expect to be back until late evening.

In her absence, Nura entrusted Miri with two important tasks. Miri did not want to let her down. The first task was an honor. She was to go to Natan's house to serve as scribe in recording the final marriage contract. Normally, Natan would employ a rabbi or his apprentice for this job, but the negotiations had dragged on all week, and since Shabbat started tonight at sundown, everyone associated with the synagogue was busy, especially with Hanina in town. He sent word last night to have Nura come to his house this morning.

They certainly have delayed this until the last minute, Miri thought. The wedding ceremony was supposed to start tomorrow night at the beginning of the new day after Shabbat. She hoped that all the details were now resolved.

Thus Natan would be expecting Nura. Miri was apprehensive about how *she* would be received in her place. "Just do as you are told," Nura advised. "Natan is a stern master of his house, but he is fair. Likely, he will be incredulous that such an important task is given to one so young. He may even be insulting. But you will do fine."

The second task was more worrisome. She was to accompany Yeshua to deliver the next batch of potion. Phasaelis had sent word yesterday through Mattanyah that this needed to be done this afternoon at the third hour after midday. Nura did not want to send Yeshua by himself for fear that he would say or do something improper and end up confined again in someone's work yard. Miri's job therefore was to keep Yeshua focused and out of trouble.

As she finished dressing in her upstairs room, the sounds of voices came through the unshuttered window from the courtyard. She looked down to see Apulia and Zibiah washing clothes while their babies slept in the shade. It sounded like the two were arguing, but in hushed tones, not wanting to wake the infants. Miri stood by the window and listened.

Zibiah's voice was soothing. "I'm sorry my beloved. I hate to leave you, but we both knew this day would come."

"*Knew this day would come!*" Mocked Apulia angrily. "How long have you known? I thought you just found out. Has he sent for you before?"

"No, my love. My husband's servant arrived just yesterday, during the afternoon when you were out. I simply meant that, as much as I want to stay here with you, I must think of my daughter. I cannot raise her by myself."

"You aren't by yourself, my lovely."

"You know what I mean. How will she marry? Who will pay her dowry? How will we manage? There will be bad times ahead."

"Marriage is overrated," said Apulia sourly. "How can you go back to that man after he cast you out?"

Zibiah exhaled heavily and collected her thoughts. She spoke slowly and evenly. "These months have been the happiest of my life. How you delight me! You are a lily among thistles."

There was a prolonged silence. Miri peeked out and saw the two women embracing. Apulia said, "Stay with me. Will your husband satisfy you the way I do? Will he cherish you? Stay with me, Zibiah. When I return to work I can make enough for us to live on."

After another silence Zibiah spoke again. "My love, the servant who came said that my husband is fasting and wearing sackcloth. He has been shamed by the rabbi and has repented. It is my daughter's only hope for a prosperous life. Surely you see that, my beloved?" She sounded like she was trying to convince herself. "Besides ..."

"What?" Asked Apulia curtly.

Zibiah sighed. "It is not a request. I am commanded to return. If I refuse, he will come and take me. And then it will be much worse for my baby."

Apulia realized that this was likely true. She was bitter. "How did he find you here?"

"The servant was clever. He traced my steps to Sepphoris and then asked around where a destitute woman and child might be staying. It wasn't hard."

Miri ducked back into her room. She descended the ladder and left the house. She did not want to disturb the two women. Miri had nothing to offer in this matter. She had no experience with husbands, lovers, and children. She probably never would.

~

They had been waiting for some time when Miri arrived at Natan's house. She was greeted at the door by a tall manservant and shown to an interior room. The large space was well lit with abundant candles. A long rectangular table took up the center of the room.

"Miryam?" Natan stood when she was shown in. "We were expecting Nura. And some time ago, I might add."

"Yes sir. I came as quickly as I could. Nura sends her regrets. She was called away for an emergency. She said to tell you that Abiyram was in need."

"Abiyram. Well. Yes of course. If *he* needs her then I suppose she must go." Natan looked doubtfully at the people in the room. Miri saw Ruth, Channah, Taletha and Yedu against the back wall. The women remained seated, but Yedu had risen to his feet with a grin when she entered. Ephrayim cleared his throat and stood up from his seat at the far end of the table. He nodded discretely at Miri.

"It would seem," said Natan to the assembly, "that we are without a scribe."

Miri tapped him on the shoulder. "Sir, Nura sent me in her stead. If it pleases you, I will perform this duty for you."

"You!" Natan raised his eyebrows in surprise. "Do *all* of Nura's relations read and write?"

Miri demurred. "No sir, I learned as a child from my brother. To be truthful, my lord, I have never before acted as a scribe. But I *can* write, and if you have patience with me, I will get the job done."

Natan frowned and rubbed his beard. "We shall see. We shall see. But first, introductions. I believe you know my wife and son. And I believe you have already met Taletha?"

By now everyone had risen. Miri took Taletha's hands in her own. "Dearest Taletha, I trust that you have been well?"

Taletha's face brightened. "Oh yes ... Miri. And you are looking well. I haven't seen you since that unhappy business last week with the soldiers. I tell you, that was quite a fright. It's good to see some color back in your cheeks, and you look like you've been eating well, though I must say the city food is not as wholesome as what we eat in the villages. I hope that you plan to come to Cana for the third day of the wedding celebration. We will give you a taste of real hospitality – oh, not that we're at all unsatisfied with our kin here in Sepphoris."

Ruth came forward and kissed Miri. "It is a pleasure to see you again dear. And Taletha, the way you talk it sounds as if you and Miri are old friends."

Miri answered, fearing her aunt's ramblings would give her away. "No, dearest Ruth, we have met but twice. But we had such a good talk, didn't we, Taletha? I feel as if I know you well. I am pleased to be an invited guest to your son's wedding."

Taletha winked conspiratorially. "Oh, yes. I have the feeling that I have known you for some time also. And now, allow me to introduce my son, who was not with us when I saw you last week." She indicated Ephrayim, who came forward and greeted her.

Natan clapped his hands together. "Well then. We shall get started. Miryam, you sit there." He indicated a seat at the center of the long side of the table. Natan and Ephrayim sat on either end. The others reclaimed their seats against the back wall.

On the table in front of Miri was a stack of wax tablets and a sharp metal stylus. She took the top tablet and saw that it was clean. She set it down in front of her and picked up the stylus.

Natan cleared his throat. "Now, let us see what kind of scribe you are. Write down what I tell you – no more, no less. You will do the contract on wax here as we work, in case we need to make changes. When we are finished, assuming we *do* finish, you are to copy the finished agreement onto papyrus, which we will both sign at the ceremony tomorrow."

Miri nodded her head.

Natan looked at the ceiling and collected his thoughts. "Scribe, write this down: On this, the twenty-first day of the month Elul in the year three thousand seven hundred and seventy four since the creation of the world according to the reckoning we are accustomed to use here ..." He saw the questioning look from Miri. "Yes I know – that is tomorrow's date, the date of the wedding – write it down. Where was I? Oh yes ... here in the city of Sepphoris in the province of Yudaea, according to the law of Moses and Israel and according to universal custom, whereas Ephrayim bar Hozai, betrothed bridegroom, is the oldest surviving male progeny and is therefore head of his own household in this matter; and whereas Natan is head of household representing the virgin Channah, betrothed bride; and whereas Hozai and Natan share common blood lineage as first cousins and have agreed prior to Hozai's death that Natan's eldest surviving daughter shall marry Hozai's eldest surviving scion, with the purpose of continuing the bloodline and keeping land and property within the clan; the two parties hereby agree to the following terms." He looked at Miri again. "Do you have that much, scribe?"

Miri was busily scribbling. She was not used to such formal language and unfamiliar with some of the words. After a moment she finished, looked up at Natan and nodded. "Would you like to hear it?"

Natan nodded. Miri read it back flawlessly.

"I see that Nura's trust in you was not misplaced," said Natan. "Very good. Now then, shall we enumerate the dowry?"

Since the dowry was to be paid by the bride's family, it was Natan who continued. "We have agreed that the items of jewelry on this list ..." He brought forth a sheet of papyrus and handed it to Miri. "Scribe, please copy this into the final contract later. ... That these items be entrusted to Channah with the stipulation that they are not to be sold, but rather passed to the new couple's female progeny as part of future dowries. If the couple produces no female offspring who retain virginity to a marriageable age, the items shall be given to Yeduthun's female offspring. Otherwise, these items may be disposed of in Ephrayim's will as he sees fit." He looked questioningly at Ephrayim. "Any objection or comment?"

Channah knew that the items being discussed included some of her mother's finest ornaments. She glanced at Ruth with gratitude.

"Very well," continued Natan. "Write this down, scribe: For as long as Natan holds a position of authority in Herod's government in Sepphoris, Natan agrees to act as primary patron of Ephrayim and agrees to advocate for him in tax disputes, should any arise."

Ephrayim and Taletha exchanged a knowing look. Although intangible, this was perhaps the most valuable item being offered by Natan. It represented insurance that Ephrayim would not lose the farm like so many others who had the misfortune of falling behind on debt obligations.

Natan noted their look of satisfaction. "Do not be too complacent, *son*. Political appointments are fleeting. I am well situated now, but that could change overnight. Indeed, they are scheming to replace Ba'asha with some new scoundrel from the east, who, I hear, is even more ruthless. I could be begging *you* for lodgings before the year is ended."

Everyone thought, or hoped, that Natan was exaggerating.

Natan clapped his hands twice and called out, "Doron, come in here!"

The same tall man who had answered the door for Miri came into the room. He had stripped off all of his clothes except for a loincloth. He stood before the group at attention, his impressive musculature on full display.

Natan tapped the table to get Miri's attention. "Scribe, the next item: one healthy male slave suitable for farm work." He turned to Ephrayim. "Son, I hope you find this one acceptable? He has served me well."

"Uh, *father*, might I make a comment?" interjected Ephrayim.

"Of course, speak your mind."

Ephrayim exchanged a glance with Taletha. "We have never owned slaves and have no facilities for caring for them. We would prefer it be written that you shall lend us the use of one of your slaves during planting and harvest seasons."

Natan raised an eyebrow and glanced at Taletha. "Is this true madam? Your husband, *my cousin*, never owned slaves?"

Taletha bowed her head. "Yes, my lord. It never seemed to be the prudent thing to do – the uncertainty of living off the land, you know."

Natan rubbed his beard and thought about this. "Very good. I suppose that's better for me. Doron, you may go. Scribe, write it down as Ephrayim suggests."

Miri nodded and continued writing. Natan asked her to read the clause back. It was acceptable to all.

Natan added, "The final dowry item is five hundred denarii." Here Natan looked concerned. "*Son,* you perhaps heard of my foolish pledge to Hanina earlier this week. That has brought me up a bit short at present. I will make good on the agreed sum, but I may need some time to collect the full amount."

"I understand, father. That will not be a problem."

"Good then," said Natan with relief. "Shall we move on to the brideprice? I will let you enumerate these items, son."

"Thank you father." Then with a smirk, Ephrayim said in an imperious tone, "Scribe! Write this down!" Miri looked up and cocked an eyebrow. She began writing again as her secret cousin spoke, "Ephrayim bar Hozai agrees to provide a future sum of no more than three hundred denarii to Yeduthun bar Natan when he reaches marriageable age and becomes betrothed. This sum is to be used toward a brideprice that Yeduthun may be required to pay. Should Yeduthun not survive to marriageable age, or fail to become betrothed for any reason, this obligation shall be abrogated."

Yedu had not known about this part of the agreement. He caught his father's eye with a questioning look.

Natan winked. "Yes. That is as agreed. Now the percentages."

"Ephrayim agrees to pay Natan the equivalent of twenty percent of olive oil and raw olives, and fifteen percent of all grain sold at market for a period of five years."

"Do you have that, scribe?" asked Natan. Miri nodded.

"Good. I think Ephrayim was worried that I was going to demand Philistine foreskins." It was a poor attempt at humor and Natan was the only one to laugh. "Very well," he continued. "Now we have certain other stipulations which must be written into the agreement. First, the adultery clause. I suggest as follows: If, after their marriage is consummated, Channah is found to have been unfaithful to her husband, the matter shall be turned over to the Sanhedrin or their representatives for examination. Subsequently, after the execution of her sentence, the sum of one hundred denarii will be returned to her surviving sibling, Yeduthun. Ephrayim agrees to faithfully raise any children given to him by Channah, including daughters."

Miri wrote this down. All the women in the room knew what the antiseptic phrase *execution of her sentence* meant. A thought occurred to her that she should sneak a symmetrical clause into the text describing what should happen if Ephrayim was unfaithful. She decided that would not be prudent.

"However," continued Natan, "if the marriage is terminated by Ephrayim by writ of divorce for any other reason, then ..."

"Father ..." Channah interrupted, speaking for the first time at the gathering. "This clause seems unnecessary to me. I know that Ephrayim would never ..."

"Be silent, daughter! I have not given you permission to speak." Seeing her hurt look, he said with softer tone, "Daughter look at me. What you say is foolish. This is a standard part of every ketubah. You are comely now, and the flames of your passion are hot. Wait until you have had a child or two and your shoulders are bent with the weight of life on a farm. That is when a husband's eye starts to roam. Then you might not be so eager to waive your right to this penalty."

Chastised, Channah nodded silently.

Ephrayim said to his betrothed, "Do not worry, my bride, I will willingly pledge any reasonable penalty that Natan can name."

Natan leaned toward his daughter with a smile. "Do you see how he equivocates even now with the word *reasonable?*"

Ephrayim sputtered, "No, I did not mean ..."

Natan waved his arms. "No need to explain, *my son*. We all know what you meant. But be careful of what words you use – especially in the presence of women. Now, Miryam, to finish the clause, where did we leave off?"

Miri read the last thing she had written. "If the marriage is terminated by Ephrayim by writ of divorce for any other reason ..."

"Then he shall return the entire dowry plus a sum of one thousand denarii, or the equivalent in land."

Ephrayim's jaw dropped. This was an astronomical sum – more money than he could ever pay. However, he said nothing.

"Very good," continued Natan. "The final stipulation that we agreed to last time: The firstborn daughter of Ephrayim and Channah shall be offered as a bride to the firstborn son of Ya'akov bar Yoceph, the eldest son of Yoceph. Should Ya'akov bar Yoceph not marry or produce a son, this obligation shall be abrogated."

As she wrote, Miri pondered that children not even conceived – indeed, Ya'akov was still but a boy – that these children have already been married off, all for the survival of the family clan.

The negotiations thus concluded, the assembly retired to the courtyard for refreshments, leaving Miri to make a copy of the final contract on papyrus. She did so carefully, in large bold letters. She left a space at the bottom for Natan and Ephrayim, along with two witnesses, to make their marks, as was the custom.

∼

After Miri finished the ketubah, she joined Taletha, Ruth, and Channah in the courtyard for a light meal of bread, goat cheese, and fruit. Channah is blessed, thought Miri. She is marrying a man with a good heart and a good mind. Ephrayim will treat her with the dignity she deserves.

The women were left alone. Natan had business in town and had taken Yedu with him. Ephrayim had excused himself to take care of last-minute preparations at the farm in Cana.

Miri looked up at the sky and judged it to be about midday. It was now time to begin preparations for this evening's Shabbat meal. Ruth asked Miri if she would like to stay and join them.

"I would, but Nura gave me one more task which cannot be

delayed. I should be back by sundown, and if it is agreeable, I would very much like to join you for the meal."

Miri took her leave and walked the short distance back to Nura's house to collect Yeshua. He had tended the pig herds last night and had arrived home shortly after dawn. She entered the barn and called. She heard his groggy answer. She returned to the street to wait for him. After a few minutes, he emerged with an apple in his mouth.

He complemented her on her fine outfit and the two set out on their way. It was an enjoyable walk. The weather was mild and they passed the time in a comfortable silence. They were nearly to the top of the long sloping road along the north side of the acropolis when they stopped to look out over the sprawling Roman encampment.

"So many," remarked Yeshua. They watched a contingent of soldiers practicing maneuvers in the field at the base of the hill. There were hundreds of them, perhaps thousands. The sophistication of the armor, weapons, and tactics was daunting. "How does one oppose *that*?"

Miri looked at him. "You cannot." She took his hand. "Yeshua, Nura worries about you. *I* worry about you. Promise me you will remember your place while we are at the palace."

"It will be fine," he said, but not very convincingly.

They finished the short walk to the gate and entered the grassy area just inside. From the sundial at the edge of the forum they saw that they were more than an hour early. The message from Phasaelis said specifically to arrive at the third hour after midday.

"What shall we do?" asked Miri.

"We could wait in the kitchen. Maybe the cook will feed us."

"Are you *always* hungry?" They stood at the edge of the long forum – the same spot where she and Nura had stood a week earlier. So much had happened since that time. She felt much stronger. She had a thought: "Show me where Ba'asha lived – where you were imprisoned."

Yeshua shrugged. "If you're sure you want to. It's over there in that cluster of villas." He motioned to the north edge of the hill. "It's back a bit, behind the others."

He led her through a maze of curving lanes a little way down the slope. They stopped in front of a particularly large villa. "This is the one. Old Ba'asha lived here with his fat wife and daughter. Hopefully, he left them something in his will. There's nothing worse than someone raised in luxury suddenly becoming destitute. Sometimes I think it's a blessing to be born poor."

They stood in silence. Miri didn't know what insight she had expected to gain from seeing her attacker's house. There was nothing here – just a house.

They became aware of a man standing on the roof of the villa returning their stare. He came toward them. They couldn't see his face because he was shielding his eyes from the sun with his hand. When he was quite near, he let his hand down and called out, "Naomi?"

Miri locked eyes with the man on the rooftop. Her whole body shuddered with recognition. It was Lebbaeus from Magdala. "What in creation is he doing here?" she asked out loud.

Lebbaeus called again. "Naomi, it *is* you. I command you, wait there!" He ran toward the back of the house. He would be here very soon, most likely with those horrible brutes of his.

Miri scolded herself for being so careless. Now she would pay for this mistake. She grabbed Yeshua's arm and pulled him hard. "Run!" They bolted off in the direction from which they had come.

Yeshua pointed to an alley leading to the right, behind another villa. "This way. Follow me." They ran to the end and stopped where a cliff face fell away before them. Yeshua pushed Miri to the left. "There. Be careful." They walked side-legged along a narrow purchase with their backs against a high concrete wall. In front of them was a forty-foot drop. They passed by another alley leading inward toward the forum.

They stayed on the ledge and proceeded past the next building. Yeshua explained that this was the aristocrat's bathhouse – a smaller version of the one in the town center. Here at least there was a wide path between the wall and the drop. It was paved, with ruts worn into the stone from innumerable wagons carting water barrels.

Past the bathhouse they came to the old wing of the basilica. Here again they had to skirt a narrow space on the outside of a concrete fence, but the slope wasn't as steep here so they felt safer, and could move more quickly.

They arrived at the back of a large building that was still under construction. "This is the new basilica. My uncle is one of the builders here. I don't know if he is here today or not. I haven't been allowed on the site since the accident with the crane."

There was an open door at the back of the building where numerous laborers came and went. In the yard behind the building lay stacks of different colored tiles, tools, piles of rough lumber, and buckets of grout. The workmen went about their tasks, ignoring Yeshua and Miri. They probably assumed that Miri, being dressed in fine clothes, was some nobleman's wife out for a stroll, and that Yeshua was her slave.

They observed men carrying buckets of dirt and mud coming from a basement door. "Tunnels," said Yeshua. "The whole hill is a warren of tunnels. They must be digging to connect this building to something else underground."

Seeing the filthy men gave Yeshua an idea. He pulled Miri into the building. They ducked into an empty alcove – an area destined to be a storage room of some kind. When they were alone, he asked with a grin. "What is it that Te'oma used to say? The female becomes male, or something?" Seeing that this elicited no response, he added, "We both need to look like workers. They will be looking for a well-dressed young lady."

Miri understood. "But ... these are Nura's fine clothes."

"She'll be more upset if you get killed."

Miri ripped the bottom of her fine white tunic off at the knee. She removed the fancy palla and silver clasp, setting them on the ground. Finally, she removed the long green scarf, revealing her close-cropped dark hair. "Face the other way," she said.

Yeshua hesitated, so Miri took his shoulders and turned him toward the wall. She removed her tunic and wrapped the long headscarf tightly around her bosom. She fastened the clasp on the side to hold it in place and donned her tunic again. "You can turn around now."

Yeshua looked at her and nodded. "Good, but we are too clean. Wait here." He went out to where the laborers were dumping excavation mud down the hillside. He took a full bucket and headed back into the building. He also picked up a couple of tools – an iron pry-bar for moving stone blocks and a small trowel. When he returned, the two muddied themselves from head to toe.

They left the bucket in the alcove and exited to the back once again, carrying the tools. Now they blended in perfectly with the other workers. They followed a path around the southern side of the building and came to the edge of the forum. Here, they were fully exposed. They still had to get across the open area in front of Herod's palace and down the side path to the kitchen.

Miri looked across the forum at the main gate through which they had come just a short time ago. There was lots of activity there now. "Lebbaeus has alerted them. They are looking for us."

Indeed, two of Herod's guards were walking toward them now. They seemed in no particular hurry, stopping people as they went and asking questions. "Quick!" Yeshua pointed to the base of a dividing fence. "Use your trowel. Bend down and dig around that stone there."

Miri nodded and did as she was told. She began scraping in the dirt at the base of the stone. When the guards were within earshot, Yeshua yelled at Miri, "No! Do it right! How stupid you are." He pulled off his rope belt and whipped her smartly across the back. She arched her back in surprise but managed to avoid crying out. She accelerated her pointless labor on the stone.

When the guards arrived, they looked bored. One of them asked in an officious tone, "We are looking for two people – a boy and a girl – well dressed. Have they passed this way?"

Yeshua feigned annoyance. "What! You want me to do *your* job as well as manage these lazy slaves? Tell you what – I'll go find your boy and girl if you run this worthless work crew for me."

The guards shook their heads and retreated. When they had gone around the corner, Miri stood up rubbing her back. She gave Yeshua a dark stare. "That. Hurt."

Yeshua ignored her, already planning the next ruse. He pointed to the front of the basilica. "Baskets! Grab one. They don't look heavy." They each picked up a large basket and walked directly in front of Herod's palace, blending in with other laborers carrying provisions here and there. No one noticed that they were covered in dirt. "Walk slowly," he said under his breath. "Act like a slave. When we finish this task there will be another. Take your time."

At last they made it to the narrow descending path on the side of the palace. When they were out of sight from the forum, Miri put a hand on Yeshua's shoulder. "Stop. We should try to clean ourselves a bit. Last week, when Nura and I made the delivery, the *queen* came to the kitchen to meet us. Here." She handed Yeshua a strip of the cloth she had ripped from the bottom of her tunic. He wiped his face and arms and handed it back to her. She did the same. "We probably still look awful, but it will have to do." They discarded the baskets and proceeded to the door.

Yeshua knocked loudly. A dour-faced woman answered before the third rap. She stood in the entrance with her arms folded. She looked doubtfully at two boys covered in mud in her entranceway.

"Afra," said Yeshua. "Afra is expecting us."

The woman gave them a look of extreme annoyance. "Ha, alud. Lagbar. Iz'zan. Q'qim!" She gestured at their filthy clothes and held her palm out, indicating that they should wait here. She called over her shoulder into the kitchen, "Afra! Ibx'xusn nek'nt bed'd letb't!"

Yeshua leaned close to Miri. "Their tongue is difficult. I know only a few words, but I think she just called us bugs."

Miri recognized Afra when she came to the door. Her oily hair was tied behind her head, her apron still stained with blood, as it had been the last time Miri saw her.

When Afra saw Yeshua her usual scowl evaporated and was replaced with a wide smile. "Yeeshew! Ibx'xusn tafq, iyyah. Z'qlil d abiba!" She grabbed his shoulders and held him at arm's length. She turned him around, looking disapprovingly at his soiled tunic. Finally she slapped his backside and broke into wild laughter. "K'sm, k'sm ... enter." She pulled him into the room.

Miri followed before the door was closed in her face. Inside the kitchen, it was just as hot and even more busy than the last time Miri had visited. Afra pulled Yeshua by the arm toward the end of a table and pushed him forcibly down onto the bench. She pinched his arm and said, "K'yin g igsan, g d'ef. Awg, awg ... that to say, eat! Ixssa g libam d hlu ami." She grabbed a wooden bowl from a shelf and took it to one of the cauldrons. Ignoring the angry look from the other cook, she scooped out some grayish porridge and set it before Yeshua. "Awg," she repeated.

Yeshua tentatively dipped his fingers into the bowl and tasted the slop. He nodded his head in approval. "Good – sweet. Ah ... Ihlwa."

His use of her language charmed Afra. She playfully ruffled his hair and gazed at him as he ate.

Miri had thus far been ignored. She now stepped forward and pulled the carved vial from her inside pocket. Remembering how Afra had pronounced it on their previous visit, she tapped Afra on the shoulder. "Pooshna ... for the queen," she said flatly.

Afra noticed Miri for the first time. She raised her eyebrows and took a hard look at her. She ran her calloused hand over Miri's cheeks and hair. She laughed and turned again to Yeshua. "Tarbat. Girl. Iyyah?" Yeshua nodded his head as he chewed. This elicited a peal of laughter from the woman. "Bid'dl im'ndir taymust? Uh, to say ... shape shifter?"

Yeshua shook his head. "No. Just a girl. Tarbat."

Satisfied, Afra took the vial from Miri and retrieved a gold coin from within her ample bosom. She handed this to Miri, and then remembering, she stabbed a finger in the air, walked to one of the tables, and returned with a turnip. She took Miri's hand and closed it around the tuber. "Taweret." she said solemnly.

Yeshua began to rise, but Afra pushed him back down. "Awg. Eat," she repeated. She took his empty bowl and once again turned toward the cauldron.

"No. Ha," called Yeshua. "Thank you, uh ... sa'ha. We must leave." He rose from the table and gestured toward the door.

Afra looked disappointed. She suddenly gripped Yeshua in a smothering bear hug and rocked him back and forth. He returned the hug, which lasted an uncomfortable amount of time. At length Miri cleared her throat.

Yeshua freed himself from the embrace. He had a thought. "Afra ..." He struggled for the right way to communicate this. He pointed to the door and shook his head from side to side. "Aesasa ... i'xatar ... danger. Rul?" He gestured now toward the inner doorway leading to the interior of the palace.

Afra scratched her head and looked at him like he was crazy. "I'xatar?" she repeated. Yeshua nodded. A look of recognition came over her face. "Eh ..." she pointed to their soiled clothes. "Alud. Iyyah? Iyyah. Tanufti ... to say, Cistern? Iyyah?"

Yeshua nodded and said to Miri, "I think she says there is a way to go out through a cistern."

Afra wagged a finger at Miri and said sternly, "Hd'u awj'jim q'qar d awi argaz'nm'i." One of the other cooks, a young skinny girl with abundant blemishes on her face, began chuckling.

Afra took Yeshua's hand and led him quickly into the interior of the building. Miri followed close behind. They took several turns until they arrived in a long corridor that terminated in a dark staircase leading down. She detached a torch from the sconce on the wall and handed it to Yeshua. "S'flid ... listen. Ankh." She pointed at the space above the passageway leading down the stair. "Ankh," she repeated.

"An?" repeated Yeshua blankly. "I don't know that word." He shrugged his shoulders.

Afra shook her head in frustration. Using her finger she traced a shape on the wall.

"Ah," exclaimed Miri. She pulled the leather cord around her neck and produced the polished ivory token that she had worn under her tunic since the day she had met the seer. "Ankh," she said reverently. "A token of Usat. It means life."

Afra's eyes widened. She looked at Miri with new appreciation. She touched the ivory figure and again pointed high on the wall. "Ujju ... b'eda nzug afla'n aman. Iyyah? Nzug afla'n aman," she said slowly.

"What is she saying?" Asked Miri.

"I'm not sure. Ujju is down, that much is clear. Nzug is walk and Aman is water. Walk on water? Then, I think she means that we should look for this symbol – the ankh."

"Walk on ... what?" Miri wanted to ask another question but just then they heard someone approaching from down the hallway. Afra shoved Miri toward the dark stairway. As Yeshua passed, Afra attempted to capture him in another embrace. Miri put her hand out to intercept. "Mine," she said emphatically. Afra retreated down the hall, cackling.

~

The staircase was surprisingly long with many turns. By the time they reached the bottom, they had lost all sense of direction. Finally, the ground leveled out. They followed a low vaulted corridor, which opened up into a cavernous space. The dancing torchlight revealed a ceiling of domes and arches extending as far as they could see. Something about the acoustics was strange, and the floor was wrong too – it was shiny, reflecting myriad glittering points of micah and quartz in the ceiling.

"Water," whispered Miri. She picked up a pebble from the dirt floor and tossed it into the room. They heard a 'plunk' and watched ripples spread out in all directions. "Akka said we are to walk on water. Here it is."

"I have heard about these underground cisterns. This is how they keep the city supplied with water in times of drought. Look." Yeshua pointed a short distance down a narrow ledge where a catwalk extended out over the pool. "Let's go."

The catwalk was a rickety affair. A lattice of ropes was attached to the arches every thirty feet or so. Wooden planks were woven into the lattice at the bottom for footholds, spaced such that it would be easy to fall through if one were not careful. Yeshua grabbed a rope and stepped out onto the first plank. It sagged deeply, causing the length of the bridge to vibrate in harmonic motion. "Wait until I get to the next arch before you step out. Do you want to carry the torch?"

"No. You hold it. But go slow."

Yeshua took tentative steps and made it to the first arch. He crouched down low, but he still could not see the other side of the water. He beckoned for Miri to come.

It was slow going. The catwalk made several turns as it went through the uneven arches. Eventually they came to another rock floor – a landing between the water and the cavern wall. Miri was thankful to step on solid ground. The 'shore' here was much wider, and it appeared to slope gently into the water. "Look!" She pointed to a low alcove carved into the wall. They went to it.

Yeshua shined his torchlight into the space. It contained four cots, a small table, and a stack of shelves with various supplies. "People sleep down here?"

They found oil lamps, spare oil, and other implements. They lit some of the lamps, improving the light considerably. At the far end of the landing they found an entrance to a low, dark tunnel. Sure enough, carved above the entrance was a cross-topped with an oval.

"I have been thinking about that," said Yeshua. "You say this ... ankh is a symbol for life. This tunnel must have been dug as a secret way to escape a siege. Other cities have them too. They say old King David managed to capture Yerushalayim because he found the escape tunnel. He led his army up through it and surprised the people living there.

"Take one of the lamps with you, in case my torch sputters," he said.

The tunnel extended back at a slight downward slope. It was not much wider than a man and it had an uneven, arched ceiling reinforced in places with shaped building stones. Yeshua led. He almost fell forward when the floor disappeared in front of him.

"Staircase," he said. "We go down again."

The steps hewn into the rock were steep, more than twice as high as they were wide. Miri found herself counting as they descended. "Twenty-seven," she said aloud when they reached the bottom.

"What?"

"Twenty seven steps. Look." The cave forked. The right branch led to another descending stairway. The other became level and angled sharply to the left. Miri held her lamp high, examining the walls. Over the right branch someone had carved: χλζζλ. She traced her finger over the letters. "What does it say?"

Yeshua shook his head. "The letters are Greek, but it's nonsense. Some kind of label, perhaps an incantation." A foul odor wafted up from the depths.

Try as they might, they could not find any carvings on the other passage. They decided to take it anyway because of the absence of odor. After a short distance the path became very rough with abrupt turns and drops. The floor was strewn with rubble. Miri heard the sound of trickling water and noticed a terracotta pipe running along the floor.

At length, the tunnel forked yet again. On the floor just inside one branch was carved a foot, a feather, and a bird. Near the top of the other, they were relieved to find the ankh. They were still on the right path. They continued, and, after a short distance they started to see daylight in the distance. Then they felt a moist breeze blowing in their faces. They emerged onto a narrow wooden platform built on a cliff face high above the road. A rickety ladder descended from the platform to the ground. Yeshua noticed an iron sconce set into the wall just inside the cave. He set his torch in it. "Put your lamp down here but don't put it out yet. We might need to go back."

Miri shook her head. "But why would we ..."

Yeshua quickly clamped his hand over his own mouth. He pointed toward the road below.

They both silently leaned forward. Three guards came running down the hill. "Do you think they are looking for us?" whispered

Miri. The question was answered when the guards stopped a couple coming up the hill – a man and a woman. The guards quickly became convinced that these people were too old to be the ones they sought. Also, they were heading the wrong way: up to the acropolis, not fleeing from it.

Miri and Yeshua ducked back inside the cave. Miri paced back and forth. "It is too dangerous. We will never make it." She looked despondent. "Nura sent me to keep *you* out of trouble. It seems that this time I have brought it."

"Don't worry," said Yeshua. "Let's retrace our steps back to the big cistern. It's not far. We can rest there and think. Maybe there is food there. We just need to wait until nightfall."

The trip up the steep stairs was more difficult than coming down. They had worked up a sweat by the time they arrived again at the edge of the underground pool. They rifled through the shelves in the alcove more thoroughly. Aside from more lamps and oil jars, they found towels, vials of perfumed oil, and a stack of clean, dry tunics. Miri couldn't be sure in the lamplight, but they looked like the same tan tunics the servants wore in Herod's palace. They found no food.

Miri dragged a bench from the alcove and sat in the gloom looking at the glittering reflections in the water. "How long do you think we should wait?" asked Miri.

"An hour. Two to be safe." Yeshua settled himself on the floor with his back to the cavern wall.

Miri sighed. "I am hungry. I was not offered any of Afra's porridge."

"Sorry." Yeshua gestured out to the pool. "We have plenty of water, and say, don't you have a turnip?" Miri ignored this. "We'll get out when it's dark. I know a back way through the woods to sneak into town."

Miri sat in silence swinging her legs back and forth. "I need to bathe. I am still covered in mud." Without waiting for a response, she stood up and extinguished all but two of the lamps. The torch had already sputtered. She removed her soiled tunic and tossed it aside. She undid the clasp and unwrapped the long scarf from around her torso. She gingerly waded into the water, testing each footfall, not knowing if the gentle slope continued, or if there would be a sudden drop.

Yeshua said nothing, not wishing to intrude on Miri's privacy. He watched her shadowy form recede into the water. At length he heard her voice from the darkness. "Are you coming in?"

~

The quartermaster tapped his foot angrily as he stared at the task before him. How were he and two scrawny slave boys supposed to unload two full supply wagons? These weren't small mule carts. *These* were the enormous wagons used by Roman troops, each one pulled by a team of six oxen. And each was as loaded as it could possibly be. One was so heavy it had damaged an axle on the way here from Caesarea.

The wagons had been left in front of the market warehouse in the center of town, guarded by a single Roman soldier. The quartermaster and his two boys had come with three small donkey carts from Herod's stables. They had been waiting for over an hour now. Ten slaves had been promised to help with the job. It was already quite late, and the quartermaster was looking forward to sitting at home by the fire with a glass of wine in his hand.

He adjusted the scarf around his neck. There was a chill in the night air. He scratched a scab on the side of his bulbous nose and stole a glance at the guard lounging on a nearby bench. The guard upended a wineskin into his mouth and wiped his face with his sleeve. Useless. There would be little chance of getting any work out of him.

And also, where was Palluw? The crooked old merchant was usually here early, especially when a shipment as good as *this* arrived. Palluw would bring his own boys to help with the loading. In the process, several items would go missing. These would be repackaged and sold at market. The profits would be shared evenly. It was a lucrative arrangement and the quartermaster enjoyed the extra coin.

He had already perused the contents of these wagons, keeping an eye out for items that came in sufficient quantity such that, if a few went missing, no one would notice. Or if anyone did notice, it would be attributed to a mistake in the manifest. There were some nice possibilities here that would bring a tidy profit.

His two boys were working hard now, but would soon tire. Where were the others? The quartermaster craned his neck to look up the hill toward the palace. You would think they would place more importance on *these* supplies, what with Herod's return from Rome and the banquet scheduled for two nights hence. Somebody messed up.

He glanced again down the side lane where Palluw kept his lodgings. Nobody coming from that way either. Perhaps the old miser didn't get my message.

He rubbed his chin as he mulled over this business arrangement. He suspected that, in their recent collaborations, Palluw was not dealing straight – that he was holding more back for himself. He would have to think of a way to check up on him. Perhaps a renegotiation of the percentages was in order. After all, was it not the quartermaster himself who was taking the lion's share of the risk?

Earlier this evening, the quartermaster had spied an area around the side of the warehouse where stacks of old crates and broken amphorae had been discarded. If Palluw didn't show up by the time they were finished, he'd have one of the slaves hide some provisions there. Then he'd send word to Palluw to retrieve them. This opportunity was too good to pass up.

He tacked the two manifests on the side of one of the wagons and surveyed the contents of the shipment one more time. Artichokes soaked in oil and wrapped in grape leaves – too perishable and not a good resale value, and too sophisticated for the Sepphoris palette. There were nine crates of fresh quinces and fourteen of plums. The quinces were always popular. One crate of each fruit would not be missed. One hundred and forty live hares and two hundred and twenty dormice. The quartermaster had to scratch his head at this one. Do we not have sufficient rodents of our own? There were eleven crates of filberts. Just one of those would bring a good price.

He continued to scan down the list: fried crickets, salted eel, sacks of some kind of fancy grain he had never heard of, forty-two jars of honey. He could probably take four of those. Eight crates containing jars of oil infused with herbs. That might be interesting, he thought. Ah – here it is: four barrels of mulsum. The quartermaster frowned as he considered this. He personally loved the honeyed wine and he knew he could water down a barrel, divide it into smaller jars, and sell them for a fine price. But since only four barrels were shipped, he worried that a missing one would be noticed. He didn't get where he was now by being reckless.

There were crates containing smaller sacks of various seeds to be ground for spices. No good – an open crate would be noticed. There were numerous pieces of furniture. Also no good – each one was separately inventoried in the manifest. Likewise for the stone sculptures wrapped in straw.

He skipped down to the last item on the list. This was the real prize. The manifest said that each wagon held fifteen barrels labeled, "Caecubum DCCXLIX Ab Urbe Conditiae." He did a quick calculation and grinned broadly. That meant the wine was now nineteen years old. He thought he could get away with taking a barrel from each wagon. He had only tasted Caecubum once in his life. His mouth watered with the memory. Making sure that the guard wasn't watching, he took his charcoal stick and scratched an 'I' between the X and the V on each manifest. It now said that each wagon held only fourteen barrels.

He took another glance up the hill. Nothing. Then he noticed two boys across the street – a good-sized one, and a scrawny one – casually sauntering by. They both wore the tan tunics identifying them as palace servants. He wondered where they had come from – not from the acropolis road but from somewhere on the south side of town.

"You there!" He started across the street. "Get over here. I've been waiting over an hour. Where are the others?"

~

Yeshua and Miri had waited until dark before descending the rickety ladder. They had come into town via the path that Yeshua knew, emerging from the woods near the tanner's shop. They were now making their way home and looking forward to a meal. Hopefully, Nura had some Shabbat bread remaining.

They turned right on the decumanus and started up the hill. As they passed the market entrance on the opposite side of the street they saw the wagons in front of the warehouse. Yeshua whispered, "Become passerby. Don't look at them."

Miri realized their mistake when a man barked out an order to them. She whispered, "The tunics ... he thinks we are palace slaves. Should we run?"

The man was almost upon them. Yeshua placed a hand gently on her arm. "No. He's got a guard with him. Just keep your face down and your mouth shut."

"Where are you two going? Did you not hear me call?"

Yeshua looked up at the quartermaster with an attitude of contrition. "Yes sir. So it was you they sent us to help. We have been looking for you." He turned back to Miri who was still lagging behind. "Come, brother. This is the man."

"Where are the others? They said *ten* strong boys. I see one ... and a half." He waved his hand dismissively in Miri's direction.

"Nobody told us about any others, sir. My brother is small but you'll see – he is a hard worker. Come, brother." He took Miri's arm and pulled her forward.

The quartermaster led them back toward the wagons. "Better than nothing I suppose. You can drive a donkey cart, can't you?"

"Yes sir," replied Yeshua.

The quartermaster explained the job. They were to unload the large wagons and set the items on the side of the street. Each one would be checked off of the manifest. Most of the items were destined for the palace and had to be loaded onto one of the donkey carts. A few of the items would remain here in storage at the warehouse.

Yeshua's hope for rest and a meal evaporated. He looked at the size of the wagons and the small donkey carts. It would take three or four trips to the palace from where they just escaped. They'd be lucky to finish by daybreak.

They worked for an hour. When the donkey carts were almost full, the quartermaster called Yeshua over. As usual, his younger brother tagged along a few paces behind. The quartermaster spoke in a calm, slow voice. "Listen now. I have a special job for you two." He waited while the two boys exchanged a glance and nodded. "You see the lead cart down the way?" Again he waited for a nod. He had learned that, with slaves, one had to explain things slowly and clearly, and get them to acknowledge every part. "I'm going to call the guard over to that cart. I'm going to ask him to drive it up to the palace. He will argue, and in the end he will refuse. Do you understand?"

"Yes," said Yeshua. "But why ..."

"While we are arguing," continued the quartermaster. "You and your brother are to take *these* items." He gestured toward a collection of barrels, crates, and sacks, which he had set aside. "Take these and hide them. Look over my shoulder. Do you see on the side of the building, where the empty crates are stacked?" He waited for Yeshua to nod. "Hide these items behind those. And make sure they are out of sight from the street. "Do you understand?"

The plan proceeded flawlessly. The quartermaster called the guard to the lead cart, saying he needed to show him something. The two then had a lengthy and heated argument. Yeshua and Miri had just enough time to hide the indicated items. They had a little trouble with the barrels. They were heavier than expected – too heavy for either Miri or Yeshua to lift. They tried lifting one together but their height difference made it awkward. They carefully set one on its side. This way, it was about knee height and could be rolled without too much difficulty. The only worry was that the old wood might crack being rolled over rough paving stones.

When they had hidden the first barrel, Yeshua noticed the inscription and pronounced the Latin words out loud.

"What is it?" Asked Miri.

"I don't know. Maybe some kind of oil."

They finished just in time. The soldier gave them an angry glance as he returned to his bench and his wineskin.

The quartermaster reappeared. "Good work, boys." He pulled Yeshua aside. "If I ask you to drive the cart up the hill, can your brother understand when I tell him what to do? I notice he doesn't speak."

"Oh yes. My brother is very smart. He has always been mute – since birth. But he understands. His name is Miykah. Just tell him what to do and he will do it."

Miri nodded but kept her face down.

Yeshua left with the other two boys, each one driving a donkey cart up the hill. Miri stayed behind and obeyed the quartermaster's commands. At one point, he handed her a hunk of the bread he had been eating. She devoured it hungrily.

About an hour later, Miri's back and feet were hurting from exertion. She was glad to see not three but six donkey carts descending the acropolis road. Alongside walked many people – perhaps fifteen or twenty.

Thus with many hands, the rest of the task was finished quickly. When the last cart had been loaded, Miri and Yeshua looked for an opportunity to quietly slip away.

Miri groaned when the quartermaster called them over again. She noticed that he had been nervously looking down a side street all evening and cursing under his breath. The quartermaster asked Yeshua, "Do you know a man named Palluw?"

Yeshua thought for a moment, and said, "I know who he is."

"Good. Do you know where he lives – down that street there?"

Yeshua nodded. "Three blocks down, on the left."

"Good. Take your brother now. Go to Palluw's house and wake him. Tell him where the goods are – the ones you hid on the side of the warehouse. Tell him to come *now* and get them. You are to help him with this task. *Then* you can go back to the palace and sleep for the rest of the night. Do you understand?"

"Yes, sir. We will do as you say."

The quartermaster gave him a hard look and decided to trust him. Normally, he liked to deal with Palluw directly, but this boy seemed capable. He nodded his head and then went to join the last cart as it started up the hill.

By now it was very late – at least a couple of hours after midnight. Miri was exhausted, hungry, and angry. And now they were starting out on yet another risky errand. "Why should we not just go home? To Sheol with this Palluw."

Yeshua said calmly, "But, we told the quartermaster we would do this."

"*We* told him? You told him. *I* am mute, remember?"

"Well, what could I do? Refuse? He would have gotten another couple of slaves to do it and we'd be in his cart on our way up to the palace, or maybe to prison."

Miri stewed on this. She saw the logic in what Yeshua had done. Still, she wasn't happy. "Well, at least let us take some of the booty for ourselves. The laborer deserves her wages, does she not?"

Yeshua stopped walking and looked at her. "What do you mean?"

Miri pondered her idea out loud. "We saw the man going over the list and picking the items, right?"

"Right. So what?"

"It looked to me like he was picking things on the spot – like he did not know ahead of time what would be in the wagons."

Yeshua still didn't understand the point. "So?"

"Think about it. If the quartermaster did not know, than Palluw could not know what has been set aside for him. We can take some and he would never know the difference."

"What would you take? What are we going to do with fancy food?"

Miri thought about this. "The barrels – you said it was some kind of oil. That would be useful. We could give it to Nura."

"They're too heavy, how are we going to move ..."

Before he could finish his sentence, he saw that Miri had been leaning against a hand cart that had been left against the wall. "Let us borrow this, move the barrels, return the cart, and *then* tell Palluw to go get his stuff."

Yeshua grinned. He loved mischief, and this plan was a good one. They took the cart back to the warehouse and hefted the barrels onto it. The cart was a bit overburdened but they were able to move it easily enough if they each took one of the handles. They crossed the decumanus and remained on back streets. They headed toward the old city – home.

As they passed behind Natan's house, Miri thought of all that had transpired this day. She remembered that she had been invited to Shabbat meal and how enjoyable it would have been to dine with her aunt and the other ladies. The meal is long over now. They will all be in their beds thinking about the wedding tomorrow evening.

"Hey, is that ... Yeshua?" A boy's voice called from within the courtyard. The bonfire was still burning vigorously despite the late hour. Yedu emerged from the gate. "And Miri too? What are you two doing out in the middle of the night? And ... what are you wearing?"

They stopped and carefully set the handles of the cart down. Yeshua embraced his younger cousin. "Yedu – Thank Alilah it's you. We've had a strange day. Why are you up so late?"

"I don't know. I couldn't sleep. I was sitting out here looking at the fire. Where are you going with those barrels?"

Miri glanced at the barrels in the cart. She said sheepishly: "These? Well, we thought maybe Nura could use them. But we are not sure what it is."

"It's wine." Said Yedu. "I remember my father had a small amphora with that same word on it 'Caecubum'. That was last year. He was raving about the taste and didn't want to serve it to guests. He wouldn't even let me taste it."

Yeshua and Miri looked at each other. "Well then. Wine it is," he said. "Do you want to help us bring it back to Nura's house?"

"That's not a good idea," said Yedu. "You stole it, didn't you?"

Yeshua laughed. "Me? Well. Some might call it stealing, but we worked hard for it – many hours."

Miri slapped Yeshua's arm. "Quiet. Yedu, why do you think it is not a good idea?"

"The barrels – with the Roman writing. Somebody will see them. People talk."

Miri said: "He is right. Let us think about this. But I have to sit down ... and eat. Yedu. Do you have any bread left from your evening meal?"

Yedu happily invited the two miscreants into the courtyard. They pulled the cart with the barrels through the gate. It barely fit. They sat by the fire and ate leftover bread. It was delicious. Miri took off her sandals and rubbed her aching feet.

She was fading into sleep when Yedu said, "How about those jars?"

Yeshua had been staring trance-like into the fire. He shook his head and looked at the boy. "Huh?" He saw where Yedu was pointing. Six large amphorae were lined up against the wall, each resting in a wooden stand. They were clay jars wrapped in rope for insulation. "Jars – what about them?"

"My father keeps water in those for cooking, and also for the mikveh." Seeing what he perceived to be a concerned look on Yeshua's face, he added hastily, "Don't worry. He's careful not to let them become unclean. He likes them because they're so much lighter than stone."

Miri understood what he was getting at. "Each one looks like it would be big enough to hold a barrelful with room to spare."

"Each jar can hold twelve hin," said Yedu with authority. "It will fit fine."

Finally Yeshua got it. "Ah. So, we dump out the water, pour in the wine, and then put the empty barrels ... where?"

"We could take them back to the warehouse," offered Miri.

Yedu could not believe the slowness of his partners in crime. "There is a bonfire right here," he pointed out.

It was easy. They pulled the cart next to the two jars farthest back. They emptied the water from the first jar into the gully alongside the house. Yedu went in the house and returned with a hand drill, which Yeshua used to open a barrel. Miri held the amphora steady while Yedu and Yeshua hoisted the barrel and poured. The aroma from the wine was heady and flowery.

When the barrels were empty, Yeshua pried the iron bands from the ends. They pulled the wooden slats apart and placed them in a stack on the fire. They were consumed quickly.

As they worked, Yeshua filled Yedu in on some of the day's events – mostly the part about being conscripted to help with the supply wagons. Yedu offered to go with Yeshua to return the handcart and wake Palluw, telling Miri that she should go home and get some rest. She thankfully agreed.

Much later, when Yeshua wearily climbed the ladder to his loft in the barn, he found Miri asleep in the hay. Trying not to wake her, he crawled in and reclined on his back next to her. She opened her eyes and looked at him.

"I have a problem, you know."

Yeshua nodded but said nothing.

"Lebbaeus – he knows I killed Ba'asha. He will not stop looking."

Yeshua nodded again. "Let's think about this tomorrow. Rest. Do you want to go back to your room in the house?"

Miri shook her head. At the risk of causing a scandal, she embraced and kissed Yeshua. They lay together in the hay and soon fell into a deep sleep.

~

The new day of Yom Rishon, early evening

Yeshua and Miri made the short walk to Natan's house, arriving just after sundown. Miri had borrowed another tunic and palla from Nura after promising profusely not to destroy them. She still had the green veil and silver clasp, salvaged from the previous day's escapades. Even Yeshua managed to find something clean to wear.

The sun had just dipped below the western horizon, and the

pinkish hue behind the acropolis made it seem like a god's palace on the hill.

The evening was unseasonably warm. There was very little breeze. All the windows of Natan's house blazed with lamps and candles. Torches mounted on tall pikes lined the short walkway from the street to his front door.

The house was already crowded when Miri and Yeshua arrived, with more people arriving every minute. The previous night, Yedu had told them that as many as one hundred people could be in attendance – a large party by Sepphoris standards. But then, Natan was a man of importance, and Channah was his only daughter.

Miri was delighted to see Yeshua's family. She greeted Mariamne and Yoceph warmly, and then spent a good bit of time listening to young Keziah relate the events of the past few days, including a lengthy description of the new outfit she made for her rag doll.

Keziah dragged Miri by the sleeve to where Chunya sat with her two young girls. A dour-looking young man stood behind her, fidgeting with the tassels on his cloak. Tahmid – Miri had only met him once before, and very briefly. She tried to engage him in conversation. This proved futile, as the man was utterly uninterested in anything or anyone here. He kept eyeing the door nervously.

As they mingled, Miri tried to remain inconspicuous. Her veil was wrapped tightly around her hair and under her chin. She kept to the shadows and corners. Her fear was that at some point Lebbaeus or one of his ruffians would walk through the door.

Miri bumped into her aunt, Taletha, who was talking with several other women from Cana. Taletha introduced her as the cousin of Nura, the town healer. She was therefore distantly related, although not by blood, to the bride. Taletha proudly told everyone that Miri had been the scribe for the ketubah. Everyone was sincerely impressed.

After she had extracted herself from this group, Miri looked for Yeshua. She saw him on the other side of the room talking to a stooped, gray-haired man who had his back to her. Yeshua looked up as she approached. "Miri, this is someone I want you to meet.

You will like him. Bustan, meet Nura's cousin, Miri."

The old man turned. Miri saw the kindly face that had protected her in her night of distress, which now seemed so long ago. As Bustan studied her face, she saw his eyes widen in recognition. "*Miri*, is it? Hmm," he said in his gravely voice. "Very well. I am honored to meet any relation of Nura's. I trust you have been well these past weeks?"

Yeshua cocked his head at the oddness of the question.

Miri took the old man's hand in hers, "Yes, Bustan. I thank you. And how are Deliylah and Yezebel?"

The man's face brightened. "Ah – good memory! They are as talkative and single-minded as ever – in the stable just down the road." He looked into Miri's eyes. "It is good to see you with your spirits back, child. You have weighed on my mind lately."

Seeing Yeshua's questioning look, Miri said. "I will tell you later. Let us just say that Bustan helped me in a time of need."

They conversed a while longer. Bustan mentioned that he happened to be coming through town when he heard about the wedding of the daughter of his old friend, Natan. He said that he could not stay for the full ceremony, but was on his way first to Caesarea, then east through the Yezreel valley to Scythopolis. After that he would travel north to a little town called Rakkat. The rumor was that Herod was going to build a grand new city there to honor Augustus.

Yeshua took Bustan out to the courtyard for refreshments. Miri saw Rabbi Eyphah standing next to Natan, laughing obsequiously at his jokes. As she wandered by, Natan reached out and took her arm. "Miri, let me introduce you to the rabbi." He turned toward Eyphah. "Rabbi, this is Miri – Nura's cousin. She did us an excellent service yesterday as scribe in your absence. I hope you get a chance to admire the beautiful ketubah she recorded for us."

Instead of greeting her, the rabbi made the pretense of seeing someone across the room that he urgently needed to speak to. "Excuse me, my lord," he muttered to Natan, and then he walked off. For the briefest instant he locked eyes with Miri. The malice she saw there was intense. So she was being shunned, Miri thought. The rabbi could not find it within him to offer a pleasant word, even on a happy occasion such as this.

Trays of olives, cheeses, fresh dates, and hard breads were being served, along with wine. The gathering remained informal for about an hour as guests arrived. After this, Natan instructed his servants to direct everyone to the courtyard so that they could begin the ceremony.

The courtyard was a large rectangular area bordered on two sides by the walls of Natan's house and on the others by high stone walls. The gate to the back street was open. A grand, cheery bonfire had been built in the corner where the two stone walls met.

Near the gate, a waist-high podium had been erected for the occasion. Natan now mounted the platform and called out in a booming voice: "Guests, relations, rabbis, clients, and friends. Please, if I could have your attention, we will commence tonight's ceremony."

Natan waited for the crowd to gather and become quiet, which took some time. Miri found a place against the wall of the house next to Yeshua. She was starting to relax. She reached over and took Yeshua's hand in her own. He responded by giving hers a gentle squeeze.

Natan forged ahead: "My beautiful daughter, Channah, has been in her chamber while we have gathered. She will join us shortly. My daughter has brought great joy in the eighteen years since Alilah blessed Ruth and me with her birth." He hesitated, looking through the crowd. "Ephrayim, come forth."

Ephrayim had been standing by the gate behind Natan. He now joined Natan on the platform.

"My guests, I introduce to you Ephrayim of Cana. My daughter has been betrothed to this young man since the twenty-third day of Av, exactly four weeks ago. The betrothal happened following arrangements made between myself and Ephrayim's father, Hozai. If only my dear cousin Hozai were still on this side of Sheol to witness these events with us. The four-day celebration that we start tonight marks the end of this period of betrothal, and the beginning of a new marriage. I know that Hozai would approve if he were here."

Several people tapped their feet politely on the paving stones to show their approval.

Natan continued: "Before we begin, let me explain that the normal seven-day celebration has, for practical reasons, been shortened to four. Today, we will start by reading ketubah aloud. I think you will all agree it is a fair and generous arrangement. The document will be posted later by the front entrance of our house for all to admire. Following the reading, the bride will make her entrance and will give her consent before witnesses. Then our good Rabbi Eyphah will bless the wine. Festivities will follow for the remainder of the evening."

Several people cheered, and laughter rippled through the crowd. Natan patiently waited for silence before continuing. "Tomorrow, the bride and groom will fast during the day. In the evening, we will hold the preparation ceremony. During this ritual, the bride and the groom will separately enter the mikveh and be cleansed to begin their new life." He gestured toward the jars in the far corner of the courtyard. "We have set aside several jars of purified water for this purpose."

Miri and Yeshua exchanged an alarmed glance. She whispered, "For the mikveh? We had better do something before tomorrow night, or they will find themselves bathing in wine."

Yeshua considered this. "Tonight, after everyone is gone, we dump the wine. Maybe we can find a cart to go refill the jars with water. I'll ask Yedu if he can help."

Natan was still speaking. "After the preparation, we will have the ceremonial transfer of the bride to the groom and the seven blessings. Then they will retire to the chuppah while we, of course, enjoy more festivities." There was more cheering and laughter, and a few leering gestures. Chuppah meant covering, or canopy. It was also what they called the room where the marriage would be consummated.

"The day after tomorrow will be the bride's introduction into the home of the groom. Several of you will travel with us to Cana. I understand that many of you will not be able to attend. The harvest is upon us and there is much to do." Secretly, Natan was glad that he would be spared the expense. "The following day in Cana will be the blessing of the house of the groom and more festivities."

This induced extended cheering and foot tapping. Ephrayim descended to the courtyard floor. After a moment, Natan motioned everyone to silence. "Now I would like to introduce my nephew, Yeshua bar Yoceph, who will read the ketubah."

Yeshua winced at the incorrect patronym. Miri gave his hand a final squeeze as he left her side to work his way to the podium. She reflected on today's events. Yedu had come to Nura's house in the morning to ask Miri if *she* would read the ketubah, it being the custom that the recording scribe would perform this function. But after the events of the previous day, Miri did not want any position of prominence, and urged Nura to do the reading. Nura demurred, saying it was not appropriate for a woman, although Miri suspected that the reason had more to do with shyness than a desire to observe protocol. Thus Yeshua was designated, being the only male in the family with a reasonable degree of literacy.

Yeshua stood on the podium and spread the document in front of him. He read in a clear, resonant voice. Miri had not realized before how much presence he commanded when speaking to a crowd. Yeshua barely glanced at the text as he spoke. Rather, he looked around the crowd, making eye contact with each person. Miri had a thought that perhaps he could one day be an actor in a theater troupe. Then she laughed at the notion. He would never have the discipline to learn lines.

When the reading was finished, Ephrayim and Natan came forward. They each took the quill and made their mark on the document. Two town elders did likewise, acting as witnesses.

Natan remained on the podium and called for silence. He introduced his daughter, the betrothed bride. To a great deal of cheering, Channah made her way to the front. She was covered head to toe in white. She wore a dazzling tunic and mantel. Her face was covered, save for her eyes, with a white veil. Even her hands were adorned with white gloves.

Channah was assisted to the podium, followed by Rabbi Eyphah and Ephrayim. The rabbi stood between the couple. He cleared his throat and spoke to the crowd in his shrill voice. "Please join me in asking the sacred questions."

Everyone intoned together: "Why is your lover better than all others, O fairest among women?"

Channah lowered her veil and faced her bridegroom. "My love is radiant, the best among ten thousand. His head is fine gold, his flowing locks black as a raven. His appearance is as noble as the cedars of Lebanon. His eloquence is sweet." She turned to the crowd. "This is my beloved, my friend, O daughters of Yerushalayim. I belong to my love, and my love to me."

The crowd responded in unison: "Why is your beloved better than all others, O fairest among men?"

Ephrayim now took a step forward. He looked into Channah's eyes. "My beloved is as comely as Yerushalayim. Her eyes overpower me. Her hair is like a flock of goats coming down the slopes of Gilead. Her cheeks are rosy pomegranates. Among sixty queens, eighty concubines and countless virgins, my dove is the only one, perfect and mine."

Channah placed her hand on Ephrayim's chest. "Set me like a seal upon your heart. For love is as strong as death. Love flashes like fire, the flame of YHWH himself."

Ephrayim echoed the action and the words, placing his own palm above Channah's breast. "Set me as a seal upon your heart. For love is as strong as death. Love flashes like fire, the flame of YHWH himself."

The two separated as the rabbi stepped between them. "Children of Israel, according to the laws of Moses, a bride must give her consent in order to be acquired through marriage. In this way, a wife is special among all the possessions of a man. He shall delight in her. The law says that even if he does not delight in her, she may not be sold for money, but rather he shall let her go where she will. She shall never be treated as a slave." He turned to the bride. "Channah bat Natan, I present to you Ephrayim bar Hozai. WILL YOU GO WITH THIS MAN?"

Without hesitation, Channah responded in her clear voice. "I *will* go with this man!"

This induced an extended period of cheering. The rabbi continued, "Let us pray to Hashem." He lifted his hands, shut his eyes and waited for quiet. "Blessed are you, Yahwiyu, king of the world. You made all that is for your own glory. Blessed are you, Yahwiyu, king of the world. You made man in your likeness and provided for the perpetuation of his kind. Through your kindness, let this bridegroom be happy, as Adam was happy in the garden long ago. May there soon be heard in the city the sound of joy and celebration, the happy shouting of men in their feasts of song. May this bridegroom and this bride rejoice together. Blessed are you, Yahwiyu, king of the world, maker of the fruit of the vine."

The rabbi was handed a goblet of wine, which he raised high into the air. After a moment, he lowered it and drank. He then handed it first to Ephrayim and lastly to Channah. The crowd erupted again in loud and prolonged cheering.

~

Following the ceremony, the bride and bridegroom were ushered into the front room so that guests could greet them individually. Many stayed in the courtyard where more food and wine were brought forth. As the guests milled about, Yeshua and Miri found themselves standing together near the water jars. They had just begun to discuss plans for disposing of the stolen wine when Yeshua's felt a tap on his shoulder. "Are you not going to greet *me?*"

Yeshua turned. "Mother!" He embraced Mariamne warmly. Miri also exchanged a kiss with her.

"When will you visit us again, son? Shimown wants you to teach him some of your tricks."

Yeshua smiled and brushed the hair out of his eyes. "I don't know. You know I am a pig herder now?"

Mariamne wrinkled her nose. "Yes, Mattanyah did mention that. A fine occupation. Any mother would be proud. Miri, Mattanyah tells me you have been spending time with my son. I hope you are keeping him out of trouble?"

Miri raised her eyebrows and placed her hand on her chest. "Oh, is that *my* responsibility now? It is too much for one person."

Mariamne caught the eye of someone across the yard and waved. She pursed her lips and then said, "Son, we haven't seen you for over a week. We do miss you."

Yeshua said wryly, "Mother, your husband does not miss me. Every time I come he has sharp words for me."

Mariamne placed her hand gently on his shoulder. "Do not blame Yoceph too much. These days he lives with one foot in a different world. Sometimes I hear him talking but there is no one there. When I ask him about it he says he has seen people long departed. Once he said he saw an angel.

"And by the way, Yoceph *has* taken a liking to that laborer you brought by two weeks ago. The big one with the limp – Esau is his name. He comes down from his cave every morning and the two are inseparable through the day. It's a wonder that he did not follow us to the wedding."

Yeshua shrugged dismissively. "I'm glad your husband has found a son that suits him."

Mariamne stroked his hair affectionately. "You look more like your father every day. David would have been proud. Have some more wine, son. Gall does not suit you."

Yeshua accepted the rebuke. He nodded and changed his tone. "As always, mother, your words make me see what is before my eyes. But speaking of gall, have you noticed this wine that Natan is serving?"

Mariamne frowned into her cup. "It is rather bitter isn't it? My sister said that all the quality stuff has been sent up to the palace for Herod's banquet tomorrow night." She asked playfully, "Did you get your invitation?"

There was a commotion inside the house. A guest of some

importance had arrived and was causing quite a stir. Mariamne offered Miri her arm. "Come dear, let's go inside and see what the fuss is all about." Miri took the proffered arm with a farewell glance to Yeshua. The two ladies entered the front room as Natan was beginning to speak.

"My dear friends and relations, we have an unexpected honor. The esteemed Hanina ben Dosa has condescended to attend my daughter's wedding." He bowed low to Hanina. "Welcome, rabbi. Now I am certain that this occasion is truly blessed."

Hanina leered as he surveyed the room. Miri noticed that his eunuch, Livianus, stood behind him, as always. Even now he was whispering something in the great sage's ear. Hanina paused, bowed toward Natan, and cleared his throat. "Not at all my dear, generous friend Natan. Rise, rise. The honor is mine. I will pray that the new couple will produce many sons."

Many pressed around, hoping to greet the great Hanina and perhaps receive a blessing. He remained in the front room, holding court as it were. A line of petitioners formed spontaneously.

Natan extracted himself at the earliest opportunity and retreated to the courtyard, followed by Mariamne and Miri. He saw his wife, Ruth, speaking with some guests. He made an apology and pulled her aside. "Can you believe the chutzpah? This party is supposed to honor the bride and bridegroom." Natan was livid.

Ruth looked nervously from side to side. "Husband, not so loud. Someone will hear." Miri and Mariamne had joined them, and a few servants were within earshot. "You know we had to rent extra slaves for tonight. They are not all loyal to us. Slaves do talk."

Indeed, Miri noticed one manservant standing at the edge of the courtyard, looking at them with a worried expression. He appeared to be waiting for an opportunity to interrupt.

Mariamne, too, tried to sooth Natan's anger. "Brother, Hanina will tire of this company soon and leave us be. Ignore him. Enjoy your daughter's special day."

Natan noticed his manservant. "What *is* it Tuval? Why are you squirming like that?"

"Master, please, I tried." He came forward and whispered something in Natan's ear. Miri glanced around for Yeshua. He had been out here a moment ago but now seemed to have disappeared. Indeed, there were very few people in the courtyard. Most had apparently gone indoors when Hanina arrived.

Natan erupted in anger. He violently pushed the servant away. "Fool! How could you let this happen? I'll have you whipped for this." The slave prostrated himself on the ground before Natan and Ruth. He began blubbering incoherent apologies, and pleading for mercy.

Ruth asked, "Husband, what's wrong? What has happened?"

Natan was beside himself. He had trouble finding the words. "This ... idiot did not buy sufficient wine. He says we are on the last amphora." He glared at his slave in disgust. "Get up off the ground! People are starting to notice you. Fool! Go out and find more. Now!"

The slave got to his feet but kept his face down. He was actually weeping. "Master I tried *everywhere*. There is no more wine in the city. I hoped what we had would be enough for this first evening. Then we can find some more tomorrow. Maybe from the villages."

"From the *villages*? You want to serve country wine at my daughter's wedding?"

Ruth said curtly: "Husband, the wine from the village of my birth is every bit as good as any you can purchase here. You never complained to my father when you were courting me."

"Wife ... and sister, I meant no offense. But let us stick to the matter. *We are out of wine!* What am I to tell my guests? And of all nights, Hanina is here. This is one more thing he will use to ridicule me."

No one offered any solution. Natan became resigned. "I will have to make an announcement and ask the guests for forgiveness ... ask them to return tomorrow." He cast a threatening glance toward the slave. "You *are* sure you can get more wine by tomorrow evening?"

The slave said nothing but nodded his head profusely.

Miri was thinking quickly. She wanted to tell Natan about the two huge jars filled with wine only a few feet from where they stood. But then she would have to explain where it came from, which would be dangerous.

Natan started toward the front room where most of the guests were still congregating. His face was red with embarrassment. As he passed, Miri had an inspiration. She laid her hand gently on his shoulder. "Excuse me sir. Have you forgotten that one of your guests is Hanina ben Dosa?"

Natan looked at her as if she were a simpleton. "Have you not been listening? Did you not hear what I just said? His presence only doubles my embarrassment."

"Sir. I did not mean to ... twist the knife. It is just that you know that Hanina is famous for miracles?"

Natan tapped his foot impatiently. "Of course, everyone knows that. What is your point?"

"My lord, I was thinking that maybe you could ask Hanina to do something. Maybe he could ... well, transform some of those water jars into wine. They say his prayers are *very* powerful."

Natan stood in thought for a moment. He raised an eyebrow and looked at Miri with new appreciation. He caught the playful curl at the edge of her mouth. *"That* is an interesting idea, young lady."

Natan did not believe for a minute that Hanina could actually perform such a miracle, but this would give him a chance to embarrass Hanina in front of a crowd. A little revenge would be sweet indeed after the huge obligation that Hanina had forced on him earlier this week.

A neighbor's daughter had just come out to the courtyard. Natan took her hand. "Young Lidia, I have a secret for you. Tell all of your friends. Rabbi Hanina is about to perform a miracle in the courtyard." The girl nodded excitedly and scampered off.

Miri searched again for either Yeshua or Yedu, but could find neither. She needed them to bring forward the two jars from the back so that Hanina would be successful. She was looking forward to the surprised look on the old fraud's face when the miracle actually worked. She followed Natan into the house. She scanned the great room but still could not find either of her confidants.

Natan waited a few moments for the rumor to spread before approaching the preacher. "Hanina, it pains me to tell you of a predicament which brings me dishonor."

Hanina looked at him curiously but said nothing.

"Hanina, we have misjudged our provisions and the ... thirst of our guests tonight. I am embarrassed to tell you that the wine has run out."

Hanina looked around the room and noticed that everyone had become quiet as they listened to the exchange. "Natan, my child. That is unfortunate."

Natan responded, "Yes, my lord it is. But I believe it is the reason Alilah has brought you to my home tonight. We all know of the powerful miracles you perform. And we have all heard your wise words, that, with a prayer rightly spoken, Hashem will grant anything. Why, you can make bread appear out of thin air. Nothing is impossible for you. Is that not true?"

Hanina became cautious. "Yes, my child, this is true. But, you do not lack for bread."

Natan smiled. Hanina had taken the bait. "But, we have water, my lord. If you can make bread from nothing, surely you can turn water into wine? We have six large amphorae filled with water in the courtyard. If you could transform but one, then our guests could all drink to contentment."

"You want me to ... change water into wine?"

"Yes, my lord. You taught us that all things are possible. Unless you think it is too much to ask?"

Several in the crowd began to cheer and shout encouragement.

Livianus once again whispered into Hanina's ear. All eyes in the room were watching them. At length, Hanina brushed Livianus away. "I will do it!" He announced. Everyone cheered and followed as Natan led Hanina to the courtyard. Even the bride and bridegroom came to watch.

Urgently, Miri looked again for either Yeshua or Yedu. They had disappeared just when she needed them. She would have to do this herself. She started pushing her way through the crowd to the side of the building where the water jars were kept. But before she could get there, Natan had already directed Tuval to bring forth an amphora. To her horror she saw that he was dragging over the nearest one – one of the four that held only water. This was happening too fast.

The crowd became quiet as Hanina mounted the raised platform and extended his hands in an attitude of prayer. Tuval placed the jar in its stand before him on the courtyard floor.

Miri felt a tugging on her sleeve. "Yedu! Where have you been?"

"I was down the street with Yeshua. We were ..."

"Hush! Never mind. Listen!" His eyes grew wide as Miri whispered into his ear, telling him about the events that were now unfolding. But it was too late to do anything about it. Her plan was not going to work.

Hanina finished his silent prayer and called out. "Someone hand Livianus a cup!"

Mattanyah was closest. He handed his empty goblet to the eunuch.

Hanina continued, "I have not yet performed the miracle. I want you all to bear witness." He turned to the eunuch. "Livianus, dip the cup into the jar. Take a sip and then pass it to the next man. Tell us what you taste."

Miri was impressed by Hanina's improvised showmanship. From where she stood, she saw that Yeshua had just returned. He stood at the open gate, watching the proceedings with a confused expression.

Livianus dipped the cup into the amphora and passed it around. Each man pronounced that it was indeed water. The last person to receive the cup was Yeshua, who drained the last few drops and, following the lead of those who drank before him, said simply, "water."

Hanina called out in a loud and clear voice "Yahwiyu! Hear me! I have faith and know that you always hear me when I call. But I speak aloud and thank you for the sake of my sons and daughters around me, so that they too will believe that it is you who acts here today. I thank you for listening to your humble servant now as you always have in the past."

He paused. Miri recalled that he had used these same words at his show when conjuring the loaves. But Hanina changed the formula when he continued: "I ask that, *if* you find everyone here to be worthy, to the last man and boy, you then listen to my humble request to transform this water into wine."

Natan had been standing behind Miri. He grumbled in her ear, "So that's his plan. The snake is preparing the crowd. When the miracle fails, he'll declare that someone here is not worthy. He'll probably point his dirty finger at me."

Miri looked up at him with sympathy. Her plan had been that the miracle would work. Now she suspected that Natan was right.

Hanina went into a trance for several minutes. At length, he groaned and reached his hands in front of his face, as if to ward off a blow. Then he fell off the platform, to be caught by Livianus. Miri noticed that he conveniently fell into the waiting arms of his servant, rather than against the hard stone wall of the courtyard.

After a moment they were able to revive him. He jumped up and called out. "The cup! Bring me the cup!" Yeshua stepped forward and handed him the same goblet. He dipped it into the jar and again passed it to the men at the front of the crowd. For each man it was the same: He accepted the cup with a hopeful expression. But after sipping, his expression would turn to disappointment. "Water," each called out. One of the men scoffed and knocked over the amphora, spilling the water over the feet of those nearby.

Hanina quickly returned to the platform, "Yahwiyu! We repent. You have found us unworthy. Perhaps it is our host you find lacking. Do you disapprove of this wedding? Perhaps there is some grievous sin among us. We must not presume. We must repent. We shall all go to our homes and reflect on what we have done to displease you."

He descended the platform in dead silence. No one said a word. It was evident that the party was over. Hanina had outsmarted them. Miri's idea had gone horribly wrong. Indeed, the celebration was ruined, as was Natan's good reputation. He may even lose his position, and be forced to leave the city.

Hanina entered the house. Others shook their heads sadly, and seeing that nothing else was to be said or done, started to follow.

That was when Yedu got his idea. Without having a chance to think it through or consult with anyone, he hopped up onto the platform. "Wait! Wait!" People paused and turned toward him. "Perhaps it is Hanina himself who is not in Hashem's favor." There was a gasp from the onlookers. How could *a boy* dare to question the reputation of one such as Hanina? But Yedu continued: "There is another here who *can* do this miracle!" Now he had their attention. Everyone looked at him expectantly. He let the tension build and then said: "I say let *Yeshua* try."

Yeshua was as surprised as anyone at this proposal. He looked dumbfounded, first at Yedu, and then at Miri. Miri winked at him with a subtle smile. Then he understood.

Natan had had enough. "No, no, no. The situation is bad enough. Let us not turn it into a circus." He cleared his throat and said in a loud voice, "Honored guests. It is in deep shame that I must announce to you that our wine has run out. My servant assures me that there will be more tomorrow. So I must ask you all to ..."

Yeshua jumped onto the platform and interrupted. "I *shall* do this for you, dear uncle. *Fear not!*" Yeshua was no stranger to showmanship. The crowd once more pressed around the podium. They all knew Yeshua. This was going to be amusing if nothing else. Several cheered in encouragement. Hanina and Livianus had come back to the courtyard to see what was happening. They observed from the periphery.

Natan left off trying to object. He waved his hand in surrender and moved to stand near the bride and bridegroom.

Yeshua raised his arms in a gesture of prayer. He stood silently for a long moment. He shook violently and then opened his eyes, grinning. "Hashem has revealed to me that if he is to do this, there must be some *payment*. The laborer deserves his wages, does he not?" He winked in Miri's direction.

Several in the crowd laughed and echoed, "Yes!" and "There must be a payment!" Yeshua fell back into his trance. They waited expectantly for him to continue.

He opened his eyes again. "This is a wedding. The wage that Hashem demands is ... a *dowry*. Hashem reveals to me that if the water is turned to wine, then Hanina must give one thousand denarii to the new bride and bridegroom."

A collective gasp swept through the crowd. All turned to Hanina, who stood in the back with a flabbergasted expression. At length, he whined, "Really Natan, this farce is beneath you. You should ..." Livianus tapped him on the shoulder and whispered in his ear. After a moment Hanina nodded. "I agree," he announced. "But he must transform not one, but two jars of water into wine. And if the boy fails, then Natan must double his pledge to me. He will then owe *me* a debt of one thousand denarii."

All eyes turned now to Natan, who sat back heavily on a chair against the wall of the house. He covered his face with his hands wondering, how had this gone so terribly awry? A moment ago he was enjoying his daughter's wedding. Then, he was facing a minor embarrassment for running out of wine. Now, he was facing financial ruin or worse. Yedu appeared at his side. He looked into his son's young eyes and saw the confidence that he himself lacked. His son nodded slightly. He stood up slowly and looked around the crowd. "Agreed," he said weakly.

Everyone's attention returned to Yeshua. Yedu scurried over to help Tuval bring forward two amphorae. He directed the slave to the two nearest the back. These were placed in front of the podium as Yeshua waited. There was scattered laughter through the crowd. This was turning out to be a very amusing evening.

"Hand me a cup!" Yelled Yeshua as he jumped down to the stone floor.

Miri was near the front. She took one step forward and bowed before him. She held forth a large wooden goblet with both hands. He took the cup with his right hand and placed his left on her head. He leaned down and kissed her forehead, thanking her.

"Open the jars!" He shouted, pointing to a young man he did not know at the front of the crowd. The young man pried the lid off of one jar and then the other.

"Hashem has not yet performed the miracle. You must all bear witness."

As Yeshua had expected, Miri had given him a cup already filled with water. He held it at the rim, with his thumb dipping inside, as one might hold an empty cup. The purpose of the kiss was pure misdirection. Yeshua now dipped the full cup just inside the rim of the jar. He pulled it out and handed it to the young man. "Take this and drink. Then pass it on. Tell us what you taste."

Several people drank from the cup until it was empty. They all agreed that it was water. Several of them spat it out. It had a stale taste, they reported – like water that has been sitting around a long time. Miri lowered her face and grinned. She had filled the goblet from a flower pot.

The last man to taste the water was Livianus. He spat it out and handed the goblet back to Yeshua.

Yeshua once again ascended the platform. He extended his arms and waited for silence. He shouted, "Abba! Emma!" This had at least as striking an effect as the the use of *the name* at the start of Hanina's prayer. His voice became soft and calm, forcing everyone to become quiet so as to hear. "I will not speak your holy name. Shine your light on us, illuminating what we do tonight. We do not need to ask, for you know our needs better than we do. *If* you find any of us unworthy, forgive us. If *Hanina* is unworthy, we shall also let go of his guilt."

Hanina scoffed from the back. He started to object but decided to hold his tongue. He was confident that he would have his satisfaction soon enough.

The prayer continued, "Nurture us, and protect us from those who wish us harm." After a long pause, he added, "Let it be DONE!"

When Yeshua bellowed this last word, Miri, who had positioned herself behind the others near the fire, tossed her little packet of naphtha into the flames. She had only just realized she had it in the inside pocket of her tunic after handing the goblet to Yeshua. A ball of flame immediately burst upward, startling everyone including Yeshua. He dropped the goblet onto the stone floor where it broke in two.

Everyone took a step back from the fire. Some looked fearfully toward the sky. Miri glanced at Hanina's face, and for the first time she saw uncertainty in his eyes.

"Hand me another goblet!" Yeshua barked. Livianus stepped forward and handed Yeshua his own cup. Yeshua bowed to him in thanks, and without hesitation dipped the cup into the jar. He handed it to a different man. "Take this and drink, but do not say anything yet. When you have sipped, pass it to your neighbor, whether it be man or woman."

The young man sniffed and then tasted from the cup. His eyes grew wide but he said nothing. He passed the cup to his wife. One by one, each person tasted the wine and became astonished. In the end, they all agreed that not only was it wine, it was the best wine they had ever tasted.

Hanina came forth angrily. "What kind of devilry is this?" He grabbed the empty goblet and dipped it into the jar and tasted. His eyes grew fearful. He spat it out. He dumped the cup and tried the other jar. Again he spat it out in disgust. His face was as red as a pomegranate. For once, the mighty Hanina had trouble finding words. "This ... This ... some kind of trick!" He became indignant and turned to the host. "Natan, I am sorely offended that you have invited me into your home and then abused me like this. You'll not see one coin of this ... this *dowry*." He cast an angry glance at Yeshua. "You, young man – I don't know who you are, but you will hear from me again!"

He started toward the front of the house to leave. He paused when he realized that everyone in the courtyard was booing, hissing, or gesturing with their thumbs. He turned and stormed out.

~

Natan filled his goblet from the amphora and took a sip. The taste was rich and earthy, with just a hint of sweetness. After a moment his tongue detected subtle notes of smoke and cardamom. It seemed stronger than most wines, but the taste was so satisfying that it would be a shame to dilute it. Natan suspected there would be more than one guest overcome with drunkenness tonight.

He dumped the wine into the fire and walked toward the gate where Yedu and Yeshua were talking. He grabbed both boys by the arm and conducted them into the street, away from the others. He stood eyeing them for a long moment. "I'm waiting," he said at last.

Yedu and Yeshua exchanged a look. Yedu said, "But father, didn't you see ..."

"Son, I have walked in enough mule shit for one evening. I've seen plenty of things in my life that count as real miracles, but not this. This one smells like a trick – like the stuff Hanina does. Something is up with you two. I want the *truth.*"

After a hesitation, Yeshua gave him the truth – or at least most of it. He omitted any mention of Miri's involvement. He told Natan where the wine came from, about the supply wagons, the quartermaster and the merchant named Palluw. (Natan knew Palluw's reputation well and winced at the name.) Yeshua told him that it was all his own doing except that Yedu helped him hide the wine in the amphorae. They didn't know that they were being used for the mikveh at the wedding. Finally, he told him about burning the original barrels in the fire.

"I wondered about iron rings behind the fire." Natan looked at Yedu. "Do not make the mistake that I am so old as to be feebleminded. I notice things that don't belong."

Yeshua added, "no one will know that anything was missing until the quartermaster goes to settle accounts with Palluw. They'll have to fight it out themselves. Why should we ..."

He stopped when Natan held his palm up, indicating that he had heard enough. After a thoughtful silence, he said to Yeshua. "You are the son of my wife's sister. You are my nephew. I have treated you generously since you arrived in the city many years ago. I opened my home to you and treated you as a son. I have wished for you a long and prosperous life, but my suspicion is that you will have neither. Yeshua, you are reckless. This is but one time among many that you have endangered my family. It ends here, tonight. Take this." He handed Yeshua a small purse. "There are fifty denarii there. It is a down payment on my pledge that I was going to give to Hanina. Spend it wisely because it may need to last you a long while. It pains me to say this, nephew, but I want you to leave. It is plain to me that you cannot change your ways. You will continue to endanger yourself and those around you until something terrible happens. Then maybe you will learn the value of caution. Learn that lesson somewhere else, and then you may be welcome back here. Enjoy the rest of the party tonight, but then, leave. I spoke with Bustan earlier. He thinks kindly toward you. He is departing to the south tomorrow morning. Perhaps you should go with him."

Natan was resolute. He turned and re-entered his courtyard leaving the two boys in the street.

~

Miri went from room to room through Natan's expansive house. Yeshua seemed to have disappeared shortly after the miracle, and now Yedu also was nowhere to be found. Perhaps they were off somewhere, like before, cooking up their next bit of mischief.

The party had been revived by the new supply of wine. Tuval quickly took charge of the two amphorae before the guests could help themselves. He now was doling out the wine in pitchers, already watered down. Miri knew that the barrels had been quite large. There would be plenty for tonight, and likely tomorrow evening as well.

As she passed through the crowd she heard people commenting on the quality of the wine. Most didn't know what to think about how it materialized. Some who had witnessed the transformation mimicked Yeshua's hand gestures and words as they related the event to others. One woman said authoritatively that Yeshua's mother had put him up to it. Several spoke scathingly about Hanina – about how he had fled the house as a coward. His reputation in this town was, at least for the time being, diminished.

Miri returned to the front room where the focus had been restored to the bride and bridegroom. Natan was at the door greeting a late-arriving guest. Miri had a hard time seeing who it was from the back of the room until Natan bowed low in a gesture of deference. Lebbaeus and his servant, Mak'ka, stood in the doorway.

Horrified, Miri quickly ducked behind two other guests. Natan was treating Lebbaeus as a superior. So that's how it is, she realized, Lebbaeus is here to stay.

Natan handed Lebbaeus a goblet of wine. She saw the tavern keeper's eyebrows rise in an appreciative manner. Then she noticed Mak'ka with his scarred face, his hawk's eyes scanning the crowd, just as she had seen him do countless times in that awful tavern in Magdala.

She turned her back and fled the room. In the passageway she bumped into Yedu. She latched hold of his arm. "Quick. Look behind me. Who is that man just arriving?"

Miri kept her back to the room as Yedu looked over her shoulder. "Oh – him. I met him yesterday. His name is Laban, or Lemek – something like that. He's new in town. He is going to be replacing Ba'asha, the one who got murdered before you arrived. My father said he is a new patron and we must treat him with respect. Come. I'll introduce you."

Miri let go of his arm. "That is what I feared. I have to leave now. Do you know where Yeshua has gone?"

Yedu's eyes fell to the floor. "He went home. He asked me to tell you that."

"But, everyone is asking for him. Why did he leave?"

Yedu answered flatly, as if evading the question. "I don't ... you should talk to him yourself. When you see him, tell him I'm sorry."

"You are sorry – for what?" asked Miri, but Yedu had already walked past her into the front room. She wondered what Yedu would have to be sorry about. She took a final glance into the front room and saw that Natan was directing his new guests in her direction. She hurried through the house into the courtyard. She ducked out the back gate and was gone.

It was not quite midnight. The streets were dark and quiet as Miri found her way through the twisting alleys to Nura's enclave. She entered the main house but did not see Yeshua in the front room. There was a single lamp burning on the table. She lit a few others, took one with her, and went to look in the courtyard. Yeshua was not there either. She looked up to the high window of his loft but did not see any light. She entered the barn and called for him.

He answered. "Miri, wait there."

He backed down the ladder and met her in the doorway. Together they walked back to the house and sat at the table. They stared at each other in the orange light, both reluctant to speak.

"I have something to tell you," Miri said at length.

"So do I," said Yeshua. "But you start."

Miri inhaled deeply and thought. She sniffed and wiped away a tear. "I must leave. I cannot stay in this town."

Yeshua stared at her open-mouthed. He did not seem upset at her news. "What?" she asked.

He reached out and touched her chin. "That," he said "is what *I* have to tell *you*."

Now it was her turn to be surprised. "But, your life is here. Why would you have to leave? Everyone loves you, especially after what happened tonight."

Yeshua withdrew his hand, shook his head, and looked at the tabletop. He told her about Natan's ultimatum. He said he did not begrudge Natan for his attitude. "He is right. I am reckless. But before now I never had ..." He became silent.

"What?"

Yeshua swallowed and looked at her. "Before now, I never felt that I had anything to lose." When Miri met his gaze, he added, "I have been in my loft, thinking that the one thing in this town that I don't want to leave behind is you."

Miri picked up his hand and kissed his knuckles. She told him about the arrival of Lebbaeus at the wedding party. "According to Yedu, he is taking Ba'asha's place. He will live here. As long as that man is here, I cannot be. I must leave – tomorrow.”

Yeshua nodded. “Then we will go together. Before I left the party, I spoke with Bustan. He’s going to wait for me in the morning. We are going to his home in Caesarea. I’ve never seen the sea. He says its so big you can’t see the other side. After that, I don’t know.”

Miri felt relief flowing through her. “We could head south – maybe find Yochanan. Follow in Te’oma’s footsteps.”

Yeshua considered this. “If we travel together, people will think it unseemly. We could say that we are brother and sister.”

“Or,” she looked at him expectantly.

“What?”

She rolled her eyes. “We could be husband and wife.”

“Yes, we could say that if anyone asks, but then ...”

“I did not mean we would *say* we are husband and wife.”

Yeshua looked at her with an uncomprehending expression.

She sighed. “Honestly, sometimes you are slow. I said that we could *be* husband and wife.”

“*Be* husband and wife?”

“Why not? I have parchment and a quill up in the library. Wait here.” She took a lamp and ascended the ladder to the room where she had stayed since her arrival two weeks ago. She fetched a box of writing implements and returned to the kitchen.

She opened the box and brought out a fresh sheet of fine lambskin. She dipped the quill in ink. “How do you want to start?”

Yeshua’s smile was wide. “Let’s start like the ketubah you wrote for Natan. It started with the date.”

Miri recited as she wrote. “On the twenty-first day of Elul in the year three thousand seven hundred and seventy four in the city of Sepphoris in the province of Yudaea.” She looked up. “What next?”

“You have to put *our* names next. How about, ‘Yeshua bar David is head of his own’ ... well I don’t really have a household do I?”

“No. Neither do I. We don’t really have anything. How about if we just say ‘free destitute person’?”

“That’s good. Say: Yeshua bar David, free destitute person and

Miryam bat ... um, who was your father?"

Miri shook her head resolutely. "I don't want to use his name. My mother's name was also Miryam. I will be Miryam bat Miryam, or perhaps just Miryam of Magdala ... also free destitute person. Then what?"

"Hmm. Natan's ketubah said something about blood lineage, and continuing a blood line."

"Such a lot of blood," she commented. "How about if we just say that we agree to be married and that we shall share all our treasures ... if we ever have any."

"Oh, we *will* have treasures."

She scribbled for a moment. "Got it. Now the other ketubah had terms – dowry, brideprice – that sort of thing." She adopted a fetching pose. "What are you willing to pay for me?"

"Wait. I do have something." He reached into his tunic and pulled out the coin purse that Natan had given him. He felt the heft of it and handed it to her. "Natan gave me this to speed me on my way. He said there are fifty denarii in here."

"Really – A fortune. Perhaps we are not so destitute."

"Write it down. But, what about your dowry?"

She laughed and tossed him back the purse. "There you go. Now we have exchanged property. It is official." She finished writing. "We each need to make our mark. Here." She handed him the quill.

He took a deep breath. "I am ready. Are you sure?" She nodded. He signed his name. She signed under his.

They were husband and wife save for one final act needing to be performed. Yeshua stood and offered his hand. Together, they went out through the courtyard and into the barn. He held the lamp while she climbed into the loft. He followed her up. They stood in the cramped space facing each other. They embraced, tentatively at first, then with growing ardor. He savored the scent of her hair, her neck. She caressed his back with her palms. They kissed tenderly, delighting in each other.

After they had removed their clothing, he held her at arm's length. "How beautiful you are, my beloved. Your eyes are like doves. How you delight me. You are a spring crocus on the Plain of Sharon. You are a lily growing in the valley."

She responded in kind. "As a fine apple tree in the forest, so is my love among sons of men. I will sit and delight in his shade. His fruit is sweet to my taste. He has taken me to his banquet room and looks upon me with love."

They lay together in the straw, making love until they were exhausted and could no longer keep their eyes open. At last, they fell asleep in each other's arms.

~

Miri gently extricated herself from Yeshua's embrace. He was sleeping soundly. She found that she was still restless. She grabbed her tunic and palla, and descended from the loft to the barn floor. From there she went outside. The air was crisp and clear. She walked through the courtyard and climbed the ladder to the flat section of the roof. The brown clay still held a little warmth from the day's sun.

She was enjoying this moment of solitude. She lay on her back, gazing up at the bright stars in the moonless night. The Romans said that groups of stars formed the shapes of animals and people. She had heard some of the names, like Aries, Cassiopeia, and Orion. She focused on a particularly bright star to the south that she knew was called Sirius. Unlike the lives of men and women, the stars remained always the same. She recalled the words of the preacher that she had read in a scroll about there being a season for everything, and that all is vanity, and that the best thing a person can do is to take joy in her daily labors. She once again recalled the memory of the first kiss she had exchanged with Yeshua after the Lamentations service. It occurred to her that this kiss had set the direction for the rest of her life. This kiss had changed everything. She was now a married woman. She wondered if she would ever have children. Perhaps one was growing in her belly even now. If so, would she have a son or a beautiful daughter? She wondered what the child would be like. She wondered about the strange road that the kiss had set her on, and where it would take her and Yeshua in the years to come.